The Lost Sheep

Book 3 of
The Good Seed, The Bad Seed Series

By

Joan Byrd

Deep Indigo Books
Published by Indigo Sea Press
Winston-Salem

Deep Indigo Books
Indigo Sea Press
302 Ricks Drive
Winston-Salem, NC 27103
This book is a work of fiction. Names, characters,
locations and events are either a product of the author's
imagination, fictitious or used fictitiously. Any resemblance
to any event, locale or person, living or dead, is purely
coincidental.

For information regarding bulk purchases of this book,
digital purchase and special discounts, please contact the publisher
at indigoseapress@gmail.com

Manufactured in the United States of America
ISBN 978-1-63066-545-6

I dedicate this book to all God's children, both the good and the bad.

There are far too many "Lost Sheep" to number and I write "The Good Seed, the Bad Seed" series in the hope of reaching those lost souls wandering down the wide path of destruction that leads to everlasting punishment.

I write these words to renew strong faith in all who believe that Jesus Christ our Savior and that He died for "all" our sins and leads us down the true path to life eternal.

When the Lord Jesus returns to judge the world, which side will He place you on?

Those waiting to be judged on His left side will be condemned by their bad choices, and those who wait on His right side have been saved by the blood of the Lamb, feeling at peace by His grace.

If your faith is like that of a child, as you approach His throne, you may hear Jesus say: "Little lamb, come and graze upon my right side."

It's never too late to ask the Lord to forgive your sins and confess your belief in Him. You can draw your answers from the pages of this book or the many witnesses out there waiting to guide you to the truth, which can be found in His holy word, the Bible.

You will find when you have Jesus in your heart, His light will shine through everything you do!

—Joan Byrd

CHAPTER 1

Ted felt the wind gently embrace him as he stepped up on the hill. The special young man always drew love and power on top of Goldsburg Mountain. "My Father." Ted's soft voice lifted up to his heavenly God.

"My son." the still small voice fell on Ted's ears. "Something is weighing on your mind. Your love one, Jenny."

"Oh, my Father, I know my Jenny loves me, of that I have no doubt." Ted grew serious. "Her love for me is great as mine is for her."

"This love I feel is powerful, my son, but yet Jenny seems distracted." The calm voice whispered. "She grows weary, even though she tries to hide it."

"Yes Father, her years on the mountain have grown long with the amount of work we share and bringing up a home filled with children and youth." Ted began to pace back and forth. "I know she loves it here, Father, loves her life with me, but yet I feel she is missing something, perhaps the freedom to come and go as she once did. Jenny tries to block these feeling from me."

"I think you need to take your Jenny on a well deserve getaway." The wind blew the voice gently on Ted's ears. "Work on the mountain has been difficult for Jenny, and the children, although they are loveable, can be trying at times for her."

"Leave? Can I be gone, if only for a short time, my Father?" Ted searched the sky. "And not just the children but my mornings on this mountain with you, Lord."

"You know I am with you at all times, my son, wherever you dwell." The wind gently blew Ted's robe around his ankles. "Listen to my wise degree, son. Take your dear love on what my people call a honeymoon, well deserved and long awaited."

"A honeymoon? But, where would I take her, my Father?" Ted glanced down the hill. The children need me and our daughters, Mary and Martha, will they accompany Jenny and I on this honeymoon?"

"Ted, my son, I see you are new to this honeymoon getaway."

1

There was almost a chuckle in the Almighty's voice as he continued. "Your precious little angels are now four years old, and yet they appear to be almost mature. Mary and Martha will remain here with the other children. Help has been called in to help with the children. And Ted…" the voice took on another tone. "There is another reason why I send you, my son."

"You have a mission for me Father." Ted's special powers alerted him of what lie ahead. "It too has something to do with children, some young, some teenagers."

"These lost children have been mistreated and abused. They have been taught bad things and we must save them." Came the still small voice with deep concern. "They need you, my son. When the time arrives, you will send for Matthew and Kathy to help you and Jenny. If I feel things grow too dangerous for you, I will send in your father."

"You speak of my real father." Ted closed his eyes as he recalled meeting his father on this very mountain four years ago. "Gabriel. It has been so long since we spoke."

"My angels keep very busy, my son, but Gabriel and Michael are always on standby to help you." The voice seemed to kiss Ted's cheek. "You are truly loved Ted. I will fill you in on where and what my plan is."

"Yes, my Father. My heart will listen, my heart will hear." Ted smiled. "I will inform Jenny about our journey. She might feel more like her old self again."

"Jenny will smile with joy, my gifted son." The voice began to fade. "You will know your destination before you step off this mountain."

"Thank you, Father, for all your many blessings." Ted closed his eyes smiling as the voice whispered before fading away.

"Go in love, in peace, dear son."

Jenny smiled as she watched Mary and Martha happily pulling off grapes. Mary handed the full bucket to her mother before grabbing an empty one.

"Mom, will dad make wine with this batch of lovely grapes? He made juice with the last bunch we gathered."

"Yes, my beautiful daughter, I will be making a rich red wine from those lovely grapes." Ted laughed as both girls set down their buckets to run into his waiting arms.

2

"Dad, did you and the Father have a nice talk this morning?" Martha winked at him as Mary squeezed his hand. "

"And just where are you taking mom?" Mary laughed when Jenny sat down her bucket and walked over in front of her handsome young husband.

"What do you mean, taking mom? Ted are those girls reading your mind again?"

Ted frowned down at the twins. "I was going to surprise you darling." He pulled Jenny into his arms giving her an invasion of butterflies. "You and I are going on a well-deserved honeymoon."

"A honeymoon? Just the two of us?" A beautiful smile fell on her face. "What brought this on and can we leave the children?"

"I think we can use some time alone sweetheart, just the two of us." He reached up and touched her face. "I love you with all my heart Jenny and I just want to show you."

"Ted Neenam, you show me every night." Jenny suddenly remembered they were not alone when she heard the girls giggle.

"Don't you want to go with me on a honeymoon, Jenny?" Ted looked down seriously.

"Yes, Ted darling, I would like nothing better." Jenny laid her head on his shoulder and felt his incredible love. "Get away, just the two of us!" she glanced up into his smiling face. "Where sweetheart? Where are you taking me?"

"The coast, the Outer Banks." Ted had heard God whisper the place as he stepped off the mountain, as promised.

"Alright, it's a pleasant time to go to the beach." Jenny wondered to herself who would watch all the children while they were away. Still in thought, Ted spoke, followed by the twins.

"There will be extra help here to watch all the children, Jenny."

"That's right mom, grandmother has been sent for." Martha took her mother's hand. "We shall be fine mom. Just have fun."

"Martha is right mom. The Father is sending Melaki." Mary beamed. "How heavenly!"

"Speaking of heavenly, can Jeffery Teddy come over for a visit while you are away, dad?" Martha blushed.

"Jeffery Teddy has unexpected company coming Martha, so he may be busy." Ted picked up his daughter and kissed her. "Kind of sweet of Jeffery Junior?"

"I prefer Jacob, dad. Jeffery is all hands!" Mary reached around

3

her mother's waist. "Why do some boys want to hug you, mom?"

"Well, innocent hugs are permitted Mary, as long as they don't start touching you in personal places they should not." Jenny gave her innocent daughter a motherly hug as she wondered if the four-year-old girls even knew what she was referring to by her statement. Martha put her questions to rest when she said with total innocence.

"You mean making advances which lead to sex. Right mom?"

Jenny's eyes grew wide as she stared down at her small daughter, shocked by her comment. "Where on earth did you learn that, young lady?"

Martha looked down shyly as she tried to answer her upset mother. "Well...I..." She squeezed her eyes shut when she felt her father take her face and lift it up.

"Martha, answer your mother."

"She heard it from Jeffery!" Mary reached for her sister's trembling hand. "You were wondering if we understood your statement, so Martha spoke up. Jeffery told us what hugging leads up too."

"Jeff Wineworth?" assuming the girls were speaking about Teddy's father, Jenny could not believe her ears. "Why on earth would a grown man tell two innocent children this very grown-up subject?"

"Relax my love" Ted tried to hide his smile at Jenny's outburst. "I think the girls are referring to the son, Teddy Jeffery." Ted wrapped his arms around Jenny's trembling shoulders as his stare had the twin's full attention. "So, Teddy, who prefers being called Jeffery now, thinks because he is the oldest at seven-years-old, gives him the authority to teach you both the facts of life."

"Jeffery said he knew a lot more and will tell us when we get older." Martha finally spoke up. "I think he is a dream."

"More like a nightmare at the moment!" Jenny got down between her little blonde headed daughters and wrapped her arms around them. "Girls, you are children of God. Remember that at all times."

"Your mom is right, my beautiful little angels, so, there are times your mother and I must protect you." Ted's attention fell on the neighboring mountain, looming up dark next to the green lands of Goldsburg Mountain. "Maybe having Teddy over while we are gone is a bad ideal. I will have a word with Jeff and Naomi before we leave."

4

"Sweetheart, if you don't mind my asking, why the coast of North Carolina?" Jenny picked up her bucket of grapes. Ted retrieved it in his left hand and gathered her hand in his right as he smiled down lovingly.

"The Father needs us to go there, Jenny. He told me so this morning."

"If God ask us to go to the Outer Banks, then it must be some kind of mission." Jenny motioned for the twins to follow them up to the house. Gathering their buckets, they walked alone behind their parents, smiling at the obvious love between them. "I guess since God ask the two of us to go alone, you thought it could be the honeymoon we never had. I am sure our heavenly God did not suggest you taking me on a honeymoon."

Ted stopped and stared down at his adorable wife before lending down to kiss her. "That is were you are wrong, my darling Jenny. It really was the Father's degree."

"Ted, get out of here!" Jenny couldn't resist laughing at the very ideal of the Holy Creator suggesting they go on a honeymoon. "You do not expect me to believe that the Almighty God, the Father of all creation, has the time to consider two lovers who have never been away from this mountain together, ever?"

"And that is why we both can tell you need some time away from the mountain and all these children." Ted looked deep into her eyes. "Admit it Jenny, you are weary of the everyday routine around here."

"Ted, I love it here, on this mountain." Tears filled her eyes. "You are here, my darling, and that is where I chose to be. I love you far beyond any words every spoken, ever written!"

"My beloved Jenny, I know how much you love me, that was never in question. My heart holds the same undying love for you." Ted's fingers caressed her face. "I also know you love your home, our life together on God's mountain. I am also aware much of our time is spent either with the children or doing duties on the farm, leaving us little time for one another. We need to get away my love."

"So, it really will be..." Ted touched her lips knowing what her question was.

"My beautiful Jenny, there will be a mission for us while we are gone, but, before the Lord hands us our work, we will have our long, awaited honeymoon, my darling."

5

CHAPTER 2

Jeff held on to Jacob while Naomi prepared the bath water. The squirming four-year-old fought to get out of his strong father's arms. Jeff Wineworth smiled down at his young son. "Son, it's just a bath. Its not the end of the world, boy."

"But papa, Teddy don't have to be washed by mama! I'm a big boy, I can take a bath when I get dirty, right papa?" Jacob looked up with his big black eyes.

Naomi stopped the water and stooped down in front of her unhappy son. "Now listen Jacob, behave this instant or no dessert for supper, got it? What's it going to be Jacob, no bath, no banana pudding!"

"Gee mama, you make it hard on a big boy!" Jacob pouted while Jeff tried to hide his smile.

"Alright Jeff, put him in the tub please." Naomi patted his head when he frowned up at his smiling father.

"Papa, mama doesn't give you a bath!" Jacob held on tight to Jeff's neck, still hoping for a rescue.

"Your beautiful mama can give me a bath whenever she feels like it." Jeff winked at Naomi as mischief shone in his blue eyes. "Then if she likes, she may tuck me into bed."

"Jeffery, behave yourself and make Jacob turn you lose." Naomi laughed and glanced up when the doorbell chimed out. "Who could that be? Sweetheart, be a doll and answer the door. My hands are full with this child."

"Sure thing, sweet one. Jacob, behave yourself for your mama or I will spank you butt!" Jeff chuckled when Jacob stuck out his lips pouting, turned and headed down to the front door. When he opened it, Jeff was staring into his own face.

The stranger on the threshold gave him a big smile, revealing beautiful, perfect teeth, no sharp canines like Jeff's or his sons. The voice proved to be almost as strong and deep as Jeff's.

"I suppose it's quite a shock to see oneself, looking back at you." Although the voice was like Jeff's, it fell very gentle on his ears. "I am truly sorry Jeffery to just show up at your door unannounced. I seem to have the advantage here." His dark eyes sparkled. "I trust mother never told you about me?"

"Mother and I did not share many words together unless they were filled with hate." Jeff stared back coldly. "Mother hated me as much as I hated her. "Too bad she had to die before she witnessed my change."

"Mother is...dead?" A sad look of remorse filled the stranger's eyes. "Mother could not have been that old. We are both in our early twenties! I was hoping to finally meet the woman who gave me a way when I was just an infant."

"Are you telling me that you are my twin brother?" Jeff stood in the doorway, untouched by this revelation by the man standing in front of him like a mirror image.

"That's right Jeffery. I am Jonathan, your twin brother, first born." He smiled. "It seems I arrived one hour before you finally made your arrival."

"Jonathan, is it?" Jeffery wasn't sure he could trust this exact copy of himself. Something just did not feel right.

"I can feel you do not believe me Jeffery, even though we look exactly alike." Jonathan pulled out a letter and a birth certificate and handed them to his twin brother. "I have brought these as proof of my identity. Mother gave these papers to the pastor she went down in town to see and ask him to find me a good Christian couple to adopt me. The caring couple decided I should know about the woman who gave me up so I could be safe. When I reached sixteen, they gave me the letter she had written, along with my birth certificate. Read it for yourself Jeffery. I think it pretty much explains everything."

Jeff's quick reading scanned over the birth certificate and noticed the date matched his. Without a word, Jeff handed Jonathan the legal document back before his long slender fingers opened up the blue stationary. After all the years since his mother's hand wrote the words in front of him, Jeff's keen smell picked up the smell of her perfume. He swallowed back his emotions as he read her words.

"My dear sweet innocent son, my beautiful baby, my Jonathan, I write this with a broken heart but it is for your own sake I must send you away. Your father is a very evil man, my sweet son. Your father has chosen Jeffery over you, sweet precious baby. This evil man saw in Jeffery, even at birth, how very much they were a like.

7

Joan Byrd

Jonathan, my brave boy, you were born one hour before your brother Jeffery, but your father pushed you aside waiting for his evil son to come out. The long hour waiting in painful labor was torture. Your brother scratched and clawed, stomped his feet against my side until at long last the little devil tore out and let out his wild animal howl. Your evil father stared down at your helpless little body and ordered me to get rid of you. While all the men were celebrating over Jeffery's birth, I wrapped you up and slipped away in the cover of darkness. I knew if you stayed up here on Black Mountain, you would not live to see the morning.

I walked all the way down the mountain road for fear of someone hearing me start the car. Especially your mean father, whose ears are keen as an animal. I was relieved to see lights on inside a small church, so, I took you inside and poured my heart out to the good pastor. After hearing your father's threating words, the pastor agreed with me that your life was in danger and he promised to find you a good Christian home, dear son. Then after I told him not to tell me his name for fear of this evil being reading my mind, the compassionate man begged me not to return to the mountain. I thanked him for his concern but reminded him about my other baby boy, waiting on the mountain and eight-year-old Gregory, whom I loved and could never abandon to face what lies ahead on top that black mountain. Before I left the church, the loving pastor ask me to bring Jeffery down for baptism. I was shocked by his suggestion but I would try anything if it would help change my younger boy.

Please know Jonathan, your life will be better now and you will be safe from your family. I do not have the strength to protect you from your father, even your twin brother, Jeffery. Jeffery is destined for a life of hate and evil. He is just an infant but Jeffery is already showing great strength and cunning intelligences. I hope you can forgive your mother. Please know I did it because I love you so very much, my son. I wanted you to know your legacy if you ever feel the need to search out your brothers. I trust you are wise enough to wait until you are an adult man, older, wiser and stronger. I don't know what the future holds, but I hope and pray life is good for you Jonathan, I love you dearly, your mother."

Jeff's eyes were wet with tears as he handed the letter back to his brother who had stood back watching the son his mother had described as evil and filled with hate, looking right the opposite. "She did love

8

you Jonathan and did the right thing by sending you away." Jeff's eyes stared pass his brother on the neighboring mountain, clothed in green and covered by the sun. "Our mother hated me and I could sense the incredible fear she felt whenever I was near."

Jonathan reached over and touched his brother's strong shoulder. "Jeffery, Mother might have been afraid of you but I could never believe a mother could hate her own child."

"It's true brother, mother hated the very sight of me." Jeff stared down at his brother. "And before you say anything, the feelings were mutual. I hated that woman and the very sight of her made me sick. The truth is, I hated all my family as well as everybody on this earth. Every tree, every flower, 'cute' little bunny rabbits, which I fed squirming and screaming to my pet wolves. Are you getting why mother wanted no part of me?"

"You paint a hellish picture of yourself brother. Mother said you took after Father and she describe him as very evil. She failed to give me father's first name but my adopted parents did tell me our last name is Wineworth." Jonathan had come back to his birthplace to get answers. He scanned the grounds nervously. "Jeffery, is father still here?"

"Walter Wineworth is dead. He met with an unfortunate accident several years ago." Jeff never broke his stare. "At the time of the accident, I admit I found it very amusing."

"Jeffery, you cannot be serious! The man practically worshiped you! You were his pick and he wanted me dead." Jonathan did not know how to take his unusual brother whose stare was unnerving. "Jeffery, just tell me when and how our father died!"

"If you must know, Walter hated my guts and the man went completely insane. While in a daze, he walked up to the top of the tower and jumped out the window on a waiting-raised pitchfork." Jeffery did not laugh this time when he told his morbid story, even at his brother's sick face. "The sad fact is, the deed has been done, regretted and forgiven."

"So, our father is dead along with his evil." Jonathan took a deep breath when he watched Jeffery shaking his head in a negative. "What, Walter didn't die?"

"Oh, my twin, Walter is very dead but our real father is very much alive and he is as evil as ever." Jeff waited for his brother to respond.

9

"But you said…" Jonathan was cut off by his brother.

"Walter Wineworth is not our father, he was mother's husband and all we got from him was his name. He only raised me then tried to kill me when I was still a small boy."

"It sounds like he too was an evil man. I see why mother sent me away." Jonathan finally looked past Jeffery and into the castle, noticing the inside did not reflect the outside. "All this evil coming from every direction, but yet as I peer inside at your charming interior, your castle looks warm and inviting."

Naomi stepped up beside her husband and stared at the man who had kept Jeffery's attention. It was like seeing Jeff looking back through a looking glass with a slightly fuller face. "Jeff, am I seeing double? I think I need to go to an eye doctor or…maybe Ted is my answer."

Jeff pulled Naomi up next to him, wrapping a strong arm around her. "Sweet one, there is nothing wrong with your beautiful eyes. You are not seeing double. This is my twin brother Jonathan. I was a little skeptical at first, thinking it was my old man's clever trick to fool me, but Jonathan has the paper to prove he is the real thing." Jeffery reached for the blue stationary in his brother's hand and handed it to his wife. "I recognized my mother's handwriting and I can smell her perfume still on the paper."

Naomi held it up to her nose, but without Jeff's keen smell, she smelled nothing and wondered if his twin smelled the fragrance. She read the touching letter and reached for Jeff's black handkerchief before handing the letter back to its rightful owner.

"I received a letter from Gloria on this very stationary and I remembered the wonderful fragrance it held. Jonathan, your mother had a kind soul and she tried to save me one time."

"I have three questions for you my dear lady." Jonathan smiled at Naomi and she noticed instantly his teeth were normal. "What is you name, how are you connected to my brother Jeffery and what did mother try to save you from?"

"I can answer your questions Jonathan." Jeff's blue eyes were cold when he looked down at his brother. "Her name is Naomi, she is my wife and mother was trying to save her from me!"

"From you brother? But, surely you could never hurt such a lovely creature as Naomi." Jonathan took Naomi's hand. "Naomi, a name from the Bible. Tell me, is it true, you were afraid of my brother?"

10

"Jonathan, when I first met Jeffery he was so much different than the man you see standing beside me. Everyone was afraid of Jeffery and his black mountain. He was strong, beyond human strength, extremely handsome..." Naomi smiled up at the man she loved when he pulled her close. "And he is even more handsome now since he came over to find love. But then, Jeff was cunning and very evil and yet there was a tenderness about him when he was with me and I was deeply in love with him."

"Not everyone was afraid of me, my dove, remember? Jeff stared down at his brother's hand still clutching to his wife's and he pulled it away into his own hand, giving Jonathan a warning look. Noticing the tension between the newly found brothers, Naomi spoke up.

"Of course, Ted was never afraid of you darling, no matter what you did."

"This Ted you speak of sounds important. You have mentioned his name twice." Jonathan looked from Jeff to Naomi.

"Ted is very important to both of us." Jeff turned quickly around sensing the boys were going to start fighting and shortly Jacob yelled out about Jeffery hitting him. "Boys, behave yourself this instant or I am coming up those steps and put an end to your picking!" Things grew extremely quiet in the big castle so Jeff turned quickly around to face his brother. "Our sons! Teddy is going on seven and thinks he's seventeen, Jacob just turned four and acts his age! You were asking about Ted. He lives on the other mountain, the one that is touched by the hand of God, so that makes him our neighbor and the best friend I have ever had. Actually, next to my loved one here..." Jeff wrapped both arms around her and pulled her in closer. "Ted is the only human friend I have ever had."

"Very touching and quite sad." Jonathan looked into his brother's cold eyes and wondered if he would ever consider him a friend and noticed a slight snarl from Jeff's lips. "Jeffery, how did mother die?"

"She created a fire, then fell into it, burning herself in its hot flames, rather than be subject to what I was about to give her." Jeff remained untouched by his brother's obvious shock and emotions.

"Mother burned herself alive? Were you truly going to hurt her Jeff, your own mother?" Jonathan stared in disbelief. "What kind of animal could do such a thing. To scare the woman that gave you

11

Joan Byrd

birth into the pain of burning in flames?"

"The evil animal that I was born to become, brother! Mother knew me, she had been caught trying to flee with my woman. I would have tortured her without mercy, then I would have destroyed her!" Jeff's eyes fell down to the floor, sadness swelling up inside his heart. "I was different then, Jonathan. All I ever knew was hate and evil. Love had not made its way into my black heart yet. I just cannot ever take back those actions from my past. I still struggle with forgiving myself but I know because of that one percent of love that mother gave me, I have been born again into Christ, Jesus!"

"You spoke of our father still being alive. You said you got your evil from him and that he is still very evil." Jonathan tried to find a ray of hope for their family. "Jeff, mother's letter spoke about how bad you would become, like she knew father's blood was bad. She wrote how he chose you because he could tell, even before you were born that you were his chosen son, not me. If you, being so evil could find salvation, surely there is a way for father to be saved as well."

"I think you need to tell him Jeff, darling." Naomi gently touched his handsome face and could read his anguish. "Tell Jonathan the truth about his father."

Jeff took around Naomi and buried his face in her hair, then turned to his brother. "Do you wish to know the true identity of our father, even though it will come as a shock?"

"Yes Jeffery, please tell me." Jonathan swallowed. "If it will shed some light on why my twin brother was so evil."

"This won't be easy to hear Jonathan! I am warning you! It's not too late for you to get back inside your car and drive away. Back to where it is safe from him getting to you." Jeff watched his nervous brother look from him to his car, then back. "Well, speak up! Do you wish to know who the hell he is?"

"Jeff sweetheart, please darling, calm down." Naomi rubbed his arm, relaxing his emotions.

Jonathan stared at his brother as he spoke up "Yes Jeffery! For God sake, tell me!"

"Our father is…" Jeff closed his eyes, trying to blot out the sneering face he had last seen. "Our father is Lucifer! Satan! The Dragon! The Devil, himself!"

Jonathan forced out a laugh. "I cannot believe that, Jeffery! Our

12

father is Satan, the prince of darkness?"

"That is right, big brother! That's how the cunning angel could see me inside mother's womb! I was his favorite, lucky for you!" Jeffery smiled, revealing his sharp canine teeth. I was more a wolf than a person! I had black eyes before I was almost destroyed by our father and was save by the Lord Jesus! My eyes are blue now, but I am stuck with these teeth." He stared at his brother. "Strange, your canines are not like a wolf's but yet, your eyes are as black as the ace of spades!"

"Yes, always strange, not only to me but everyone I met." Jonathan's attention fell on Naomi. "Naomi, you saw something in Jeffery, my dear, that apparently no one else did. You fell in love with him despite his evil and hate."

"I fell in love with Jeff the moment I saw him, when he saved me from one of his wolves." Naomi smiled. "And my love for Jeff has grown over the few short years I have known him. He is a wonderful father to Teddy and Jacob and the most loving, giving, husband any girl could dream possible."

"Your little boys, do they—" Before Jonathan could finish his sentence, Jeff had read his thought and answered.

"Both Teddy Jeffery and Jacob have black eyes, Jonathan, just like I had. Jacob, our youngest still hasn't grown into his canine teeth yet but our oldest, Teddy Jeffery, is overjoyed to have teeth like mine."

"My name is Jeffery Teddy, papa!" the brash seven-year-old stepped from the shadows where he had been listening, Destiny, his pet wolf, setting beside him observing the stranger closely. "So, you are Uncle Jonathan! We finally meet."

"You seem to already know me, son." Jonathan smiled at the handsome boy who resembled his brother and him. "Excuse me for asking, but, is that a wolf beside you?"

"It is sir! A gift from my grandfather! We named him Destiny!" Teddy smiled, revealing his sharp teeth, then looked up at his parents who were watching him closely. "And yes, mama and papa, I knew about Uncle Jonathan even before he showed up."

Naomi reached down and took her son's small hand. "Son, how could you possibly have known? Your father did not even know his twin brother would be coming." She turned to Jeff, whose attention had not left their son. "Jeff, you did not know, did you?"

13

Joan Byrd

"My love, I was never told about Jonathan, either by mother or this evil man I call father." Jeffery took Teddy by the shoulders, his gaze never leaving his eyes. "Alright son, out with it! I strictly forbid you to speak to your grandfather ever again!" Both stared at each other coldly. "Did you disobey me? Did you speak to that devil, boy?"

"Jeff, darling, surely our Teddy would not go against your wishes and speak to someone he knows is evil." Naomi dropped to the floor in front of her boy. "My darling son, please tell your mama you have not spoken to your evil grandfather."

"Mama, you have always told me to never tell a lie as has papa and my Ted." Teddy's little strong hand gently rubbed his mother's face. "I had a dream one night. An angel in red warned me about a man named Jonathan, coming to Black Mountain to take papa's place."

"That just is not so!" Jonathan laughed. "That child has some imagination! It is the craziest thing I have ever heard! It is far-fetched! Way out there in the end field!"

"The end field?" Teddy's eyes grew big as he asked, "Do you play baseball, Uncle Jonathan?"

"Baseball?" Jonathan looked confused briefly, then remembered his statement. "You are referring to, way out there in the end field! As a matter of fact, I could have played all-star baseball if I had not chosen another profession." Jonathan and Teddy started laughing while Jeff and Naomi still looked serious, still not sure what their son's dream meant. "Hey, you two lighten up! I think Jeffery and I are bonding!"

"Teddy, one second ago you thought your uncle was out to take my place?" Jeff's stare remained cold. "Which one of my positions son? As your papa? As your mama's husband?" Jeff's eyes flashed fire. "As Lucifer's favorite son?"

"Jeffery, Jeffery! Please brother, I seek neither." Jonathan smiled to reassure his twin. "I came with the hopes of finding my brother and getting to know him better. As for your sons, I feel honored to be their Uncle Jonathan. As for Naomi, your lovely wife, just be glad you found her first. I am truly happy for you Jeffery and I respect wedding vows deeply." Jonathan grew serious. "As for wanting to replace you as Lucifer's favorite son, I would rather disappear from ever existing than have that place! I was brought up

14

in a strong Christian home and I am a true believer in the word of God!"

"You told our son you could have played all-star baseball but you chose another profession." Naomi held tight to Jeff's hand as she asked. "What is this job you do Jonathan?"

"Believe it or not, I am a minister in the Methodist Church." Jonathan laughed softly by their surprise expressions. "I wonder how father feels about that, Jeffery?"

"He probably regrets not killing you himself when you were a baby instead of ordering mother to do it." Jeff looked over at the black sedan. "Your luggage is in the trunk. You will stay with us."

"If you will have me." Jonathan walked toward the car, Jeff and Teddy close behind him. "The church bishop has given me some time off before placing me in a permanent church. I recently graduated from Duke Divinity University. I preached at my first church for training and built up the small congregation to almost double before a permanent minister took over."

"So, did you grow up in North Carolina or just attend college here." Jeff carried the heaviest bag in and Teddy was handed the smallest.

"As your home is resting on this mountain connected to the Blue Ridge, my home was on the other end of North Carolina, near the Outer Banks." Jonathan followed his brother and nephew inside the big castle. He took in the high ceilings and stone floors. Jeff knew he was looking around in wonder so he asked his brother as he turned to face him.

"Is this your first castle, Jonathan?"

"It is and I never dreamed they could be so big inside!" Jonathan grew excited. "It is like living in a fairytale! Princely and charming!"

"This place was anything but a fairytale castle until my bride graced these walls from dark and gloomy to bright and airy." Jeff's stare made his brother tremble. "Before my Naomi came into my life, most everyone who entered those doors below, never left." He smiled. "At least alive or with their own mind."

CHAPTER 3

"Jonah, come to mama, sweetheart." Kathy held her hands out for her crying three years old. "You mustn't draw on Ruth's picture. Mommy has got you a sheet of paper, just for you." Kathy smiled up from the floor as Ted and Jenny came inside with their twin girls. "Wow! You girls have picked a fine harvest of grapes. I can almost taste your daddy's wine!"

The girls giggled as they handed their buckets to the parents and got down next to Kathy. Mary picked out a red crayon and handed it to the three-year-old.

"Can we help you watch Jonah, Aunt Kathy? Mom and dad will want us to stay close to you and Matthew while they are away."

"Are you two going away somewhere?" Kathy stood up, brushed off her pants, and took her friend's hand. "Alright Jenny, out with it?"

"Ted is taking me on a little vacation." Jenny gushed with excitement. "Just the two of us."

"It's a honeymoon, Aunt Kathy! The Father thought they needed some alone time." Martha smiled up at her parents. "A time to hold hands, make goo-goo eyes at each other, kiss a lot and..." she giggled, "make love!"

"Martha Neenam! That may be what we will be doing but you do not have to announce it to the entire Christian family!" Jenny looked up at Ted for help.

"Is this some more of Teddy's teaching, Martha?" Ted picked her up and let his hand run over her blonde head. "My beautiful daughter, remember you are only four years old and I would like you to be my little girl a while longer, understood?"

"You bet dad! I love being your little girl!" Her little arms encircled his neck as she kissed him. "You are the best dad ever! Right Mary?"

"The very best!" Mary got off her knees and jumped up to hug him as she smiled up at his handsome face. "The very best and the best looking!"

"Well girls, there is no mistaking that you belong to him. You

16

both are two adorable angels!" Kathy patted their blonde locks. "And Jenny, you and Ted deserve some alone time. Very romantic alone time!" Kathy moved up close to her friend and whispered. "I'm just glad my little Jonah is a normal three-year-old."

"I know what you mean Kathy." Jenny watched Ted's eyes twinkle when he glanced their way and her daughters giggle, before he got down on the floor and passed out the crayons. "Unfortunately, so does Ted and the girls." Jenny laughed at her friend's head shaking. "We all forget they can hear us or read our minds, but Kathy, I would not trade what I have for nothing in this world."

Matthew made his way from the kitchen drinking a big glass of water. "Hey ducks, did I hear that you guys are going on a romantic get-away?"

"Matthew, did Andrew relieve your sheep duties so soon?" Ted stopped playing and walked over to the young man. "I ask you to stay out until four."

"You did Ted and I had planned on staying out my full time." Matthew knew Ted probably already knew why he was standing there instead of watching the sheep as told.

"Never mind what I know Matthew, just answer my question!" Ted's eyes stayed on Kathy's young husband.

Matthew glanced nervously over at his wife, before answering. "Well, I sort of ask brother Andrew to take over for me today so I could take Kathy somewhere special for her birthday."

"Birthday!" Jenny grabbed her mouth and looked helplessly at her best friend. "Oh, Kathy, it slipped up on me!"

"We knew it was Aunt Kathy's birthday mom. That's another reason we told her we would watch Jonah for her." Mary looked up dreamily into Matthew's smiling eyes. "I think what Matthew's got plan for Kathy is very romantic."

Kathy's eyes lit up and she made her way over to her handsome-rugged husband. "Just what have you planned for us this evening, my dashing shepherd?" she moved in close and quickly backed away from the smell. "Whatever it is, as soon as you wash that sheep smell off, we might go through with it."

"A romantic night of dinner and dancing and then…" Matthew looked over at Ted, whose eyes had stayed on the young man. "I thought it may be nice to get a motel room for the night, you know, a little privacy."

17

Joan Byrd

"WHAT'S WRONG WITH YOUR OWN ROOM MATTHEW?" Leah had been listening from the bottom step. "IT'S NOT LIKE YOU HAVE NEVER DRIVEN UP THE MOUNTAIN IN THE DARK BEFORE AND YOU AND KATHY NEVER LET US KIDS DISTRACT YOU BEFORE!"

"Leah, will you ever outgrow that big mouth of yours!" Matthew felt like his beautiful gift to his wife was being ruined by this red-headed monster

"Matthew, take Kathy out for her birthday." Ted pulled the money box down and held out several bills. "There is enough here to take her out for a fine meal and dancing..." Ted eyes twinkled as a smile fell on his lips. "And by all means, you deserve a quiet romantic night so there is enough here for a room at the Goldsburg Inn, much nicer than a motel." Ted turned away from a shocked Matthew to a nervous red-headed teenager. "Leah, you are a young lady now and it's time you start acting your age. You can start by speaking softer."

"Having a big mouth is not lady like, I know. I am really sorry Ted for blasting off! It is a bad habit and I can see how much I hurt brother Matthew." Leah looked down shyly. "I'm sorry Matthew. I guess I'm just a little jealous I don't attract boys."

"Come over here and give your brother a hug!" Matthew lifted her up in a brotherly hug. "And don't you go worrying about getting a boyfriend. I bet if you took down those pigtails, you would have your choice of boyfriends."

"Thank you, Matthew. I hope you and Kathy have a wonderful time." Leah gave Kathy a hug before going outside. "Happy birthday Kathy!"

Matthew took the money Ted was holding out then gave him a hug. "You and Jenny deserve that honeymoon more than any couple I know. And don't you worry about the kids or the farm work while you're gone. Kathy and I will make sure the older youth help us with the kids and work and don't worry, I'll do my share of watching the flock."

"I know I can depend on you Matthew, but when the time comes, I will be calling you and Kathy to join us." Ted noticed Jenny's confused eyes as he took around her. "First the honeymoon, as promised, then the mission. It is God's plan that we call them in for help."

18

The Lost Sheep

"I understand darling and any amount of time we have together will be cherished." Jenny's attention fell on all the children filing in for lunch and gave a sigh. "Who on earth is going to watch all these children while the four of us are away?"

"On earth, my mother is on her way and from heaven, God is sending someone great with children to help out." Ted motioned for the girls to remain silent for he felt them read his mind and heard their giggles.

Jeff watched from the window as his newly found brother was bonding with his oldest son. A smile fell on his lips when he sensed his wife coming up behind him. He reached back and took her hand, pulling her beside him at the big window.

"My beloved, it appears our Teddy has taken up with my brother and they are becoming real close."

Naomi looked down at the pair laughing as they threw the baseball back and forth. "I think it's good you have a brother darling since the rest of your small family are gone." She gave him a loving hug as he caressed her hair.

"I have all the family I need or want, my beautiful Naomi, you and our boys." Jeff stopped speaking as he tilted his head, sensing someone near. "Ted is coming down the path to speak to us. It has to do with Teddy's behavior with his girls."

"What sort of behavior has our son been up to, Jeff?" Naomi looked out at their seven-year-old puzzled.

"Boys will be boys, sweet dove." Holding tight to his wife's hand, he led her down the steps to the front door and opened it, in time to see Ted step out of the forest. Destiny and Thorn came running to the door and spotting Ted, began growling. Jeff snapped his fingers, and the wolves moved obediently next to him. Glancing toward his brother, Jeff noticed Jonathan never looked to see who had the wolves upset.

"Ted, what has my son been up to?" Jeff asked as he gave Ted a welcoming hug, then stepped back so his wife could greet the other special man in her life.

"Yes Ted, please tell us if Teddy has said or done anything wrong with Mary and Martha." Naomi looked upset. "Teddy has been acting up. At seven you would think he were seventeen by some of his actions and words.

"Sweet angel, it's not as bad as you are imagining." Ted's smile

19

reassured his beloved adopted sister. Your son seems to know a lot about sex and he likes to share certain facts with the girls. This morning Martha came out with some of the words Jeffery Teddy, which he prefers being called, told them."

Naomi looked up at her smiling husband in dismay. "Jeff, did you know Teddy was interested in...sex?"

"Most boys are, sweetheart. It only natural for the male sex to get interested in it at a young age." Jeff smiled broadly at Ted. "Perhaps, Ted was the only kid who never thought of sex growing up."

Ted blushed, knowing how true Jeff's words were. "Jenny was a new experience, that's the truth, my brother." Without looking, toward the stranger playing with young Teddy, Ted continued. "So, you have a twin brother, Jonathan." He grew serious. "Watch him! Both of you!"

"I have sense it too, Ted." Jeff felt his brother at last looking their way, and he knew he had heard their quiet words. "And I feel sure he knows we sense it."

"There is no doubt, my friend." Ted finally turned to face Jeff's identical twin. "I can easy tell you two apart and its not your slimmer face." Ted gave Jeff's brother a warm-genuine smile as he made his way over with Teddy. "Jonathan, so, you are a man of God?"

"Yes I am. A minister of the Methodist faith." Jonathan returned the incredible man's smile. "You must be Ted, I have heard so much about. They failed to mention your striking resemblance to our Lord. Amazing."

"I resemble my father Jonathan and yes, I am Ted, Jeff and Naomi's friend and closes neighbor. Welcome to Goldsburg." Ted looked down at the young boy whose eyes were cast down to avoid Ted's stare after overhearing their conversation about him and the twins. Jeffery's sharp hearing had taken in every word, so he felt relieved by Ted's statement to him. "Teddy, I see you like your Uncle Jonathan."

"I like him very much, Ted." He looked back down and kick at a rock. "Uncle Jonathan is teaching me to play baseball. He could have been a pro but he gave up the bat for the Bible."

"So, he is teaching you?" As if in slow motion, Ted turned his gaze on Jeff's brother, causing Jonathan to tremble involuntary,

20

then reached down, taking Teddy by the hand. "You wish to be called Jeffery Teddy now, son?"

The young boy rolled his black eyes up. "I do Ted. Teddy sounds so childish! So innocent."

"And you think that is bad, young man?" Naomi took his arm. "Get inside that house this instant and wash off! Then you can explain why you have been telling Mary and Martha things they are too young to hear!"

"Sorry mom. It's that they are so hot!" he lifted his shoulders "I still cannot decide which doll I want!"

"There's time for that boy! Just get inside like your mama told you!" Jeff's cold stare gave his son the chills so he turned quickly toward the house, his father calling after him. "And stay away from Goldsburg Mountain until your mama and I can go with you!"

"Sure papa, whatever you say." Jeffery ran up the steps to avoid any more words from his father.

"Kids pick up so much trash watching television these days." Jonathan tried to make excuses for the young man's actions. "It's a good ideal to keep close tabs on what the boys watch."

"That is very interesting brother." Jeff remained cold. "Good try in defending the little demon's actions but it won't fly here! We do not own a television, nor do we wish to! We make our own entertainment and ours is a lot more interesting." Jeff turned his attention to Ted. "So, my busy friend, you are finally taking Jenny on a long-awaited honeymoon?"

"A honeymoon?" Naomi threw her arms around the man who had saved her and helped bring her to God. "You both deserve some alone time together. I know! I was a part of that big family and I know how they take up a great deal of your life. We will see that Teddy stays home while you are away."

"Thank you, angel." Ted turned his attention on Jonathan. "It is good to meet you Jonathan. How long will you be visiting our town?"

"I really couldn't say Ted but Jeff is the only real family I have left and I would like to know him better." He appeared sincere. "If we have the chance to bond, I might just move here if the bishops can find me a church."

"The town of Goldsburg is a friendly town and most all those living down below are good Christian people. I am sure your leaders

21

can find a good church for you here." Ted shook his hand, patted Jeff on the shoulder and hugged Naomi before heading in the woods blocking the thoughts that came to his mind. "There will be a church open for you Jonathan Wineworth, but will it be Christian?"

Jeff watched Ted disappear in the forest, then took his wife's hand and started back inside the castle. "Coming Jonathan?" He could hear his brother walking up the steps behind him as he too blocked his thought from his twin. "Yes Ted, we shall see just what sort of preacher this brother of mine is."

CHAPTER 4

Blaze looked around to make sure no one had followed him and his younger companion Devin. He silently motioned him forward as the handsome youth cast his attention down to the squirming cat in his hands. "My anxious little friend, soon you will meet your end!" Blaze laughed out as he glanced behind him to find Devin's was smiling broadly.

"I think the master will be pleased with this offering, Blaze. It's far better than that sick kitten we sacrificed last week." Devin admired his leader, the sixteen-year-old who walked ahead to their hideout in the forest.

"Devin, give the signal to let Fire know it is us." Blaze ignored the younger boy's remark about the sick kitten. It made him feel like a failure in front of the pack. "See that you do not speak about that ill cat again, you little creep!"

"Sorry Blaze. I will light my won so Fire will see it." The young boy held the lighted won high and waved it back and forth until he saw movement ahead. "She has spotted us Blaze and has pushed back the hidden passage door."

"Will you two, hurry and get in here before someone sees you!" Fire's black outfit made her hard to see as she waved them in with her long black nails.

"What gives girl? Do you take me for a fool! No one followed me!" Blazed pushed past her and smiled to himself when he heard her slam the door shut. "Beautiful, you know I am always careful! I cover my tracks, sweetheart!" He smiled at her stone face. "Cheer up Fire! We stole a perfect sacrifice this time!" Blaze held up the scared black cat. "Satan will be please this time."

Fire took the shivering cat and gently rubbed its soft fur. "You won't be sacrificing this cat tonight or any night partner. Haven't you noticed how perfect he is for me? His fur is shiny black and he has eyes that are a devilish green!" the black hair beauty reached over and patted the boy's cheek. "Thank you for my birthday present, even if you forgot I turned sixteen today."

"Birthday?" Blaze narrowed his eyes. "Then you must find us a

23

Joan Byrd

sacrifice for tonight birthday girl or explain to Lucifer why you decided to withhold his sacrifice."

"Relax lover boy, my sacrifice for us makes yours look like child's play." Fire led both boys to the small opening and pointed at the goat grazing outside in the dark. "We might have to wait until tomorrow night to offer our sacrifice though." She turned and walked deep into the cave, Blaze right behind her.

"Look fire, I give the orders around here and I say we make our offering tonight, Friday the 13th!" Blaze felt the younger boy on his heels and turned to push him back. "Look creep, stop following us around and get loss!" Blaze grabbed Fire's wrist and pulled her around. "Are you going to tell me what the hell is going on, Fire?"

"It's Patches and Blake! They have run away again!" Fire flopped down in an old stolen chair and began rubbing the content cat's back. "I went to get some firewood for the sacrifice and took Willy with me to help carry it. Marble stayed behind to keep the kids busy, but the little buggers tricked her and slipped out when she had her eyes closed."

"What is wrong with those brats?" Blazed grabbed a hot beer and took a big sip, making a face. "Shit! That is offal! What good is stolen beer when we don't have power for our ripped-off refrigerator?"

"Stop complaining and tell me what we can do about those no-account kids? If someone finds them, they can scare them into leading the cops to our hideout!" Fire grabbed the warm beer and took a sip making a distasteful face before handing the can back.

"If they know what's good for them, they will stay hidden! "Fire shot from the young man's eyes. "I will tan their hides good this time! Do you think they went for help?"

"Who do they know besides us and Blackheart? I cannot see them going to him. They hide whenever he comes calling. Not that I blame them," Devin had been waiting a few steps away and asked nervously. "They're your family Fire, you should know their moods."

"Only Patches, dumb ass! Blake is Willy's brother and as black as the ace of spades!" Fire made her way to the secret door and peeked out in the darkness. "They are kids left on their own, just like us, remember? Our mama was a drunken prostitute and God knows who fathered me and Patches!"

"I have a mother." Devil puckered up trying not to cry in front of his leader. "I just lost her, that's all."

24

The Lost Sheep

"Are you stupid or something Dev?" Blaze slapped his face for showing weakness. "Your bitch of a mother got screwed, had you and left you at a dumpster to rot! Stop dreaming and face the facts pal! You are just like us, born to losers!"

"Blaze, do you have to be so mean?" Fire put her arm around the younger boy who was staring down, tears dropping on his old worn-out shoes. "This kid looks up to you, you, heartless creep!" Fire lifted the sad boy's face. "It's alright Devin. Come on with me, let's go search for Patches and Blake."

"We will all go to search, except Marble. That little failure can stay put and let us back in." Blaze yelled out for the frighten girl that had been hiding ever since she let the kids escape by her. "Marble, get your ass out here now!"

She moved out from behind a stack of boxes and stood trembling "I...I am sorry Blaze!" Marble swallowed back her fear. "I never meant to...I mean Patches and Blake wanted to play hide and seek and they ask me to be the finder. I closed my eyes and counted to twenty and when I opened my eyes. I thought they had hidden but..."

"They tricked you?" Blaze stared down.

"I ran toward the door and not seeing the banana peeling from Blake's banana, I slipped and fell hard on my seat!" Marble blinked back her tears, fearing the worse.

Blake reached over and rubbed her round butt. "Poor baby. Does that hurt?" Mischief showed in his lustful eyes. "I promised to make it feel all better tonight." His fingers moved over her breast as Fire rolled her eyes up in disgust. "For a twelve-year-old, you're well-endowed beautiful."

"Thanks Blaze." She smiled down shyly. "I would really like that tonight."

"Of course, you would, you little harlot!" Fire faked a smile. "By the way, your breast, are big because you are almost seven months pregnant, to God knows who's baby."

Blaze laughed and took Fire by the hand. "Coming sweetheart. Are you jealous?"

"Hardly! Let's move before it gets daylight." Fire jerked her hand free and headed out the door as she yelled back to the pregnant twelve-year-old. "Marble, watch the damn place and let no one in but the pack!" The small search party disappeared into the darkness.

25

CHAPTER 5

Jenny pulled their new white SUV to a stop in front of the public parking lot for the ocean excess and climbed out. When Ted spotted the vast ocean in front of them he stopped and gazed out with fascination. As Ted looked out he took Jenny by the hand and started walking toward the water.

"God's world is vast and breathtaking! I have heard many people speak about the ocean, Jenny, but I never dreamed it could be as beautiful as the mountains."

"You have never seen an ocean before darling? Surely you must have came to America either by ship or an airliner." Jenny smiled into Ted's child-like face as he looked out.

"Jenny, I arrived at Goldsburg Mountain in a flash of light, not a ship or a plane. I had no doubt the ocean would be so beautiful, for God the Father created it." Ted finally looked down at Jenny. "But, in the first day of creation and in the days of Noah, the entire earth was covered with water. One round ball of water."

"So, this is part of that vast water that once covered all the earth." Jenny pondered the notion that was the reason for most of the earth being surrounded by bodies of water to this day. Then it became apparent that Ted could not climb God's mountain while they were gone. "Ted, you are aware that there is no mountain near the coast, except the high ones that still lay under the ocean.

"When the Lord is ready to speak to me, dearest Jenny, He will call me. Either to the edge of the water or up a small grasses knoll. My Father is with me wherever I am, just like He is for you, my love." Ted's gaze wondered up and down the quiet beach. "It appears we are the only souls on this beach this evening. There's no one in sight."

"Good! There is nothing like having your own private beach." Jenny's eyes lit up with mischief. "It's too bad the beach won't be light much longer and there's the fact we have got to find our motel."

"Our Motel is just up the road two miles on the right. It appears to be almost new and we can drive up to our room and park." Ted casually walked her back to the car as she stared up at him with amazement wondering if he knew what their room looked like. "Our room? It is a cozy little end room with a very large bed." Ted took her in his arms smiling. "I hope you don't get lost from me in that giant bed darling."

"That will never happen, Mr. Neenam. I will be sleeping right beside you no matter how large that king size bed is." Jenny held his hand as he helped her behind the wheel.

"That's good Jenny." Ted reached over and kissed her as she turned the car on. "The motel appears fairly small, ten units. I can see a good place to get our meals as well, and just in walking distance from the motel."

"Small does not matter, being in the end room is nice, car parking outside the room means secure and a romantic dining spot in walking distance will permit us to have a good bottle of wine with our meal and we will not be bothered with a red-neck sheriff pulling us over while driving impaired "Jenny laughed at Ted's uncertain expression. "And the best part, lover boy, is that king size bed for making love!"

"Jenny, we never get drunk! It is against our beliefs." Ted watched her chuckle. "You are just pulling my leg, you sweet little..." Ted stopped speaking and looked from the car window as his eyes froze on a thick, overgrown forest. As Jenny observed his strange behavior, he held a hand up for her to stop. "Jenny, could you pull over for a minute?"

After checking her rearview mirror and seeing no car in sight, Jenny quickly pulled over on the shoulder of the highway. "What is it, Ted? Is something out there or can you hear God calling you?"

Ted put his window down and stared out into the woods, not saying a word. He slowly closed his eyes and spoke softly. "I understand Father." Jenny knew to remain quiet until Ted finished conversing with the Holy Spirit. Ted opened his eyes and turned to face his wife. "We may leave now Jenny, but I must return to this spot in a few days."

Jenny drove to a stop in front of a big sign reading, The Ocean View Motel. It was exactly as Ted had described, down to the ten small rooms. Before they got out, Ted warned Jenny about the owner.

"A Mr. Blackwood is going to wonder about the two of us." Ted

27

Joan Byrd

got out and walked around to help her out, the perfect gentleman, Jenny thought. "He does not think we go together. You know, the perfect mates."

"How could a stranger possibly have that stupid observation?" Jenny laughed as she followed close behind her handsome young husband, admiring how good Ted looked in his jeans and white cotton sweater. The way Ted's long shag hair seemed to glisten in the late evening's sunlight.

Ted glanced around at her. "Trust my words Jenny. I just know for a fact Blackwell will think we do not go together." Ted opened the door and walked up to the desk where a middle-aged man stood, reaching for his glasses for a better look at the couple that just walked through his office door. First, he studied the beautiful, sophisticated lady with the incredible body then moved his attention to the young man, who was obviously a left-over hippy, then he motioned Jenny up.

"Do you have a reservation, my dear?"

"We do sir. Mr. and Mrs. Ted Neenam. I reserved a room last week." Ted pulled Jenny up next to him as he smiled at the bewildered man. "Is there anything wrong, Mr. Blackwood?"

"You know my name, young man?" The motel owner could not understand why this elegant lady was married to an obvious hippy and he watched in horror when she wrapped her arms around his waist.

"I remembered your name when I called for reservations Frank." Ted put his arm around his wife. "And I assure you sir, I am not a hippy, whatever that is."

"A hippy?" Jenny frowned at the skinny man. "My husband just happens to be very religious and he has friends in high places! Very high places! So, Mr. Blackwood, before you have another misguided thought, may I suggest you tell us the number of the room on the end and let my husband have our key, please! It has been a very long drive and I intend on going to bed early tonight."

"Very good, Mrs. Neenam." Shaking his head in total confusion, he reached for the key to room number 10. "Here you go, room 10, last room on the north side. I hope you both have a restful night."

"Oh, I'm sure we will Mr. Blackwood." Jenny followed Ted to the door and smiled back at the red-faced man. "Just after I have

28

made love to my wonderful, sexy husband for a couple of hours." She walked out smiling, leaving Frank Blackwood completely speechless. She ignored Ted shaking his head at her as she climbed behind the wheel and drove around to the end of the building. Still shaking his head over Jenny's comments, Ted opened the back of the SUV and pulled out Jenny's two bags. Setting them down to unlock the door, he glanced over at his smiling wife.

"Jenny, what am I going to do with you?"

"I can think of lots of things you can do with me, handsome. And before you start preaching to me about what I said to that inconsiderate room keeper, I had every right to defend my man!" Jenny walked inside with her smaller bag. "I just wanted that jerk to know just how well we go together!" Jenny watched Ted sat her big luggage on the bed and open it for her. "Ted, I still cannot believe that you did not pack a single thing for this trip, not even toothpaste!"

"Jenny, the Lord will provide as always." Ted gave her a kiss before staring down at the king size bed. "Jenny, are you sure you want get lost in that bed?"

"Not on your life, my darling husband." Jenny threw her arms around his neck and gave him a passionate kiss. "I'll be laying way too close to your hot body to get lost. You roll, I roll!"

"Alright!" Ted looked around for the bathroom and started over. "Do you mind if I go first Jenny? I really need to be excused."

"Sure, thing sweetheart. I'll just put away my things so they won't get wrinkle" Jenny blew him a kiss as he hurried to the bathroom calling back.

"I shouldn't be long Jenny. Just hang your things next to mine in the closet."

"Sure Ted, next your invisible clothes." Jenny laughed to herself until she opened the door to find two pair of jeans along with two cotton sweaters, one blue, one lavender. She hurriedly hung her clothes next to them and walked over to check the drawers in the small vanity. Just as she expected, Jenny found a stack of white boxers along with sky-blue bathing trunks."

"They even gave him a bathing suit, so, I guess we will be swimming." She mumbled, not noticing Ted behind her.

"Jenny, are you talking to yourself darling?" She turned to see Ted had brushed his teeth sparkling clean.

"I was just admiring your swim trunks darling. When did you learn how to swim? When you were small?" Jenny picked up her vanity suitcase and bedroom slippers.

"Swim?" Ted pondered the question for a moment. "I guess I haven't learned yet Jenny, but it appears I will be learning how tomorrow." Ted noticed her staring up at him, unsure of his intentions for learning to swim the following day. He gave her a gentle push toward the bathroom. "Jenny, could you speed this up beautiful. I really need my wife." Jenny watched Ted turn down the covers and pull off his clothes and lay down.

"And I need my husband." Jenny stared over at him, still worried about his attempt at swimming. "And not just tonight darling! I need you to be with me for a very long time! Ted, do you know how long it takes most people to learn how to swim? I was a fast learner and it took me four days to feel good about diving into the deep end."

Ted fluffed up the pillows and pushed himself up. "Jenny, I will dive in and start swimming. It will come naturally!" Ted let his hand run over the big bed. "Wow! This thing makes our bed at home look like a baby bed."

"Ted, stop changing the subject!" Jenny was getting flustered over his lack of concern. "You can't just dive in and start swimming Ted! It takes lessons!"

"Yes, I know darling. And that is why I will watch you go in first." Ted climbed from the bed and walked over to take her hands. "Jenny, just trust me please and get your butt in that bathroom, then hurry back!" Jenny glanced down at his manly readiness and swallowed. "I will be waiting for you in bed."

"I can see that Ted darling." Jenny dashed off to the bathroom mumbling to herself. "Turn me on, you, handsome sexy husband, so I will stop arguing with you about swimming." She finished quickly and stepped out unbuttoning her blouse, her attention on the watchful waiting husband. Turning to face the mirror to avoid his stare, she climbed out of her pants then removed her underwear, smiling to herself when she heard him sigh and turned to see his erection. "I am glad to know I can still turn you on Ted."

"Jenny. My beautiful Jenny." Ted held out his arms to her and she made her way slowly to the large bed. "You will always turn me on my dearest. Never doubt that. I am completely devoted to you and my love is overflowing."

Jenny smiled as she climbed onto Ted's lap, throwing her legs on either side. With passion swelling in his eyes, he pulled her down for a passionate kiss as his hands moved around over her perfect round breast. As if by magic, Ted was inside her, moving with slow motions. As their passion grew hotter, Ted threw her over to move faster until they both reeled with complete satisfaction.

They lay contented for a few minutes, then Jenny yawned and gave Ted a kiss goodnight before rolling over. Ted admired the smooth curves of Jenny hips and her perfect butt and he could feel himself getting aroused again. For a brief moment his thoughts turned to Jeff and how he claimed having gone several times in a single night and thought Ted might have that same gift. He knew, without a doubt, he could please Jenny and himself again but how would she take being woke up. Ted reached over and let his hand move over her hips and butt, causing her to stir before turning over to find Ted ready and waiting. He bent down and kissed her while climbing on top of her.

"No sleep yet, my darling lover. We are on our honeymoon, remember, and I need more of you."

Jenny pulled him close, feeling the need for him awake her body. "My wonderful husband, we need to honeymoon more often."

So as the distance waves crashed gently along the shore, the couple in room 10 was making waves of their own. One powerful wave after another.

CHAPTER 6

Jeff and Naomi made their way to the vegetable garden, buckets, hoes and rakes in hand. Although Jonathan had volunteered to help out with the weeding, Jeff insisted he enjoy his time off and perhaps watch from the garden bench.

Teddy and Jacob helped pull weeds for a short while until they started picking with each other and began to race around the garden, kicking dirt on their parents as they ran past. Jeff looked down at his wife to see dirt in her hair and with one strong jab, stuck the hoe up in the dirt as he reached out and grabbed a boy in each hand.

"Boys, if you are not going to help your mama and me, then get your butts away from this garden before you drown you mama with dirt!"

Both boys glanced down to see their mother looking up as she wiped dirt from her hair. They felt their father's fingers dig in their arms. "We never meant to sling dirt mama! We are sorry papa."

Seeing the frightened boys shaking from their father's anger, Jonathan waved them over. "Look fellows, since you don't feel like pulling weeds, how 'bout you come with me and pick some flowers for your mama to show her just how much you love her and to make up for kicking dirt in such beautiful hair."

"Can we papa? Can we go with Uncle Jonathan and pick some flowers for mama?" Jacob called out hopefully, knowing it would make him feel better to show his mama how much he loved her.

"Jacob, besides the roses your mother planted in the rose garden, there are no flowers on Black Mountain. I put a curse on them before I met your mama because I hated them same as I did songbirds. Have you ever seen anything other than crows, ravens, owls or bats?" Jeff yanked the hoe from the soil and stared coldly at his brother. "If you wish to help where those boys are concern, just keep them over there where we can see them!"

"Jeff, you are wrong about the flowers." Jonathan stood up to take around each boy and nodded his head up a small hill several feet away. "Growing just at the top of that hill is a large bunch of wildflowers. They either escaped your evil curse or the very breath and light that reflects off dear Naomi must give them a reason to thrive."

"You may tag along with your uncle boys, but I am telling you that hill will be bare." Jeff returned to the weeding as he called back to his youngest. "Jacob, stay off that hill son! You are too little to be climbing."

Naomi had stood up to check out the hill they were going to check and knew instantly it wasn't safe for children to climb. "Jacob, you heard your papa! No climbing son. And Teddy, please be careful and listen to Jonathan."

"My name is Jeffery, mama and don't worry about me, I climb really good!" To the oldest boy's delight, the hill was completely covered with red flowers with black centers, shaped much like a daisy. "Hey papa, you must be blind! This hill is covered with red flowers!"

"Just be careful going up that hill son and find somewhere to tuck the flowers so you will have both hands to come back down!" Jeff's keen eyes focused in on the red hill as he shook his head with disapproval before looking down at his worried wife. "Naomi, my beloved wife, I just this morning looked from our window across those hills and they were bare as always! Not a flower in sight!"

"How strange." Naomi shielded her eyes as she watched Teddy climbing up. "Flowers just don't grow that fast. Do you know any reason they might grow all of a sudden Jeff?"

"It would take someone with magic skills, and since Ted is not on the mountains and I am certain it wasn't me, my guess would be my twin brother, although he would never admit it." Jeff stared coldly at his twin who was observing Teddy going to the top.

Jacob tugged at Jonathan's sleeve until he glanced down to see the tears forming in the young boy's eyes. "Uncle Jonathan, I really want to pick mama some flowers too. Will you let me go up, please?"

"Jacob, your papa and mama don't want you to climb that hill by yourself." Jonathan glanced over at the vegetable garden and found his brother busy hoeing out weeds while facing their way and noticed Naomi down on her knees pulling morning glory vines from the bean poles, glancing up occasionally.

"Then, can you take me up, Uncle Jonathan, please. I'm not very heavy." Jacob pleaded as Jonathan took his hand, pointed up

33

on the hill toward a disappearing Teddy, pretending to find a better spot to watch him, made his way around the base, out of view from the parents. Jonathan smiled down at the pouting boy then swung him up on his back. "Just hold on tight Jacob and let's go find Jeffery."

"Thanks a million, Uncle Jonathan! Now I can pick my mama lots of pretty flowers too!"

They had reached the top when Jeff finally spotted them. He threw down his hoe and helped Naomi stand up, pointing to the three figures standing at the top of the hill, bent over picking flowers. "It would appear our clever four-year-old got his uncle to climb him up. I hope brother Jonathan is as good bringing him back down with a handful of stupid wildflowers!"

"Oh Jeff, they look so high and they seem so small." Naomi shielded her eyes from the sun as she watched Teddy spotting them and waving proudly from the top. Naomi moved closer so she could call out to her boys. "You kids be careful up there and listen to your Uncle Jonathan!"

"It was a piece of cake, mama!" Teddy cupped his hands around his mouth and yelled down. "And boy, I can see a lot from up here! Goldsburg Mountain is in plain view over there!" Teddy pointed toward the green mountain.

"Just finish picking those flowers for your mama and get back down here before I swoop up after you!" Jeff had made his way to Naomi's side, garden tools securely in his fist. "I finished getting those damn weeds sweet one, now the garden can flourish this summer."

"Jeff darling, I am afraid the weeds will be non-stop this summer." Naomi noticed his cagey smile. "Jeff, what did you do?"

"I considered my curse upon innocent little flowers and thought getting rid of the weeds would be twice as rewarding." Jeff stopped speaking and stared up at Teddy descending from the hill, Jonathan moving slowly behind him carrying Jacob on his back.

Never taking her eyes off her children coming down the high hill, she, lend over to ask the obvious. "Jeff, tell me you didn't curse those weeds out of our garden."

"Although I was tempted my adorable wife, I knew I should not." Jeff enjoyed her relieved smile, then turned in time to see Teddy reach the bottom of the hill. "Almost down! So far, so good."

34

The Lost Sheep

Near the bottom, Jonathan's foot slipped but he quickly caught himself, causing Naomi to grab Jeff's arm. They watched him set Jacob down on a smooth rock and tried to hear what he was telling their young boy. "Jacob, we're almost at the bottom." Jonathan smiled reassuringly to the frightening boy, holding tight to his bunch of wildflowers. "Now listen son, I will jump down then hold out my arms so you can jump. Remember, I'm great at catching balls and you're almost as light as any ball I've ever caught. What do you say champ? Think you are brave enough to jump buddy?"

"You bet, Uncle Jonathan! I'm a good jumper, just ask Teddy Jeffery!" Jacob answered as he looked down at the ground nervously then at the wildflowers in his small fist. "I might drop mama's pretty flowers when I jump, Uncle Jonathan."

"We would not want you to lose your beautiful mama's flowers, Jacob." Jonathan held out his hand. "I will carry them down with me and give them back to you after you jump, alright." The little head bobbed up and down as he carefully released his loving gift.

Jonathan made the jump easy, then handed the flowers to Teddy before holding out his hands. "It's your turn Jacob. Jump and I will catch you. I promise."

"Jeff!" Naomi jerked her hand away and started running for the hill, Jeff close beside her. "What if he misses? That's still too high for Jacob!"

"Jonathan, let me catch my son!" Jeff was beside his brother in a flash, but Jonathan would not budge. "I can catch him, brother! I took him up there, let me help him down!" Jonathan wanted to prove himself worthy of family as he stared up into the boy's scared eyes. "Jacob, I love you. I would never drop you! Please trust me and jump."

Without another thought, Jacob closed his eyes and leaped from the smooth rock. On the way down, Jacob's foot hit a rock sticking out and started a rockslide toward Jonathan. Without thought for himself, Jonathan jumped up to grab the frightened child, pulling him to safety just as a good size rock hurled down. Jonathan slung his body around, putting Jacob out of harm's way while the heavy stone slammed down hitting Jeff's twin on his leg.

"Just lie still Jonathan." Naomi was on her knees beside him, trying to keep him calm." Jeff is bringing the car around. I have called Doctor Ward and he will meet us at Goldsburg Hospital's emergency room." Jonathan squeezed his eyes shut in pain as he managed to ask.

"Jacob? How is the boy?"

"Jacob did not even get a scratch, thanks to you Jonathan. You saved his life. We will be forever in your debt by your heroic actions." Naomi lifted his trembling hand and looked up when Jeff ran up. "Jonathan has come too darling and is in great pain."

"The rock broke his leg." Jeff leaned over and stared down at his brother. "Hang on! We are going to rush you to the hospital."

Jonathan tried to look around, but his whole body seemed to be aching with pain. "The boys? Who...who will watch Jeffery and Jacob?" Jonathan cried out in pain when Jeff lifted him up and carried him to the car. Laying Jonathan gently down on the rear seat, Jeff shut the door and ordered his family in the front.

"Lie still and don't move! The kids are safe with us!" Jeff sped out the long Wineworth driveway and down the mountain. Within minutes Jeff pulled up to the emergency entrance and two aids were waiting with a stretcher. With no assistance, Jeff had his brother on the stretcher in seconds.

"Jonathan, I am going to park the car, see Naomi and the boys are safe in the waiting room and I will be with you shortly."

"Thank you, Jeff." Before Jeff could leave, Jonathan took his arm. And Jeff, please tell Naomi you both are not in my debt for saving Jacob. Jacob is part of my family too. I would lay down my life for those two boys and you guys."

"Would you, brother?" Jeff remained cold toward his brother. His strong senses warning him something wasn't right and things different from how they appeared. The men waiting were getting nervous watching the identical brothers. Jeff felt their uneasiness and looked down at them. "Take him in. I will be along shortly." Jeff could not resist his soft chuckle when the men hurriedly wheeled Jonathan inside. With two big steps, Jeff was behind the wheel.

36

CHAPTER 7

Ted watched Jenny walk out in a red bikini bathing suit and turned to model it for him. He walked over and touched her stomach. "Jenny, is that all there is to that swimsuit? It looks as if the middle is missing."

Jenny laughed at his innocents. "Darling, this is a two-piece bathing suit. Very popular and stylish, if you have the figure to wear one." Noticing how well Ted looked in his blue bathing trunks, Jenny gave a little whistle. "And you look as good as I thought you would in your swim trunks. Blue is a good color for you, handsome."

"I see you chose red." Ted pulled her into his arms. "Jeff would approve."

I am not trying to please Jeff, Ted. Just my sexy husband." Jenny grabbed two towels and walked to the door. "The same sexy husband who has never swam but says he is going swimming."

"Jenny Neenam, just get moving to that pool and jump in and swim." Ted walked by her to open the door, took her hand and headed out to the motel pool. "I guess I will have to show you how fast I can learn and I will jump in and swim."

"But, you said you couldn't swim and you never have." Jenny walked toward the pool looking back over her shoulder at Ted.

"I haven't, swam, ever Jenny. I do not lie!" Ted stopped short when Jenny suddenly twirled around to face him. "Jenny, will you please relax honey. I will swim after watching you."

"Oh brother! I'm just glad you're not heavy!" Jenny threw her towel on one of the chairs as she mumbled to herself. "I think I can pull you to safety when you start flapping and sinking!" She spotted a man with big muscles sitting on the edge of the deep side of the pool. Breathing a sigh of relief, Jenny took Ted's towel and threw it next to hers. "Good! I've got help pulling you up and out when you get in trouble."

Ted shook his head, knowing Jenny wasn't going to take his word this time. "You're just not going to make this easy, and it's obvious you do not believe a word I am saying. So, it would do no good to let you know that man will be of no help."

Jenny looked up at him and made a face. "You are really going through with this then?" she looked to see the man smiling her way and it was obvious he could be of help.

"Jenny, have I ever lied to you before?" Ted gently turned her face toward him. "As a matter of fact, have I ever lied before, period?"

"No, you have not! It is not in you to tell a lie, Ted Neenam, but, to quote the Bible: God helps those who help themselves! And, unless you are a fish that just found water, you need lessons! God gave us the gift of choice and right now, you need to rethink your choice!"

"Just jump Jenny, before I push you in!" Ted was getting upset.

"Very well, Mr. Fish! Watch and learn!" Jenny made her way up the diving board and looked down to see if he was watching. "I will make it a simple dive, but if you prefer, you may dive in feet first."

"No, I will do it just like you. Just jump before it's time to go back to bed!" Ted stood staring up at his beautiful wife, determined to make a dive exactly like hers.

"Before it's time to go back to bed! Very funny!" Jenny walked to the end of the diving board. "Well, here goes!" Jenny dived gracefully into the water, came up and swam out in the middle of the pool before turning around to see Ted. When she noticed the spot empty where he had been standing, she wondered if he had chickened out until he called out from overhead.

"Jenny, up here!" Jenny's head flew up toward the diving board and saw her fearless husband waving from the end of the board. "Make room darling! I'm coming down!"

"Oh shit!" Jenny bit her lip, glanced quickly to make sure the stranger was still sitting nearby before looking back up in a panic. "Just be careful sweetheart. I am here for you."

Ted smiled, sprang twice and made a dive down into the water. He surfaced for a moment, gave his wife a smile, then went back down. Taking a deep breath, Jenny dive down after her husband and found him sitting on the bottom, looking around. Ted pulled Jenny down into his lap giving her another smile. "It is beautiful and cool down here Jenny, darling." He spoke easily enough as Jenny's eyes grew wide.

The Lost Sheep

"Wha…" Jenny motioned to the top and she struggled with her breathing, giving herself a kick off of the bottom, she swam up quickly, coughing up water. Ted sprang up beside her, looking worried as he hit her back lightly.

"Jenny? Are you alright? What happen to you down there?"

"Ted, I got strangled by water when I tried…" Jenny stared in disbelief. "Ted, what just happened down there?"

"I don't know what you're talking about Jenny." Ted looked confused. "Did I do something wrong?"

"First, you gave me a big smile, but there have been others who can hold their breath and smile." She had seen it but she couldn't believe what she had witnessed. "But sweetheart, you talked under water!"

"Doesn't everyone?" was Ted's innocent reply.

"Ted, everyone else has to hold their breath under water." Jenny touched his face lovingly. "No one has ever been able to breathe under water until now."

"Excuse me, my dear." The strong man sitting on the edge had been watching and listening to the young couple. "Maybe this young man had on an invisible oxygen device."

Ted leaned close to Jenny and whispered. "Sweetheart, maybe my talking under water is something only I or Jeff can do so maybe we should not let this news get out."

"I agree Ted. Let me handle this interested party." Jenny gave the stranger a beautiful smile. "I am truly sorry if our little game made you curious, but you see, my lover and I enjoy creating little fantasies when we go on vacations." Jenny could see Ted frowning at her so she moved over to whisper in his ear. "Do you have a better ideal sweetheart? Maybe, the truth." She watched Ted close his eyes and shake his head. "I didn't think so. I've been known to tell a few innocent tales in my time, only under the right circumstances. Do I have your permission to finish my story, Mr. Neenam?"

"By all means, Mrs. Neenam. I will give you this one because it's our honeymoon and I'm feeling extra generous." Ted touched her hand under the water. "You are a literary major so, this should be a good fiction."

Jenny gave him a kiss and turned back to the waiting man, who sat kicking his feet slowly in the water. "Sorry, I needed his permission before I revealed one of our favorites." Jenny swam up

39

closer so other sunbathers could not ease drop on what she was about to make up. "This is where my lover pretends to be an alien from out of space and he comes to earth to seduce an American woman, drag her to his spaceship and make wild passionate love."

"Oh, how delightful!" the stranger laughed out. "I get it! This young man pretends to be from another planet, meets you under the water where he pretends to speak, and not being human gets you all excited, then he takes you to bed, I mean, his spaceship and wow!" the man's eyes grow wide. "How exciting! What imaginations you have!"

"That about sums it up, right darling?" Jenny turned to find Ted swimming across the pool. "Shit, he was right!"

"Right about what, my dear?" the strong man continued moving his feet in the water.

"Oh! He said he felt like taking a swim." Jenny noticed the man hadn't been in the water except for his feet. "If you don't mind my asking, are you ever going to get in and swim or just sit there and kick your feet?"

"Well, since you asked, I'll give it a try." He jumped in, went under the came up in a panic coughing and calling for help, before going back under.

Jenny made a dive for the man, only to find Ted had reached him first and they both lifted him to the service. Ted gathered the man, twice his size, in his arms and carried him up the pool steps and laid him by the pool, laying his hand over his mouth. The man started spitting water out and blinking his eyes sheepishly.

"I thought I was sitting at the shallow end. I can't swim."

Jenny felt very perplexed for believing this man could have helped her with Ted, and it worked out just the opposite. Ted had saved the strong man from drowning. She finally got the courage to face her husband and found him smiling down at her.

"Jenny darling, always remember, things don't always seem to be as they appear."

CHAPTER 8

After having a light lunch at the local diner, Ted and Jenny walked hand-n-hand down the beach. Occasionally Ted would stop and look out at the vast ocean and close his eyes. After watching him repeat the same thing over and over again, Jenny finally broke the silence.

"Ted darling, what are you doing? You walk a while then stop, look out and close your eyes, as though you're in a dream like state."

"I am taking pictures of the ocean and beach, the sea birds and jumping fish, in my mind, so I can share them with all the children when we get home." Ted looked down at his wife, reading her thoughts before she could respond to the obvious. "No camera is necessary Jenny, so stop worrying about forgetting yours."

"How do you know I forgot my camera?" Jenny stopped, shook her head knowing he could read her mind. "Alright, so you know everything. But darling, it would have been nice to have a few real photos of us on our honeymoon."

"Why would you want pictures when you have me." Ted teased. "Besides the pictures I am taking in my mind, we are making beautiful memories to hold in our hearts forever."

"That is a beautiful way of saying I love you." Jenny pulled his head down to kiss him. "Its just that when I'm old, I can look back on this honeymoon and cry and smile."

"Why cry, my love. This is a beautiful time we share." Ted looked down innocently.

"Yes darling, it is." Jenny reached around his waist and gave him a hug. "Its just the part about growing old that makes me sad."

"Jenny, my Jenny. I will keep you, young darling." Ted pulled her into his arms. "There will come a time you may appear old, but only on the inside. When you are in my arms, you will feel just as alive and young as you do today. My love, you will see yourself forever young when we walk into God's kingdom together, forever, side by side."

"With you, forever young." Jenny repeated his words, took his hand and continued down the beach. Ted had pointed out four sea

Joan Byrd

gulls dancing on the beach but stop suddenly and stared out in the water. Jenny followed his eyes to a lone swimmer out in the ocean, a long way out.

"That young man is about to get into trouble. He is about to drown." Ted spoke calmly. "No one around, nor his friends who are busy flirting with some girls, will see him in time." He kept his eyes on the young man as he squeezed Jenny's hand. She looked around at the beach goers and noticed no one was watching the man in the water. "Even if they hear him cry for help, they won't be able to reach him in time."

Jenny once again took in those on the beach and noticed the chatting teens, several families with children and all of them oblivious to others around them. She noticed the lone swimmer seemed to be doing fine, but Jenny knew Ted, and she knew he sense immediate danger for the teenage boy, drifting out on his float.

"It will happen...NOW!" Ted released Jenny's hand as she looked out, hearing a far away cry for help.

Everyone stopped what they were doing and looked out in the water for the one in trouble. One of the young men cried out as he raced down to the water's edge, followed by his friends.

"My God! Its Jay! He's in trouble!"

"They can't make it in time!" a mother grabbed her child in her arms as she looked out helplessly at the thrashing young man, yelling for help. "Please God, help that young boy! Send your angel!"

"Ted, you were right! Are you..." Jenny stopped and stared at the empty spot beside her, then looked around for him. He had simply vanished. Then she heard the excited voice on the beach call out.

"Where did he come from?" one woman cried as her small son said with big eyes.

"Could he be an angel?"

"He seems so young, himself and is it just my eyes or does he..." an elderly man had managed to make it to the water's edge. "he looks like..."

"Jesus! He looks like Jesus!" a little girl sang out, jumping up and down happily. "Mommy, its Jesus! Will he walk on water to bring that boy in?"

Jenny ran up in the crowd and stared out in the ocean at Ted and

42

the young man, now calm. "That man out there saving that young man is my husband!"

"Your husband?" One of the women looked at Jenny with uncertainty. "Then could you tell us how he managed to get way out there so fast?"

"She's right lady! When we looked out there all we saw was our friend yelling for help. Your 'husband' just appeared from out of nowhere! Can you explain that?"

One of the teenage girls checked Jenny out and instantly noticed her knock-out figure in the red bikini. "You are married to that heavenly hunk? He's really hot!"

"Such talk young lady!" the elderly man raised his white eyebrow. "Can you not see how God sent that young man out there to rescue that boy in trouble while his friends were flirting with you three girls? We are obviously witnessing an honest to goodness miracle!"

Jenny watched as Ted swiftly made his way back with the young man, then she gazed around at the excited crowd as she mumbled to herself. "Ted, you have some explaining to do for all these curious witnesses!" she held her breath as he easily helped the young teen reach his friends. They laid their towels down for Ted to lay him down. No one took their eyes off the man with the long hair and heavenly blue eyes. The large crowd gathered around Ted as he looked down at the smiling youth and took his hand.

"God is happy you have come home Jason. Be more careful from now on when you go swimming."

"Thanks Ted. I promise I will never do anything foolish again, like that!" Jason could not take his eyes off the man who rescued him, both body and soul. "God sent you to save me, not just from drowning but my life forward."

"Hey Jay, what happened out there, man?" one of his friends helped him stand as Jason watched Ted walk over beside the beautiful woman in the red bikini and take her hand. As if nothing had happened, Ted said softly.

"Let's go shower and get dressed for a romantic dinner, darling."

The three young girls looked at one another with dreamy eyes as the rest of the interested crowd stepped over to the handsome couple, full of questions. Ted gave them his beautiful smile as he spoke.

43

Joan Byrd

"My friends, I know your heads are brimming with many questions." Looking into every face, the witnesses suddenly felt a peace rush through them, causing them to relax and just listen to his words. "What I tell you is this. Listen and except with your heart. God, the Father, ask me to save this young man from drowning, both in the ocean and in his life's choices. This was His purpose for teaching me to swim this morning. When the Father ask of me, I go!" Ted turned and started walking back down the beach with Jenny, leaving the crowd speechless.

Ted, dressed in white pants and a white shirt, escorted his beautiful wife, dressed in a long blue sundress, into a very romantic French restaurant. Everyone dining inside stopped to admire the handsome couple who had entered. The woman watching marveled at the young man's charming manners as he helped Jenny in her chair. They thought what a perfect couple they were and how lucky the lady was to have a man so young and handsome. Ted bent down to her ear to whisper.

"Those ladies in here are right, you know. The thoughts they are thinking."

"What exactly are they thinking, darling?" Jenny reached across the table and touched his face. "That I am a lucky woman to have such a handsome young husband."

Ted blushed. "I must admit they were thinking that too, but what I was agreeing with is the fact that we are a perfect couple, Jenny." Ted reached over, lifted her hand and kissed it. "I love you Jenny."

"I love you too Ted." Jenny blew him a kiss, then picked up the menu and found everything was in French. She peeked up to find Ted trying to make out the words and she reached for his menu and patted his hand. "May I order for us, darling? I learned French in college and I really could use some practice." Noticing Ted's relieved smile, Jenny placed their order. The waiter brought out a basket of warm French bread, along with a fine French wine. Before the waiter could open the wine, Jenny picked it up and looked at the label, noticing it was a very expensive wine George Pennington used to order for them. Jenny handed the bottle back to the waiter and smiled. "There's been a mistake here. I'm so sorry but I believe you brought us the wrong wine. I ordered…"

"Yes madam, I am aware of your choice but it would appear your entire meal has been paid for, right down to this magnificent

44

wine." The waiter smiled, keeping the, giver a secret as promised and opened the bottle.

"How did George find out about are trip here?" Ted looked up at the bewildered man standing over them. "It was George Pennington who paid for this meal, correct?"

"A...Why, yes sir, it was Mr. Pennington. But how?" Jenny interrupted the confused man.

"Trust me when I say, don't ask?" Jenny smiled at Ted. "Good old George must have got a tip from someone on the mountain. It's just like George to pay for the entire meal including one of his favorite wines."

"Your friend Mr. Pennington must really like you because he has also paid for " The waiter was cut off by Ted.

"The entire, honeymoon vacation!" Ted shook his head. "I knew God would provide! He led George to call the mountain and Matthew filled him in." Ted sat back as the waiter poured a small amount of wine into his glass for him to taste for approval. Not knowing the custom, Ted stared up at the smiling man.

"Is this all I get? I assure you sir, I am old enough to drink wine. I have been making it for years on our mountain and drinking it since I was twelve."

Jenny couldn't control her chuckle as she glanced up at the flustered waiter. "Ted darling, you will get more after you sample the wine first to see if you like it."

"Where is you sample Jenny?" Ted looked over innocently

"Could you just pour me a little taste as well." Jenny smiled up at the ruffled waiter. Jenny drank down her sip, then watched Ted enjoy his before she gave the waiter what he was waiting for. "The wine is excellent!"

"Then it's excellent, Mr. Cromer! Pour away." Ted did not look at his questioning eyes but he did read his thoughts. "I am certain you introduced yourself to us, Mark."

"Of course, sir, whatever you say sir." The nervous waiter hurried away mumbling to himself. "Well, Mr. Pennington did tip good!" He started to enter the kitchen when he heard the diners grow silent and looked around to find the young man getting ready to pray.

"My heavenly Father, with a happy heart I give thanks for my life with Jenny, our beautiful daughters, Mary and Martha, my friends and extended family. For all these new friends who dine among us, for those who serve us as I hope they serve you. For the food that is set before us and the caring hands that made it. Bless each one here this night with a love fill and giving heart and thank you for your tender mercies and grace, Amen."

CHAPTER 9

The Wineworth's had returned to the castle with Jonathan. After Jeff helped Naomi out of the car, he opened the back door and easily lifted up his brother, who wore a cast on his right leg from his ankle just above the knee. Teddy had been observing his father's strong muscles when Jeff caught him staring.

"Teddy, run and catch up with your mama so you can open the door back when she unlocks it."

"Alright papa!" the young boy smiled up with admiration. "And the name is Jeffery, papa. I want to be strong one day, just like you!"

"I have no doubt you will be just as strong, Teddy Jeffery, but for now, do as I say. Now, get moving!" Jeff was running out of patience with his oldest boy insisting for the name swap. The last thing Jeff wanted was to hurt Ted's feelings.

"You cannot blame the boy Jeffery, for wanting to be named after his papa." Jonathan watched Naomi and their sons moving in front of them as his strong brother carried him as though he were just a boy himself. "Your son admires you and just wants to take after you."

"The new me, I hope." Jeff made his way up the stone steps to the guest room and smiled at his pretty wife for having the bed unmade and the pillows propped up for a more comfortable rest.

"Alright sweetheart, just tuck Jonathan in and I will head for the kitchen to start supper." Naomi looked down at her brother-n-law and smiled. "The doctor said you needed to rest the remainder of the day so we will bring you a tray up tonight. Jeff will get your wheelchair out of the car as well as the crutches for later. There's a bell by your bed if you need us."

"Thank you, Naomi. You are truly an angel." Jonathan watched her closely as she walked out, then smiled up at his brother. "You're a lucky man Jeffery to have such a beautiful, caring wife, and two great kids, who love and admire you."

"I am aware how lucky I am Jonathan." Jeff switched on the bedside lamp and handed his brother the book he had started reading. "If you will excuse me, I am going down to the kitchen to

47

Joan Byrd

assist my beautiful caring wife right now." Jeff turned toward the door and without a smile, walked out.

Teddy had carried over the pan of potatoes his mother asked for and watched as she washed them off. "Mama, remember when we were waiting for Uncle Jonathan to be taken care of in the hospital and I took Jacob to the men's restroom?"

"Did something happen to you boys in there?" Naomi stopped washing the potatoes to listen to her son.

"There was this man in there, washing his hands and staring at me and Jacob. The whole time he was watching us he was thinking mean thought about me, Jacob, and daddy. I could tell Jacob was getting nervous and that made me real mad! I wanted to send the man flying into the mirror!"

Naomi took Teddy hands in hers and looked at him tenderly. "Son, you must never think mean thoughts just because someone else does. We must treat others the way we would like to be treated. Do you wish to share with me what that stranger was thinking?"

"His bad thoughts were, those boys belong to that evil man that lives on top of Black Mountain. Why God allows men like that to have children is beyond me! They both should have died at birth!"

"That was truly a mean and cruel thing for anyone to think, darling." Naomi sat down and pulled her seven-year-old in her arms. "There will always be people son, who judge others, never really knowing anything about the ones they are putting down. They are breaking one of our God's commands for judging others.

"But mama, I think Jacob heard his thoughts too." Teddy looked over at his younger brother under the table pushing a red truck. "Mama, Jacob is little and it's up to me to protect him. He started shaking real, bad and when I ask him what was wrong, Jacob started crying."

"Why was your brother crying, Teddy?" Jeff had walked in, overhearing his son. "What did Jacob tell you?"

"Jacob pulled me over to the end sink and whispered that man don't like us or our daddy!"

Jeff stood over his oldest boy, staring down, reading the stranger's thoughts and seeing what Teddy Jeffery had done to the man. Jeff knew not sharing it with Naomi would be wrong, no matter how much it hurt her. She had to know what her son was capable of. "Yes son, I know what you did." Seeing fear in Teddy's

48

eyes and uncertainty in his wife's, Jeff gripped his boy's shoulder. "Tell your mama Teddy Jeffery, she has a right to know."

"Teddy, what on earth have you done?" Naomi felt for Jeff's hand as they both watched him, neither noticing the other interested listener. Jacob had stopped playing and had crawled out from the table to see if his brother was going to tell the truth.

"I approached the rude man and told him he was very mean to make my little brother afraid! Then I told him to never speak bad about my family ever again or bad things would happen to him." Teddy suddenly felt brave and his eyes turned cold. "I really hate that man!"

"Teddy, you must never hate anyone! God wants us to love one another." Naomi looked up at Jeff, suddenly afraid she might lose her oldest son to the evil side. "Please Jeff, tell me our son did not kill that man!"

"No Mama! Jeffery did not kill that bad man!" Jacob ran over and grabbed around his big brother. "That mean man laughed in his face, then pushed him out of his way. He walked out the bathroom door laughing and then we heard a loud scream. That bad man tripped and fell down the steps."

"Jeff?" Naomi's trembling hand covered her mouth as Jeff pulled her into his arms, eyes still on Teddy.

"Sweetheart, Jacob is right! The man had an accident on the stairs. I was down with Jonathan when paramedics rushed in with a man who had had an apparent heart attack and fell down the back stairwell." Jeff knew in his heart it could easily have been his son who had put a curse on the heartless stranger, striking him with great pain which led to his falling down the flight of steps. But Jeff did not think his loving Naomi could handle those cold facts about her innocent little boy, and as always, Naomi came first in Jeff's heart.

"The postman just brought these two letters for you Jonathan." Naomi took the breakfast tray and opened back the curtains to let in the morning sun. "I thought you might enjoy the sunshine. Isn't it a beautiful day?"

Jonathan had been watching Naomi closely and as she opened the curtains back, smiled at her perfect body as she gazed up at the blue sky. "It is very beautiful, Naomi." His eyes went to her face when she turned around.

"Well, enjoy your mail. I hope it's good news. Jeff will be up

Joan Byrd

shortly to help you get up." Naomi smiled and left Jonathan to his letters and thoughts.

"You certainly have brightened up my day, Naomi Wineworth!" Jonathan spoke softly as he ripped open one of the envelopes and started reading, "Blackheart, Blaze and I have been arrested and cannot get out until you come for us. Sorry to interrupt your 'family' visit, but we don't know how the kids are fairing or if they have been found by the police. Patches and Blake ran off and as far as Blaze and I know, they are still missing. Please come soon! We hate this stinking jail! Fire." Jonathan shook his head as he tore open the second letter.

"Reverend Wineworth, those kids you have been in charge of and trying to help, have gotten into more trouble. We caught them stealing food from a convenience store, taking a dog from the kennel, and conducting indecent behavior in a public place, not to mention, under-age drinking with wine stolen from the same convenience store. Request you come at once to retrieve these young delinquents or they will be tried and sent to the youth prison for a long time." Signed Randy James, Chief of Police. Outer Banks Headquarters.

Jonathan's dark eyes stared angrily at the first letter before hiding it inside the book on his lap. He folded the sheriff's letter and tucked it inside his shirt pocket. "Yes, I know what I must do." Smiling, he forced himself to move to the side of the bed and whispered. "Get those kids out of jail and bring them here."

Moments later, Jeff had arrived to help his brother in his wheelchair and he had filled him in on the troubled kids he had been helping and them getting arrested. "Jeff, I would never ask you if I could make the trip myself. Those kids need me. I have made them my responsibility. All I'm asking is for you to go after them for me." Jonathan looked pleadingly at his twin. "It shouldn't take but a few days."

"You want me to go to the Outer Banks, the coast of North Carolina?" Jeff spoke more to himself than his brother. "If I go, Naomi goes with me!" Jeff looked down at his brother coldly, sensing feelings he didn't like.

"Of course, Jeff. You could take Naomi, but if the boys stay here with me, I would need help with them since I cannot walk without aid." Jonathan tried to keep his real thoughts blocked while

50

he continued to speak. "Perhaps, someone from Goldsburg Mountain could come over to help with the cooking and watching the boys."

Jeff's eyebrow went up, knowing Jonathan was avoiding his real thoughts. Sensing Naomi approaching, Jeff turned to smile at her when she entered. "Sweet one, Jonathan has asked us to travel to the coast and rescue two of his troubled young teens. He says they are his responsibility and they have gotten into trouble with him gone."

"Would we take the boys with us. Jonathan cannot watch them, nor can he do any cooking for either himself or Teddy and Jacob." Always thinking of others, Naomi looked down at her helpless brother-n-law, sitting in the wheelchair. "Jeff darling, as long as Jonathan is unable to fend for himself, he needs help. The coast isn't very far away sweetheart, so it shouldn't take you but a couple of days. Maybe it would better if I stayed here to see to everyone."

"That just will not happen, Naomi." Jeff noticed the hopeful look fade from Jonathan's face. "You 'will' come with me or I will let those juveniles rot in jail!"

"Jeff, sweetheart!" Naomi took the letter Jonathan handed her to read. After reading Chief James's report, she took her husband's hand. "Jeff, they're just troubled kids, like the ones Ted took in. I was one of those young teens. We cannot be responsible for them being sent to prison. If Jonathan cannot help them, I know Ted can."

"Ted will already be there, on his honeymoon." Jeff pulled her close. "I'm sorry if I sounded cold and uncaring, my love, but I just cannot leave you at home. I need you."

Naomi looked into his loving eyes and smiled. "If you want me by your side my love, I will come with you. I will find someone to help around here while we are away."

"That sounds great! Thank you both very much." Jonathan sat back relaxed. "I will keep the boys busy and out of trouble. Absolutely no climbing while you're gone. I truly love Jeffery and Jacob."

"We know you do Jonathan." Naomi handed him back his letter. "We will need for you to write up a letter asking Chief James to release the children in our custody?"

Most certainly. I will write my request immediately with the reason I could not come in person." Jonathan reached for their

51

hands. "Thank you both for doing this for me. It really means a lot." His black eyes met Naomi's. "And you might not want to refer to Blaze and Fire as children in front of them. They will find it offensive. They consider themselves adults and even if they're not, it's hard to convince them otherwise."

"If I were the one responsible for the little heathens, I would immediately change those demonic names!" Jeff, took his wife's hand and left the room.

CHAPTER 10

Ted had sent word for Matthew to bring Kathy and join them on the coast, giving him the directions and name of their motel. He knew the honeymoon was almost over, although he and Jenny would have enjoyed a few more days together, God's work would always come first.

Rising just before dawn, Ted made his way down the quiet beach knowing God, the Father was waiting to speak to him. His warm beautiful blue eyes scanned the horizon, noticing the first rays of sunlight coming up slowly above the water.

"Father, I heard you call. You wish me to find these children that have been left on their own, two lost from the others."

"Yes, my son. Sweet precious children that have been led astray, lost and afraid." The morning breeze blew gently through Ted's long hair as he listened with patience. "There are seven in all, different ages and they have fallen prey to the evil one."

"So, these children have no family or unfit parents they ran away from?" Ted could feel the pain in the children's hearts and he knew of the two, smallest separated from the others.

"Some ran away from an abusive parent, one throw away at birth, the rest from foster homes not much better. You must find them and take them up the mountain while there is time, my son."

"I know you will show me the way, Father. I have sensed their souls in a patch of woods. I have yet to sense the youngest two." Ted suddenly sensed the arrival of Jeff and Naomi. "I see two loved ones are coming to retrieve the oldest two lost."

"True, my son, the oldest two are the deepest in the cult, even though they are just sixteen." The Father's voice came warmly. "Jeff and Naomi are not aware of the situation. It has been blocked from their mind, although Jeff's keen senses knows something has been blocked from him. Their mission here is to help out a brother."

"Jonathan." Ted grew serious, remembering his strong doubts about Jeff's twin brother. "I know I must love everyone, my Lord, good or evil and my heart does love. But there is something about Jeff's brother that bothers me and I cannot find trust in him."

53

Joan Byrd

"With good reason, my son. Watch him closely." Came the still small voice.

"Teddy and Jacob, their little ones, have been left with him." Ted searched the sky for answers. "His leg, he claims has been broken." Ted grabbed his chest and looked out at the rising sun with distress. "Jonathan has sent for Ester to help him. She is innocent and pure."

"Ester, she has turned seventeen." Came the strong voice.

"She turned seventeen this month, Father. Her Christian beliefs are strong and righteous." Ted felt God in action and smiled. "You have sent John with her. Thank you, Father."

"Brother Jonathan could not complain after he was informed that Hannah would not allow one of the girls to come on their own and it was her understanding that Mr. Wineworth needed a young man to help him dress."

"As always Father, you shower us with your blessings! It is hard for me to be in two places at the same time without leaving my Jenny." Ted closed his eyes remembering their night of love. "I'm aware I could have been back on the mountain in a flash, but I could never leave her side in a strange place."

"And I would not ask you to, my loving son. It was I who sent you here in the first place to have some much-needed time alone together. Your gracious mother and the young angel I sent have been doing fine so you may concentrate on Jenny and the lost children. That is enough to keep you busy at the present." There was a slight chuckle in the Lord's voice as he said. "You spoke earlier of not being able to sense the two smaller children. I tell you true, you will find them today in a most unusual place, my son." The laugher grew a little louder as Ted looked up, wondering out loud.

"What sort of place could be so funny, Father?"

"Let me just put this plain." The voice began to fade. "The honeymoon is over son, as of this morning." The voice seemed to ripple in the waves. And Ted, good luck with Jenny."

Ted knew the Lord was hinting at something as he ran his hand through his hair. "Good luck with Jenny? Where can those kids be hiding?"

Ted stood over Jenny, smiling as she talked in her sleep. He could barely make out her mumbling words but knew she was dreaming about them making love.

54

The Lost Sheep

"Mumm Ted, yes darling, oh yes there, my love." Jenny moved her body as though she were feeling pleasure. Just watching her made him grow excited but he immediately remembered God's warning: The honeymoon is over son.

"What exactly did the Lord mean?" Ted never meant to whisper out loud but his voice brought Jenny out of her dream and she opened her sleepy eyes and focused in on her husband, up and fully dressed.

"Ted darling, have you been out for breakfast again?" she sat up and stretched. "I just had the sexiest dream. We were making love and I was getting very close to fireworks when I heard you whispering." Jenny stopped speaking and stared at a confused Ted when the sound of children's giggles came from somewhere close by. "Ted, did you hear that? It sounded like…children giggling?"

Ted put his finger to his mouth and pointed to the floor beneath their bed.

"Don't be silly darling. There isn't any room under us." Jenny pulled the cover nervously over her naked body. "This motel is on the ground level."

"I am well aware of that, Jenny." Ted spoke softly as his lips moved in silent conversation. "Under the bed."

"WHAT?" Jenny jumped from the bed and grabbed around her husband as she whispered. "Under our bed?"

"This morning, before I left the Father, He informed me the honeymoon was over." Ted got down on his knees and pulled the bed skirt out. He gazed into the eyes of two frightened children, cuddled together. "How long have you two been hiding under our bed?"

"Oh, my God!" Jenny's thoughts flew back to the previous night of hot sex with her husband, never knowing they had runaways hiding under their bed taking in every tiny detail. Ted read his wife's thoughts, then the children's thoughts.

"Jenny, it was hot darling and yes…" Ted looked at each child. "Both of you witnessed everything, something that should have been private and only shared by the two of us, who are in love."

"I'm sorry mister." The small girl spoke nervously. "We never meant to listen to you. We thought this room was empty, you know, not rented out."

"Yeh! This is where we come to hide when we run away from

55

Fire and Blaze!" The young black boy blinked. "There's never been anyone sleep in here before, cept one other time and all they did was fuss and snore."

Jenny laughed as she reached for her clothes. "Ted, keep them under that bed until I get dressed. Make sure those two did not sneak out to watch us making love."

"We didn't miss, honest. It would not have been anything we hadn't seen before if we had though. We've watched two people have sex before." The little girl yawned. "My sister, Fire and Blaze."

Jenny walked out combing her long hair as she shook her head over the little girl's comment. "Who is this Fire and Blaze? Sounds like names from a bad cult movie."

"Fire and Blaze are cult names, Jenny and I afraid these innocent children have witnessed a lot more than they're telling us." Ted reached under the bed and pulled the kids out. They were dirty and smelled as though they had not bathed in months. Ted wrinkled his nose from the odor. "I am not sure why I did not sense your presence, but why I never smelled you is beyond me."

"Ted darling, I can answer that last part." Jenny smiled at him holding both children at arms-length. "I was wearing a lot of perfume last night and nothing more."

The kids giggled as Ted frowned up at his wife. "And that was the other warning from the Father this morning! Good luck with Jenny."

"Just what did he mean by that?" Jenny pouted and sat down to put on her sandals.

"Like me, the Lord knows my beautiful wife sometimes says things or does things without thinking it out." Noticing her embarrass smile, Ted reached over and gave her a kiss as the two children he was holding, smiled at one another. Ted sat down and pulled them up close. "First, I want you to tell me why I did not sense you because I know what you did." The children could feel Love flow into their hearts and body just by his touch. "After your confession, each one of you will get a bath and a new set of clothes as we toss out those smelly rags you're wearing. Then, Jenny and I will treat you both to breakfast. What do you say, my little friends?"

Once again, the inseparable twosome smiled broadly at each other then up at Ted. "We blocked ourselves from you so you would not feel us." Blake twisted his fingers in an unnatural way and rolled his eyes back to demonstrate the black magic they had learned. "It is black magic Blackheart taught us to defend ourselves from being found."

"Blackheart?" Ted grew serious. "Patches, you go with Jenny to get a bath. Jenny, there's a trash bag waiting inside the bathroom for the soiled clothes. New ones are hanging up behind the door."

"New clothes, for kids our age? But where did they come from and how do you know my name?" Patches grew nervous, her eyes wide with disbelief. "Are you like Blackheart?"

"Blackheart is an evil man who works for Lucifer, the devil." Ted remained calm as he gently touched her small hand. "Relax Patches, I am a servant of the living God. My heart is filled with love as yours will soon be, little one." Ted laid Patches' hand in Jenny's. "Make this child clean on the outside, my darling, I will make her clean on the inside, in the name of Jesus."

"You will not recognize Patches when we get finished." Jenny led the happy girl to the bathroom as the small child smiled up at Jenny, admiring her beauty.

"I'll never be as beautiful as you are Jenny."

"Oh? We shall see about that!" Jenny glanced back and gave Ted a wink. "I just bet, after we wash away that dirt, you will go from a rag-a-muffin to a fairytale princess!"

"I guess I'm next! Baths are not my favorite thing, but for a new set of duds and breakfast, I'd say it's a fair trade." The boy smiled up at Ted.

"A very fair trade, Blake!" Ted smiled at the boys surprised expression. "Yes Blake, you will clean up into a very handsome fellow and with those new 'duds' you will be ready to dine with other folks!" Ted chuckled when the boy's stomach growled loudly. "I would say that hungry lion needs a big breakfast!"

Blake laughed and threw his arms around Ted lovingly. Ted returned the hug, not caring that the dirty boy smelled like he had just been sleeping with pigs and wallowing in their mud.

CHAPTER 11

Jeff and Naomi stood looking out at the most water either of them had ever seen. The ocean seemed to stretch out and around into forever and the big crashing waves made it feel even bigger. This was a new experience for the couple that had never been outside Goldsburg.

"Isn't this beautiful, Jeff?" Naomi reached for his strong hand, never taking her eyes off the ocean captivating her attention. "Next to our mountains, it's the most beautiful thing I have ever seen."

"You are the most beautiful thing in my life, Naomi. Nothing compares to you in my heart. Neither this ocean nor the mountains we call home." Jeff spoke so softly, Naomi looked up into his alluring eyes. They had been focused on her instead of the new scene that brought them down to the beach first. "Neither will anything or anyone replace what I feel for you, my love."

"Jeff darling, your words do comfort my heart. There are times when I feel I am not pretty enough for such an amazing man like you." Tears laced her brown eyes. "I am truly blessed to have your love and my love for you is every bit as great!" Seeing his head lowering for a kiss, Naomi closed her eyes as he covered her lips in a fiery kiss. Taking a deep breath as she felt passion sweep into her veins, Naomi pulled gently away. "How easy it would be to find myself lost in your embrace, but we must not get distracted. We have a mission waiting here."

Jeff smiled lazily as his hand brushed over her breast. "It would not take much to have my way with you, my sweet dove, right here on this beach. And, believe me dearest one, you are incredibly beautiful and it is I that feel blessed that you could have loved someone like me."

"I truly feel God brought us together so you could be saved and help Ted in this fight with your father." Naomi saw the passion still building in her husband's eyes, so she thought it best to change the subject. "Is Ted and Jenny still on their honeymoon? I know you must know if they are."

"You change the subject, sweet one." Jeff slipped his arm

around her waist and smiled. "As for Ted and Jenny's honeymoon, it would appear their time alone is over. They have little ones to deal with."

"Little ones?" Naomi looked up at him puzzled. "Surely they didn't bring Mary and Martha."

"The twins are on the mountain with their Grandmother Hannah and some young angel God sent to help out. Ted has a mission, much like ours, only he has been sent to help seven lost children." Jeff checked his watch. "It's time to go to that meeting with Chief James. We will meet up with Ted and Jenny later today."

"Do you know where they will be?" Naomi followed her tall husband back to their car.

"Not yet, my love, but I will when the time is right." With one last kiss, Jeff helped her in and left the beach behind them.

Ted and Jenny smiled at one another as they were seated in the small café across from the motel. As Jenny studied the breakfast menu, Ted noticed the children had their menu's upside down and he lend over to Jenny.

"Jenny, Patches and Blake cannot read." He nodded his head toward their menu's then spoke up as he retrieved them. "Permit me to order for all of us."

Looking relieved, the children smiled and sat back to hear what threat they would be eating. Knowing the kids were hungry, Ted smiled up at the waiter. "We will have bacon, scrambled eggs, grits, gravy and biscuits. Bring plenty of butter and Jelly please. We have some hungry kids here. Three tall glasses of milk for me and the children and my wife would like coffee with cream and a small orange juice." Ted's smile went from the happy-face kids to his beautiful wife, shaking her head in disbelief. "Did I do alright Jenny?"

"Very well done, Ted darling. You ordered the things I was going to, right down to the small glass of orange juice." She got the children's attention to show them how to unroll their cloth napkin then place the silver ware correctly. The waiter brought out the plates of food and a big basket of biscuits with plenty of butter and Jelly.

As soon as the waiter left, Patches and Blake grabbed a biscuit from the basket only to have Ted collect them and lay them on their plate. "Children, we say grace before we eat. Then you can dive in."

Joan Byrd

"Say grace? What's grace?" Patches could smell the bacon, causing her mouth to water.

"It is a blessing. A prayer, to the Lord, thanking him for the food." Ted took her hand and motioned for Patches to take Blakes as Jackie smiled and gripped the small boys right hand before taking Ted's left hand.

"Wow! Did God make this food Ted? Is that why we are thanking him?" Blake asked sincerely causing Ted to smile before he reached over to close each child's eyes.

"Blake, God, our Father, has created everything good on this earth, including food. I will tell you all about the Lord later. Now keep your eyes closed until I say amen. Heavenly Father, we give thanks for this food, in which we are about to receive. Guide Jenny and me in caring for these two children, as well as the other five. Enrich their lives with grace and love as you show us the way to guide their footsteps and hearts to you. Bless all those here within these walls as you love and protect them. In your holy name, Jesus we pray, amen."

Patches and Blake glanced up at each other, both feeling a sense of hope but yet wondered why their wonderful new friend Ted used so many names for God. God, the Father, the Lord, and his holy name is Jesus.

Ted smiled and pointed to their plates as he handed them their forks. "My little ones, please eat your breakfast. I will tell you everything you are wondering about later, I promise." One taste of the food, brought one bite after another as they dug in. As Ted happily watched them enjoying their breakfast, he thought, this was probably the first real meal they have ever had.

CHAPTER 12

Jeff and Naomi waited outside the office of Chief Randy James, trying to avoid the cold stares from the officers and staff workers. After waiting fifteen minutes over their appointment time, the sheriff opened his office door and waved them inside.

"I am sorry it took so long to check out your driver's license Mr. Wineworth, but I swear, you look exactly like your brother, Reverend Wineworth! Only thinner in the face and slightly taller." Mr. James never cracked a smile as he glanced back up, first at Jeff then Naomi, an unlikely woman for such a moody dark man. "Do you mind my asking what your occupation is, sir?"

"I would not consider what I do an occupation, Mr. James and I cannot see that is any of your business. As of now, I am not into killing and winning souls for the wrong side. I am merely here at the request of my brother who broke his leg saving my son." Jeff stared over coldly, giving the tough man the shivers. "One good deed replacing another."

"So, you are not in the religious field like your brother?" Randy James looked down at both brother's pictures on his desk. "It is amazing how much you resemble."

"That is as far as the resemblance goes, Mr. James, Jonathan and I are nothing alike otherwise. At lease, not anymore!"

"Then you use to be a good man like him?" The man faked a smile at this unsmiling man.

Jeff laughed sarcastically. "I'm afraid you got it all backward! But believe what you will and just tell me when we can get those kids out and take them to my 'reverent' brother."

"Patience, Mr. Wineworth." Randy James turned his attention on the beautiful quiet woman, sitting close to the scary man. "My dear, things like this cannot be rushed. They take time. I trust you understand." Still observing Jeff's wife and avoiding the tall man's cold stare, the sheriff continued. "Mrs. Wineworth, the good reverend described you to a tea."

"He should be able too! Jonathan looks at her enough!" Jeff's eyes blazed. "So, James, I gather we both pass the look test?"

61

Joan Byrd

"There is no mistaking you being Reverend Wineworth's twin nor this lovely lady being your wife." The chief of police handed Jeff an official paper to sign. "After signing this document which states you are responsible for the two delinquents who go as Fire and Blaze. We will have you meet the main guard this afternoon at the town jail house around two o'clock."

Jeff slide his chair back and stood his tall frame up, towering over the six-foot sheriff "We will be there, two sharp! Just have those kids waiting!" Jeff took Naomi's hand after he speed read the document before signing it, then walked to the door, James following close behind.

"Since you have a few hours to wait, why not take it the tallest lighthouse in America. Cape Hatteras." The police chief showed them to the door. "It's worth the climb and a great view at the top, if heights don't bother you.

"Thank you, sir. The, light house sounds enchanting but we have friends here to see." Naomi felt Jeff's strong grip pull her out the door. His eyes softened when they were alone.

"Sweet love, we can do both. Look up our friends who will be standing at the top of Hatteras."

"Making the climb up the 193 ft light house was the easy part for the small group. When they reached the very top, Ted stepped out, feeling the wind blow through his long shag hair and breathed in the fresh air that made him feel light-headed. Smiling, feeling safe in the arms of his Lord, Ted held out his hand for Jenny to join him.

"I don't know Ted. It's really high up and to step outside…" Jenny took a deep breath, trying not to show panic around the two children who stood watching her. "let's just say, I might faint!"

"Jenny sweetheart, trust me. I will have you and my promise is to keep you safe as a baby in its cradle." Ted's face was so pure and tender, Jenny let go of her fears and taking his hand, stepped out beside him. "Just stay close to the structure darling and don't venture out around the short guard rail." Ted's attention fell on the two children, watching with wide eyes.

"Kids, it will be safe for you to join us. Patches, take my hand and Blake, you may hold Jenny's hand and help her feel safe." Ted gave the smiling boy a wink. "That's what brave boys like us do for sweet girls."

62

The Lost Sheep

Feeling safe with Ted and Jenny, Patches grew excited and pointed out at the water in front of them. "Wow! I can see way out in the ocean from up here! Is that a boat?"

"That is a fishing boat, several miles out Patches." Ted smiled down at the small girl whose fears had slipped away. "Do you see the fishing boat Blake?"

"It looks more like a toy boat from way up here!" Blake yelled against the strong wind then watched with amazement the brave people who were standing near the rail looking down. "Aren't those folks afraid the wind will blow them off?"

"I would prefer not watching them!" Jenny gazed down at the children. "And if some of those people have children, lets hope they watch them closely!"

Ted squeezed his wife's hand lovingly to take her attention off the dare devils. "Jenny, we are about to get company. Jeff and Naomi are on their way up."

"What? But how...?" Jenny shook her head laughing. "Jeff and Naomi are making their way up the light house right now."

"Jenny, Ted, Jeff said we would find you up here." Naomi peered out, feeling nervous with the wind striking her face, causing her to take a deep breath to calm her fears. "I knew 192 ft. would be high, but I never dreamed heights would make you feel this dizzy."

"I won't let nothing happen to my girl." Jeff stepped out, causing Patches and Blake to grow tense and quiet. They looked at each other with wide eyes of fear. Jeff immediately felt their great fear of him, as did Ted. Lowing his tall frame to look them in their eyes, Jeff spoke softly.

"Small ones, you fear me? I can assure you, I have not come to hurt you."

"Patches, you and Blake have nothing to fear from these two-loving people. Jeff and Naomi are our friends and neighbors." Ted touched then gently, making them feel safe. "Perhaps you are mistaking Jeff for his twin brother Jonathan."

"Why should they fear your brother, Jeff?" Naomi looked at the two small children clinging to Ted and Jenny. "Do you think they know Jonathan?"

"We know him miss." Blake's voice trembled. "He...sometimes helps us, that's all. We ran away and he don't like that." The small boy didn't want to tell them the truth about Blackheart for he

63

Joan Byrd

knew they would get a beating.

"Blake's right! He is a preacher miss and takes care of all us kids." Patches' big eyes checked out the pretty short hair girl who was stroking her soft curls. "Miss, you are beautiful! Like Miss Jenny."

"Then that makes three Patches, because, you are very beautiful yourself!" Naomi took her hand and patted it. "You and Blake are in very good hands now. You need never be afraid again. I know. Ted took me in when I was in trouble and helped me. Children, you will grow to love Ted and Jenny, and everyone else living at the home on Goldsburg Mountain."

"The home?" Blake looked up at Jenny. "Miss Jenny, where is this home on the mountain this pretty girl grew up in?"

"Our big beautiful farmhouse sits on the most beautiful mountain in the state of North Carolina. It is named Goldsburg Mountain because the sweet little town that sets below it has the same name." Jenny glanced up at a smiling Ted. There are lots of children of all ages and many beautiful people who call the mountain home. The very best part of living there, you sweet darlings, is the love we all share and the heavenly fact that God reveals Himself on the very top."

"My little ones, as soon as we gather up the other three hiding in the wooded cave, we will be headed home, and you may see for yourself." Ted could feel Jenny and Naomi observing him with questions. "Care to explain this one to the girls, Jeff?"

"It would be a pleasure, dear friend." Jeff smiled broadly, revealing his sharp teeth, causing the children to shiver and back behind Ted and Jenny. "Ted is referring to the five youngest out of seven lost children. He has seen the vision of a wooded cave where three are hiding and the oldest two await me and Naomi at the jail. They will return with us to Black Mountain."

"Bla...Black Mountain?" Patches swallowed, remembering Blackheart's teeth were just as sharp as this twin's. Is that a scary mountain where witches and vampires live?"

"Our mountain is anything but scary, sweetheart." Naomi smiled and the girl relaxed. "Jeff and I live there with our two little boys, Teddy Jeffery and Jacob. Our mountain is next to Ted and Jenny's mountain."

"Where is your brother, sir?" Blake tried to sound calm. "We

64

haven't seen him in weeks"

"At the moment my brother is on Black Mountain. He is spending some time with us, little one." Jeff could sense their fear of his brother but somehow the kids seem to have the reason blocked.

"Did you leave him alone with your sons, sir?" Patches slipped out from behind Ted, suddenly feeling fear for these boys.

"So young and so thoughtful, Patches." Jeff marveled at this small child's compassion. "My brother is there but he has a broken leg, so we got two helpers from the home."

"That's good!" was Patches' short reply. "How old are your sons, sir?"

"My, aren't we full of questions." Jeff read her thoughts and smiled. "I suppose that's fair, to know if they are close to your age." Patches eyes flew open, wondering how he knew why she wanted to know. "Teddy is seven and Jacob is four."

"We're right in the middle! I am six and so is Blake." Patches smiled down shyly. "Mr. Jeff, is your Teddy as handsome as you are?"

The four adults laughed at the girl's bold question. Naomi bent down to face her. "I can answer that one, Patches. Young Teddy is very much like his handsome mysterious daddy and so is our Jacob, so far only in looks."

"That is enough questions for a while kids. It is time to go to the hidden cave in the woods." Ted took one last look out over the ocean, thinking this high place would be the perfect spot to converse with the Lord.

"How did you know about our hidden home in the woods, Ted?" Blake frowned down at his friend. "Patches, you told him, didn't you?"

"I did not!" the small girl placed her hands on her hips. "It was probably Black..." She caught herself and looked down nervously.

"Blackheart?" Ted finished her thought and turn to Jeff. "We must be careful. Things could get bad on Black Mountain."

CHAPTER 13

Tracy Reynolds re-read the letter in her hand, then looked to be sure she was still alone on her wrap around porch. Tracy had been checking her personal mail every day before her husband got home, hoping she would get a letter from Jonathan. It seemed like such a long time since they were locked in each other's arms, then he left for a town called Goldsburg to visit a brother he had never met.

"Oh, Jonathan." Tracy spoke softly to herself, fearing her husband of almost twenty years would come home and find her with a letter from her lover. With trembling fingers, she lifted the long-awaited letter and started reading it again.

"My dearest Tracy, oh, how I miss you my darling. I would give anything to have you in my arms, kiss those beautiful full lips and make passionate love to you. If only you were here, my love. I have decided to stay awhile, but the thoughts of you being so far away, haunts me. A church has come open my darling and the town of Goldsburg is a quiet charming town. I was hoping perhaps you and Joseph could come for a visit, perhaps a vacation. I checked my calendar and find that it's past time for another council meeting between you both. We mustn't let Joseph get suspicious over our arrangements since these meetings seem to be working in his mind. Joseph just hasn't caught on that you are my woman, not his. Tracy, you are my clever girl and I know you will think of a way to convince your husband to come here. My address is included so please, let me know what you have come up with. Yours Always, Jonathan."

Tracy jumped when she heard the front door shut and her husband call out. Tracy quickly tucked the letter in her pocket, and grabbed her water can as she answered the familiar voice. "Joseph, I'm out on the side porch." She commenced to watering her hanging plants as her husband stepped out.

"Tracy darling, the servants can get those. You must not bother yourself with small jobs." Joseph walked over to kiss her cheek bringing out her smile.

"I enjoy my plants, Joseph. They give me delight watching them

66

grow. Besides, they give me something to do."

"Then, if it makes you happy dear, water away!" The business man loosened his tie before pulling out a big colorful brochure and handed it to his wife.

"What is this, Joe?" Tracy sat down the watering can and flipped through the pages, revealing the Caribbean. "It is a lovely place Joe, but what this about?"

"Now dear, surely you're joking." The slightly balding man pointed at the luxurious hotel. "Trace, our twentieth anniversary is next week and this is the perfect place to take my beautiful wife."

"Everything looks lovely Joe." Tracy folded the brochure and handed it back to her smiling husband. "Darling, don't get me wrong. I love the Caribbean, but we have gone to different islands for the last two anniversaries and they all look the same. I would really like to go somewhere completely different this year. Somewhere quiet and small, an old town somewhere near the Blue Ridge, perhaps.

For a moment, Joseph looked at his wife seriously, then shook his head smiling as he tossed the brochure in the porch swing. "Somewhere different sounds interesting, but I'm thinking somewhere like Paris or London. Across the pond and old as well. What do you say?"

"Joe, we have been across the 'pond' many times and this anniversary, someplace more simple and charming is where I would rather spend our time." Tracy waited for a response, but he only could stare at her, unsure of her sudden change. "Joseph, I have been scanning the internet and found a charming small town near the mountains of North Carolina. The perfect place is Goldsburg."

"What is so special about this small town, Trace?" Joseph pulled out a cigar, smelled it before lighting, then took a big drag.

"It looks like some of the old towns you see in movies, such as Peyton Place, only this town sits in the shadow of two mountains, connected but completely different in an appearance. There are no skyscrapers, just quant little shops along a tree line drive and church steeples nominate the sky." Tracy had read up on the town that had taken her Jonathan away and if she had answered her husband's question honestly, she would have stated: "This town is special because Jonathan is there." But she would keep that little part a secret. "There is this enchanting bed and breakfast on the edge of

Joan Byrd

town which sounds absolutely dreamy. The perfect place for our twentieth anniversary."

"I can see you have your heart set on Goldsburg." Joseph stopped, recalling hearing that name before. "Goldsburg? Why is that name so familiar?" then it hit him and he laughed out. "I remember now! Isn't that the town Reverend Wineworth went to recently?"

Tracy looked as though she was trying to remember as she picked up her watering can to finish watering her plants. "Come to think of it Joe, I believe that was the town the pastor was going." She gave a little laugh. "Small world."

"Yes, it is! If that will make you happy Tracy darling, by all means, call and make reservations at the bed and breakfast. This will be a new experience for us! Might be fun after all!" Joseph took the can from her hand and opened the wide door. "Enough work young lady. You might not be the only wife that saw that delightful bed and breakfast on the internet."

"You are right as always Joseph." Tracy squeezed his hand and pointed to the lit cigar. "Enjoy that smoke on the porch and I'll see you for dinner." She almost danced inside, feeling relieved that she convinced her husband to go to such a small town. Tracy also knew she should feel guilty for deceiving her trusting husband, but her deep love for the man waiting in Goldsburg was too strong. She would make all the arrangements and let Jonathan know she was on her way to him.

68

CHAPTER 14

Jonathan was resting comfortably on the garden bench watching Teddy and Jacob at play, cheering them on. As each boy threw the ball in the net, Jonathan would clap, bringing out big smiles from his nephews. When they missed the net, he would offer convenience in their next shot, making them try even harder.

Esther walked up quietly, observing the handsome man nervously as she remembered how he had brushed up against her the previous night when no one was watching. She took a deep breath and stepped up next to him. "Reverend Wineworth, sir, I thought you might like some lemonade."

"Thank you, Esther, but I do wish you would call me Jonathan." When he took the glass, Jonathan noticed her hand tremble. "Esther, are you afraid of me, my dear?"

The sheltered girl knew Ted had told them to always tell the truth and never lie. She glanced over at Goldsburg Mountain and felt relaxed. "I have never been around you before sir, I mean Jonathan. Strangers make me feel a little uncomfortable."

"That is understandable Esther, but I can assure you, I am perfectly safe. My brother Jeffery got all the bad traits from our father, not I." Jonathan smiled, revealing perfect teeth. "Look, I had the boys to bring a yard chair around in case I found a cheering partner. Would you join me and watch my nephews show off?"

Esther laughed softly as she pulled up the chair and gazed out at the boys playing. As she observed their competitive rivalry to gain their uncle's respect, Esther found their bonding appropriate. She smiled over at the handsome man next to her. "Jacob and Teddy seem to have taken a liken to you, Jonathan. Will you be staying in our town for long?"

"Yes, I plan on staying here Esther." When Jonathan spoke her name, he made her feel beautiful and special. "After meeting my brother and his wife, Naomi, the boys and a very special young lady with silky brown hair, why should I want to leave?" Jonathan's words made this shy girl feel warm, but she could not fandom such a handsome mature man deciding to stay because of her. Never thinking twice about Jonathan being able to read her mind, Esther sat up when he said softly. "Esther, do you feel unwanted sometimes? Surely a girl as pretty as you must have a boyfriend."

"A boyfriend? No sir, I have not got a boyfriend. As for feeling unwanted, I can assure you Jonathan that in a house filled with over a dozen of people, I have never felt unwanted. Ted makes everyone feel special and very much loved and wanted as does his wife, Jenny. All of the family care for one another deeply."

"Esther is right Jonathan." John had overheard Jonathan's statement and Esther's response after stepping up to pull her from the chair. "Kido, it's bath time. Let's get these kids inside. Supper is almost ready, despite losing my helper." John reached inside his shirt pocket and pulled out a pink envelope, handing it to Jonathan. "I almost forgot, this came for you. I'd say a female from the perfume smell and pink envelope!" his eyes fell on Esther, to find her staring at the good smelling mail." Just stay put Jonathan and enjoy your letter. I'll be back to fetch you later."

"You're a good man, John and thank you, I'll be find." Jonathan waved for his nephews to go with the two, young people. "I'll be in shortly boys. Run alone and get a bath before dinner." He watched them until they were out of sight, then tore open the good smelling envelope. Recognizing the perfume, he smiled broadly as he began to read.

"My dearest Jonathan, my heart started beating again when I received your letter. I was beginning to think you had found another and had forgotten all about me." Jonathan smiled to himself as he whispered.

"Never, my dear Tracy, never." Then he continued the letter.

"As luck would have it, Joseph wanted to take me to the Caribbean for our twentieth. I was able to change his mind and talked him into the small town nestled beneath two mountains near the Blue Ridge. It was really quite easy convincing Joseph. His love for me is so pure. I believe he would try and give me the moon should I ask it of him."

Jonathan sneered. "Pure? Joseph is anything but pure, Tracy Reynolds!"

"As of now my love, I have made reservations at this adorable old inn that sits at the edge of Goldsburg. It is called the Picket Fence, should you wish to look it up. We will be arriving next Friday by car. I have your number, so it's best that I call you to arrange our first meeting. I cannot wait to be in your arms again, darling. Your Tracy."

Jonathan smiled to himself as he put the letter in his pocket. "Tracy Reynolds comes to me of her own free will and soon I will have more than her beautiful sexy body. Soon, my father, Tracy's soul will belong to me as well!"

Joan Byrd

CHAPTER 15

County Jail: Outer Banks, North Carolina

Blaze and Fire had been brought to the departure gate and stood silently watching the tall handsome man who looked exactly like their cult leader, Blackheart. If Jonathan had not written them back, informing his students of the black arts, that his twin brother Jeffery would be coming to pick them up, they would have mistakenly called him Blackheart, giving their fearless leader away.

Jeff had sense them watching when he entered the release block and instantly knew they had blocked any thought they were having from him. Jeff knew his brother's power was already great. He could easily control others, especially children whose minds were still developing. Perhaps his advance mind skills could just as easily draw adults to commit sins, especially women. Jeffery Wineworth knew how easily a devil's son could become filled with the desire to win souls and how easy it was to lure women into their lustful trap.

Jeff glanced over at the young teens and they quickly looked away to avoid his penetrating stare. The sound of his deep dark voice made them glance back his way, to see him speaking to the warden. "There are the papers, all signed! May I take those kids now?" Jeff tried to remain civil as he stated bluntly. "My wife was ordered to remain outside these walls and wait for me! I do not like to leave her alone in this place!"

"Mr. Wineworth, I can assure you, nothing will happen to your wife here. This place is highly guarded by armed officers." The officer in charge stepped over to the locked security door and ordered the jailer to bring the juveniles out. "Alright you two, I am releasing you in the care of Mr. Jeffery Wineworth, the brother of Reverend Jonathan Wineworth. He will be taking you to his brother, so, I trust that you kids will behave yourself and listen to this man and his wife." The warden put out his hand toward Jeff, who shook it, never taking his eyes off the troubled youths. Two officers escorted the teens out behind Jeffery as he made his way to Naomi. She looked behind him at the sixteen-year-olds and smiled, getting

72

nothing but stares in return. Glancing up at her husband, she whispered.

"This is not going to be easy." As they walked to their car, she checked her watch. "Jeff, it is already three in the afternoon. Do you want to start back now or get a room, have an early supper, then get up early and drive home?"

"It has been a long day, sweet one and staying the night then getting an early start sounds the best." Jeff opened the back door and waved the kids inside before shutting the door. After helping Naomi in, Jeff walked around, slid behind the wheel and left the jailhouse behind.

The loving act Jeff had shone to his wife had not gone unnoticed. Fire watched the love given and considered the fact that she had never witnessed Blackheart show that kind of love to anyone. He had sex with many women, including herself and twelve-year-old Marble, but that was because he lusted for it. This twin seemed to have the same scary manners toward others, but such love and devotion shown his wife made him right the opposite from Jonathan.

Ted led Jenny and the two children through the dense forest until they came to what appeared to be a dead end. "I can sense three children, just inside this camouflage door."

Blake and Patches wasn't sure what camouflage meant as they looked on with wide-eyes. "It's a fake door made of small trees, Ted."

"Yes, I know Patches." Ted touched her cheek and the warm feeling swept through her as she hugged herself, trying to keep it in. "There's a password or a signal you give to let them know it's safe to open. What is it?"

"A wand, our leader gave each of us one." Blake pulled out the torch-like object and lit it, then moved it from side to side. Seeing the wand through the crack, Devin assumed it was Blake and Fire and opened the door and stared into Ted's loving eyes. The scared boy started to slam it back shut when Patches and Blake stepped up in front of Ted.

"Dev, it's alright." Blake smiled at his friend as Patches took Ted and Jenny's hands.

"Devin, these are our new friends, Ted and Jenny. They have come to help us."

Joan Byrd

The young boy looked skeptical at the two strangers. "Hey bro, you know what the reverend said. We should not trust anyone! Especially police."

"Reverend? Jonathan Wineworth?" Jenny looked surprised at the troubled young teen. "Look son, if it helps your trust in us, we know where Jonathan is staying. He is visiting his brother Jeffery and Naomi, Jeff's wife. They are our friends and we live on the connecting mountain in Goldsburg."

"Jenny is right Devin. There is nothing to fear." Ted's voice calmed the young man down. "God has asked me to bring you and the other two hiding inside, back to Goldsburg Mountain." He looked past the big-eyed teen. "You may tell Marble and Willy to come out. I know Marble is under the old bedframe and Willy is in the makeshift bathroom."

"What's wrong with you brats! You told them what all our names are?" Devin felt nervous around this man with the long hair and heavenly blue eyes. He could sense good flowing from him and he felt like he was an angel. "You're wrong mister! They are not here. There's nobody here but me!"

Ted walked past Devin, knowing he was lying, and made his way to the makeshift bathroom and opened the poorly hung door. Willy was trying to pull out a loaded gun from the closet. Ted comely stared at the black boy. "Willy, the gun is no use on me. Even now it falls apart in your hand," The wooden handle came apart in the boy's shaking hands as the barrel rolled to Ted's feet. He bent down and scooped up the bullets. "Children should never play with loaded guns. You will learn right from wrong my poor innocent children."

"I am not a child sir." Marble walked out from where she had been hiding under the bed. It was obvious the young girl was very pregnant. "I cannot remain a child when I am having one, can I?" Her eyes looked bloodshot and tired for a twelve-year-old.

Jenny walked over next to the young girl and shook her head. "Who did this to you child? How old are you?"

"Marble is twelve, Jenny and I'm not sure she really knows who the father of this baby is." Ted looked at her sadly.

"I'll not tell you who the daddy is, ma'am!" Marble looked coldly at the perfect shaped woman standing over her. "And I do not need your pity! "Marble sized up Ted's handsome body.

74

The Lost Sheep

"Handsome, you're right about not knowing who this baby's daddy is. I'm really not sure which man I screwed is the daddy."

Jenny looked up into Ted's sad eyes, then back to the young child who had spoke such vile language in front of complete strangers and small innocent children. "Sweetheart, can these children be saved?"

"Jenny, my love, you know that answer." Ted took her into his protecting arms. "One percent of good can win over one hundred percent of evil. Love is God! God is love!" the couple repeated in unison, bringing out smiles of hope from them both.

Ted looked around the dirty surroundings, then turned to face the five children. "Alright, if you have anything you wish to bring with you, go get it now." Ted spoke, with authority. "There will be no discussions about this. If what you bring is needed and good, it will arrive with you. You may not bring anything with you evil, but should you attempt to hide something non-exceptionable by the Lord, you will find, it will not go up that mountain with you."

All five kids scattered to gather their personal items. Patches packed what few clothes she had and an old doll, Blake packed a favorite pair of jeans and shirt and left the old worn-out clothes on his pile. He started to bring the wand, but remembering who gave it to him, Blake threw it down and walked over by Ted. The other three, Devin, Willy, and Marble packed most of their clothes and a few prized items they stole. When the boys walked out to join the others, Marble slipped a box of new condones in a stolen shoulder bag belonging to Fire and hid it with other items before coming out, puffing from the weight of her two bags.

Ted got her attention when he took the bag with the clothes and stared into her eyes. "You are leaving with much, Marble, but you will arrive with a whole lot less." He had the group to file out to the car and they drove away, leaving the hidden cave behind.

75

CHAPTER 16

Tracy Reynolds sipped slowly on her wine as she thought back to the evening she met their new preacher at Oak Grove Methodist Church in the small coastal community on Ocracoke Island, where she and Joseph had bought one of the old homes after vacationing there one summer. The members of Oak Grove were a close-knit church family, all neighbors and friends. Tracy's friends on the-staff parish committee had met Jonathan Wineworth and called her all excited about the handsome young bachelor who was chosen for their church. They informed Tracy that the pastor would be making his rounds to meet members of the congregation.

Jonathan had called their home the night of his arrival and spoken to Joseph on the phone about dropping by to meet them and introduce himself. Tracy had chosen a black jumpsuit with a single gold cross neckless that dangled around her hidden breast. When she opened the front door, Tracy wasn't prepared for just how handsome her new preacher was when he smiled down with those dark alluring eyes. Jonathan spoke her name and her heart melted. She could not remember what the conversation was about between Jonathan and her husband, but occasionally their eyes met and Tracy felt as though this incredible man was looking deep into her very soul.

When Sunday rolled around each week, Tracy made sure she found a seat near the front so she would be able to looked into the preacher's alluring black eyes. Then the night of a yearly tradition came to celebrate Valentine's day. The church held a community dance and dinner, which was always a sale out on the small island. Tracy had purchased a new long red dress to wear, hoping to impress the new minister but when she came down to model it for her husband, she noticed he wasn't dressed for the dance.

"Trace, I'm sorry precious, but I have come down with a slitting headache." The devoted wife reached down to check his forward for fever. "I just took some pain med's that have made me drowsy, so I will sit out this year's dance, but darling, I wouldn't want you to miss out on the event."

The Lost Sheep

"Nonsense Joseph. If you're not feeling well, I will skip this year's dance." Tracy placed a realistic smile on her lips. "Besides, what fun is a dance if your valentine is at home and you've no one to dance with."

"I'm pretty sure there are several male friends who would love a dance with my beautiful wife. I have seen how men look at you beautiful." Joseph chuckled and quickly grabbed his head. "Seriously darling, you have been looking forward to the dance all week and even bought this sexy little dress to outshine those other wives, just to please your old man." Before Tracy could object, Joseph held up his hand. "I insist! Who knows, if the new pastor didn't invite a date, you might even get a dance from him."

"Joseph Reynolds, don't be ridiculous! "Tracy looked in the mirror to check her make-up, then smiled down at her trusting husband. "I will go, only because you insisted and I did get all dressed up! Instead of standing around looking like a wall flower, I will volunteer in the kitchen."

"In that dress?" Joseph motioned toward the door. "My innocent bride, you will be the bell of the ball! It's a good thing I trust you." He blew her a kiss. "Now go and have fun!"

Joseph had mentioned their many men friends who would want a dance with this beautiful brunette, but Tracy had only one man in mind. Her and every female there at the dance. Tracy had noticed the long line forming around the handsome minister when she arrived and how he had looked her way. Feeling foolish and like some school girl having a crush, Tracy offered to help in the kitchen.

She found herself slicing pieces of cake and placing them on red paper plates when she felt a hand touch her shoulder. Thinking it was one of the other women helping in the kitchen, Tracy turned and looked up into the minister's piercing black eyes.

"Tracy, I was waiting for you out there." Jonathan continued to stare at her, making her grow warm and suddenly she realized how quiet the kitchen help got and looked around to find her and Jonathan alone. "Don't you want to dance with me, Tracy?"

"It looked like you had more than enough ladies wanting that honor, reverend."

"Jonathan! Please call me Jonathan, Tracy." Her name seemed to roll off his tongue like magic. "Those other ladies are no interest to me. It is you I wish to dance with, Tracy."

77

"Then, I would be honored to have a dance with you, Jonathan." She returned his smile as he swept her to the dance floor. To the other women's dismay, Jonathan danced every dance with Tracy Reynolds until the evening was over. As they played the last slow dance, Jonathan pulled her so close to him she could feel just how turned on he was.

The lights were turned off in the fellowship hall and the people were making their way out to the parking lot. Jonathan had followed Tracy out to her car and before she knew what was happening, she found herself alone with him down an abandon road.

"It's alright Tracy, your husband is sound asleep and he won't wake up until the morning." Jonathan's lips met hers in a fiery kiss and at first, Tracy felt guilty for having lustful feelings for her minister, but God help her, she knew she was falling in love with him.

"Oh Jonathan, I shouldn't be, we should not " Tracy breathed heavily as he removed her clothes, then his own.

"My darling Tracy, I love you! I need you." Jonathan's hot kisses went down her neck as he whispered breathlessly. "Do you want me to stop, dearest?" once again, his lips were on hers with hot passion.

"To stop? No, oh, no Jonathan! I need you too, my darling." Tracy looked into his eyes as she felt him enter her and she knew at that moment, she would never be the same. Her need for him was powerful and without a doubt, she belonged to him.

Jonathan lay holding Tracy in his strong embrace. He had read her thoughts and knew she belonged to him now. Her body lust after his and she had committed adultery. First, her body, next, her soul, for all eternity.

Jeff and Naomi had settled in the motel bed where they had made passionate love, knowing the two teens in the two adjacent rooms would not disturb them after Jeff's stern warning. He also knew if they tried to run it would be when they thought the couple was sleeping. Naomi snuggled in her husband's strong arms as she thought about the troubled teens.

"I cannot help but feel sorry for those young kids, Jeff. They should be enjoying what sixteen-year-old kids should be doing. Learning in a good high school, participating in all the school's activities and just being kids. During supper, they never one time looked at us. They either stared down at their plates or at each other."

"Those two ungrateful brats were quite rude while you were praying. The little devils never realized I could see them with my eyes shut." Jeff smiled down at his wife's questioning eyes when she looked up. "Yes, sweet one, if I choose to watch someone without their knowledge, I can focus through my eyelids. The idiots plan to escape to night while we sleep, but they won't get far. I will catch them and give them a reason to never try again."

"You won't hurt them, will you Jeff?" Naomi covered her yawn and she nestled down on her pillow.

"There's nothing for you to worry about, darling. I want have to do much to scare them." Jeff smiled down on Naomi's naked body before pulling the sheet over her. "Sleep peacefully, my love. I will behave."

Jeff sat up when he sensed Fire and Blaze sneaking out of their rooms to run away. He slipped quietly from the bed so he would not wake his sleeping wife, gave her a kiss, put on his clothes and disappeared.

Blaze and Fire made their way quickly down the street toward the patch of woods that would take them to their hideout. Blake kept looking behind them to make sure they had not been followed by Blackheart's scary brother. Fire pointed to the row of tree's just a few feet ahead.

"I hope we did the right thing, running away Blaze. There's something about this Jeffery that scares me more than Blackheart. We both know Blackheart has powers. Do you think his twin obtains the same abilities?"

"I say they are nothing alike!" Blaze glanced behind him before adding. "That woman of his said a blessing before we could eat! A stupid blessing! Can you believe it?"

"That would make her a stinking 'Christian'!" Fire made a distasteful face. "I say Blackheart has more power to do things better than that brother of his!" The bold girl tensed up when she felt a strong hand grip her shoulder and lifted her completely off the ground. "What the?"

Blaze felt himself being raise in the air as he struggled against his assailant. "Hey, what's going on?" The one responsible twirled both teenagers around to face him. Blaze and Fire stared directly in

79

the tall man's black eyes as their feet dangled in midair.

"You misguided stupid girl, I have got ten times the power of my older twin brother and I am not afraid to use it! Do you understand?"

"What…what are you going "Before Fire could finish, Jeff continued her thought.

"Do to you?" Jeff turned coldly on Blaze as he read his thoughts. "No Blaze, I will not take you back to jail at this time. But try another stupid stunt again, you can spend the rest of your ungrateful lives behind bars for all I care!" Jeff noticed their scared wide eyes and knew he had convinced them, but he wanted them to promise. "Are we clear with that?"

"Yes sir, Mr. Wineworth! We promise we'll come with you, and cause no more trouble." Blaze relaxed when Jeff lower them to the sidewalk. "Where did…a"

"Did I come from, since you kept looking back to see if I was following you?" Jeff smiled, revealing his sharp canine teeth. "Do you really think someone like me would follow the normal way?"

"We're sorry sir. It won't happen again." Fire looked away to avoid Jeff's cold stare.

"Then it's settled! We will go back and you will NEVER do anything to upset my wife again!" Jeff gave them a light push to the motel. "And the next time my wife gives a blessing, you will respect her faith, you little heathen! I have been on both sides, evil and good, and believe me, the faith my loving wife has is the greater choice! Are we good here on respecting my Naomi?"

"Yes sir, whatever you say, Mr. Wineworth." The teenagers made their way quickly to their room. "What time do you want us ready, sir?"

"Six o'clock sharp, six hours from now! Do not be late!" Before Jeff shut their doors, he smiled. "It's Breakfast and on the road back home to Black Mountain!" He left Blaze and Fire staring at the closed door.

CHAPTER 17

Ted and Jenny walked into their motel room exhausted after getting the five run away orphans fed and bed-down for the night. They had rented the two rooms next to their end room, one for the children, who were used to bunking together, and the other room for Matthew and Kathy, who had not arrived and were very late getting there.

"When those two love birds arrive, I will have a few words with them." Ted sat down by the door. "They have let us down because their better judgement did not avail."

"Do I have time to shower before they show up?" Jenny pulled her top over her head and threw it across the bed, knowing Ted already knew the exact time Matthew and Kathy would be pulling in. Before she could take off anything else, Ted looked over and shook his head.

"Put your clothes back on Jenny. They're pulling into the motel parking lot right now. They have spotted our car." Ted walked over to help his upset wife with her top. "I'll get the door."

Jenny shook her head as Ted opened the door to Matthew's raised up hand, preparing to knock. He gave Ted a shaky grin.

"I guess there's no need in knocking." Matthew blushed as Ted stared into his eyes. "Sorry we're late. We sort of made a wrong turn and got lost."

"Was that before or after you decided to stop for lunch at that bed and breakfast, enjoy a bottle of wine, grew romantic and convinced each other just one night there wouldn't make you too late." Ted motioned them inside their room and shut the door. "Care to tell us all the story?"

"I am certain you already know everything." Matthew bit his lip when he felt Kathy hit him. "Sorry Ted."

"Then, may I refresh your memories." Ted pointed to the sofa and Jenny, knowing not to interrupt her husband, could only smile sheepishly at her best friend. "Yesterday morning, you got a late start, because passion over came you and you made love, so that put you late. Then half way here, you spotted that romantic little B&B

Joan Byrd

sign on the highway, declaring the perfect place for a romantic night, so you chose lunch there instead of the McDonnel's right off the road you were traveling. So far, so good, right, lover-boy?"

"It was getting late and we thought that if we got to bed early, then we could get an early start and make it here around noon." Matthew tried to sound upbeat but noticed Ted was not smiling back.

"Cute Matthew! Good try!" Ted frowned. "You got your very romantic room at the B&B and it came with another complimentary bottle of wine and chocolate cover strawberries. It was still early so you both decided to enjoy the wine and strawberries which led to another night of love making!" Ted stared down at them. "Do you know where I am going here?"

Matthew looked down at his hands, feeling guilty. "Yes Ted, I do. Ted, I am a young man who has needs and a very sexy wife to supply those needs for me."

"You may continue Matthew." Ted joined Jenny on the side of the bed and took her hand.

"Kathy and I made love again." Matthew glanced up to find he had everyone's attention. "Then when we woke up," He swallowed. "We went again, took a shower together, got hot all over again, and afterward, showered separately, to make it safe. We had breakfast and got on the road and about an hour later, we made the wrong turn that got us lost for a while." Matthew teared up as he looked innocently over at Ted. "I am really sorry I let you down, Ted."

"Well, you're here now, so there will be no more sex until we return to the mountain." Ted stood up and made his way to the door. "You are on a mission Matthew. I trust you will remember that. I shall need your assistance tonight at twelve sharp."

"Twelve a.m.? Why so late? Haven't you got any of those runaway kids yet?" Matthew retrieved his and Kathy's luggage and followed Ted to their room. They stopped at the middle room and Ted whispered.

"Matthew, our five runaways are inside that room right now pretending to be asleep but they will make a run for it tonight at twelve and we will be ready to stop them."

"But how?" Matthew shook his head. "I'll be ready Ted."

The five children had dressed and slipped from their room. Patches was crying as Devin pulled her along with the group. Before

82

they could make another step, Ted and Matthew stepped out of the shadows.

"You children will turn around this instant and return to your room." Ted spoke softly. "You will be coming with us tomorrow."

"Suppose we choose not to come mister?" Devin stepped forward, his bottom lip pushed out in deviance. "You can't make us!"

"No son, I cannot." Ted's eyes held total love as he spoke tenderly. "But, God can Devin, and it's for your own sakes that we do this."

"Yeh kid, do you think we want to be up at this time of night?" Matthew stepped back behind Ted when he heard him clear his throat. Marble stepped up for a closer look at Matthew and ran her hand over her hair.

"Where did you come from? You're real cute in those tight jeans."

Matthew stared down at her round belly and stepped close to Ted's ear. "Is that kid pregnant or is she just plain fat?"

"She is expecting a baby Matthew and the father could be any low life man or boy."

"Shit!" Matthew grabbed his mouth when Ted stared down at him.

"Matthew, let me do the talking." Ted turned his attention back on the children and noticed Patches had been crying as he whispered at Matthew. "Stay clear of that twelve-year-old girl and the girl called Fire. They're both driven by lust and don't care if the man is married or not." Ted bent down in front of Patches. "Patches, it was wrong for Devin to slap you child because you wanted to come with me."

Patches ran over and grabbed Ted around the neck, causing Matthew to jump back. "God Ted! She is touching you?"

Ted looked up at Matthew, almost laughing at his scared face. "Matthew, relax! Patches is, an innocent child. What can she do to me? Hug me to death?"

Matthew blushed as he looked down at the six-year-old girl looking up confused. "You told me to stay clear of the other girl, so I just assumed since the other girl is about to pop out a baby, you meant this one was fire."

Ted stood up laughing and lifted Patches in his arms as he

83

walked past the other four children toward the motel. He called over his shoulder. "Follow me."

Not knowing how or why they began walking behind him, the small group followed Ted right inside their room and stayed there until Ted came for them when the sun came up.

Jeff pulled his car up at the gas tank and switched off the silent motor. Before climbing out he lean over to give his wife a kiss. "Sweet one, stay in the car with these, heathen and I will fill up with gas and return as soon as I pay." Jeff turned to stare coldly at his riders. "I expect you both to behave and remain inside this car, understand?"

"Yes sir." They echoed in somber unison.

After paying for the gas, Jeff started for the car when he was stopped by a middle-aged redhead with an ample bosom. "Jonathan, my dearest, I see you are back!" Before Jeff could respond, the woman quickly past him a note before waving for the man walking their way. "Harry, Reverend Wineworth has returned from his trip. Isn't it wonderful?"

"Welcome home, reverend." The man took his wife's hand. "See you at church." They walked away as Jeff stared after them then down at the secret note for Jonathan.

Jeff placed the note in his pocket for future reading and headed for the car. Before getting inside, his eyes locked with the wide-eyed redhead who had mistakenly handed him the note and Jeff could tell by her wild expression she realized she had handed her personal words to the wrong man. Jeff gave her a smile, climbed in and drove away, chuckling.

Naomi looked over at her husband after witnessing the strange behavior of the woman who had approached him. "Jeff sweetheart, what just happened back there?"

"Mistaken identity, my love." Jeff reached for Naomi's hand and gave it a kiss. "The broad just assumed I was Jonathan. I think my 'religious' brother is having an affair with a married woman." Through the rearview mirror, Jeff noticed the teens in the back seat sat up, wide eyes, and whispering to one another.

"An affair with a married woman? Oh Jeff, he is a minister!" Naomi whispered. "He should know better! I know he is human, but to break one of the ten commandments!"

"I think brother Jonathan knows better darling, but he does not

84

hold to your religious beliefs. To be honest, I think little miss redhead is not the only one on Jonathan's love list of married women." Jeff's eyes met Fire's "Not to mention, fresh kids!" Jeff pulled the note out for Naomi to see, then tucked it back in his pocket. "A little reading for later."

"Now, I understand why that woman looked so upset when we drove away." Naomi sat up. "She mistook you for your brother and handed you her love note before her husband saw you."

"It appears my brother Jonathan is more like my old self than he lets on." Jeff kept his eyes on the road ahead as he added. "My love, be careful around him and never catch yourself alone in his presence."

Ted and Jenny drove up to the white farm house on Goldsburg Mountain. Jenny reached over to pat her husband's knee, feeling proud of him. "Like everything you've set out to undertake, you have learned how to drive a car as good as a horse drawn wagon."

"Well, I figure it is something my son will want me to teach him when he's old enough to drive." Ted climbed out to avoid Jenny's questioning eyes. "Everyone out of the car and stay with me. Matthew is finally coming up the road and will be in view…now."

All three children looked at each other puzzled as to how he knew the exact moment. They hadn't even heard a car coming in on the sandstone drive. Patches pulled at Ted's sleeve and he smiled down at her bright smile.

"Ted, it is beautiful up here! Just like you and Jenny!"

"And you will make it even more beautiful with that bright smile, Patches." Ted waved for the other two boys to get out of Matthew's car and join them. Devin and Blake's brother Willy walked lazily behind Kathy checking out her body and whispering about how hot and sexy she was."

"Boys, there will be no talk like that up here on God's mountain!" Ted took each boy by the arm. "You will respect all the ladies and young girls here while you live among us."

"Say mister, why can't we live on that other mountain?" Devin felt like the leader when Marble and Willy agreed. "It doesn't look as cheery as 'God's' mountain. Dark and mysterious, more to our liking! Right gang?"

"I like cheery Devin!" Patches gazed at the front door when she saw four children running toward them from the house. Two were blonde headed girls who looked just like Ted. The twins threw their arms around Jenny and Ted as Mary welcomed them.

"Mom! Dad! You are home from your honeymoon!"

"We are so glad you're home!" Martha added as exchanged places with her twin sister to hug her father. Martha climbed up on Ted's shoulders as Mary got between their parents and took their hand. Ted smiled happily over at Jenny's beautiful smile.

"We have been missed, darling."

"So, it appears, daddy." Jenny thought to herself, knowing Ted was capable of reading them. "Son? Do you know something I should know, Ted dearest?"

Ted smiled at her and whispered. "Yes, wonderful news, Jenny. A son in eight months."

"Eight months?" Jenny's eyes grew wide from the shock. "On our honeymoon?"

"First night!" Ted could sense everyone standing around silently were confused except for the twins and the young blue-eyed man walking toward them from the house. "Melaki, how does it feel watching more than one?"

"For me, these children are loving and well behaved. You have done well my brother." The handsome youth looked over the new arrivals. "I see you have won over the two small ones, Patches and Blake but the other three will take some time to clean out the dirt!" Bright blue eyes smiled over at Jenny. "The grandfather is very happy it will be a boy this time, Jennifer, although he would love to spoil Mary and Martha as well!"

"The grandfather?" Jenny looked up at Ted for answers but received only a kiss on the cheek.

"Later Jenny. At the moment we've got to get these five, settled in." Ted, held out his arms for Ruth and Rachel who stood back waiting for their orders. They ran up happily in his warm embrace. The front door slamming caused everyone to look and see Leah running out, pigtails flying behind her.

"TED, JENNY! MATTHEW, KATHY! YOU'RE HOME!" Leah ran from one to the other giving them each a hug then stood back smiling, glad they got home safely. "BOY, I'M GLAD TO SEE YOU! THOSE BOYS HAVE BEEN HARD TO HANDLE!"

Ted looked around to find everyone holding their ears, except him and Melaki. Ted pulled her over and pointed out all those holding their ears to block out her loud mouth. "Leah, sweet girl, can't you see how your loud voice affects other's around you? Now, tell me where you saw Teddy and Jacob."

"GOLLY! I NEVER SAID WHICH BOYS!" Leah grabbed her mouth when she noticed Ted's frown and continued in almost a whisper. "Sorry. Teddy and Jacob were at their house when Hannah sent me and Miriam over to the castle to take Esther the items she was low on."

"Leah, where is Miriam now?" Ted already knew the answer when he looked out toward the garden to see Robert hoeing with Andrew. "Why is she still at the castle?"

Esther had been listening from the screen door and made her way out slowly to face Ted. "It's my fault Miriam is at the castle Ted. I hurt my arm playing with the boys and when Miriam brought the things I ask for, Jonathan…I mean Mr. Wineworth ask her to take my place."

Ted listened quietly, but knowing the truth Esther was hiding, he took her hands and looked into her eyes. "You did not hurt your arm playing with Teddy and Jacob. Jonathan kiss you and…" Ted could see everything in her eyes as he spoke softly. "Esther, go up to your room and wait for me. Understand?"

"Yes Ted." Tears ran down her cheeks as she raced off to find a place free from all the questioning eyes watching and listening to them.

Jenny stepped up next to her husband and took his hand as she watched the young girl flee into the house. "Ted, did that jerk rape our Esther?"

"You might call it rape, but when it was given willingly, it could be described as a bad choice." Ted had kept his voice down so those standing around could not hear his words. "We have no way of proving his gilt and it is obvious the man who claims to be a preacher will deny it ever happened."

"I knew young Esther had gone astray Ted." Melaki looked at him peacefully, as though he had witnessed many others falling to temptation. "Would you like me to speak to the young lady for you, Ted?"

"Thank you for your loving concern, my brother, but Esther is my responsibility. I will trust you to take these five children and guard them closely." Ted gave him a knowing smile. "Since you're

87

an expert at that very thing, it should come easy." Ted took Jenny's hand and walked to the house.

"Ted, do you think Miriam will be safe? She can be easily sucked in by flattery."

"Her heart is with Robert. Miriam has learned to be strong." Ted touched Jenny's face, reflections of their honeymoon running through his head. He gave her a loving smile before facing the stairs. "Jenny, you can come with me. I never enter our girl's rooms alone. Besides, you could be of some help."

"Thank you darling for letting me help out with our family." Jenny wrapped her arm around his back as they made their way to Esther's room, where she waited nervously.

CHAPTER 18

"I'm so sorry Ted! I don't know what came over me." Esther sat between the quiet couple as she poured out her heart. "I went to the kitchen for a glass of milk. I thought everyone had gone to bed. I recall John telling me how he had helped Jonathan with his pajama's, then saw that he got to bed before going in to sleep with Teddy and Jacob, due to Teddy's behavior toward Leah. Earlier in the day when Leah and Miriam brought my groceries, Teddy had forced himself on Leah, trying to kiss her before pushing her on the ground and climbing on top of her. Jonathan was there watching but because of his broken leg he couldn't get up, so John heard her screams for help and raced out to pulled the laughing boy off.

As I was saying, thinking everyone was in bed asleep, I got my milk, drank it and turned to leave when I saw Jonathan, standing in the doorway, blocking my exit. I noticed instantly the cast was missing and Jonathan was completely better. I cannot explain why, but I froze in my tracks and then he put his hand out to me. I could not control myself. I walked straight to his arms. Then I felt his burning lips on mine." Esther covered her face, sobbing. "Oh God, Ted! Why? Why did I go with him to his room?"

"Jonathan had you in his spell, Esther. He willed you to have sex with him and you did." Ted pulled her into his arms and let her cry. "My dear child, God will forgive you. Just ask him. He knows you love Him."

"And I do, Ted!" Esther sniffed as she got down on the floor with Ted and Jenny. "Dear Father, I have sinned. Please, forgive me and wash me clean Lord Jesus and I promise to never break your heart nor Ted's ever again."

Jenny lifted the trembling girl up off the floor and gathered her in a loving embrace. "Esther, sweet child, let us go and wash off that evil mans lust from your beautiful Christian body."

"That's my girl!' Ted kissed Jenny's cheek as he patted Esther on the head. "While you wash away your sin, I will go down and see to our new family." He smiled and walked out, knowing Esther was in good hands. The Lord's and his Jenny's.

Joan Byrd

Jeff and Naomi led the two teens around to the back of the castle after hearing lots of cheering going on and their sons laughing out. When the small group walked around, they noticed Jonathan was not alone cheering. Miriam sat beside him, touching his hand while rooting on each boy when they made a score. Jacob scored a point and jumped up and down with joy as Teddy laughed sarcastically.

"Ha, little brother! I let you win that one just to see you go ballistic!" Teddy knew he had hit a nerve with his brother. "Get ready to get creamed!"

"No one will cream the other, Teddy Jeffery!" Jeff moved in quickly and grabbed the ball away from his oldest son's hands. "What have I told you both about being good sports!"

"Jeffery, you're back!" Jonathan stood up to kiss Naomi, noticing Blaze and Fire watching him closely. "I see you got these kids out. Did they co-operate with you?"

"I was about to put the ungrateful punks back behind bars!" Jeff reached down and picked up his youngest as he stared at the two teens coldly. "I think we understand each other now."

Jonathan's dark eyes drew the teen's attention. "Blaze, you and Fire need to be grateful that my brother Jeffery and his perfect wife took the time to come after you! You will be under their roof for a while so you shall behave and act like the grownups you claim to be!"

"I'm sorry, reverend." Fire looked him up and down as she blew a big bubble. "It's just hard to trust adults after being molested and raped! Beaten and slapped around!"

Blaze smiled as his voice took on a hint of mockery. "Boy Rev., you sure did heal up fast! Most people take several weeks to mend broken bones. It must have been a miracle!"

Jonathan stepped in close to the fresh teenager and got in his face. "We will have none of that, boy! I will see you to your rooms Miss Miriam prepared." Jonathan turned to Naomi and Jeff after plastering on a smile. "As for sportsmanship little brother, I taught the boys to play to win! Be strong, brave, and do your best! Following my advice, the boys are becoming great ball players!"

"Papa, Uncle Jonathan has taught us a lot about winning." Jacob wrapped his arms around Jeff's neck. "But papa, I think you're still the best coach."

"Thank you, Jacob." Jeff looked down to find Teddy staring down at the rock he was kicking, and rubbed his oldest son's hair.

"Teddy Jeffery, what does my number one son think."

"You are a great coach papa." Teddy continued to kick the rock. "Uncle Jonathan is great too! He actually played baseball in school and college, so he has taught us some really cool stuff."

"Well son, we will discus all this later." Naomi reached down and pulled him away from the rock to give him a hug and kiss. "Now Teddy, be a good big brother and take Jacob inside and wash the dirt off of you before we eat. John said supper was almost finished." Naomi had watched Miriam get up and stand next to her brother-n-law. She pulled her to one side and whispercd. "Just what are you doing here? What happened to Esther?" Naomi drew in closer. "And why aren't you inside helping John with supper?"

"Naomi, I happened to help brother John in the kitchen and we we're almost finished when your son, Teddy, called me to come to the back door. He said Jonathan would like for me to help root on the boys and it sounded like fun. So, I informed John, went out and started cheering loudly. Jacob and Teddy have gotten real, good at ball."

"It's called soccer, Miriam." Jeff had over heard their whispers. "And that was not the only reason you came out. You have got a full-blown crush on my brother and if you keep flirting around with him, Jonathan will have you in his bed! Is this what you're after and if so, what about poor Robert we saved because of your deep love for him?"

Miriam forced a laugh. "No! It is nothing like that Jeff. I am Robert's girl. We plan to get married soon." She laughed again, to hide her true feelings for Jonathan and how she felt drawn to him. "I love Robert. Now, that you're back home, I'll be going back to the farmhouse tomorrow morning. I only stayed after delivering groceries because Esther hurt her arm while playing ball with those rough boys of yours."

"Correction, my dear Miriam. Esther hurt her arm having rough sex with Jonathan!" Jeff stared down into her wide-surprised eyes. "Change of plans Miriam! You are going home tonight after supper! I will take you myself!"

Naomi stared wildly from Miriam to Jeff. "Ted knows! No one from the home is safe here, Jeff! Please, take John with you and do it now! Get them home quickly!"

"Keep the boys by your side at all times while I am away, my dearest one." Jeff took them quickly away.

91

CHAPTER 19

"I assure you brother, I do not know what you are talking about." Jonathan looked hurt by Jeff's accusation, accusing him of taking advantage of Esther. "Jeffery, I would never take advantage of any woman who was not willing to have sex with me." Jonathan knew what his brother was thinking. "Of her own choosing Jeffery and never anyone so young." His dark eyes looked at Naomi pleadingly. "Naomi, when I became a minister, I took my vows serious. I am innocent here. I cannot explain what made that sweet child accuse me of having sex with her. Perhaps she had a realistic dream or something. I do not wish to put my brother down, my dear, for I only met him and have grown to love him, but maybe these girls from such a sheltered home have always had secret feeling for Jeffery and could never show them because he was married to one of their sisters."

"Jonathan, I know girls can have day dreams about mysterious handsome men, but with Miriam, her dreams were always about Ted, never Jeff. Then she met and fell in love with Robert." Naomi wished for her husband's sake that Jonathan could be telling the truth and all this was just young girls imagination.

"Are you referring to Robert Perkins?" Jonathan walked to the window and gazed out into the darkness.

"How do you know Robert Perkins Jonathan?" Jeff stared at his brother. "Have you ever spent time in the witches Salem?"

"Heavens no! But, a young man named Robert Perkins came by my parsonage requiring if I might be Jeffery Wineworth. I informed the young man I had a twin brother who lived in Goldsburg, North Carolina and he thanked me and left with two older gentlemen."

"Those gentlemen were Robert's evil father and grandfather, long gone to father." Jeff watched his brother closely. "Robert has chosen good, Jonathan, so leave him alone!"

Jonathan turned around and laughed. "If you are through with your interrogation Jeffery, I'm off to bed." His eyes fell warmly on Naomi. "I know it's hard for you to believe me, you, angelic girl, but sometimes the devil makes a good person appear bad to break up a relationship between brothers. I came seeking my lost brother and found a loving family I was hoping to be a part of, but it appears to be falling away. For you, dear lady, I will pack my bags in the morning and be gone with the trouble teens. I bid you both goodnight." Jonathan walked away quickly to his room and shut the door.

"I will give my brother one thing." Jeff sneered. "Jonathan can act so well, he could fool a great many people." Jeff looked down at his wife, tears spilling from her beautiful eyes. "Sweet one, Jonathan has touched your heart with his lies. You must not believe a word he speaks."

"But Jeff, what if it is the devil, your father, wanting us not to trust Jonathan." Naomi laid her head on Jeff's strong shoulder. "I feel pity for him, either way. Whether he is good as he claims, or bad like you say."

"My very loving wife, you might not believe me when I tell you I too have pity for my brother. I only want good for him, like I received." Jeff pulled Naomi in his arms. "I will do all that is in my power to win Jonathan over to our side, but until then, he must stay here at the castle so I can watch him. If he leaves this place, he can and will have an ally. Satan himself and the people of Goldsburg will be in grave danger."

Jeff had decided to pay his twin a visit before he went to bed, so he knocked lightly on Jonathan's door and walked in. "Jonathan, might I have a word with you before you turn in and switch off your light?" Jeff's cold stare gave his brother a slight chill as he waved him inside. "I promise, it won't take lone."

"By all means Jeffery, say whatever you came in to say." Although feeling a little nervous around his tall, calm brother, Jonathan felt hopeful that things might work out. "I truly am sorry about the misunderstanding, but if my leaving makes your charming wife feel better, I'll take my leave."

"That is what I have come to discuss with you Jonathan. After talking it over with Naomi, my 'charming wife', I decided to ask you to stay with us. You are right about the two of us just finding each other, and family ties have become important to me ever since I found love. Teddy and Jacob have grown fond of you and I'm sure they would want you to remain with us on Black Mountain." Jeff forced a smile, to match his brother's. "I would not bring this up in

93

front of my angelic wife, but I know girls do have a way of flirting with us men and if tempted enough, they become irresistible to us. Before I found love with Naomi, I could take any woman I desired, but now, my little woman is all I need." Jeff put his strong arm around his brother's shoulders. "We both know you had sex with that little virgin, but I trust from now on Jonathan, you'll control your apatite for sex." Reaching in his pocket, Jeff brought out the note he received at the service station. "I almost forgot, some lady, with curly red hair, mistook me for you at the coastal service station, and slipped me this note. Just by observing her shock when I got to my car, I'd say, the married broad was in her mid-sixties. I see you like them older too, big brother." Jeff chucked as he walked out, recalling what the adulteries had written in her note.

Jonathan stared at his brother until he walked out, shutting the door. He walked to the bed and yanked the note out to read. "My darling Jonathan, has it been four weeks since you left? For me, my adorable hunk, it seems timeless since you held me in your arms. I miss feeling you body next to mine and the hot passion between us. I been thinking about what you told me darling, to leave Frank and take him for all I can get, for us. Jonathan, if that is what you still ask of me, I will do it, my wonderful lover. I will give up everything for you Jon, even my very life."

Jonathan angrily pulled open the dresser drawer and tossed the tell-tell note inside with the other letters he had received since arriving at the castle. Looking up in the mirror, his eyes caught his reflection, angry for getting caught by his brother, yet turned on by Rose's offer to give him her life.

"Jeffery knows I am not what I claim to be! He knows I seduced Esther into having sex with me and he knows I have the hots for Naomi and if I could find the opportunity, I would make love to her." Jonathan walked slowly to the bed and removed his pajamas before laying down to stare up at the ceiling. "If Jeffery knows all this about me, then why is he asking me to stay? Why can't I read my brother's thoughts like I do everyone else." Jonathan's eyes burned with hate. "Now that my stupid brother has chosen the good side and GOD has his soul, why, does that black wolf of a brother still have more power than me? Why?"

CHAPTER 20

"Miriam, you will never be alone with Jonathan Wineworth again! Do I make myself clear, young lady?" Ted spoke softly. "Dear girl, he is not what he claims to be. Miriam, do you trust me?"

"Teddy, you know I trust you more than anyone I know." Miriam looked hurt. "Please Ted, tell me, what did I do wrong?"

"As of now, sweet girl, you've done nothing wrong." Ted gently reached for her hand. "Jonathan has many of the same powers his twin does, Miriam. He is very capable of making you do his bidding. The man is already gaining your trust and it's just a matter of time, Jonathan will lure you in his bed if you let down your guard."

"Teddy, Jonathan seems like such a sweet man. The way he treats his nephews is priceless. He has never offered to touch me in an improper way." Miriam was sincere as she added with a smile. "Jonathan is a man of God, Ted. A preacher and I swear, we are just friends, nothing more."

"Miriam, Jonathan is a preacher only by title and your words to defend him only prove my point. The man has already gained your trust." Ted watched Esther walking toward them and she found her place beside him. "Thank you, Esther, for helping your sister. I know this cannot come easy for you but you will find strength in God."

"It must be told to help Miriam know the truth about Jonathan Wineworth." Esther reached for her sister's hand. "Miriam, I pray my words will save you from my fate. I trusted Jonathan, just like you. He had a way of making me feel special, even beautiful."

"You are special Esther and the beauty of the Lord shines through your beautiful face." Ted put a loving arm around her trembling shoulders, causing her to relax from his touch. "Go ahead, sweet girl."

"Ted, Jenny is so lucky to have your love." Esther lend her head on his shoulder as she continued. "And yes, you are lucky too, to have Jenny's beautiful love."

"I am very lucky to have such a wonderful woman as Jenny to love me, Esther. Thank you for acknowledging her." Ted smiled as he nodded for her to continue her story for Miriam.

"Miriam, Jonathan had me in a trance. I could do nothing but follow him to his bedroom. His kisses inflamed my body with desire for him and we had sex. I..." Esther stopped as tears fell down, her, whole body trembling as she recalled what happened." "Go ahead Esther, it's alright to confess how you felt." Ted spoke softly, calming her fears.

"I enjoyed the things Jonathan was doing to me. I never dream sex could feel so amazing. He made me feel hot and..." She looked shyly up at Ted and saw total love shining through as he nodded to go on. "He made me feel sexy. The more he gave the more I wanted. I felt myself moving with him, to bring on that special sensation that I was delirious for. Jonathan was demanding, a rough lover, pulling me in all directions, but I gave him all he needed." Esther sobs as she poured out her heart. "When I got back to my room, I felt so dirty and ashamed. Jonathan followed me, then grabbed me into his arms, wanting more. He slung me across my bed and we did it, over and over again. He became like an animal, slamming me around until I heard my arm snap, but even then, I wanted more of him." Esther buried her head in her hands. "I fell asleep around two a.m., completely exhausted. The next morning, I hardly recognized myself in the mirror. I hated myself and wanted to die! My only hope was coming home, to Ted and find some sort of peace and God willing, forgiveness." Esther could not control her sobbing as she fell in Ted loving arms.

"It's alright my daughter, my sister. That was not easy but Miriam needed to hear what she was about to get herself into if she hung around Jeff's brother."

Esther stopped crying and gave Ted a thank-you smile before looking at her Christian sister. "Miriam, please listen to Ted. You've got Robert and he loves you. I know he would marry you today if you would just give the word." She waited for Ted to help Miriam up when they noticed Jenny waiting on the steps for Miriam, so she could offer her own female wisdom about leaving 'bad boys' alone and be grateful for the one that loved her.

"Why must we go to church, rev?" Fire pulled at the Sunday dress as she looked at her reflection. "You know it's against our beliefs!"

"She's right, B.H.! If the rest of your creepy brother's Christian friends are as scary as he is, I rather go skinny dipping in that creek we drove over coming up the mountain." Blaze stared at the necktie his fingers were fumbling with." How the shit does this thing go?"

Jonathan stared coldly at the fresh teenagers, then he yanked the necktie from the boy's hands and began making it look perfect. "The trouble with you brats is, you do not know how to take orders without making rude remarks! When I say we go to church, I have a damn good reason!" Jonathan shoved the silent youth in a chair and got in his face. "Boy, you are not to question an order I demand you to do! Have I made myself clear or do you wish to feel the pain of disobedience?"

"I have behaved badly sir. I will obey all your commands, Blackheart." Blaze shook with real fear, knowing what this man was capable of doing to someone who upset him. "Seeing your kindness around the small boys and your brother's wife, I just assumed..."

"That I had changed?" Jonathan sneered, as he pulled his gums back over his sharp teeth. "Never let appearances cloud your vision son. Beneath all the preacher act, I am still the man you fear!" He moved to the dresser and pulled out his caps, placing them over is canines. Jonathan smiled at his reflection, pleased with his reverent look. "If you kids must know why we go to church, it is to mislead those around us into believing we are what we claim to be." His eyes fell lustfully on Fire as she pulled up her panty hose. "I am a preacher, a loyal big brother, a devoted uncle and you, my poor unfortunate misguided juveniles, have been placed in my care, to help you find the right path."

"So, we appear to others that you are leading us down the path of goodness and righteousness." Fire smiled and walked over into his arms. "While you are really leading up to hell and damnation."

"Such a smart girl." Jonathan's lips melted over her in a flaming kiss. "Tis a shame there is no time for sex! My body lust for yours in a powerful way, my Fire."

Fire gazed up into his black eyes, seduction written on her young face. "Then, I will make up for our loss tonight. I will be yours, completely, Blackheart, as always, body and soul."

Jonathan smiled and led them out the door. The three would be going to church, but their minds would be wondering down the wide lustful path.

"Do you really think Jonathan took those kids to a church

Joan Byrd

service in town?" Naomi helped Jacob and Teddy get out of the car then took their hands. "Alright boys, straight to the chapel. We are running late."

"Ted won't mind, as long as we're here, my dove." Jeff helped Naomi keep up with their running sons. "As for brother Jonathan, he is just putting on a good front to the citizens of our fair town to win them over whenever he gets that church he claims he's getting." Jeff bent down to whisper, to keep the boys from hearing. "All the other church's in Goldsburg will find a drop, in attendance when Jonathan opens his doors and starts preaching."

"Papa, why didn't Uncle Jonathan come to church with us this morning?" Teddy held open the heavy door for his family. "No one preaches as good as Ted."

"I agree son, Ted has been gifted by the Lord Himself." He whispered to Naomi, blocking out the boys from hearing him "This is the only church that won't be affected by brother Jonathan. He is afraid of Ted, and with good reason. Jonathan can sense Ted's over powering love flow from him. He's afraid to let those two young brats near Ted and risk losing control of them."

The youth choir was just finishing "Sweet Hour of Pray" when the Wineworth family found their seats. Even though Jeff and Naomi were outside the church door and the children were singing, Ted could hear the conversation about Jonathan clearly. Ted's thoughts were directed into Jeff's as Matthew read the scripture.

"You are aware your brother cannot set foot on my mountain unless I allow it! He has proven my doubt in him by dishonoring our Esther. We will deal with the lost teens that are in his possession at the present. Jonathan has an agenda that involves your father and he has already set the course for many lives who have and will fall into his trap. My vision sees ahead and the time of salvation or damnation is near for Jonathan's actions. Look toward the Christmas season, my friend. The time for miracles."

"Surely there's hope for Jonathan if I could find salvation! "Jeff sent back his thoughts.

"Jonathan was different from you Jeff. He had only known love, while you knew only hate. His heart led him into becoming a minister for all the right reasons. Jonathan's faith was real. He had confessed to believing in Jesus as his Savior. Your father knew Jonathan was alive, a believer and wanted no part of him as long as

98

he had your devotion. The fact that your twin looked exactly like you, made Lucifer seek him out and change him slowly to be a substitute for you. The more power Satan released into Jonathan, the greater his hate became, until all the goodness he knew turned to complete evil."

Ted could still see the stone faces of Willy, Devin and Marble as the children sang the first hymn, joined happily by Patches and Blake. There were seven total lost children that had been led astray by Jonathan's teaching. The two smallest had found their way home, but the other five were still lost sheep that needed bringing back into the fold. And if possible, bring Jonathan back to the narrow path that leads to life.

CHAPTER 21

The picnic was laid out by the brook where Ruth had almost drowned a few years back. Ted raised his arms, signaling for everyone to find a place around the long table spread lying on the ground. He smiled down at Jenny as he helped her down next to him, Naomi on his right. Jeff managed to get his long legs into a comfortable position before glancing over to Miriam when she found a place beside him, Robert at her left. Miriam gave Jeff a warm smile before making a comment.

"Jeffery, I cannot get over how much you and Jonathan look exactly alike."

"We are identical twins Miriam but that is were the our being alike ends." Jeff could read more from Miriam than she was letting on. "Do you and Robert have a date set yet? You cannot keep old Robert waiting forever girl."

"I keep telling her the same thing Jeff." Robert reached over for her hand. "I think Miriam enjoys watching me suffer."

Miriam gave a soft laugh and hit his hand. "Robert Perkins, that's just not true! I am just planning the perfect wedding, that's all."

"Miriam, it's not a big wedding that makes you happy, it is finding and marring the right man." Naomi had been listening as she reached across Jeff and touched her face. "Dear sister, it is being together that makes life perfect."

"Naomi is absolutely right Miriam." Jenny added as she watched her twin girls playing by the water. "Sharing your life with the one you love is what keeps you happy. Having children together and knowing they came from that beautiful love you share." Jenny sat up on her knees when she noticed Teddy trying to give Mary a kiss. "Mary Neenam, you and Martha get yourself over here this instant and sit down! Daddy is about to say the blessing."

"Coming mom!" Mary called out as they raced over, kissed their parents and she flopped down next to Devin. "Dev, you're in for a great picnic." Mary heard her father clear his throat, a sign for her to close her eyes. She whispered. "Before we eat, Dad prays so close your eyes." Noticing the stone face of Devin had kept his eyes open, Mary closed hers as she willed the rude children's eyes shut as their words froze, then smiled at her father. "Go ahead dad, they're ready."

Ted shook his head as he looked up to heaven. "Most loving Father, whose care and guidance leads us through each day, we open our humble hearts with thanksgiving for all your good gifts. May we love as you love, Holy Lord. Amen."

The food was past and everyone ate in silence. Seconds before, Marble had wobbled up next to Matthew and ask him sweetly to help her down. As he passed her a dish, she let her hand touch his with each passing. After receiving the last dish, she thanked him and continued to smile up at him shyly throughout the meal.

Matthew tried to move as close to Kathy as possible, causing her to laugh softly and take his hand. "Sweetheart, it's alright to talk to Marble. She's only twelve-years-old and very pregnant, for heaven's sake. What can she do? Mash you with her stomach?"

"Kathy, Ted did warn me to stay clear of her." Matthew looked helpless, then down at the smiling girl. "I guess as long as she is pregnant, I will be safe."

Kathy continued to laugh as she picked up her sandwich and took a bite. "Matthew, you are bigger than that little girl. Take away the baby fat and all that's left is a kid, so just relax and enjoy your lunch."

Matthew mumbled close to his wife's ear. "A kid with an appetite for s-e-x! Kathy, she knows the 'S' word! The kid does not even know who this baby's father is!"

"The 'S' word?" Kathy looked thoughtful. "Shit? No, sin? I've got it! Sex!"

"Neither Kathy! The kid said...Screw!" Matthew laid his head over on his wife's shoulder. "Can you believe a girl that young using that kind of language?"

"Maybe the kid likes screwdrivers and hammers! Nails and screws." Kathy laughed when Matthew looked up bewildered. "Relax honey, I'm kidding. I know what you're referring too. Ted is right! Stay clear of little miss hot pants!"

Devin and Willy stood by a tree line path throwing a baseball at one another as they watched Mary, Martha, Patches, and Ruth splashing in the shallow brook. Devin fastened his attention on Mary.

Joan Byrd

"That little blonde is about the prettiest girl I have ever seen."

"You are kidding, right bro?" Willy chuckled as he watched the identical twins kicking water on each other and laughing. He tossed the ball back as he shook his head. "Those blondes look exactly alike, so how can one be prettier than the other?"

"Its in the eye of the beholder, dimwit! Mary has got something special and it makes me feel real, good!

"Hey punk, you're talking about my girl!" Teddy marched over and gave Devin a hard push, causing him to stumble.

Devin turned on him, fist in the air. "Hey kid, watch it!" Devin stared down at the boy five years his junior. "I have decided Mary is my girl!"

"Like hell she is!" Teddy yelled, causing the adults to look their way. Jeff jumped up and with four big steps, he grabbed his son off the ground, black eyes staring angrily into his.

"Teddy Jeffery, we will not have that kind of language from our son!" Jeff slung his attention on the frozen boys. "As for you little demons, stay clear of those girls! Mary and Martha may seem older but they are only four-years-old!" Jeff's finger punched each boy in the chest. "And stay clear of my son! He may be younger than you both, but take my word, you would not want to make him mad!"

"Jeff" Ted spoke softly as he placed his arm around his angry friend's shoulders. "Let me speak to these young men." Jeff could read the warning in Ted's gentle eyes and was aware of how easily he had grown angry, a bad sign.

"Ted, sometimes I fight my old feelings. I know I must stay strong." Thoughts given only to his friend before looking down at the scared teens. "I'm sorry boys if I was too harsh, but I know my son's strength better than either of you. Just listen to the wisdom of Ted. I will take my son home now."

Ted nodded his approval for his friend's words, then placed a hand on each boy, who felt the strong sensation of a warming love. "Devin, Willy, my daughters are off limits to you both. They are still very young and in their mama and daddy's care until they reach the age of eighteen."

"What about that demon's boy? He claimed your daughter as his! Is he any better than us?" Devin's voice shook.

"First, Teddy Jeffery is not the son of a demon. Teddy has been our friend ever since he came into this world." Ted's eyes grew misty, causing the two boys to ponder his emotions. "For Teddy's father Jeff, sometimes life gets hard to do what is right. If you knew where he came from, you might understand his struggles." Ted turned to lock eyes with Jeff, then watch him walk away with his family. "Jeff Wineworth is my trusting friend. He is my brother by faith. I will never turn my back on him no more than he would on me. Life is a constant struggle, but with God, all things are possible."

Ted had left Jenny fast asleep. He knew he could find peace on the mountain top. The day before had been very taxing on him. First, learning more about Jeff's brother, then the incident with Teddy and the two lost boys and the fact that the argument was over his daughter Mary.

Ted had reached the top and felt the gentle breeze blowing across his brow. "My son, many things are of trouble to you."

"Father, there is much to be done." Ted spoke softly and with reverence. "With each passing day there seems to be more and more lost sheep finding their way to our small town. They all seem to be connected to one man."

"Jonathan." The wind whirled around Ted's ears. "His dear mother Gloria thought she had made him safe by sending him away. It nearly broke her heart. Lucifer was glad to be rid of the son he never wanted. Nothing escapes my once beautiful angel. He is clever and smart."

"Then, I'm right about Lucifer having a hold on Jonathan." Ted reached down to pick Jenny a daisy. "A replacement for his favorite son, Jeff. Yet, he waited four years to bring him forward."

"Lucifer takes his time to gain the trust of those he wishes to possess, then he molds them into what he desires them to become. It is a fact that the once beautiful angel of light wanted Jeffery to be his number one son!" the heavenly voice grew strong with a warning. "Beware my son, Lucifer still wants Jeffery! Jeff has shown his temper! He must watch his anger! The blood of my powerful fallen angel still flows through his veins. The two six's that are made permanent on my son Jeffery can never be removed. One more six, and the mark of the beast will have his soul forever. Beware the devil's lies about honoring his son by making him the Anti-Christ!"

"Lord, why go after Jonathan if it's Jeff Lucifer is after? Just

103

Joan Byrd

because he is his son and the image of Jeff?" Ted knew the answer, but wanted to reassure himself. "It's because Lucifer has substituted Jonathan for Jeff in case he cannot win over his favorite son."

"You know correctly, son." The soft voice fell over Ted. "But beware, Jonathan is not the only one Satan might choose."

"Teddy. The boy is already showing signs of evil, although his innocents keeps him unaware of it." Tears swelled in Ted's blue eyes. "Such a sweet innocent child but as he grows he is finding his powers and strength. Naomi, my angel, will be heart broken if Teddy Jeffery choses evil over good."

"The lad calls for his name to be switched to Jeffery. He has stated boldly: I want to be just like my papa."

"Teddy is only one part of why I'm troubled. Please help me make the right decisions Father. There are already so many souls here and many more yet to come." Ted's legs trembled by the weight of what lay ahead and he felt they were going to collapse when strong hands took hold and lifted him up. Ted relaxed when he recognized the familiar voice behind him.

"Ted, my son." Smiling, Ted turn and saw his angelic father smiling back at him. "There is much work to be done down here and since you seemed to be outnumbered, the Holy Creator has loving sent me to assist with gathering His lost sheep. Ted, my boy, you and your friend Jeffery, are not alone on this journey. I, your father Gabriel, will be beside you as will many more brothers of mine when the time arrives." The tall handsome angel chuckled as he draped his arm around his son's shoulders. "Now, tell me about my new grandson? When will little Gabriel be making his arrival?"

CHAPTER 22

Jenny had awakened to find Ted missing from bed, but his absence never bothered his pretty wife. She knew his morning tradition was to climb to the mountain top and converse with the Almighty. After taking a quick shower, Jenny got dressed and slipped from the quiet farmhouse, leaving the smells of Hannah's baking bread behind. Jenny had her own tradition when the weather was favorable like this morning. She would make her way to the mountain path and wait for her husband on her favorite rock until he came down to walk her home.

But, before Jenny could step onto the path that headed up, she stopped after hearing someone call her name. "Jenny, let us wait for Ted here on this bench this morning. He is already on his way down the mountain path and he will not be alone this morning." Melaki seemed to light up when Jenny let him help her sit down. "I have come to prepare you Jenny."

Jenny tried to smile as her thoughts went back to seeing this young man for the first time and Ted promising to explain who this outspoken young man was. Had Ted forget to tell her, she thought to herself, or did he will for her to forget about it, until now.

Reading her thoughts, Melaki took her hand and peace filled her instantly. "You are wondering about me, Jenny. Ted will tell you when you are ready to hear."

"Can Mekaki read thoughts like Ted?" Jenny pondered the thought as she said "Melaki, are you an…"

The handsome youth jumped up and pointed at Ted and the tall man walking close to him. Except for the stranger being much taller than her Ted, they looked almost identical and both wearing white robes. Jenny stood slowly, realizing, this stranger with her husband had been able to set foot on Ted's mountain, the same mountain no other human was allowed to climb. With one exception, she thought. Her magical wedding day. Then it dawned on Jenny who this glowing man was. Could she actually be looking at an angel?

"Yes, Jenny, an angel." Ted took her trembling hands. "Not one, but two."

105

Joan Byrd

"Make that two and ¾'s angels Ted." Gabriel smiled at a confused Jenny.

"Ted?" Jenny's eyes grew wide as she stood slowly and looked from the tall angel to the young one.

"Jenny darling, what I am about to share with you must not go beyond this point." Ted helped her back down and joined her on the bench. "Do we have your word, dearest?"

"Whatever secret you share with me Ted, I will keep safe inside me, I promise darling." Jenny could feel her heart pounding from a different kind of fear. Not one of danger, but seeing the unknown.

"Remember, to have faith, Jennifer, believing is seeing and seeing is believing." The tall angel pulled her up and put his arm around her. "I am Gabriel, Ted's father."

"And I am Melaki, your daughter Mary's guardian angel." Suddenly Jenny realized the powerful truth she had just been told. Although she already knew her husband was part angel, she never dreamed his father was such a high-ranking messenger of God, nor the sweet young man who had been sent to help out was her daughter's guardian, but the truth that made Jenny began swaying was the words spoken by God's messenger angel himself. This very angel that brought Elizabeth and Zachariah the news of John the Baptist's birth and the glorious news to the virgin Mary, that Jesus, the Son of God, was to be born of her.

Gabriel had proudly informed Jenny that his son Ted was ¾'s angel, making him only ¼ᵗʰ human. Jenny felt her surroundings spinning and before she fainted to the ground, Ted caught her in his strong arms.

Jenny slowly opened her eyes and knew she was lying in their bed. Had it just been a dream, she thought, a very real dream. Before she could sit up and look around, Jenny felt Ted gently run his fingers through her hair.

"Jenny, my love, it was no dream. My father and Melaki have been sent to help us gather the loss sheep. The bad shepherd has led them astray and the number is too great for me and Jeff to save alone.

"Ted, who will you introduce your father as, sweetheart?" Jenny sat up and Ted pulled her into his embrace. "Will he stay robed like you?"

Ted chuckled and wrapped her tighter. "I'm sure Gab will find

106

an outfit more suitable for his job. I will introduce him to the children as one of my teachers, from my youth." Ted could read his wife's thoughts questioning the truth in his statement, knowing he never told a lie. "I speak only the truth, darling. I cannot lie."

Jenny blushed, knowing he read her doubts. "It's just that you only met your father, so how on earth can you honestly claim he taught you as a youth?"

"From his voice, Jenny. As I was growing up, I would climb the hill behind my home where this intelligent unseen angel taught me many things I put into practice even today." Ted remembered back. "I heard from three heavenly beings while growing up. God, the Father, Gabriel, and my Lord and brother, Jesus, Christ. I never questioned why I was different, nor why I had powers I could not explain. The Lord told me I was born for a great purpose and when the time came, it would be revealed to me. As for now, my chosen purpose is to help the forgotten children and all who are lost from the Almighty." Ted smiled down into Jenny's beautiful face and kissed her tenderly.

"My personal purpose in life is to be a good husband and father. I love you Jenny, with all my heart, and had I the time, I would make love to you at this very moment. But, the family has awakened, getting dressed and pretty soon we will hear lots of little feet marching down the stairs, hungry and ready for breakfast."

"I knew I was married to a very special man, Ted Neenam. Thank you for sharing your past and your love for me." Jenny ran her fingers down his chest, causing him to take a deep breath. "We may not have time to make it under the sheets now darling, but I'm sure you will show me a good time tonight." Jenny moved up close to him, and could feel his manliness before jumping from bed and walking to the door, still dressed. "Well sweetheart, are you coming with me or do I remove these clothes and climb back in that bed with you?"

Ted jumped up and was by Jenny's side in a flash. "My tempting bride, you are really in for it tonight woman!" With one last kiss, he took her by the hand and pulled his surprised wife out the door.

CHAPTER 23

"Jonathan, can you meet me at the town library in one hour?" Tracy Reynolds spoke softly as she listened for the water running in the shower where her husband was bathing.

"I would love to meet you there, Trace." He whispered, his voice low and seductive. "I'd rather meet you at the Goldsburg Hotel."

"Soon my darling." Tracy felt herself growing excited just from hearing his voice. "I just need a little time to think of something to tell Joseph. So far he hasn't become suspicious "The attractive woman closed her eyes as she pictured lying next to Jonathan. "Soon, I promise. God, I need you!"

"I'm glad. I will meet you in one hour, Trace, at the sexy novel section." Jonathan smiled to himself as he replaced the receiver in its cradle. "Poor misguided Tracy. She thinks she is the only one I'm having an affair with." He pulled on a black pair of pants and matching black top. "The little adulteress is glad that poor old Joe hasn't got suspicious." Jonathan stood back to admire his reflection, tempting and sexy. "Stupid bitch! She hasn't a clue I've set her faithful husband up with his own sexy demon. How delightful!" Jonathan slid his billfold in his back pocket then turned, right into his brother.

"Jonathan, what is so delightful to cause your face to glow with joy?"

Jonathan was disturbed that he had not sensed Jeff come inside his room and wondered just how much he had heard. "I just found out that two of my church members from the cape are in town for a visit. A delightful couple." Jonathan knew how to put on a real smile when needed. "I was on my way down to ask if I may borrow your car. Mine appears to be low on gas and I did promise to meet the Reynold's in town in one hour."

"So, you can drive then? The leg is completely healed!" Jeff never drew his attention off his brother's face.

"It wasn't broken after all as we feared. It is quite strange the doctors made the wrong call and put on that cast." Jonathan waited a moment before asking. "The car, may I borrow it, just this once?" Jeff reached in his pocket for the keys. "Feel free to fill up your car when you return, brother. I feel sure you have spotted our big gas tank at the barn." He tossed his keys in the out reached hand. "Be careful Jonathan. You are not as wise as you think. I am very capable of seeing through your transparences "Jeff turned and walked from the guest room, leaving his brother staring after him.

Ted walked in the back door of the farm house and noticed Robert was sitting across from Esther playing a card game. Being caught up in the excitement of the game, neither player had seen Ted observing them. "Having fun, you two?" Ted glanced down at the cards Esther was holding and she smiled up.

"Hi Ted! Robert is teaching me how to play rook." She raised her cards and pointed to the black crow, then giggled. "This card is the one to avoid. Looks like it 'flew' right into my hands."

"It certainly sounds like you are enjoying the game." Ted looked around the empty den and knew these two were alone. "Robert, where is Miriam? I thought she might be with you. I have been looking for her to help mother in the kitchen."

"Miriam went to town with Matthew and Kathy, about thirty minutes ago." Robert propped up on his elbows as he laid down the cards to speak. "She had some books to return to the library and wanted to pick up a few more to read."

Jenny walked from the kitchen drying her hands on a dish towel. "Hi sweetheart! Hannah needed a hand in the kitchen so I volunteered since Kathy and Miriam left for town."

Ted pulled her over and gave her a thankful kiss. "Good girl. It appears Miriam changed my orders to help in the kitchen for a trip to the library."

"You know how Miriam likes to avoid work around here when there's an opportunity to do something easier." Jenny took his hand and pulled him away from the young couple playing cards. "Hannah sent Matthew and Kathy to town to shop for needed items, soap, shampoo, sugar. Miriam grabbed her over due library books and ask to ride along." Jenny glanced at the couple laughing. "Ted, I see you noticed Robert and Esther together. I have been observing them and they seem to be growing very close."

"Miriam keeps putting Robert off." Ted looked their way to find them exchanging smiles. "That girl's head is always in a cloud,

109

Joan Byrd

Whenever I try to read Miriam's thoughts, she starts quoting the 23rd Psalm in her head."

"Why on earth would she hide her thoughts from you? What's that about?" Jenny pulled the curtain back to see her twins still swinging with Patches, Ruth, and Blake. "Do you think Miriam is having second thoughts about poor Robert?"

"I think our Miriam is having thoughts about someone else." Ted looked down, his eyes serious. "I fear it may be Jonathan Wineworth."

"Even after you and Esther warned her about him?" Jenny was aware of how selfish Miriam could be if she wanted something and how she thought of only of herself at times.

"I do not think Miriam will go looking for Jonathan but men like Jeff and Jonathan have a way of knowing when women are drawn to them. Jeff was better at that art than any man and he knew if he wanted to take a woman, all he had to do was make her fall into his trap." Ted could not resist his chuckle when he added. "Jeff was not prepared for the trap Naomi held for him. Love is a powerful thing and Jeff Wineworth is living proof that 1% of good can win over 100% of evil." Ted's thoughts returned back to the flirty blonde who had tried to win him for herself and a tear came in his blue eyes. "If Jonathan thought for one second, he could have Miriam, a virgin and Christian under my roof, he would not stop until he had her. Jenny, the children mean the world to me and if I were to lose just one to Satan, it would cut me deeply."

Jenny took around Ted in a loving embrace. "I will pray for our Miriam, Ted darling, that she listens to the only man who ever loved her, even after being the selfish, outspoken, girl she has always been."

"My Jenny, my dearest love, I can see you love this selfish girl yourself and your prayers are always welcome." Ted took her hand. "Would you like to walk with me to the feeding pastures, to check on Devin, I sent him out to help watch the sheep with John and Thomas." He smiled when his wife smiled shaking her head yes. "Willy is with Rachael and Andrew, gathering vegetables. Marble is supposed to be picking grapes with Leah and Elizabeth. Due to her delivery date coming soon, I cannot push her into any strenuous job."

"Poor child." Jenny followed her husband to the back door and

110

walked along the path that would take them to the sheep's field below the grape vineyard. "The pain she must endure in childbirth for someone so young, will not come easy."

"Yet, one so young had sex willingly, again and again, never thinking about the outcome." Ted looked out to see the three girls filling their buckets with the plump grapes. His attention fell on the pregnant twelve-year-old, her fingers moving at a snail's pace. "Then there's that little soul to be born from this young girl."

"Poor little thing. What will become of the baby Ted? Will it be raised here, like baby Ruth was when we met?" Jenny felt Ted's gentle squeeze as he glanced down at her.

"I have been praying on the matter, Jenny and the Lord has given me His answer." Ted stop to take her hands. "You and I must raise this little baby boy as our own, dearest one."

"Adopt the baby?" Jenny was wide-eyed, knowing that Ted had already informed her about her getting pregnant on their honeymoon, first night. "What about Marble? Do you think she will fight to keep her baby?"

"Marble is almost a baby herself darling and I am just glad her evil leader didn't have this baby aborted." Ted looked out at the young girl with compassion. "She won't fight us Jenny. Marble will be relieved to be rid of what she feels is a burden. Besides, this unborn baby has no chance if he stays with that girl."

"Very well darling, we must follow your heart and give this baby 'boy' the chance he deserves." Jenny laid her head on Ted's chest. "The girls will be a big help with their brothers. We've had experience before raising two babies at the same time."

"Jenny, I love you so much. Two sons born several months apart will give us time to give our first son the time he needs to feel loved. Our son will be born on Christmas Eve and his name will be Gabriel. After his grandfather."

Jonathan spotted Tracy Reynolds looking down the racy-romantic book section as she pretended to be looking over the titles. He smiled at her shapely figure as he moved up behind her and touched the back of her neck. Tracy shut her eyes and smiled as he spoke softly in her ear.

"So, Joseph came with you to our little library?" Jonathan turned her around slowly and she gazed up into his seductive dark eyes. "I see you found the naughty section. Let me help you find the perfect book to prepare you for our evening under the sheets." His long fingers ran along the shelf as he continued to stare down at her. They stopped at a red book and he laid it in her hands and he whispered, "Page 666, the time and place! I cannot wait to have all of you!"

Seeing her husband moving down the history isle, Tracy tucked the red book under a previously found book on gardening to throw off Joseph when they checked out of the library. "I looked forward to reading what's in this book on page 666." Tracy whispered as she nodded toward her husband checking the back of a book. Getting his attention, she called him over. "Joseph darling, look who I ran into"

"Well I be! If it's not Reverend Wineworth. It is a small world!" He chuckled as he shook hands. "How is the visit with your brother going?"

"It couldn't be better, Mr. Reynolds. Thank you for asking." Jonathan tilted his head to see the title of the book featuring airplanes in the business' man hand. "Another book on planes Joe. You're really into flying." Jonathan playfully slapped the shorter man on the back. "I recall you enjoy going to the exercise club to keep in great shape." Jonathan tried not to laugh when he heard Tracy get choked. He pulled a card from his wallet and handed it to Joseph Reynolds. "I found a private man's club just off Main Street Joe and this one is for you. I think you will like it a lot!" Jonathan winked and pulled Mr. Reynolds to one side, as he motioned for Tracy to go check out her books. Thinking Jonathan was distracting her husband for her, she smiled and walked swiftly to the book checkout. Jonathan draped an arm around the businessman. "The directions are on the back. I have you registered as Frank Smith from L.A. I think you will be very pleased with this 'lady Joe."

Joseph Reynolds twisted around to find his wife waiting by the library door. He smiled broadly and stuck the prized card in his pocket. "Jon, how can I ever repay you? I just cannot get enough! It looks like I've become addictive to sex, in all forms, thanks to you."

"Glad I can help feed that appetite of yours, big boy! Just have fun." Jonathan glanced over to find Tracy had turned to page 666 and was happily reading his note. "A happy church member is a cheerful giver!" Both men laughed as Jonathan moved past Joe at the book counter and stood next to his wife.

The Lost Sheep

"Tracy, I told Joseph about this great men's spa in town and he's anxious to try it out. I hope you don't mind him skipping out this evening at two p.m."

Tracy recalled the note stating: Meet me a two this afternoon at the Goldsburg Hotel, room 666. Even though the same devilish number came up in both the book and the room number, Tracy convinced herself it was just a coincident and gave the tall handsome man beside her a bright smile.

"I think that is exactly what my darling husband needs. He has been wound up in knots ever since we arrived and a spa treatment is just the right medicine for him." Tracy gave her husband a quick kiss as she added. "And knowing how much Joseph hates taking me shopping, he can enjoy the spa while I enjoy all the charming little shops this beautiful old town has to offer. Joe, you can drop me off on your way to your spa."

"Then that settles everything. You're both set, doing things you enjoy." Jonathan took a seat by the window and opened the book he had been holding. "I will have a word with my brother Jeffery and his lovely wife, Naomi about having you over for dinner soon, if you like."

"I would love to meet your brother Jonathan, to see if there's any family resemblance." Tracy placed her library books in her oversize shoulder bag and smiled down, wishing she were sitting in his lap.

"Family resemblance, you may be surprised, Tracy." Jonathan winked. "Have fun you two. Joseph, I hope you start feeling great" he gave him a thumb's up, then turned, his burning eyes on Tracy. "And I 'pray' you get everything you desire, Mrs. Reynolds." His eyes followed them outside and froze on the blonde climbing from the white S.U.V. "It appears to be my lucky day! I will stick around and see if pretty little Miriam needs any assistance finding the right book.

CHAPTER 24

"Miriam, check your watch. Kathy and I will be back in exactly one hour. That should give you plenty of time to return those books and find a few more to check out." Matthew looked around the library and all appeared normal. "No wondering off to some shop! Remember to go straight to the Christian novel section and avoid the trashy isle."

"Matthew Christian, do not be so exasperating! I know Ted would never allow me to bring home an X-rated novel! Get real and get going, before I scream!" Miriam threw her shoulder bag on and patted Kathy on the back. "Poor thing! Being married to our Matthew!"

"My honey just likes to keep us all straight, Miriam." Kathy laughed before adding. "While you're in there, check out the children's books and choose some for different ages." Kathy's attention was drawn to the sound of a familiar bell. Two ladies were stepping from the lady's shop where her and Jenny used to shop for modern clothes. She gave a sigh and settled back in the bucket seat.

"I'll be watching for your return in about an hour. Please pick out some good smelling shampoo Kathy." Miriam waved. "Don't let Matthew pick it out!" she stated as she pushed open the heavy library door, walked in and returned the books before heading for the Christian section.

Miriam was in deep thought as she rummaged through the many novels lining the shelves and didn't hear the man step up behind her until he said her name softly. She turned to see Jonathan towering over her and it made her heart start to flutter.

"How good to see you, Miriam. You left the castle in such a hurry I never had the chance to say farewell." His dark eyes smiled down. "Do you need help finding a book? I think you will enjoy reading my suggestions."

"Jonathan! What a nice surprise!" Miriam tried to sound normal although she felt nervous being so close to the man Esther had described. "So, you like to read too."

"Doesn't everyone." He continued to smile as he took the book she had been checking out. "Interesting! Hannah Finds Love. This one looks good and clean."

Miriam blushed from the comment and took the book back. "That's what I read Jonathan. Ted would never permit me to read a regular romance novel "

"Admit it Miriam, haven't you ever wondered what they talk about in those regular romance books? Many of them are beautifully written and can help an inexperience young lady learn how to make love instead of looking completely out of touch with what's happening." Jonathan remained very gentlemanly as he gently touched her face. "Such innocents. Tell me Miriam, do you know how to make Robert happy sexually on your wedding night, if you don't mind my asking such a personal question? I am a minister and I council young people all the time, so you can be open with me."

"To be honest, I haven't the foggiest ideal what I am suppose to do, Jonathan." Miriam smiled shyly, feeling more relaxed by his manners. "Ted never talks about sex with us, and I have been too afraid to bring up the subject with his wife, Jenny. She would help me, I have no doubt, but I feel sure Ted would object and Jenny would never go against his wishes for the world."

"Miriam, this is something every bride needs to know and if you have no mother to let you in on what to do, then let me help you, my dear." Jonathan took Miriam's hand, sending warmth through her body. He felt her trembling. "Miriam, I am a preacher. I only wish to help you." Jonathan dropped his head and shook it sadly. "I know you have heard some bad things about me, especially concerning Esther. Miriam, what you've heard has been twisted." Jonathan noticed the librarian look up at them, so he pulled her over to the reading table and pulled out a chair for her. "The truth is, Esther had a crush on me. I could tell by her actions. She became flirty and then one night, she showed up at my bedroom door saying she needed to talk. After letting her inside, Esther confessed her love for me and said she needed me." Jonathan looked up pleadingly. "Miriam, I swear the girl's hands were all over me while she tried to kiss me. The next thing I know, Esther was removing her clothes and locking my door. What was I to do! I am a man for God's sake and I had not been with a woman for a very long time. I felt myself growing with desire and I pulled her into my arms and started kissing her back. When I realized what I was doing, I threw her

115

clothes back on and sent her away. I wanted to make sure she got back into her room without being seen, so I watched her run, blinded by the tears. As she rounded the corner, she slipped and fell, and that's when she hurt her arm." Jonathan reached for Miriam's hands. "I swear Miriam, I never touched her sexually. Just that kiss."

"I believe you Jonathan." Miriam looked into his dark eyes and could only see truth. She could also feel passion sweep through her body, just from his touch. "Maybe" she thought. "She was feeling real love." Miriam touched his handsome face. "I'm sorry for all the misunderstanding, Jonathan. Esther has been known to dream before as does all girls who fantasize having the perfect mate."

"Tell me sweet Miriam, is Robert the perfect mate you dreamed about?" Jonathan's hand squeezed hers.

"You are the perfect man for me Jonathan." Miriam knew she felt it but never dreamed she could actually say the words to his handsome face. She looked down, feeling flushed from embarrassment. "I am truly sorry Jonathan. I was too out spoken. Sometimes I say things before thinking it through."

"There's no need for you to apologize for the way you feel Miriam." Her name rolled off his tongue perfectly. "To be honest sweetheart, I cannot explain my feelings for you. I find you beautiful, sexy, and I believe I am falling in love with you darling."

Miriam sat up, her heart racing after this perfectly wonderful man confessed he was falling in love with her. "Jonathan, I love you too, from the moment I saw you cheering on your nephews." She finally had it out in the open and from the way he reached over and covered his lips over hers, she had no doubt about her love for him.

"What time are your friends picking you up sweetheart?" Jonathan's dark eyes held her in a trance before she jerked alert and glanced down at her watch, noticing she had only fifteen minutes to complete her task before Matthew drove up.

"So, my girls got only fifteen minutes?" Jonathan knew by her shocked expression Miriam was aware that he had the same gift for reading minds that Jeff and Ted had. "That would not give us enough time to seal our relationship, unless..." Jonathan pulled her up, taking the books from her hand. "Grab those children's books stacked up there and let's get checked out. I have an ideal."

"What ideal Jonathan? I simply cannot be late! Matthew will tan my hide!" Miriam's mind was racing as she thought. "What did

Jonathan mean by sealing the relationship? Whatever it is, Ted will be able to see everything from me and know why I was late."

"They will never know darling our act made them late." Jonathan kissed Miriam before rushing her in front of the clerk. He gave the librarian his handsome smile, causing her knees to buckle. "My girlfriend will check out these books Miss. If you could speed it up, we have an appointment to make."

The middle-aged woman smiled dreamingly up at the handsome man. "Yes sir. I shall check these books out promptly."

"I will wait over by the door for you darling." Jonathan moved over by the door and placed his hand on his temple. "Demons of the underworld, delay this couple who's face appears for one hour." He smiled, hearing the response in his head.

"We hear and obey! The couple we see will be delayed for you, son of Lucifer."

CHAPTER 25

"Kathy, didn't you say the shampoo was down isle four?" Matthew pointed to the cleaning products lining the shelves. "Unless we intend to wash our hair in Ajax or Clorox, I think they have moved the merchandise around since we've been here."

"Oh, sweetheart, I said at the end of isle four." Kathy marched him down and pointed to the big display of shampoo lining the shelf. She grabbed up her favorite and put it in the cart. "Now get eleven more bottles while I get the soap."

Matthew started counting bottles of shampoo and placing them neatly in the cart when he felt a tug on his pant leg. He looked down at an innocent wide-eyed young boy. "Hey Kid, what are you doing?" Matthew squatted down to be level with the scared boy. "Hasn't your mama ever told you about approaching strangers?"

"You don't look strange to me mister, just normal." The young blonde-headed boy blinked when Kathy stepped up laughing.

"My Matthew normal?" Kathy stopped laughing when she noticed the little fellow's knees were shaking. "Young fellow, are you lost?"

He teared up, lips trembling. "Yes ma'am. My mama was looking at dog food for Sparky, our pet hound dog, when I saw the word toys on the end row. I walked over to check out the balls and when I turned around to show mama, she was gone."

Matthew looked at his watch and mumbled. "Oh crap! We are going to be late picking up Blondie! Only ten minutes left to purchase this stuff and get back to the library and we run into a lost kid!"

"Well Matthew, we cannot leave this little boy alone until we locate his mother. She couldn't have gone far. I'm sure she's still inside the drug store trying to find..." Kathy took the boy by the hand. "Son, what is your name?"

"Mama told me to never tell strangers my name." He looked up innocent.

"Look kid, just a minute ago you said I didn't look strange!" Matthew bent down and stared in his eyes. "Are you saying my wife looks strange?"

The Lost Sheep

"That hot chick is your wife? Wow!" The boy looked up at Matthew surprised. "I'm five years old! How old are you, mister?"

"None of your business bee's wax, kid! Just tell us what your name is so I can shout it to the roof top and alert your mama that you're missing." Matthew knew Miriam would be giving him a hard time for being late. "Name, spit it out!"

"Billy." The boy blinked nervously when Matthew stomped his foot.

"Billy what?"

"Not Billy What, mister! My name is Billy Boston!" he squinted his eyes up at Matthew as he stuck out his tongue.

"Oh shit! This kid is driving me nuts!" Matthew stood back up, cupped his hands round his mouth and yelled out. "Is Billy Boston's mama in this store! Your brat is on isle four!"

"Matthew, what on earth are you doing?" Kathy made an apologetic smile at the customers standing near-by. "We need to take this boy to the manager and let him announce his name on the loud speaker."

"Who needs a loud speaker when your voice carries all over the drug store!" The manager rushed up and scattered the growing crowd. "Let me help you find the missing boy's mother, young man."

"Look sir, this kid has been giving us a hard time and I am certain if his mother is in the drug store, she heard me like everyone else.!" Matthew frowned down at the smiling boy. "Maybe she left you on purpose, kid!"

"No sir! I think she's probably in the lady's room." The boy smiled up at Kathy. "She has to go a lot!"

"The poor dear." An over weight lady had been listening to all the commotion and the big group of spectators turned when a frantic blonde came running up and grabbed the boy's arm.

"Your mama, son?" the manager gave a shaky smile at the gathering customers.

"Yep! That's her alright!" the boy laughed and jumped behind Matthew.

"Billy Boston! You scared the living daylights out of me!" She frowned down at the laughing boy. "I told you to stay put! You never listen to me, always going around with your head in a cloud!"

"She will be alright." The boy took Matthew and Kathy's hands.

119

"Thanks a million, you two."

"Billy Boston, did you tell this nice couple you were lost?" she reached over and hit him. "And how old did you say this time, Bill? Four, five?"

"Billy is five isn't he, Mrs. Boston?" Kathy looked confused. "Although he talks like he's much older."

"That's because this little twenty-year-old midget is an adult!" the woman grabbed his hand. "Why I married a joking midget is beyond me!"

"Well lady, your five-year-old husband made us late!" Matthew took Kathy's hand and headed the cart toward the check out. "Miriam will never believe a twenty-year-old midget acting five, held us up!"

"It was original, you must admit." Kathy pulled the cash out to pay, then glanced once again across the street at the little dress shop her and Jenny had done business before marrying Matthew and Ted. "I wonder if our friend still owns that little dress shop across the street?"

Matthew knew Kathy or Jenny hadn't bought any new clothes since moving to the mountain and getting married. He looked over at her, feeling helpless, wondering if she was missing her old life. "Kathy, I wished I could buy you pretty things." Matthew, spoke from his heart. "You know with Ted and the family, we buy only what we need."

Kathy reached over and touched his face lovingly. "And that's the way it should be darling. You don't need to buy me beautiful things to wear Matthew. I've got you and that's all I need to make me happy."

"I love you Kathy Christian." Matthew picked up the bags and headed for the car, thirty minutes late.

"Wineworth, room 666." The buzzer sounded and the door clicked open. "I got this room to come to whenever I needed to get away from the castle." The key in his hand opened the door. "I come for various reasons. To meditate, write my sermons, just have a little privacy away from family."

"Ted should like my falling in love with a preacher." Miriam walked inside the dark room and looked around. The huge bed in the middle of the room caught her eye. Its bedspread was a rich deep black and she watched his hands pull down the spread refilling

120

blood red sheets. Jonathan's eyes wondered up her body as he smiled.

"Does my girl like my choice of colors? I find them warm and sexy, like you."

Miriam swallowed, as she began to worry. "They look very warm Jonathan." She looked away as she thought. "I shouldn't be here in his room, alone. Something seems wrong."

"You should be here Miriam, if you love me as you claim." Jonathan walked to the window and looked out. "Did you lie to me, Miriam?"

"Jonathan, can you read my thoughts like Ted can? And like?" Miriam felt for the chair behind her and sat down.

"Jeffery!" Jonathan walked over to the dresser and pulled off his caps. "There! Now I can taste those beautiful lips and tongue better, my dearest Miriam."

"Jonathan, do you wear some sort of braces? "Miriam asked nervously, afraid to look at him.

"Miriam darling, because I love you far too much to hide anything from you, I, like my brother, have sharp canine teeth." Jonathan sat down next to her and smiled, revealing his wolf-like teeth. "Dearest, I was born with them, just like my black eyes." He took her hands. "Is it my fault my mother slept with the devil?"

"The...devil?" Miriam started to get up but Jonathan easily held her down and started kissing her with hot passion.

"Miriam, my beloved! Why can't you love me for me?" Jonathan continued to kiss her between words and she felt her body growing hot and excited. "Naomi married Jeffery and he was evil. I, on the other hand, am a good man who is in love with a woman. You my Miriam."

"Jonathan." She whispered his name, lost in his trance as his hand moved over her breast. She took a deep breath, needing more.

"Do you love me Miriam? If you do, give me your body and let it be mine forever."

"Yes Jonathan, yes!" Miriam's fingers ran down his bare chest and it did not matter to her when he found time to remove his shirt. "I give you my love. I give you my body." In her fiery lust she felt Jonathan removing her clothes and lifting her in his strong arms, laying her across the red sheets. Fire raced through her body as he thrust himself deep inside her, taking her virginity. Jonathan brought her to complete satisfaction over again and again until he moaned out his own fiery fireworks.

Miriam had lost her chance to be a virgin on her wedding night, but she knew she had gained the sexiest man to make her happy, forever.

"My girl is in a trance?" Jonathan asked as he gently slapped her butt. "Let's get you dressed. Your ride will be coming by the library soon."

"Ride? Library? Oh my God!" Miriam slid her feet into her shoes as she checked her watch. "Darn! I'm fifty minutes late! Matthew will kill me! Ted will..." Miriam sank back down, feeling terrible. "Oh no, I've let Ted down."

"Miriam, don't make such a big deal over making love to me. You love me, remember? It's not the end of the world." Jonathan turned her around to button her blouse.

"Not the end of the world? It is to me!" Tears ran down her cheeks as she spoke between sobs. "Ted will hate me!"

"Ted hate?" Jonathan laughed out as he replaced his caps over his sharp teeth. "That would be priceless! That would prove he is a human, not some angelic being." Jonathan pulled Miriam into his arms. "Stop fretting darling. I love you woman and you love me. It's perfectly natural for two people in love to have sex. There is nothing for you to be ashamed of darling. I should know, I am a preacher for God sake."

Jonathan took her hand and pulled her up, grabbed the books and headed out the hotel and down the street. "Look Miriam, if it would make you feel better, I will prove I love you." He pulled her around to face him. "Marry me!"

"Marry you?" Miriam's eyes grew wide, surprised by the sudden question. She wiped her eyes and smiled up at him. "Jonathan, do you mean it? Do you really want us to get married?" Miriam could not wrap her mind around a man like Reverend Jonathan Wineworth asking her, a poor orphan girl, to become his wife.

"I ask you, didn't I?" Watching the light change, Jonathan helped her across the street to the library, and Miriam noticed instantly Matthew and Kathy where not in front of the building waiting on her.

"Oh no! They left me!" Miriam looked in panic up and down

the empty streets. "Ted will kill me!"

"Ted kill?" again laughter came from her tall companion. "Now, that would be a dream come true."

"What?" Miriam stop searching for the white S.U.V. and stared up at the man she declared her love to. Was he serious or was he making a joke from her statement.

"I am joking Miriam." Jonathan turned his head to hide his smile and his attention fell down the street where he could see Matthew stopped at a stoplight. "Your ride is coming up the street so I will vanish." He bent down and gave her a kiss. "I will be by to see you soon. You better break it gently to old Robert."

"Robert?" Miriam felt sick as she watched Matthew pull the car up next to her. "She turned to tell Jonathan goodbye. True to his word, he had vanished. Miriam moved nervously to the car and swallowed when she saw Matthew climb out. Taking a deep breath, Miriam started to apologize for being late when Matthew started confessing.

"Just don't rub it in Miriam. I know we're late, for one solid hour but we have a good excuse." Matthew took the stack of books and laid them in the back with the shopping bags, then turned back, noticing how flushed her face was. "My God, Miriam, your face is as red as a beet! How long have you been standing in this heat?"

Matthew had given her the answer she needed. "You said it Matthew, one solid hour! I thought my feet were going to go to sleep standing here." Miriam frowned and slid into the open door, Matthew staring down in disbelief.

"What made you wait out here in the open sun, Miriam? There's shade next to the building or better still, air conditioning inside the library. You could have watched for us from that big window overlooking the sidewalk!"

"And let you jump me for not standing by the curb when you pulled up?"

Kathy turned around in her seat and shook her head. "Miriam, it has been a very unusual day. What should have been a simple shopping trip, turned into a nightmare. Almost as if some wicked force put a spell on me and Matthew, delaying our every turn."

Miriam suddenly recalled Jonathan's words, "I have an ideal. They will never know our act made them late." What did you do Jonathan? She thought before asking Kathy. "What happened? Did you have car trouble or a flat tire?"

"We didn't have any kind of car trouble, Miriam. That would have been a lot better than what we went through." Matthew got back behind the wheel. "First, there was a five-year-old kid pretending to be lost, which turned out to be a lame joke! He turned out to be a twenty-year-old midget comedian! Then this whooper of a woman crossed the road in front of us and dropped a large bag of apples. Apple Annie started flapping her flabby arms around and waving for the cars to stop, screaming loudly, 'don't run over my apple pie!' Perish the thought!"

Kathy could not control her laughter over Matthew's description of their day's events, as Miriam joined her in laughter, trying to speak between chuckles. "Did the poor woman rescue her apple pie? That is way too funny!"

Matthew rolled his eyes up looking discussed with his passengers for laughing. "Now, you see why we're late! That and the fact that every stupid stop light in this town turn red when we came to it! I can almost guarantee Ted will never let the three of us go shopping again!"

"Ted?" Miriam sank down in the back seat and gazed nervously out the window. "Ted will be hurt and angry."

Kathy turned to look at Miriam and noticed the girl looked nervous and upset. "Are you alright Miriam? Ted will understand why we're late. He won't be angry. Knowing Ted, after hearing Matthew retell our dilemmas he will join us in laughter. There's nothing to worry about."

"Kathy is right Blondie! Unless you ran off with a strange man and lost your prize virginity, Ted will have no reason to blame you for anything." Matthew teased.

"Oh Matthew, just lock it shut!" Miriam folded her arms to keep her hands from shaking, then closed her eyes to block out his words, that were more-true than he realized.

CHAPTER 26

Ted had filled the large wooden basket with ripe red grapes and had the ones chosen to stomp wash their feet before climbing in. Robert walked up and climbed easily in before helping Esther. Ted ask Devin to climb in and help Rachel. The rough boy yanked Rachel down almost dropping her into the grapes. Robert pushed the fresh young teens hands away and help lower the young girl.

"Devin, Rachel is a young lady, not a bag of feed! Treat her with dignity!"

"Robert is right Devin, so I will be watching you very closely." Ted put more grapes in the basket as Robert and the girls started stomping them, Devin watching with a frown on his face. "I suggest you start moving those feet Devin and behave if you want supper."

"Sure thing!" he mumbled. "As long as I can have a glass or two when I'm through being a slave."

"So, you feel as though you're being treated like a slave?" More of a statement than a question. "Son, we are family here and we farm this mountain to survive. We grow what we eat and sell what we don't. Everyone pulls his share of the work and as long as you're under my roof, you will carry your load and do it with a cheerful attitude like all the other children who feel blessed to have a home and people who love them."

"Alright! You want cheerful!" Devin gave a loud laugh and started dancing over the grapes. "Maybe, a partner in this dance!" He reached out and grabbed Esther's hand. "Alright doll, show me your moves!" he pulled her close.

Robert Perkins gritted his teeth as he pushed the fresh boy so hard he fell into the bottom of the grapes. "Keep your filthy hands, off Esther! Got it?"

"Shit man! You'd think that broad was your girl instead of the blonde!" Devin stood up angrily, grape juice dripping off his entire body.

"That is enough!" Ted called out. "Devin, get out of the wine basket right now! Thomas?" Thomas, six-foot, slightly heavy, yet strong, walked over and stared down at the trouble maker. "Go with

Devin and see that he has a bath, then bring him back to me!"

Thomas looked down at the five-foot boy and gave him a light push. "Move it along to the house buddy! We've got grapes to make into wine and no little squirt is going to slow us down!"

Ted shook his head then returned to filling the basket with grapes when Matthew came running from the house. Before Matthew could say a word, Ted put down his bucket and looked up at the house. "So, Marble is going into labor." Matthew rolled his eyes up, drooped his shoulders and followed behind Ted Mumbling.

"I could have just stuck my head out the back door and waved! Saved all those footsteps!" He felt Ted touch his shoulder. "Sorry Ted."

Ted called back to those stomping in the basket. "Keep working. I will return as soon as Marble's baby is born.

"I'll keep these girls busy stomping Ted!" Robert called out. "Take all the time you need." He smiled into Esther's eyes while thinking. "Maybe Esther and I can have a little fun without everyone thinking we're flirting."

Miriam had overslept due to spending a good deal of the previous night lying awake thinking about Jonathan and how wonderful he had made her feel. She sat up and stretched. Her head turned toward the clock and she slung her feet to the floor. It was already ten o'clock and she wondered why no one seem to miss her at breakfast. A knock drove her from bed as she stared at the door.

"Miriam! For the third time, wake up and open this door!" she recognized Kathy's voice and wondered why she was whispering. When she opened the door, Kathy pushed her way inside and shut it. "I thought you would never get up!"

"Can't a person sleep in around here once and while? Do you need me for something?" Miriam covered a yawn.

Kathy gave her a light push down on her bed. "Miriam, I couldn't sleep last night, so I got up at two a.m. to go down for a glass of milk when I overheard you talking to yourself."

"Well, I couldn't sleep either Kathy. I had something on my mind and I just couldn't stop thinking about it." She pushed her way up and sat down to brush her hair. "I must have fallen off around three this morning. Almost the same time Ted gets up to climb that mountain."

"Miriam, do you need someone to talk to?" Kathy walked over

and took her hand. "You seemed upset yesterday when we picked you up in front of the library. You jumped Matthew when he picked on you about losing your virginity. You know Matthew says things he doesn't mean."

"I know. I suppose I was just hot and cranky." Miriam smiled. "I will apologize to Matthew the moment I see his joking face."

Kathy walked to the door. "Miriam, I really mean what I say about listening if there's anything you need to talk about. I'm a good listener." She started to open the door, then added. "It's probably nothing, but your Robert and Esther seem to be spending a lot of time together. As of right now, they are stomping grapes in the wine basket."

Miriam forced a laugh. "Stomping grapes is anything but romantic, Kathy." Jonathan's words came back to her about letting Robert down easy. "Don't worry Kathy, I am on my way to see Robert right now. I can assure you he and Esther are just good friends." She watched Kathy shrug her shoulders and walk out.

"Jonathan, my man, Ms. Cameron was excellent yesterday." Joseph Reynolds spoke softly, remembering his two o'clock meeting with the sexy woman who had performed many kinky sex acts on him. "I wouldn't mind seeing that sex kitten again and soon."

Jonathan smiled as he rubbed the wolf's head. "I knew she would be to your liking Joe. So, Tracy enjoyed the little tea house as well?" He remembered how they grabbed one another the moment she shut the door to his hotel room, never knowing the well-paid maids had changed the sheets from his previous lustful romp with Miriam.

"Oh yes, Tracy was overjoyed, to say the least!" Joseph laughed. "She plans to go back there today around two. She met two charming ladies and became fast friends." He looked around to see if his wife was still getting ready. "How convenient for me! That's why I called. Can you set me up with Ms. Cameron again today at two?"

"It's short noticed, but I am sure I can convince the lady she has another happy customer who would pay her handsomely for a romp in the sack." Jonathan checked his watch. "Go there, Joe, you won't be disappointed." Jonathan put the receiver down smiling and pulled out a white silk shirt and black slacks.

Joan Byrd

"Destiny, you, handsome devil, how do I look?" The wolf sat up, ears perked and turned his head to one side then gave a woof. "I know, devilishly handsome." Jonathan turned when a knock sounded on the door and he gave the wolf a wink before stating "Yes, Jeffery, your wolf is paying me a visit." Jonathan walked over to let the boy in. "We enjoy each other's company, Jeffery. You have a smart wolf here."

Teddy Jeffery stared up at his father's twin and walked over, then knelt down to hug his big wolf. "You're right Uncle Jonathan. My Destiny is very smart and extremely clever. He doesn't like most people."

Jonathan picked up a comb to straighten his long hair. "I hear your grandfather gave you the wolf a few years back, as a gift and told you his name was Destiny." He glanced through the mirror and smiled.

"Uncle Jonathan, my papa forbids me to speak about my grandfather." Teddy stood up and led the wolf to the door. "You are on your way to meet a lady. Is she pretty and sexy, uncle?"

"Not words one hears from a seven-year-old, Teddy Jeffery." Jonathan joined him at the door and picked up his car's keys. "It's good to have my Jag back now that's it filled up with gas. I won't have to drive your father's black monster anymore."

"Papa didn't mind loaning you our car, Uncle Jonathan." The young boy looked up knowingly as he turned to go. "Have fun with that lady!"

Jonathan frowned, knowing his brother's oldest son was growing stronger in power everyday and he knew he had to work harder to win his father's approval before the kid became a challenge.

"What is it with you Fire? You keep looking at Blackhearts brother!" Blaze pulled her around to face him. "I know Jeff looks just like our leader, but, he is not him! If anything, this twin brother of Blackheart is even scarier than he is and appears to be ten times stronger! The guy is weird!"

"And you think Blackheart is not weird?" Fire pulled her wrist away. "You cannot pretend to me, Blaze Foster! You are afraid of Jonathan just as much!"

"That's real refreshing coming from a girl who runs into Jonathan's arms every time he wants sex with you! You don't act

128

afraid then!" Blaze shot back. "You damn well enjoy it! I've got eyes, I can see!"

"Wow! That's big!" she laughed out. "You, watching me and Blackheart while at the same time you are screwing little Miss Marble or humping Devin or Willy!"

"Shut your face bitch!" he yelled. "God! I hate you woman!" Blaze grabbed Fire and kissed her. She struggled for a few minutes before throwing her arms around his neck, returning the passionate kisses.

"I hate you too Blaze!" Fire said breathlessly as she pulled her top off and watched him rip off his shirt. The young couple stared at one another briefly, standing in the middle of the attic where Jeff had sent them to straighten up. His hands fondled her young breast as she breathed deeply. "Blaze...just do it!"

Blaze pulled Fire down on the hard attic floor and they started making out until they reached the fiery climax. She closed her eyes to block out the sweat dripping down her face and whispered "Blaze, I—"

"I know Fire. I feel the same way." He took his shirt and gently wipe her face and eyes. "I have loved you for a long time."

Fire smiled as she put her arms around his neck and spoke softly. "I love you, and Blaze, I really got to pee." Hearing the door open, they jumped and stared into each other's eyes.

"Look you two, do not think for one second I don't know what just happened up here!" Jeff stood over them, looking at the half clean attic. "This floor is too damn hard to be having sex on and by the way you're both sweating, I assume you have found out it's hot as hell up here!"

"Get use to it, Jeffery Wineworth!" Blaze got up to help his girlfriend, and pulled on his jeans. "Your father will stop at nothing to get you back!"

"Mr. Wineworth, forget what Blaze said sir." Fire stepped in front of Blaze after taking his hand. She could tell by the owner of the castle's demeaner that Blaze's comment rubbed him the wrong way. "Sir, may we both be excused. I really need to use the bathroom."

"Go! Both of you!" Jeff's eyes blazed. "The next time you get horny, find a damn bedchamber!" he pushed passed them and stormed out.

129

Joan Byrd

"Fire, what just happen up there in that attic?" Blaze was sweating from unnatural fear. "What made me say those things to Mr. Wineworth? I could not control my words! It was as if someone else was speaking through me!"

"Holy shit! Blaze, I think the devil took control of you for a while." Fire looked worried. "Remember Blackheart's chanting. 'Speak through us, my father. We are yours!"

"Oh shit! It really works!" Blaze turned white, having believed all the chanting was just a hoax." The devil really is their father!"

CHAPTER 27

"Melaki, why can't Martha and I watch Marble have her baby?" Four-year-old Mary Neenam listened as the young girl screamed out in pain.

"You are not much more than a baby yourself, young Mary." His eyes came alive with lights. "You must remain a child for a while longer, unlike your daddy who was years ahead of his age."

"That is because our daddy is more angel than human Melaki, same as Jeffery and Jacob's papa." Martha swung her short legs from the dining room chair.

"That's right, sister Martha. Except daddy's father angel is good and Uncle Jeffry's father angel is very bad." Mary took her guardian angel's hand. "Is this not so, Melaki?"

"Yes, sweet angelic girl, I fear so." He looked toward the dark mountain. "Darkness veils the mountain. Evil has returned and we must pray for your Uncle Jeffery not to fall into temptation."

"Melaki, if all God's children have a guardian angel, where is uncle Jeffery's angel?" Martha's blue eyes glanced toward the gloomy mountain.

"Jeffery is different from most of God's children, dear one. The Holy Creator did place the soul in the wee baby, but Jeffery's father, Lucifer made certain that only fallen angels had access to his favorite son." Melaki knew these small girls understood the danger he spoke of, so to assure Martha she wasn't left out, he added. "My brother Dalaki is present with us Martha, but he must stay invisible."

"Then, Delaki is my guardian?" Martha sat up and looked around her smiling, trying to feel his presence. "You said he was your brother."

"One of many billions of brothers and sisters. We each have a purpose and for many, like myself, we are sent as guardians, to protect, help guide and remain with our ward throughout their life journey on earth."

"Then you take your ward home to heaven to live forever with Jesus?" Mary smiled.

"There are many we rejoice with on the way to eternal love,

131

sweet Mary, but alas, many others we must sadly take down below, to everlasting punishment, such as Marble, Devin, Willy, Blake and Patches, lost children who have gone astray." The angel touched her sad face. "But, some children find their way home, through faith and a guiding hand."

"Like our daddy! He is so full of love for everyone." Martha felt around her, hoping to touch her angel. "If anyone can help these loss children, it's Ted!"

"Out of the mouths of babes!" Martha felt inviable hands hugging her. "I'm sitting on your left, by the way."

Martha giggle and smiled up at the unseen angel. "You may come out if you like. I don't bite!"

Melaki laughed. "Sweetie, it's not that brother Dalaki doesn't want to appear before you, God ask me to help for a while, that's all."

"But, I heard him speak to me and give me a hug." Martha looked confused.

"You heard my brother speak to you in spirit talk and the hug was a loving gift." Melaki smiled. "Speak to him in spirit, then listen, sweet Martha."

Martha looked at the vacant place beside her and thought. "I know you are beside me Dalaki. I love you and I am happy you are my guardian." She giggled "I hope I pronounced your name right."

My sweet baby girl, you spoke my name beautifully." The voice filled her head, causing her to smiled broadly. "I love you too!" Mary and her guardian laughed softly, knowing that Martha was conversing with her guardian.

Jenny held tight to Marble's hand as Hannah had the twelve-year-old to give one last push. Ted stood by the window praying for the young mother and newborn. Hannah's gentle words and touch guided the young mother through the worse pain she could have ever imagined.

"Sweet girl, I can see the baby's head so push hard, then it will be over."

"All right!" Marble was dripping with sweat as she screamed out in pain when Hannah's expert hands gently pulled the baby out so it could breathe his first breath.

"Good girl. Rest now, you've earned it." Hannah smiled up as Ted walked over to look at the small bundle in her hands.

The Lost Sheep

"Mother?" Ted watched as Hannah handed the baby to him. "My son." Ted looked at the miracle laying in his hands, then held out his hand for Jenny. She smiled down at the cute little fellow who appeared to be smiling at them. "Your name will be Noah Neenam, from this moment forth. I am your father." He pulled Jenny down "This is your beautiful mother. You are our son."

Ted looked lovingly at his wife. "Jenny darling, are you ready to know who fathered this child?"

"You know?" she closed her eyes, wondering if it was Jonathan's. That would make them parents to the devil's grandson. "Yes, I'm ready."

Ted placed his hand on the baby's closed eyes. When he opened them, Jenny looked down into two small eyes, the color of midnight.

Rachel excused herself to go to the bathroom, leaving Robert alone with Esther. Robert began picking with her when he slipped and fell in the mashed grapes. Esther doubled over laughing at the funny sight.

"Robert Perkins, one big grape! I think I will step on you and make lots more juice!"

"Step on me, will you?" Robert grabbed her foot and pulled her down next to him." Now, who's a grape? Why Esther Christian, I swear, you look good enough to bite!" He started tickling her.

"Robert?" Esther was giggling so much she couldn't hardly speak. "Robert? Stop it! Ted will...fire us!"

"What a shame! Loose all that good pay we had coming!" He stood up, then pulled her out of the juice, both laughing at each other. "We're just a couple of dripping grapes stompers!"

Esther laughed as she remembered Matthew slipping into the juice and went on telling Robert how he had been watching Kathy hanging out some clothes in her short shorts. "When Kathy pulled out her underwear and started hanging them up, poor old Matthew tried to stand on his tip toes for a better look and down he went" She chuckled loudly. "head first!" Esther suddenly noticed Robert had stopped laughing and was still holding her in his arms. His eyes looked warmly into hers as he lowered his head. "Esther. I"

"Robert?" Miriam called out as she made her way across the lawn to the wine press basket. She stopped short when she noticed the couple dripping in juice. "Good Lord! What on earth happened to you two?"

133

"What does it look like Miriam? We are crushing grapes and not just with our feet." His hands slipped off Esther's shoulders but one remained holding her hand. "We have learned how to mash grapes quicker with more parts of our body."

"Very funny Robert." Miriam laughed. "Just admit it. You slipped and fell. We have all done it before, except..." her eyes fell on the blushing girl. Except Esther. I guess there's always a first time Esther."

"It happened so fast I simply lost my balance." Esther smiled up at Robert. "The truth is, when Robert started falling, he pulled me down with him."

"Not very gallant, I must admit. Just a bad reflex reaction." His gaze fell on Esther. "I must have grabbed her while I was trying to catch my balance."

"Well, Ted is on his way down here." Miriam finally noticed Robert holding Esther's hand, causing her to frown. "Go ahead and stick to that story, you two, but if it's a lie, Ted will see right through it!"

"Robert, I see you and Esther have been fooling around again. See what it gets you!" Ted smiled at the dripping pair "I guess anything to make a chore more fun."

"I'm sorry Ted. I was showing off and slid down." Robert knew only the truth would work with Ted.

"And I was laughing at his misfortune, so he pulled me down with him." Esther gave a weak smile, afraid to look toward Miriam.

"Well Esther, if Miriam hadn't slept in until ten o'clock, she could have stomped grapes with her boyfriend." Ted turned toward the nervous blonde. "Letting your mind control your sleep is bad for you, young lady, especially when the thoughts are bad for you as well."

"What does that mean?" Robert climbed out and took hold of Miriam's arm. "What's going on with you, woman?"

"Not now Robert!" Miriam pulled away, acting as though she was the one mistreated. "Go get a shower, and you do not need Esther to help you with that!" she stormed off.

Robert shook his head, then helped Esther out of the basket before walking silently to the house. Esther looked sadly after him.

"Ted, what is going on with those two?" Esther was genuinely concerned.

"Robert and Miriam are pulling apart." Ted watched as Robert disappeared inside the back door, Miriam in the front. "Miriam is flirting with danger and Robert" he took Esther's hands. "Robert is falling in love with you."

CHAPTER 28

"Trace, my love, I won't be able to meet you tomorrow." Jonathan ran his hand over her large breast. She was still out of breath from their heated love making but Jonathan seemed as relaxed as he was before they started. "Something has come up. Alas, some church business." With one last kiss on her neck, Jonathan rolled out of bed. "Rest up, my cherished possession. Our sex will be twice as powerful the next day."

The attractive brunette sat up and slipped into her clothes. "Waiting will be hard Jonathan. It appears I need you more and more with each passing day."

"Good! Then, I shall have you whenever I desire you." He walked her to the door, kissing her one last time. "I did speak to my brother Jeffery and his wife about your coming for dinner and they have agreed. We shall be with one another tomorrow evening at Wineworth Castle, even though we cannot have any hot satisfying sex with one another." He smiled as he opened the door and walked her down the street. "Dinner, seven sharp!"

"I'll be there." Tracy smiled and touched his strong chest. "With Joseph, of course." After climbing in the cab, Jonathan watched it drive down the narrow street.

"Poor sweet Trace, my church business will consist of a trip up to Goldsburg Mountain, where my hot little blonde Christian awaits her future husband."

"Who is Miriam seeing, sweetheart? I know you know." Jenny brushed through her long chestnut hair as she watched her husband staring out the bedroom window. "And before you mention Jonathan Wineworth, do you really think Miriam is that careless?"

"I don't think Jenny, I know." Ted walked over and flopped down on the bed, his eyes on his beautiful wife. "Miriam had sex with him Jenny and she was up all night reliving it."

"You heard her?" Jenny swirled around on the dresser bench. "Was you in the hallway outside her room?" she got up and joined him.

"No Jenny, I was in our bed lying next to you." He rubbed his

136

face through her hair. "Mum, you smell good sweetheart."

"Ted, are you saying you heard Miriam from in here?" Jenny realized her husband had special powers but to hear someone talking to themselves late at night, probably in soft whispers, seemed impossible.

"Jenny, you tend to forget, everything is possible with God." He laid back and closed his eyes. "Miriam saw Jonathan in the library. It was all innocent at first, then one thing led to another. I'm afraid Miriam is weak when it comes to the Wineworth brothers. They ended up in his hotel room and had very hot sex. He has asked her to marry him."

"Marry him? After just one time together? You are kidding?" Jenny touched his arm when his eyebrow went up "Ted, I'm aware you don't kid. That is just a phrase people use when you've been handed a bombshell."

"My darling Jenny, you do have a way of brightening my darkest mood." Ted laughed.

"You're welcome, I think." He continued to laugh so she joined in then remembered the marriage proposal "Ted. Miriam is engaged to Robert. Surely she didn't except Jonathan Proposal." Jenny shook her head in disbelief. "She just met the man a few days ago. Now, if he was your twin, then I might understand her excepting, but Jonathan, after what Esther told her."

"Jenny, the Wineworth brothers can be very appealing to women." Ted put his arm around his wife and pulled her down. "If he goes through with this proposal, my answer may be yes."

"Yes? But, Ted" he cut her off.

"Jenny, Miriam is pregnant."

Jeff chopped the lettuce as he watched his wife scurry around the kitchen, preparing for Jonathan's guest. "Sweet one, I wish you would have let me get you some help for tonight."

"I will be fine Jeff. I'm used to fixing supper for a big group, remember?" Naomi turned and blew him a kiss. "It would be lovely if you could get our boys to stop chasing each other around my kitchen though."

Jeff jumped up and grabbed each boy, his voice stern. "Boys, stop running this instant, before I tan your back sides. Teddy Jeffery, how many times have I told you to keep that wolf out of the kitchen! Now, both of you, get up to your rooms and get ready for our company!"

137

The boys knew their father was true to his word, so Teddy grabbed Destiny and headed out the door quickly. Jacob walked over by his mother and looked up apologetically.

"Mama, I'm sorry for running. I'll go up to my room and wait for supper." The shy boy turned to his tall father and looked up. "Papa, I'll behave at the table, I promise."

Jeff dried off his hands and scooped up the small boy, giving him a hug. "Jacob, I'm sorry too, for yelling at you and Teddy." He kissed his son's cheek and sat him down for Naomi to give him a kiss.

"Papa and I will be finished soon Jacob and we'll come up to get you sweetheart. Just wash up and be ready."

"Yes ma'am!" Jacob smiled and raced out the door, happy his parents weren't mad at him.

Naomi took off her apron and put the salad away, before taking her husband's hand. "See sweetheart, all done. Your help is all I needed to get everything done on time. The last dish is on the table and the bread is warming in the oven."

"My beautiful together bride." Jeff pulled her into his strong arms. "If I kiss you, I'll get hot! And if I get hot, I'll want to make love." He gave her a big squeeze. "But alas, our guest, have just arrived and are about to ring our bell." With that, the bell ran out and Naomi smiled up at her handsome husband.

"Do you think I will ever get use to you knowing things before they happen, like Ted?"

"Just don't dwell on it, sweet dove." Jeff took her hand and opened the door. Tracy Reynolds stared at the couple holding hands as Naomi broke the ice.

"Welcome to Wineworth Castle." Naomi could sense the woman was putting on a fake smile. "Would you be Tracy and Joseph Reynolds, Jonathan's friends?"

Tracy, assuming Jeff was Jonathan, could not understand why he was acting so distant. "Yes, very good friends, Miss?"

"It's Mrs., Mrs. Reynolds." Jeff's stare held her firmly. "Mrs. Jeffery Wineworth."

"Oh!" the attractive brunet seemed relieved to Naomi for she quickly changed her demeanor. "What a lovely place you have here Mrs. Wineworth."

"Please call me Naomi." As always, the beautiful girl gave an

The Lost Sheep

angelic smile. "May I call you Tracy and Joseph?"

"That would be lovely, Naomi, and if you wouldn't mind my asking, where is your husband, Jeffery?" Joseph had also thought their pastor was acting different.

"My husband? Why, Jeffery is standing right in front of you." Naomi couldn't control her laughter, realizing the couple had mistaken Jeff for Jonathan. "I guess Jonathan forgot to mention he and my husband are identical twins."

"Only in looks, I can assure you." Jeff waved them inside. "Please come in. Jonathan should be down soon."

"Did someone say my name?" Jonathan stepped up beside Naomi, closed his eyes to smell the aroma of the food waiting to be served. "Something smells rewardingly delicious sweet sister."

"I hope you all like it." Naomi was noticing Tracy Reynolds looked from Jonathan to Jeffery, obviously admiring their bodies. Jonathan had noticed his beautiful sister-n-law observing his lover and knew he had better do something.

"Let me fix you both a drink before we dive into Naomi's delicious dinner." Jonathan led the way to the bar and pulled out two glasses. "White wine for Trace, brandy for Joseph." Passing the glass to his lover he touched her hand slowly, then fixed himself a scotch.

"Jonathan never forgets what we like." Joseph Reynolds looked around the large dinning room, lively lit by wall sconces and two crystal chandeliers, gracing both end of the long table. "From the looks of the outside, you would not expect to find such a bright, luxurious room."

"We like things cheerful, Joseph." Naomi felt her husband squeeze her hand lovingly when she looked up at him smiling. "Jeff, my wonderful husband of eight years, turned his gloomy castle into a sunny-happy home where we live with our two sons. So, just enjoy your drinks while I go and fetch the boys."

"I'll keep the fires burning until you return my love." Jeff spoke softly in his wife's ear making Tracy feel drawn to him, which Jeff sensed instantly. "I am a very happy married man, Mrs. Reynolds."

Suddenly she grew hot from embarrassment, sensing this brother was a carbon copy of Jonathan and could read her mind. Jeff smiled down at the confused woman and spoke softly. "Mind reading is a gift Tracy. Besides me and Jonathan, there is one more

139

capable of doing it madam. My best friend and neighbor on the adjoining mountain."

Before Tracy could respond, Jonathan walked over, smiling at the pair. "Looks like you two are bonding." His dark eyes burned into Tracy's as he took her arm. "There is something I'd like to show you before we sat down to Naomi great dinner." Jonathan placed his hand on his brother's shoulder. "Jeffery, will you visit with Joe here until we return. It won't take long."

"See to it!" Jeff knew his brother was wanting some along time with this married woman and it was obvious the husband did not suspect anything. Jeff knew, this was not the first time Tracy Reynolds had been alone with his brother Jonathan.

Just out in the rose garden, Jonathan was giving Tracy Reynolds a hot burning kiss, then released her, still spinning with desire for him. He coolie wiped off her lipstick and reminded her the rest of the diners were waiting on them to return. Inside, he merely informed them how much Tracy loved roses so he took her out to see them before they ate.

"And did you like the roses Tracy?" Jeff ask coldly.

Tracy glanced over at Jonathan who was busy chatting with her husband. She sensed this brother knew their secret and was playing with her emotions. Taking a deep breath, she looked up into his dark stare. "The roses were very fragrant Jeffery. So many lovely colors. Did you plant them?"

"Me? Hardly, flowers aren't my thing, but my angelic wife loves flowers and she has the green thumb when it comes to planting flowers. Tell me Tracy, did you like the black roses?" Jeff knew the woman was unsure if there was such a color for a rose and Naomi was quite curious as to what her husband was up to.

"To be honest Jeffery, I must have missed the black roses. It was getting a little dark outside and black would be hard to see." Tracy felt please with her answer. "I should like to see the black rose. It sounds like such an unusual color.

Jonathan had overheard Jeff's questions and knew instantly he was on to them. "Jeffery, why not tell Tracy what the black rose stands for?" the brothers stared coldly at one another before Jonathan ask "Do you prefer I tell this dear lady and why you would never permit your perfect wife to plant even one in her garden?"

"By all means Jonathan, tell Mrs. Reynolds about the cursed

black rose!" Jeff smiled slowly, revealing his sharp teeth and Joseph Reynold let out a gasp and sat back, out of the way. Tracy was obviously not bothered by this sudden revelation, a fact that even Naomi noticed as she moved over next to the woman.

"My husband's teeth do not seem to bother you, Tracy." Naomi reached to pulled Jacob's elbows off the table. "They frighten most people the first time they see them."

"I, well..." She glanced down at her plate, knowing how frighten she had been the first time she saw Jonathan's sharp teeth, but later she grew to enjoy them and how they turned her on when he smiled. "I guess my mind was so focused on the black rose, I never noticed."

Jeff suddenly gave a chuckle, knowing Jonathan had the same sharp canines he had. "It's a family trait we got from our father, right Jonathan? Even my first born has grown into his. Show them son."

"Gladly!" Teddy sat up beaming and gave a big smile, revealing sharp-wolf-like canines. "I'm super proud of mine! I am just like my papa!" Teddy looked over at Tracy before facing his uncle. "By the way Uncle Jonathan, I forgot to ask you if you had a good time yesterday with your 'friend'?" Teddy gave Tracy a wink when she stared over at him, then she turned to Jonathan.

"Jonathan, will you please tell me what the black rose stands for so I can enjoy this great meal."

"The black rose stands for the rose of darkness, evil and sin." Jonathan glanced over at Naomi and noticed her shaking. "My dear sister-n-law, there are no black roses in your fair garden, nor will they ever be. Your husband was merely making a poor joke."

"Do not get too relaxed in your choice hobbies, Mrs. Reynolds. You never know when a black rose will show up at your door, nor from where it came." Jeff stood up, dropping his napkin on the table. "Come family, this meal is over for us." Jeff gave his brother a warning look. "Jonathan, when you've finished, show your guest out." He collected Naomi and his two sons and left the visitors staring after Jonathan's unusual brother.

CHAPTER 29

"Come here slut and remove your clothes!" Jonathan's attention burned on the young sixteen-year-old girl. "You are mine, Fire! Your body and soul belong to me!"

"Yes, Blackheart, I am forever yours." The young girl walked over removing her top, revealing her firm breast. Blaze sat in the corner of the room, pretending not to watch, but, his eyes kept going back to the tall strong man standing over the girl he had confessed to love. Jonathan instantly sensed the young man's thoughts and slung his head around to stare at him. Blaze quickly pretended to be fixing a broken box when Jonathan spoke loudly.

"Blaze, take that box and get the shit out of my room, now!"

"Blackheart, I won't watch you, I promise. I'll turned my back and stay busy." Blaze did want to leave his girl alone with this sex-craved animal.

"I NEED MY PRIVACY, YOU LITTLE PERVERT! NOW LEAVE THIS PLACE BEFORE I THROW YOUR SORRY ASS OUT THAT WINDOW!" Jonathan's eyes flashed with fire as he pushed Fire on his bed and yanked his clothes off, never bothering to watch the scared boy flee from this devil.

Fire felt her pulse racing with both fear and with sexual excitement, knowing what this man was going to be doing to her. "Now bitch, spread those leg and prepare for my entry!" Jonathan climbed over her, forcing himself deep inside as she moaned in pain. He continued to pound her mercilessly until he let out a deep low cry, releasing his evil inside her."

"Now slut, don't you get pregnant like that stupid Marble! Understand?"

"I know how to abort a baby, remember? Marble is just a child Blackheart. She had no clue how to fix it." Fire was so sore, she could hardly move and she felt relieved to see him smile down at her in his friendly way.

"I'm sorry Fire, if I got too rough with you. You know how that turns me on and you're the best at letting me do what I desire to do!" Jonathan helped her up. "Where I'm going today is no place to get

142

The Lost Sheep

horny, so I relieved myself on you. Sweetheart."

"You've got my curiosity up, Blackheart." Fire got down at his feet to help him with his shoes. "Can you share with me where you are going?"

"To Goldsburg Mountain, my hot Fire, to court one of Ted's girls." Jonathan laughed at her expression before standing up. "I must be on my best behavior. Think no bad thoughts, just good holy ones befitting a minister. This Ted cannot be easily fooled and I must convince the goodie Bible thumper, I am the real thing."

"I am certain you will do find, Reverend Wineworth." Fire gave him a reassuring smile to set the mood and Jonathan always liked how this young girl could make him feel the part he was playing. "I will pray that everything works out for you pastor."

Jonathan laughed out and gave her a kiss. "Sweet girl, you may or may not believe this, but damn if I don't love you!" Giving her a wink, Jonathan walked away humming a hymn.

"Miriam, we need to talk." Ted placed his hand on her shoulder, pouring love inside. She closed her eyes as her fingers stopped on the piano keys. "You need to tell Robert about Jonathan. Everything Miriam."

"Then you know about Jonathan." Miriam turned on the piano bench to face Ted and only saw concern in his loving eyes. "I never meant for it to happen Ted. I resisted Robert's advances, that is until he gave me the rape drug."

"Jonathan is not the same as Robert, Miriam." Ted took her hand and sat down beside her on the sofa. "Jonathan is Jeff's twin brother, Miriam. That makes Jonathan Lucifer's son too."

"Yes, he told me." Miriam ran her fingers nervously through her blonde hair. "I have fallen in love with the devil's son! I'm in the same boat as Naomi, aren't I?"

"Not exactly dear one. Jeff has changed and for him it will be a constant struggle to remain on the good side." Ted cast his eyes on the black mountain connected to theirs. "There are ones we love living on that mountain. Naomi, my angel and her sons. Teddy thinks he is already grown and little Jacob is still innocent of any bad thoughts. Jeff has become to me a dear friend and brother. I love him dearly and know he would do anything for me." Ted turned back to the worried girl. "Miriam, I know you love this ideal of a life with Jonathan, but is Jonathan capable of loving you in return?

143

He knew love once and became a minister to show how much he loved the Savior. That was before Lucifer decided he had another son who looked exactly like his favorite, so he began molding him into another Jeff, promising his reward would be the chosen Anti-Christ, deceiving him with another lie."

"Then, you're saying Jonathan is now the evil son! What should I do Ted, besides confess to Robert?" Miriam cast her eyes down sadly. "I never meant to hurt Robert. I thought I loved him enough to marry him, then things kept holding me back."

"By all means, you must tell Robert everything. It won't come easy but you may be surprised if Robert seems to be a little relieved that you have found somebody else." Ted knew Miriam and he knew he had hit a weak spot in the blonde headed young woman. Miriam could dish it out but those who she thought loved her should never do the betraying.

"Why would Robert be relieved? Has he been seeing someone behind my back?" she spoke angrily, stomping her foot. "Of all the nerve! And him claiming to adore me and wanting me to set the date!"

"And what about your affair behind poor Robert's back? Are you so good you can do whatever you like but good old Robert will still be there waiting for you." Ted gripped Miriam's hands. "You pushed Robert away Miriam. That young man was crazy about you! He was ready to marry you because he loved you! But as always, you could not decide what you wanted. Don't go blaming Robert Miriam. You pushed him into another girl's arms and couldn't even see it happening because your head was up in a cloud!"

"Esther?" Miriam blurted out. "Robert's been making out with Esther behind my back!"

"No Miriam, open your selfish eyes!" Ted's strong voice filled her ears, then he grew soft. "Robert has been faithful to you. Not once has he offered to kiss Esther. As far as Esther knew, she and Robert were only good friends who enjoyed each other company. Yes, he held her hand, put his arms around her and almost told her he loved her, but that was as far as he went. You, on the other hand, had sex with Jonathan Wineworth. He took your virginity and made you pregnant, all in one short hour."

"What? Me, pregnant?" tears flooded down her face as reality sat in. "Jonathan said he wanted to marry me. Was he serious? Do you think he knows he made me pregnant?"

"Jonathan is coming here today to see you." Ted pulled her up. "Go, wash your face." Ted gave her a brotherly hug. "Then you must tell Robert. I will let you know what to do, but you must trust me."

"With my life. Ted." Miriam felt relieved to have it out in the open and to know that Ted had not abandoned her. She would wash her face then go face Robert.

"So, he is coming here today, to see you?" Robert sat holding his ex-girlfriend's hand. "Things always have a way of working out, Miriam. I truly did love you but I could feel you slipping away. You became so distant and Esther was there to fill that empty spot where you once stood."

"I know Robert and I am truly sorry that I let you down. I loved you too." She looked at him sadly, knowing this chapter in her life was over. "I guess my love wasn't as strong as yours or I wouldn't have fallen so completely in love with Jonathan."

"I hope and pray you're doing the right thing Miriam." Robert genuinely felt scared for the girl he had loved. "You know what he did to Esther. Can you really trust what the man tells you?"

"Robert, I'm having Jonathan's baby." She searched his eyes to see any reaction. "Ted told me this morning."

"Then you slept with him willingly." Robert spoke softly. "I thought I would be the first with you sweetheart, but someone stole that honor when he stole your heart."

"If it's true that Jonathan made love to Esther, you have lost that honor with her as well." Miriam smiled with regrets. "If you truly love Esther, and I believe you do, this won't matter to you as long as she loves you in return."

"You are right love. Esther came as a surprise to me. First we were very good friends and I could confide in her about our problems." Robert stood up and walked over to look up the steps, knowing Esther had left them to talk. "Somewhere along the way, I fell in love with her."

"Then tell her Robert. I am certain she must love you just as much." Miriam stood up to join him at the foot of the stairs. "I am truly happy for you Robert. You deserve to be totally happy. Maybe now I won't feel so bad about myself and how I treated one of the finest fellows I grew to love."

145

Robert touched her cheek before kissing it one last time. "We can always be friends, Miriam."

"I'd like that very much Robert. Very good friends." Miriam hugged him and turned to find Ted watching, a smile on his heavenly face.

CHAPTER 30

Miriam stood staring out the big hall window when Ted and Jenny came down the steps holding hands. "Get away from that window Miriam." Ted's voice fell soft on her ears. "Jonathan is coming into view."

Miriam jumped back and ran over to the large hall mirror to check her hair. "Miriam, you look beautiful. Far too beautiful for Jonathan." Jenny put her arm around Miriam's shaking shoulders. "Try to relax, sweetheart. There's no need to be nervous as long as Ted and I are near you."

"Thank you, Jenny. You have been so gracious to me, even though I probably don't deserve it from the way I use to treat you before you married Ted." Miriam gave Jenny a sincere hug. "It means the world to me that you and Ted are here with me."

"Well Miriam, I, for one, would never want to be a long with either Wineworth brother." Jenny smiled over at her husband. "Besides, we look after our own, right Ted darling?"

"My beloved Jenny is right Miriam. Jonathan cannot or would not even think of hurting you as long as we are present." Ted walked passed the girls to the door. "He knocks." And on cue, the heavy knock fell on the front door as Jenny and Miriam exchanged smiles. Ted opened the door revealing the tall handsome man smiling just beyond the threshold.

"Ted, we meet again." Jonathan put out his hand. "It was good of you permitting me to come over to your beautiful mountain. This is such a bright spot compared to Jeffery's gloomy place. I'm sure you can imagine, it took some getting used to."

"I would think such places would suit you better, Jonathan." Ted never looked away from the dark eyes staring back. "The church you attend below in the town is the newest one built. Just this year, correct?"

"Very good observation Ted. I noticed your quant little chapel just beyond the rock path. I'm sure it can accommodate your large family along with Jeffery's small brood." Jonathan looked past Ted to smile at the girl he came up to see. "Has Miriam told you about us, Ted?"

Joan Byrd

"I know all there is to know about you Jonathan and my sister Miriam." Ted stepped back to let Jonathan come inside. "Tell me Reverend, you would never take advantage of a girl just because she cared for you, would you?"

"I would say our feelings are mutual, isn't that right Miriam?" His eyes held hers.

"Yes, they are. I wasn't forced into doing anything I chose to do." Miriam watched Jonathan closely. "I love you Jonathan."

"There! You see Ted, it's true love." Jonathan smiled with assurance. "I have been searching for the right mate for me. Not only someone to make my lonely nights, happy nights, but a woman with good Christian values capable of being a minister's wife. And not just any girl," he took Miriam's hand. "This girl!"

Miriam swooned before she spoke. "A minister's wife, me. What a lovely ideal." Miriam ran over to Ted "You would like that choice for me, wouldn't you Ted?"

"A man of God who is true in his faith and beliefs would be perfect for you, Miriam. A man who truly believes what he preaches." Ted's attention never drifted from the tall dark man, who was watching him equally as close.

"You doubt my faith Ted?" Jonathan looked hurt. "Ask my congregation! My church leaders! They will tell you what you need to know."

"Jonathan, I know what I know. Sometimes things are not what they appear to be." Ted was aware Jonathan's heart had grown cold and in his present state he was not capable of loving anyone. The loving man also knew Jonathan was capable of putting on a good front and could fool the average person with his suburb acting skills. Much like the one coming after him.

"I know what you think of me Ted and why you cannot trust me or my chosen profession. I am Jeffery's twin brother. Therefore, I cannot be faithful to the Almighty God if my father is the devil and his evil blood runs through my veins!" Jonathan had a sincere look about him as he continued to defend his faith. "You are right about one thing Ted, things are not as they appear. I may look exactly like Jeff, but that as far as it goes. My saintly mother, rest her soul, stole me away in the cloak of darkness when I was just an infant and sent me away, far from the evil that reign within Wineworth Castle."

"So, after all those years of staying safe, you show up at your

148

The Lost Sheep

brother's doorstep, not knowing if the evil still reigned within those walls. You chose to take a chance and hopefully reunite with the brother your mother had warned you about." Ted spoke, knowing the real reason but preparing to get another lie.

"I did take a chance after finally receiving the letter my mother had written me. I found out I had brothers and I wanted to look them up." Ted witnessed a small amount of true devotion from Jonathan when he spoke about his departed mother. "I found my family Ted. My heart ached to see them, especially my dear mother, only to find out she had died. An apparent suicide to keep Jeffery from torturing her before painfully killing the woman that saved my life."

"You do not hold Jeff to blame for your mother's death anymore, do you? You are one happy family now, right Jonathan?" Ted knew Jeff didn't trust his twin any more than he did. "And Teddy and Jacob, I hear you are getting close to them."

"My nephews are very special to me Ted. Naomi has been very kind and giving. A very charming lady and easy to love." Jonathan looked down. "My brother keeps his distance. I do not think Jeffery trust me anymore than you do."

"And, what are your plans regarding Miriam? Do you really wish to marry her and be a faithful husband, only to her?" Ted finally broke away to look toward Miriam, who had been taking in all their words.

"I wish to marry her Ted, with your permission of course." Jonathan answered politely as his gaze turned on the smiling girl. "I'll make her happy and as for being faithful, I live the ten commandments diligently every day."

"Do you?" Ted remembered the thoughts Miriam was having about Jonathan bringing her to satisfaction again and again. "So, you will make Miriam happy? Yes, I think there are ways you make the girl very happy, Jonathan."

Miriam froze, blushing by Ted's comment, knowing what he was referring to. Jenny moved over and draped her arm around the gilt ridden girl as she whispered softly. "Whatever happened between you and Jonathan inside his hotel room, Ted knows. I know how you must be feeling right now."

Miriam squeezed Jenny's hand when she heard Jonathan's next question. "Then, I may have Miriam's hand in marriage, Ted?" Jonathan's eyes misted up with tears. "I do care about her deeply

149

and my love for her is real."

"Very well. First, you must date her for a respectable time and there will be no more sex until after the wedding." Ted calmly walked behind a small table and poured two glasses of his best wine, then two glasses of rich-red grape juice, handing each lady a glass before giving Jonathan the wine. "I toast your willingness to abide by my demands Jonathan."

Jonathan had watched silently as Ted poured the grape juice and handed a glass to his wife, then Miriam. He lifted the wine glass and tapped Ted's, then the women's juice glasses before stating "I will make that toast Ted, and agree to follow your rules, but I cannot understand why my fiancé is having juice instead of wine."

"Miriam cannot drink wine for another eight and a half months, Jonathan." Ted watched him closely to see if he could figure out she was having his baby.

Jonathan gave a sarcastic laugh as he sized up the small man in front of him. "Ted, surely you don't expect me to wait eight and a half months before I marry this woman. And what's with this cutting her off wine so long? Is this some kind of religious ritual you believe in Ted?"

"No Jonathan. I have nothing against a woman having wine unless it's not good for her health. Pregnant women should never drink alcoholic beverages or smoke during this time." Ted could tell by Jonathan's demeaner that he had hit a nerve with him. "That little affair ended with a nice little gift attached. Jonathan, you're going to be a father. Congratulations."

Ted and Jenny had settled down in the small room adjacent to the living room, where they left Jonathan and Miriam to speak in privacy. It was obvious to Ted that Jonathan was struggling with the ideal of having a baby and he knew this was not part of the man's plans. Ted had hoped that this revelation might resort in Jonathan's breaking off the wedding, but Ted doubted this would deter Jonathan's determination to marry one of Ted's girls.

"Miriam, I never dreamed you weren't on birth control. Most girls go on the pill in high school." Jonathan's look was far away, as though he were trying to sort out a decision in his head. "I guess I should take the blame and have used some protection, but God, I hate to have sex with a damn rubber blocking my feeling."

"Jonathan, I was just as shocked as you were when Ted

informed me that I was having a baby. I felt like dying, right then and there!" Miriam touched his hand, finely getting his attention. "Maybe, you wished I had died. I don't think you want any thing to do with this baby, Jonathan."

"A baby is something I am not prepared for Miriam." He pulled her over to the sofa and sat down. "And God forbid that you die, Miriam."

"Jonathan, if it's freedom that you choose, then I will let you go and raise our baby right here in this loving home." Tears formed in her eyes. "He will never go without anything he needs, especially his mother."

"Miriam, I guess abortion is out of the question?" Jonathan was holding her hand when she yanked it free.

"God forbid I kill my innocent baby! I would never destroy the gift that God entrusted me with. Not for you, not for anyone! Jonathan, how could you even suggest such a horrible thing of me. It's obvious you don't know me at all!"

"Miriam, I never meant to sound cold and heartless. Little babies are precious and like the Lord, I love the little children." His eyes held real sadness. "I guess it was the shock of knowing I was going to become a father before I became a husband. See how this will look in front of my congregation. They look up to me and respect my values. I guess you hate me now."

"Hate you? Jonathan, I love you more and more and now that we are going to have this baby, it has brought us even closer." Miriam realized she had a hard road ahead if she married this handsome man seated beside her. Did she make a big mistake by letting Robert go? It was too late to second guess her choice.

"Miriam, do you really believe that I am a bad choice?" Miriam knew Jonathan could read her thoughts as she listened to him. "I know you don't trust me or my motives for making you my wife. I know you think you made a mistake by telling Robert it was over. I only ask that you do not give up on me and give me the chance to prove how much I love you."

"Do you love me Jonathan? Really love me, or am I a pone in some strange game you're playing?" Miriam did not back away, feeling safe with Ted waiting nearby.

"Miriam, my one and only, I know it must seem odd that I fell in love so fast with a girl I hardly know anything about." Jonathan

151

had the look of love on his face as he concluded. "Miriam, do you believe in love at first sight?"

"I must, for it happened to me too Jonathan." Tears collected in her blue eyes, wanting to believe his words but still unsure of his motives after speaking with Ted and Jenny. "Jonathan, if you love me as you say and really want me then you must want our baby. If you love me, you must love your baby in the same way."

"Darling, it's true I am having a hard time getting my head around all this and the fact that I would have chose living a few years with my wife before having a family but" Jonathan gathered her hands in his. "I will want and love our baby and will welcome it into my heart. Father will be pleased."

"Father?" Miriam trembled, thinking he was referring to Satan.

"My adopted father, Ronald Fulton. He and Grace have been after me to get married and start giving them grandchildren."

"I'd love to meet your parents Jonathan." Miriam felt relieved talking about family. "Do they still live on the coast of North Carolina?"

"They bought them a beautiful old home at South Port, a charming coastal town. I rarely get back to visit since pastoring a church takes up my time." Jonathan relaxed, feeling his chances with Miriam had greatly improved which would delight his real father. "Why don't we go there on our honeymoon. South Port has several romantic bed and breakfasts."

"South Port sounds wonderful Jonathan, if Ted approves." Miriam thought she noticed a scowl come to his handsome features and assumed he thought Ted had too much authority over all those living under his roof. She would jump at Ted's defense no matter what it cost her. "Jonathan, except for Jenny and Kathy, every young person living here grew up under Ted's care and we respect his wisdom and guidance with 100% loyalty. After you have grown to learn Ted, you cannot help but love him. Ask your brother Jeffery. Once they were complete opposites. One living to ruin the lives of innocent people through lust, evil and hate and the other one, fighting to bring lost souls home to the Lord, through love. Now, they have joined forces to fight Lucifer, your evil father and win with that 1% of pure love over his 100% evil." Miriam gently touched his face. "You can love him too Jonathan. If you just let go and let the love of Jesus show you."

152

The Lost Sheep

"Young lady, there are two things I must insist on if we get married." He pulled her up close. "First, let me preach the sermons. No wife of mine will ever preach to me. Second, I am sure Ted has been a wonderful influence on you, but when you become Mrs. Jonathan Wineworth, you will belong to me. As your husband I will guide you and be the man of the family, as the Bible says. You will be treasured and always devoted to only me." His eyebrow went up. "Do I make myself clear, woman?"

"Very clear Jonathan. You will wear the pants in our family. I will be your loving, adorable wife and your children's Christian mother." She glanced Ted's way and noticed him smiling back. Miriam knew her first love, the one who could never return that same love to her, was pleased with how she had handled Jonathan Wineworth. She closed her eyes and started saying in her thoughts the 23rd Psalm to block out from Jonathan the words dancing through her head "My Teddy is pleased with me."

Joan Byrd

CHAPTER 31

Many members from Jonathan's old church at Kill Devil Hills had moved to Goldsburg to join his new church. All of them came for different reasons. Many of the married women, old and young alike, lusted for the handsome sexy preacher and many had committed adultery with him, unbeknown that they weren't the only one. Over half the men in the congregation, including Joseph Reynolds, had affairs with prostitutes or other married women in the church. The young people who attended the sinful church fell right in with the adults. Two young teenage girls had become shop lifters and three of the young men bragged about the number of banks they had successfully robbed while they filled up the collection plate with stolen money.

The members didn't mine that their new church wasn't affiliated with any other denomination, Methodist, Baptist, Catholic, etc. All they cared about was the fact their leader was the preacher there. Jonathan had hand picked the large congregation because each one was easily persuaded to commit sin under his leadership, in return, the tempting minister was winning souls for Lucifer. The faithful flock never question their leader for choosing the very same name for his new church, Kill Devil Hills Church.

Jonathan looked around at the growing congregation and smiled down at the young girls who always chose the front row to sit, where they would temptingly part their legs, revealing no panties, to flirt and please the one they had enjoyed in bed. He knew once he brought Miriam with him, he would have to ask his young fans to dress appropriate and behave like perfect little ladies in front of his bride.

Jonathan lifted up his eyes over the crowd for any visitors and noticed two new faces at the back. Today he would have to preach a normal sermon, to feel the new ladies out. During the hand shaking after the service, he planned to ask their name, but for now, Jonathan must dwell back to his old sermons.

"Good morning, my brothers and sisters in Christ. Welcome to the house of God and any visitors among us, we welcome you with

154

love. I would ask that our caring members greet the new faces among us properly this morning." Jonathan smiled out warmly at the older woman, wearing white gloves and an old fashion hat atop her white bun. His attention fell on the middle-aged woman who resembled someone he had seen recently. Thinking back, there was a photo, sitting on a side table, with these very same women standing with Jenny Neenam in that children's home. Jonathan watched as the younger woman reached up to push in her falling hair pin and he smiled at her old fashion dress. "This one could be a challenge but there hasn't been a woman I couldn't tempt. Jonathan's eyes fell on Kris O'Donnell. He smiled slowly, with warmth and luring romance.

Kris blushed, feeling herself grow warm by his stare. She glanced over at her mother who was checking out the unusual hymnal. Sitting straight as usual, Kris bent down to whisper in Bessie's ear. "Mother, I believe my hot flashes have come back." Another look at the handsome preacher reviled he hadn't taken his eyes off of her. "Mother, I do believe that young preacher is flirting with me. He hasn't taken his eyes off me during this strange new hymn the congregation is singing."

Bessie O'Donnell glance up at the pulpit before lending toward her very proper daughter. "Kris, really! I am quite certain you are imagining things dear. It's not like you to even notice such things." The loving mother patted her daughter's gloved hand. "He appears to be caught up in the music the choir is singing."

"I am sure you are right mother." Jenny's aunt adjusted her glasses. "I been meaning to have my eyes checked. These old glasses surely need replacing after having them for ten years." Kris gave a sigh as she listened to the choir. "I'm just a silly old woman."

"Kris darling, you are not silly or old. You're just lonely and set in your ways." Bessie had hoped her younger daughter would have found a mate by now but she was content to remain an old maid just to give her mother companionship.

"Me lonely? Really mother. How could I be lonely when I have you. "Kris reached over to take her mother's fail hand. "Besides, we are doing just fine without a man around to give us orders."

Jonathan had watched the two ladies throughout his sermon on Angels and Demons and why God allows evil things to happen in His perfect world. He was somewhat amused when the offering

155

plate got around to their pew and how their eyes grew wide at the large amount of cash already collected. Jonathan locked eyes with Kris as he spoke. "If this were a perfect world my friends, then there would be no need of heaven. Evil and good abide, side by side together, for as long as this earth is here. So, is there a heaven? Most certainly. It is where God abides but the way to heaven is down a narrow path and you must live a good and perfect life, without sin. Is there a hell? I can guarantee everyone attending today, hell does exist but it's path is wide, to welcome the sinners in it's alluring evil kingdom." His dark eyes remained on the two visitors as he announced the last hymn. "Please turned in your hymnals to page 666 as we sing, The Path to Follow."

After the service, Jonathan greeted all those in attendance and when the O'Donnell women stepped out, Jonathan reached for Kristine's hand, holding it firmly. She smiled up shyly.

"Reverend Wineworth, that was a very different sermon from what we're use to, but it was very moving. You made it easy for us Christians to know which path to trod down."

"I'm glad you enjoyed it young lady." Jonathan knew what to say to charm the women, no matter their age. He released Kris to welcome her mother. "I am glad you came today, dear lady. What did you think about my word?"

"Interesting Reverend, most interesting." She pulled her glove up when he released her hand. "I was a mite confused about which path was built up the most. I couldn't help but noticed you never led the people to go down the right path, reverend."

"You observe me well, madam. It's true I did not instruct my congregation which path to take. Like the good man upstairs I let my people make their own choice which path to take, hoping of course, they choose the right one. I can teach them the word but I cannot live their life for them, now can I Mrs. O'Donnell." Jonathan had been introduced to them earlier by one of the ladies on the welcoming committee.

"Why, certainly not reverend." Kris looked down critically at her mother, who simply shrug her shoulders. "It's up to each and everyone of us to live the life we believe in, although I do hope all these good people here chooses to follow Jesus example like my beloved nephew, Ted. If anyone needs an example of what a Christian should be like, he is the one." Kris nervously straighten the strap on her hand purse. "Sometimes I even see Ted as an angel."

"Yes, one might get that impression of Ted Neenam. I had the honor of meeting him and his beautiful wife Jenny, who I believe is your niece Miss O'Donnell and your granddaughter, Bessie."

"Yes, my granddaughter married Ted a little over seven-years-ago and their love has blessed them with two adorable twin girls." Bessie beamed. "Perhaps you saw their four-year-old daughters running around when you met Ted and Jenny. You couldn't miss them. They are the spitting image of their father."

"I never saw the little girls who take after their father. It must be a family trait. I hear the religious young man looks exactly like his father." Jonathan knew Ted was the son of the angel Gabriel, but he was certain these two relatives knew nothing about his birth father.

Both women looked at one another confused, uncertain as to where he got his information. Kris whispered to her mother. "Let me answer this one mother. I'm not sure where you got your information Reverend Wineworth, but Ted has no resemblance to either one of his parents. We just assume he takes after a distance relative."

"You might say, a very distant relative my dear Kristine." Jonathan smiled, pretending to explain, when he knew for a fact Gabriel was created before the beginning of the earth, making him very distant. "I was referring to how Ted looks and dresses. Like someone who just stepped from the pages of the holy book." Noticing their smiles, he knew he had fooled them. Jonathan also knew the grandmother, Bessie O'Donnell would be all but impossible to win over, but her daughter, Kristine was obviously starved for love and affection. He knew he could easily win this one's soul and make his father proud of him. Blocking out everyone waiting for his attention, Jonathan gazed down deep into Kris's eyes, half listening to her words of praise for him. He was hatching up his plan to win and change Kristine O'Donnell's life forever.

CHAPTER 32

Ted had rolled over in bed to prop up on one elbow as he smiled down lovingly at Jenny, sleeping soundly. They had made passionate love the night before dropping off to sleep, naked in each other's arms. Ted traced her face with his fingers, lifting a fallen curl from her forehead before kissing it. Smiling, Jenny opened her eyes as he spoke softly. "Good morning, my sleeping angel." It was still too early for the first rays of sunlight to shine through the window shade and darkness filled the sky.

"Is it morning already sweetheart? It seems as though I just shut my eyes." She yawned.

"The clock will soon strike four, my nearest Jenny. I awoke with the need to make love to you before climbing the mountain." Ted's gaze was so serious, Jenny once again felt the flutter of butterflies invade her body.

"Then, by all means, my beloved romantic husband." Jenny kicked off the sheets and held up her arms. "Your wife is more than willing to assist you with your request."

Smiling, Ted climbed over on her and began kissing her with so much passion that Jenny felt as though she would burst if he did not become one with her. Sensing her strong emotions, Ted made the connection and they began moving in perfect rhythm until minutes later they both reached the highest level of passion.

Ted happily kissed his wife before stretching. "Jenny, would you like to walk with me to the mountain this morning?"

"I would like that very much Ted." Jenny sat up next to him. "It's quiet and peaceful this time of the morning and my nice rock seat will be waiting for me at the foot of the mountain."

"That's right, little mama, not to mention the long walk will be good for you." Ted helped her up and to the shower.

After reaching the rock seat, Ted kissed Jenny and continued his climb to the top as the first rays of sunlight drifted through the trees. When Ted reached the top, the Lord was there waiting. "Ted, my son, I know you feel danger ahead and are concerned for the many lost souls that have come to the town below. They follow the one who led them all down the wide path to destruction."

"I feel Jonathan has won many unfortunate lost sheep for Lucifer." Ted searched the brilliant blue sky. "The children you put in my care are a challenge, all but the smallest two. Patches and Blake have found love and desire to be a part of us."

"You and Jenny have given Noah a place in your hearts as your own son. The boy will not suffer like his twelve-year-old mother, even though he is Lucifer's grandchild."

"Marble is head strong and has a selfish lustful will that may doom her in the end. Even now she is old enough to know right from wrong and she has been brainwashed into believing her fate will be rewarded instead of punished." Ted felt his tears burning for the lost child. "Even now just days after giving birth, the girl flirts openly with Matthew and Andrew."

"The girl's eyes are set for you my son as will the young women named Fire. They will look at you with lust in their eyes and seek to tempt you." God's voice remained soft and loving to the one he was proud of. All three boys, Blaze, Devin and young Willy, are checking out the older girls, including your Jenny and Kathy. Devin also has his eye on your Mary and cannot be trusted around her."

"I have noticed his attention toward her, as has young Teddy Jeffery, who already claims our daughter as his own." Ted paced back and forth, anxious about Mary's safety. "I have warned all the home girls about keeping their distance from the new boys and what their intentions were toward them. I have a deep dread that something bad is going to happen to some of our family. Miriam is already in dangerous territory where Jonathan is involved."

"The once good son is responsible for many of our problems, young Ted." The Lord's voice grew in volume. "All your fears are bonded in truth. Besides Miriam, there will be other members of the family, yours and Jenny's, who will be greatly tempted. If their faith wavers for one second, they could find them self, traped in the devil's web."

"Be with me, my Father. Help me to know the right way to defeat your old foe and when he will strike." Ted felt peace on top the mountain but he knew he must go back down and face the trials to come. "Father, I ask you to be with my brother Jeffery, in these trying times. It's easy to see Lucifer is only using his brother to get to him. It grieves my heart to see Satan has his eyes cast on the young boy, Teddy, even more than he does his own son Jonathan."

"Jonathan seeks to be is father's number one son and dreams of becoming his Anti-Christ." The voice grew sad. "It was not long ago this same lad was filled with a different kind of fire. The fire of the Holy Spirit! My son Jonathan was on his way to becoming one of the greatest preachers known to man."

"How easily he slipped from grace and all for the power of becoming the devil's anointed one. Now Jonathan is aware of Jeff's two six's and he has grown even more jealous of his twin. It's my worst fear knowing my most trusted friend is marked already by two of the three marks and one more would doom him as the beast." Ted looked up, hand lifted as though he were pleading a case in the court of law. "If Jeff, marked with two six', can be saved, surely there's hope for Jonathan. I will not rest, my Lord, until I fight to win back every lost soul taken from you and that includes Jonathan, your prodigal son."

"My faithful son, in your wisdom I find hope for my lost children." The wind blew over and around Ted. "Jeff has a strong will and he is your closes help. Gabriel will be helping you fight the fight and as the time grows nigh, many great forces from heaven will reign down upon my old foe and his fallen comrades. You are never alone!"

Ted closed his eyes, feeling the strength and the power rush through him. "Blessed one, thank you. Knowing you are always near, it is easy to press forward, armed with your mighty shield and powerful words." His voice softened. "Be with my Jenny and little girls, loving Father. Protect them and keep them safe while I go to battle this evil that lies ahead."

"You have my word that your family, including young Gabriel not yet born, will be protected from all evil forces as will you, my beloved son." The voice seemed to whisper in the breeze. "Go in perfect peace. Your loving Jenny waits for you and I see one approaching her from behind that could cause danger. Go quickly!" with the warning, Ted vanished.

Jenny sat patiently, repeating the song in her head Ted sang the day they got married on top the very mountain he had climbed. She glanced down at her watch and glanced up the path. "Ted has been gone only thirty minutes so, I'll read some more of my book." Jenny shuffled around to another position on the hard rock then opened

The Lost Sheep

her latest book, Billy Graham's ANGELS. "I'm sure there's something in here about Ted's father." Before she could get started Jenny jumped when she heard a limb snap loudly behind her. Turning around quickly, Jenny noticed an unfamiliar young man walking toward her. She jumped to her feet dropping her book.

"Sorry miss, I never meant to frighten you." The young teen bent down to retrieve her book, his attention falling on the cover. "You believe in angels, miss?"

"I should hope so." Jenny reached for the book as she thought to herself "Married to an angel whose father just happens to be Gabriel. "Don't you believe in angels, young man?"

"Me? Sure, do miss. Mostly fallen angels like the powerful Lucifer." His words startled Jenny even though his appearance seemed innocent enough. "What's a beauty lady doing way up here alone so early in the morning?"

"Before you arrived, I was meditating by reading Billy Graham's classic book on the different kinds of angels." Jenny glanced up on the mountain path, hoping to get a glimpse of Ted. "You sure are filled with questions son. I could ask you why you are here, so early in the morning, obviously lost."

"Not exactly lost, miss. I'm a guest on the neighboring mountain and I enjoy taking early morning walks." The boy's curios eyes followed hers, up the steep path going to the top. "Waiting on someone, miss?"

"Young man, do you always leave the pronoun I, off all of your sentences?"

"Pronoun's are a waste of good grammar, miss." He laughed.

"Not if you are an English teacher! To answer your last question, I am waiting on someone. My angelic husband, who should be coming down that path any moment now." Jenny had secretly hoped she were right but she knew if she felt danger all she needed to do was whisper Ted's name.

"So, your old man climbed to the top and left you down here. Why didn't he just let you go up there with him?" The young teen cupped his hand over his eyes and stared upward. "It is a long climb but I bet the view at the top is worth the climb."

"My very young husband took me up once, but I cannot tell you anything about the view." Jenny remembered only the incredible heavenly wedding service on a rainbow and the fragrant flowers.

161

Mostly, she remembered Ted, holding her hand as each one of them said their magical marriage vows. She came out of her memories when she noticed the teen walk over close to the path.

"I think I'll make that climb and see for myself how great the view is." The cocky teen looked over his shoulder at Jenny. "I might just tell you how beautiful your neighbor's mountain looks from up there." He started forward when Jenny grabbed his arm to stop him. "Hey, what's with you lady? Does you husband own that mountain top?"

"By law, yes, he does, but that is not the reason I stopped you." Jenny let him go when he stared down at her hand. "The truth is, that mountain belongs to God! No one is permitted up there except my husband." She narrowed her eyes when he laughed out. "Look kid, if you ever read the Bible, you may know the story of Moses being the only one able to climbed the mountain of God where he retrieved the Ten Commandments. Well, this is sort of the same deal."

"First of all, the Ten Commandment are worthless on me and this crap about your husband being the only one permitted to climb this stinking mountain in the state of North Carolina is totally ridicules lady." His eyes burned on her as he bragged loudly. "I'm going up so don't stop me!"

"By all means, go for it!" Jenny stood back arms folded and waited for the scream that she knew would be coming.

Before he could take one step forward, a force of electricity hit him, knocking him backward with a thud, on the hard ground. The shocked teen trembled uncontrollable for several minutes and carefully tried to sit up, his head spinning in circles. "Hell! What the shit just happened?"

"You did not want to take my good advice about staying off God's mountain! That's what happen buddy boy!" Jenny tried hard to hide her laughter.

Finding his feet stable, the youth grabbed Jenny and started shaking her. "Laugh at me, bitch! I ought to kill you!"

"And find yourself in great pain again!" the teenager felt a hand pull him off the ground and sent him sailing through the air where he landed in a bed of clover. When he rolled over, he saw the source of his assailant. A man, barely six-foot, long blonde hair, dressed in a white robe, the spitting image of Jesus. "I know who you are boy, just tell my wife." Ted stared into the sixteen-year-old's face.

"How do you know my name mister?" he spoke nervously. "I don't know you?"

"I'm waiting son. I know you are visiting the Wineworth family, next door and I know you are a student of Jonathan Wineworth. You and your friend, your very close friend, Jasmine, by birth but goes by Fire." Ted took his wife's hand, his attention never leaving the teen. "I'm sure you don't wish for another round in the clover, Marshall."

'Shit man, you know our real name!" Marshall was sweating when he looked toward Jenny. "Blaze! My chosen name is Blaze, miss."

"It's Mrs. But you may call me Jenny, Blaze." Jenny turned to Ted. "This is the Blaze and Jasmine? The other two Jonathan got a hold on?"

"Reverend Wineworth is our friend lady. The only one that's ever loved us or given us any help." Blaze relaxed as he watched the love between the couple in front of him.

"Son, how many years have you been with Reverend Wineworth?" Ted reached for his hand and Blaze felt love flowing through him as he was lifted off the ground.

"Six years sir. I was ten when Jonathan took me in. He was still at Duke, studying to be a preacher. Jonathan was a kind and caring young man." Blaze glanced back up the path that had sent powerful shock waves through him, then back at Ted. "You walked up that path and it did not knock you back?"

"Blaze, remember I told you Ted was the only one permitted to go up on the mountain." Jenny had seen a small change in the outspoken boy since Ted touched him.

"Ted?" He soaked in the angelic man standing in front of him. "So, you're Ted."

"Marshall Foster, just what do you think you are doing harassing Jennifer Neenam?" Jeff appeared from out of nowhere and took the young man by the arm. "Did I not warn you about coming near this mountain?'

"Yes sir, Mr. Wineworth." Blaze trembled at the sight of Jonathan's mysterious brother. "I guess my curiosity got the better of me, sir."

"No harm was done Jeff, but thank you for coming over to

check on the boy." Ted draped his arm around his neighbor's shoulder. "We have got our work cut out for us, my brother. Many are coming, many more have already arrived."

"I too have been sensing their arrival. My brother is quickly filling his new church with old members and a few unexpected visitors." Jeff and Ted exchanged their thoughts, both knowing there where members of their own family that needed watching. "Yes Ted, we shall watch them carefully."

The young teen stared at both men, knowing neither had spoken out loud, yet Jeffery answered as though he had heard Ted say something. "Excuse me sir, but did I miss something? Ted never said anything to you about watching somebody."

"Boy, keep quiet while Ted and I are discussing something very important. You do not need to know our business!" Jeff pushed him down next to Jenny, who had sat back on the rock to wait while they spoke in silent secret. Jenny smiled over so sweetly the teenager calmed down.

"Blaze, try to relax and don't waste your time trying to figure out why these two men can discuss something without anyone else hearing them. It took some time for me to get use to it, but it comes natural now."

"We both know to watch Miriam and Teddy, but there is another one close to us, a most unlikely person for Jonathan to seek out. It hasn't happened yet so I cannot make out who it is." Ted listened to Jeff now as he thought back his answer.

"I too sense Jonathan is just before retrieving another good soul and like you, this one is going to be a shock."

"Jeff, as soon as I know, we'll be there to help them." Ted spoke softly. "The Father will send help in due time."

"Then I will listen for your call Ted." Jeff motioned for Blaze to follow him.

"As I will yours, Jeff." Ted lifted Jenny up and draped his arm around her waist. "Give Naomi our love as well as Teddy and Jacob."

"My pleasure Ted and please kiss those adorable girls of yours for me." Jeff gave a low laugh. "That would make Teddy Jeffery mad with jealousy, now that he claims Mary for his own."

"Wow! This Mary sounds neat! Any baby you two made would have to be super good looking. I'd really love to meet that chick."

Blaze followed behind Jeff, day dreaming about a shapely blonde. "Why am I just learning about her?"

Jeff turned so quickly, Blaze ran right into him and stared at his chest. "Look boy, for starters, Mary and Martha are only four-years-old, so hands off!" Jeff gave him a push down the path as two of his wolves fell in beside him. "If you know what's good for you, you will start listening to me instead of my brother. Jonathan."

"And, what if I choose not to! What are you going to do about it!" Blaze looked straight ahead, knowing that he would chose to follow Blackheart.

"What am I going to do if you choose to follow Jonathan?" Jeff turned him around to face him. "I'll stand back and watch you fall to the evil side and in return...burn in hell!"

CHAPTER 33

Jonathan looked up from his office work as the church secretary brought in Kristine O'Donnell. Smiling, he rose from his chair and walked around the desk to greet her. "Kristine, I see you got my message." The handsome pastor pulled out the chair that faced his desk as he motioned the secretary away.

"Yes, I received your message asking me to come in and help you with a sermon you're working on." Kristine felt her heart flutter at his touch. "I must admit reverend, this is the first time I've been asked to help with a sermon."

"Jonathan! Please, Kristine, call me Jonathan." He flashed her a brilliant smile and the usually outspoken woman felt flushed just admiring his handsome face. "The title of my sermon is called Never Too Old. I hope that does not offend you. Believe me, that was not my intention, my dear young lady."

Kristine couldn't resist a chuckle as she said "Good Lord Jonathan, I have not been a young lady in quite a few years. It is obvious I am very mature so I can honestly say I am not offended from the title."

"That just seem like the perfect topic for a sermon, having several middle-aged members in the congregation. Take you for instance. You see age climbing in years and you just assume you're old. So, you dress and act the part." Jonathan stood back up and walked around in front of her. "Maybe if you start by taking down your beautiful hair instead of wearing it pulled up in that tight bun. It is pulled smoothly back, away from your face of which you wear very little make-up."

"Well, I feel this look seems to suit me Jonathan." Kris couldn't understand why this extra special young man cared about how she looked, but he had made her curios and she wished to hear more. "What do you suggest?"

"May I have your permission to show you?" he smiled when she nodded. "For starters, let's take down your hair." Jonathan's fingers gently removed all the hairpins that held up the tight bun, causing her hair to fall down over her shoulders. He then ran his hand through her dark brown locks, greying only slightly around the temples, until it hung full and shiny around her face. "Kristine, my dear, you have beautiful hair and with it down, you are already looking younger." Looking in her eyes, he touched the top button on her blouse. "If you would permit me to undo a couple of the top buttons and apply a small amount of make-up, I believe the reflection you will see looking back is the real Kristine O'Donnell waiting to come out."

"I trust you Jonathan. I haven't even looked at myself, but I already feel younger just from hearing you talk." Kris gave him a beautiful smile, the same youthful smile she had given to the boy a younger Kristine had loved and lost many years ago. For a long moment, Jonathan was captivated by her haunting smile. Jonathan pulled up a chair and started applying make-up to her face. Within minutes, she had been transformed into a very sexy Kristine O'Donnell. After opening the top three buttons, he lifted her collar for the finishing touch.

"Now sweetheart, let's have a look at the new you and be honest, let me know how you like it, beautiful Kristine." Jonathan took her hand and led her to an adjoining room which displayed a full-length mirror. "Beautiful lady, meet the new Kristine." Jonathan walked her in front of the mirror where she gave a gasp at the vision looking back. A much younger, even sexier Kris

"Oh Jonathan, is that really me?" Kris O'Donnell could not believe her own eyes.

"You have been hiding yourself long enough darling." Jonathan's voice grew so seductive, Kris felt her knees shaking. "You have devoted your life to your mother so long you have become her. Have you ever been in love with a man, Kristine?" He pulled her around to face him. "Tell me, dearest, have you ever made love to a man before?"

"Oh, heavens no!" Kris swallowed before giving a soft laugh. "Who would have me, Jonathan? Look at me."

"I am looking at you Kristine and I'm captivated by what I see. If I weren't already engaged to be married" Jonathan's eyes burned into hers. "I would have you, Kristine. I would find it a pleasure to make love to you, beautiful lady."

"Jonathan, I'm at a loss for words." Kris felt numb. "No one has ever said those words to me before."

167

Joan Byrd

Jonathan pulled her into his arms. "Kristine, I feel like kissing you! To feel my lips parting over yours is suddenly burning in my flesh." His lips came within an inch as he whispered. "I am not married yet and my need for you is great Kristine."

"Jonathan...I" Before she could say another word, Jonathan's lips melted over hers in a passionate kiss. Kristine O'Donnell was feeling something happening. A new sensation that filled her with feelings she had never felt before. A passion so strong she wanted to experience more from this very sexy man.

Jonathan knew he was winning Jenny's aunt over. He could feel the lust she was experiencing was new to her and Jonathan knew he had Kris O'Donnell right where he wanted her.

"Kristine, do you want me to stop before I cannot control my body?" Jonathan breathed heavily.

"I know I should stop Jonathan." Her heart was pounding with new emotions. "This thing that I feel, I cannot explain. It seems wrong in one way and incredibly right to be in your arms."

"This thing you're feeling is love Kristine. You are falling in love with me and that's why it feels right." Jonathan pulled her against him so she could feel his manhood, causing her to quiver. He smiled to himself as he asked. "My darling, do you want me to make love to you?"

"No! Yes! Yes, Jonathan, yes!" Kris clutched his bare back and wondered when he had removed his shirt.

"Let me lock the door darling." Jonathan walked over, locked the door then dropped his pants. Jonathan was standing naked in front of a full eyed Kristine O'Donnell.

Kristine was still tingling from the sex she had enjoyed with Jonathan. Now she knew what Jenny and Kathy had been experiencing all this time while she had sat at home being a goodie two-shoes. She never questioned Jonathan about having a bed in the wall when he had let it down before undressing her. Now, sitting behind the wheel of her car, she mused that she should be feeling ashamed, but she smiled at the reflection of herself in the visor mirror before climbing out. Jonathan had suggested that she put her hair back up as he buttoned the blouse for her, while kissing her neck. He thought the sudden change might upset her mother Bessie and she should slowly change into her new self.

Kristine had made plans to visit that little dress shop down town

168

The Lost Sheep

that had intrigued Jenny and Kathy before they got married and buy herself some new outfits. She would set up an appointment with a hair stylist and pay a make-up artist to help her with applying make-up. Kristine felt beautiful as she waltzed inside the front door and kissed her mother's cheek.

"Somebody is in a cheerful mood. The meeting with Reverend Wineworth must have been successful." Bessie smiled up from her knitting.

"It was a very good meeting mother. Jonathan is the nicest man to work with, such a gentleman." Kristine couldn't wipe her brilliant smile off her face.

"With the looks of you darling, I'd say Reverend Wineworth made quite an impression."

"That would be an understatement mother." Kris laughed. "We hit it off beautifully, so I've decided to change my membership to Kill Devil Hill church very soon."

"Change your membership? But Kris, you have been a member of Goldsburg Methodist for your entire life. You can't just up and quit over one meeting with that new minister. You can't be serious." Bessie sat up and laid down her knitting. "Promise me you won't rush into this darling."

"Mother, I will give it a little more thought if it will make you happy. But what I choose mother will be for myself. You need not change the church you love." Kris hopped up and walked to the cabinet, then pulled out a bottle of wine that she had received when she retired from the city bank. "Wine mother? I think it's time I learn to drink more wine. I hear its really good for you."

"Kris, are you alright dear. I never seen you acting like this before." Bessie could not understand the change in her youngest child.

"I would say, I am the best I have ever been mother." Kris poured herself a glass of wine and took a sip. "I am ready for a new me mother, so prepare yourself." She picked up her glass and walked to the stairs, smiling back. "A new hair style, new clothes, a little make-up, in short mother, a new Kristine." Laughing, she blew her mother kiss and walked up the stairs singing I Feel Pretty.

Bessie shook her head in disbelief, not sure what had gotten into the prim and proper Kristine. Bessie liked the fact that her daughter was happy, happier than she had been in years. The only other time

169

Joan Byrd

Bessie could recall her acting this way was when she had just graduated from high school and her love for Johnny James, the only boy she ever had a crush on, ask her to marry him. He went off to war and never returned and the happiness in her eyes died with him.

Upstairs, Kris danced through her bedroom door, switched on the table lamp, then locked her door, something she had not none in years. After taking a sip of wine, Kris sat down the glass and took a seat in front of her mirror. Just as she had done every night for years, Kris removed her hair pins and started brushing her hair out. Her attention fell on the hair band that usually wrapped the end of her long pigtail. But things would be different from now on, Kris would leave her hair down around her face the way Jonathan liked it. Pulling open her gown drawer, she made a face before saying, I will buy some new gowns tomorrow as well." Searching through her t-shirts, she found one large enough to sleep in and pulled it out. She took off her blouse and long skirt, tossing them aside before staring at her underwear.

"Lord, look at these-old-underwear. I must put some new undies on my list as well. It's a wonder Jonathan didn't burst out laughing over these worn out things." She undone the bra and slid the soiled underwear to the floor. Catching her reflection in the mirror, Kris stood back and turned around, seeing her figure for the first time. "Not bad for a forty-eight-year-old woman." Kris had always been thin, so her waist looked good and with a little help from the YWCA down town, she could get back in great shape. The large bust sagged very little and actually still looked sexy, she thought happily. Still timid, Kris reached up and touched them, remembering Jonathan's touch when he had caresses each breast and let his tongue run over her nipples. The thought along brought back the passion she had felt for him.

She walked back for another sip of wine and starting to feel the effects of the red drink, she carried it over to the bedside table. She glanced down at the T-shirt lying in the chair near her vanity. Giggling to herself like a school girl, Kris pulled down the covers and climbed in bed naked.

"Maybe I will dream about Jonathan tonight." She drank down the remainder of the wine before switching off the light. Lying there in the darkness, feeling her head spinning with the wine, she relived her first ever love making with a man. Not just any man, Jonathan had been so gentle with her as he removed her clothes and laid her across the bed. Her heart once again fluttered as she recalled looking into his black eyes as his lips parted over hers bringing out the incredible passionate feelings flowing through her body. The fire that swept through her when he parted her legs and climbed over on top of her. Neither one of them uttered a word the entire time Jonathan took control of her as he made love. Then the unexpected, the magic that happened inside her when she felt the ecstasy explode and heard him whisper in her ear "Never too old, Kristine. You are mine!"

Kris O'Donnell smiled as she said softly "Yes Jonathan, I am yours forever."

CHAPTER 34

"Jonathan, I hear you are really building your church" Jeff's eyebrow shot up "down below."

"Yes, many of my old members seemed to have missed their minister and followed me." Jonathan looked up from writing a letter, overlooking the cutting remark from his brother, "It appears I will be making Goldsburg my home."

"Do you intend to live with me and Naomi awhile longer?" Jeff looked around the guest room and noticed Jonathan had replaced the new paintings Naomi had put up with some of Jeff's old evil paintings. "Jonathan, what's with my old paintings. I thought I had put them up in a safe place."

"I find them very haunting, Jeff. It's like having a recording of your past. You have captivated things you have done." Jonathan stood up and walked over to the largest painting. "Take this one. It is a man's torso, strong and muscular, very naked with a very erected penis with two sixes just above it."

"Like it, do you?" Jeff showed no emotion over the indecent drawing. "What do you think it means?"

"You appeared to be wishing you would receive the three sixes from father, then you would become Satan's Antichrist, correct brother?" Jonathan smiled calmly as though he had merely asked him which soft drink was his favorite.

"I did not have to dream about getting those sixes, brother. I painted that picture the day I was branded with my second six." Jeff stared coldly. "If I had chosen evil over good, I would already have the final six on my abdomen, brother."

"Well, damn brother, I won't doubt those facts since you were always the chosen one!" Jonathan stared back just as coldly. "Our father wanted to destroy me and anoint you, but the sad truth for the old man is" Jonathan laughed out "he ended up with two saved sons."

"Are you saved Jonathan?" Jeff knew his brother was lying and sooner or later he would slip up. "Or, are you really hoping to become our fathers number one anointed son and be Satan's Antichrist?"

The Lost Sheep

Jonathan laughed out mockingly. "That's just a lot of crock, Jeffery. It was you who was the evil son. The one that received two of his marks and needed only one more. Look at your precious works of art Jeff. Evil drips from ever single drawing. Never me, brother! I was raised by good Christian people. I stood a chance to become something meaningful, but you never got that chance. Instead of being number one, you have settled for number two, the puppet for Ted Neenam. He's the one who is in charge. Connected to the Almighty God! Even though they saved you, they still watch you closely, because of your connection to the devil. I feel sorry for you Jeffery."

"Save your pity brother." Jeff's emotions did not change. "I don't need it now and I never needed it then! I know I am watched by all those who love me and it is because I need watching as long as Lucifer wants me for his number one. Ted treats me as an equal, not a second-hand puppet! He helped save my mortal soul, along with Naomi. It's with admiration I witness his one-on-one talks with the Lord on that mountain top and if being his second means following him through the battles we will fight for the Lord, then I am proud of my position! I had rather be the last soldier in the line of battle than to be Lucifer's anointed king!" Jeff turned to the door. "When you move from this castle, take down my pictures and put them back where you found them! I will not have my sons looking at them! Understand? And start praying for the Lord that saved you as an infant to save your soul now!" Jeff stormed from the room.

Ted watched as the children were finishing their supper, reached under the table for Jenny's hand and whispered "I love you." She smiled and whispered the words back to him. Looking back at the children, he noticed they were all smiling at the loving couple.

"Alright my dears, now that you have finished nourishing your bodies, I would like to discuss the town's big picnic in the park. Jenny has convinced me that it will be a fun outing for our family, but before we go, I must set a few rules."

The smaller children whispered with excitement while the older teens smiled at each other. Leah, overjoyed by the news forgot her promise to use her inside voice when she shouted "I hear there's going to be rides, like the fair!"

"Leah, please pipe down! We are not outside kid!" Matthew rubbed his fresh headache as he patted her red pig-tails.

173

Leah made an "I'm sorry" face and tried to calm down. "I really heard they do have rides and all sorts of games to play."

"Leah is right. There will be a few rides dear." Jenny winked at Kathy who had helped her get the tickets for everyone. "There will be a carousel, pony rides, hayrides, and a small roller coaster."

Kathy chimed in. "The games will include, bingo, pin the tail on the donkey, shooting at duck's game, guess your age, dunk the clown and hit the bell with the hammer."

"Why would anyone want to hit a bell with a hammer?" Matthew stared over at his wife. "Forgive me sweetie, but that sounds like a really stupid game."

"No silly, you don't actually take a hammer and hit a bell! It's a game of strength, Tarzan. You take a really big hammer and hit a weight that moves up a tall poll to the bell at the top. If you ring the bell, you are a winner!" Devin laughed out. "Boy, are you stupid!"

"Devin, that will be enough smart talk." Ted looked at the young teen seriously, causing the boy to look down to avoid his stare. Ted glanced around at the other quiet children. "We will all partake in the town picnic together, so be on your best behavior. A fair warning, if anyone of you misbehaves I will take the entire group back home. Is that clear children?"

They all nodded politely except Marble who was busy chewing her gum, blowing and popping bubbles.

"Marble, we do not chew gum in this house! Especially at the table!" Ted handed her a paper napkin. "Spit it out please and hand me the remainder of your pack."

"And if I refuse!" she lifted her head in defiance, then noticed she had everyone's solemn attention. "Well, it is my last piece! Can't I at least get the flavor out first?"

"Marble, no one else has gum to enjoy in this family. We cannot afford such luxury here." Jenny frowned at the twelve-year-old, while thinking to herself "And to think, she was going to be a mother?"

Ted read Jenny's thoughts and patted her knee gently before smiling into her eyes. He focused on the young girl, still chewing and staring down at the napkin in her hand. "I will not tell you again, young lady. Take out that gum or stay home."

"Oh, alright!" She mumbled and spit the gum inside the napkin. "At least I got most of the flavor out." She noticed Ted was holding

174

out his hand, so she threw the napkin over in it. She watched him throw it down and put his hand back out. "What? I told you that was my last piece of bubble gum."

"Do you enjoy being left behind when the rest of the family are having fun?" Ted did not budge. She gritted her teeth and pulled out a pack with one piece missing and reluctantly handed it over. "Thank you."

"You are not welcome! At least I can still taste the flavor from my first piece." Marble stuck her lips out.

"Gee, aren't you the lucky duck." Matthew made a face at the rude girl and instantly noticed Ted's unsmiling face, so he quickly changed the subject. "Ted, are we suppose to trust these five to behave in that large crowd of people down town?"

"They had better behave Matthew. We will not be alone at the fair." Ted glanced down at Jenny before continuing. "An old teacher friend of mine is coming to help and no one gets away from him. You will respect him at all times and he, likes to be called Gab." From Ted's side vison, he could see her looking at him, remembering who Gab was. "Are there any questions?"

"Ted, can we do all the things Miss Jenny and Miss Kathy told us about? All the rides and games?" Patches spoke softly as she gave him a sweet smile.

"Sweet child, you may play the games meant for little children and you will be supervised on the rides. We must all remain together for the meal and be with at least two adults from our group at all other times." Ted reached over and patted her cheek.

"Jenny, do we wear our school clothes or our Sunday clothes?" Esther squeezed Robert's hand under the table.

"That is a great question Esther." Jenny smiled over at her friend, who had helped her with the big surprise. "You will be wearing neither school clothes or your Sunday outfits. We have a nice surprise for all of you. Our good friend, George Pennington, sent us a check to help purchase not only school clothes and supplies for everyone old enough to attend school but because Kathy and I are such good shoppers, there was enough money left over for not only a new Sunday outfit, but play clothes that fit in at the family town picnic and fun day!"

Everyone around the table clapped with excitement except for Devin and Willy, who felt sure the clothes wouldn't be hip enough for them to wear. Devin glanced over to make sure Ted was preoccupied before he managed to get Mary's attention and give her a wink. She frowned at his advances and shook her blonde curls, then turned to her father.

"Daddy, will Teddy Jeffery and Jacob be at the fun day picnic?" she smiled when she heard Devin grunt.

"Yes, sweet one. The Wineworth brothers will be there, with their parents." Ted's eyes fell on Devin, who looked down wondering if he had seen the wink to Mary. "I might even let you and Martha ride the carousel with Teddy and Jacob. Would you like that darling?"

"Yes, thank you daddy." The twins said in unison before Martha whispered to her sister. "Maybe we can convince dad to let us go on the hayride with the boys."

Ted smiled, first at his girls then at Jenny before lending over to whisper to her. "Mary and Martha want their daddy to allow them to go on a hayride with the brothers. What does their mama think?"

"Mama thinks, the girls may go on the hayride as long as their mama and daddy are sitting right there with them, watching." Jenny laughed softly. "I know what you're thinking Ted Neenam. By my wanting to watch them when they are with boys, proves the girls have some of me in them after all, finding ways to be alone with their fellows."

Miriam had been listening quietly, wondering if Jonathan was avoiding her by not calling asking her to go with him to the town picnic and fun day. She jumped when the phone rang out and her eyes met Ted's, knowing he knew who was calling.

"Yes Miriam, it's Jonathan on the phone so you may answer it." Overhearing Ted, Marble, Willy, and Devin exchanged glances, wondering why Jonathan would be calling that girl and how Ted knew it would be him. "Never mind how I know things, young ones. Just see that all of you behave proper tomorrow by following my little one's behavior and manners and learn." Ted got up and helped Jenny with her chair. Esther and Rachael smiled an approval to his loving act. Robert noticed their interest, and stood up to help them. First Esther then Rachael.

Kathy smiled before punching Matthew's arm. "See how a gentleman helps a lady out of her chair, sweetheart. It's never too late to start."

The Lost Sheep

"You bet, pet." He hopped up, nearly knocking over his chair and without so much as a glance in Ted's direction, he quickly recovered, then graciously pulled back Kathy's chair. "My beautiful lady, is there anything else I can do for you before I'm off to my manly duties?"

"Manly duties? Watching stinking sheep?" Willy laughed mockingly.

"Yell kid! It takes a tough brave man to tend the sheep! You must always be on watch for wolves, mountain lions or wild dogs! They're always after a nice lamb meal!" Matthew frowned at the trouble maker. "You'd be safe out there though kid! Animals of prey hate the taste of rotten meat!"

"Matthew, may I speak to you a moment." Ted took his arm and pulled him toward the back door. "Matthew, you need to set a better example around these troubled kids, my friend. I know you feel like boxing their ears. There are times, I would." He patted Matthew on the back. "Just practice more patience. We can't undo evil work if we ourselves act bad."

"I'm sorry Ted. I just don't like the way that group treats you." Ted saw sincerity in Matthew's face. "It makes me lose my cool."

"Matthew, you know perfectly well I am capable of taking care of myself." Ted cast his attention inside to the small group, who where secretly talking and making jesters with their hands. "It's Mary and Martha I'm concerned about. Devin cannot keep his eyes off Mary and I am afraid Teddy is going to lose it and someone will get hurt."

Matthew frowned over at the fresh teenager. "Surely that sixteen-year-old jerk wouldn't hurt a seven-year-old boy over a four-year-old girl!"

"No Matthew, but a seven-year-old grandson of Lucifer can do major damage to a delinquent young punk." Ted took his arm. "Pray for Teddy, Matthew. He must never feel the power he has at his young age. It could turn him to the evil side."

"Shit!" Matthew grabbed his mouth. "It slips out, I'm sorry Ted." Then Matthew turned and caught Devin holding his wife's hand. "What the crap is that jerk think he's doing? I'll knock the shit out of him this time!" Before he could take one step, Ted had pulled him outside.

"Matthew, just watch the sheep and let me handle this. You

177

must cool down and think about what you just said, then pray about it." Ted gave his young friend a light push. "Don't worry about Devin Bates. I'll take care of him." Ted watched Matthew slump his shoulders, then turned and walked away, mumbling.

"I bet if it were Jenny getting groped he'd sing a different tune."

Ted shook his head and went through the door and was on Devin so fast, he didn't know what was happening. "Mr. Bates, you are going right now and apologize to Mrs. Christian."

"Apologize? For what, you goodie-two-shoes?" the rude boy spit out and watched Ted calmly wipe off his face.

"I know what you were doing young man and what you were planning after her husband was out of sight." Ted stared into the scared eyes of the teenager as Kathy watched, wondering why Ted was being so strict with the kid.

"Ted, Devin offered to help me with the dishes to make up for being so mean to Matthew. I thought that was terribly sweet of him."

"Yes Kathy, he may have offered to help with the dishes, but washing dishes was the last thing on his lustful mind, right Devin?" Ted's gaze became hypnotizing. "Answer the lady."

Devin gave a smirk. "I hate doing dishes! That's girl's work." His eyes fell down Kathy's body. "I thought, why waste all this sexy broad. She needn't wait to be laid when I'd be pleased to bang her."

"You, underage bastard!" Kathy drew back her hand, ready to slap his face when Ted caught her hand.

"Sweet Kathy, do not give him what the devil desires of you." Ted's gentle voice helped her relax as Jenny walked over and placed her arm around her friend.

"Come with me Kathy and let Ted handle this misguided jerk." Ted smiled to himself at Jenny's words then he took a firm hold on the ungrateful boy's arm.

"You are coming with me son!"

"Coming where?" Devin moved uncontrollably beside the angelic figure until they reached the valley where the sheep grazed. "Hey, what's the big ideal bringing me to the stinky sheep pasture?"

"I changed my mind. You will be watching sheep tonight. Devin." Ted motioned for Matthew. "You are right about Kathy Devin. She doesn't need to be alone tonight. Kathy needs her husband."

Matthew broke into a big smile and he realized he had been out

178

there pacing back and forth for no reason. Devin's eyes grew big, the thoughts of being out there with night time falling and wild beast creeping up to kill a lamb or even him.

"But, what about me man? You can't leave me alone way out here in the dark."

"You won't be alone son. It seems my help has arrived." Ted smiled as he felt his father walking up behind him. He turned and gazed at the tall angelic figure wearing blue jeans and a t-shirt. "It's good to see you Gab." Ted fought to keep from laughing at Gabriel's attire.

"Ted, long time no see." His blue eyes sparkled in the moonlight. "I see my wardrobe amuses you, son."

Matthew and Devin stared in wonder at the extraordinary tall man with long blonde hair and matching beard standing beside Ted. The twinkling stars and full moon gave both men a warm glow that surrounded them. Both men had the same blue eyes, the color of a crystal clear blue sky after the rain and their resemblance was astonishing to the two witnesses.

"Gab, this is my old friend Matthew, who has been with me on the mountain from the start," Ted pulled a stiff Matthew up.

"So, a you're Gab? You taught Ted?"

"Many things" his voice was low, but strong. "I'm more into giving announcements but with Ted, it was more long distant lessons, right Ted?"

"Very much. I was gathering my wisdom from a great many good sources while growing up." Ted smiled up at his father who couldn't resist hugging his son. "It will be a joy working along side of you Gab." Ted motioned Devin up. "Then, I will leave you with young Devin, Gab." Ted returned his father's hug and motioned for Matthew to follow him and noticing his young friend had been in a trance watching father and son hug, Ted took his hand and pulled him down the path, Gabriel sending them on their way.

"Don't you worry none about me and old Devin here." Gabriel chuckled. "We'll do just fine with these sheep. I've always wanted to try my hand at being a shepherd." He winked at the boy. "Now, I've talked to a few in my time. Gave a very important message one winter's night, long time ago. Yay, I saw quite a few shepherds, just never been one."

"Never? Hey buddy, me either." Devin looked as Ted

179

disappeared down the path. "Maybe this isn't such a good ideal Gab. Neither of us know shit about watching sheep."

"This word sounds like it might be foul. Young man, I make speeches in my profession, my given field, chose just for me, and never in all my many years of bringing messages to God's people have I used foul language. Not once, and I've given a great number of messages." Gabriel put his arm around the frighten teen's shoulder making him feel relaxed. "First, we need a little fire wood to make a nice warm fire. Even the summer nights grow cold on top of a mountain."

Devin looked around and noticed a snack of fire wood, brought up for the shepherd's. He walked over and got several and placed them on a pile. "I made fires for our members when we lived in the cave." He searched his pockets. "Damn, no matches."

"Son, you must break the need to use foul words. Now, you say we need matches. What are they used for?" Gabriel looked innocent enough so the teen did not laugh.

"To strike and make fire for the wood, Gab."

"I see." Gabriel suddenly pointed to the boy's left, causing him to look in that direction nervously. "It was nothing son, I must be seeing things." Devin turned back feeling relieved then noticed the fire burning before he could ask the obvious question,

Gab chuckled and cut him off. "It appears I have matches after all, just not the kind you carry in a pocket." They sat warming their hands as Gabriel spoke words to comfort the frighten young man. "Keeping watch over God's flock is just the same as keeping watch over small children." Devin felt at peace looking into the tender blue eyes of this very special man. "You guide them home, to their place of rest and watch over them as they slumber, making sure one doesn't go astray."

"Gab, what happens to them if they go astray? Maybe they just want to feel free." The teen looked around at the sheep as they laid down, one-by-one.

"Sheep, like God's children, when one goes astray, they will permit the evil in the darkness to snatch them and do much harm, even death. Then they are lost from us forever."

Devin felt safe with this mysterious stranger and suddenly he had the urge to please him by watching for a stray lamb. He sat up when he noticed a baby lamb wondering out of sight, its mother sleeping soundly. Without so much as a thought about his own safety, the young teen jumped up and raced after it. When he returned smiling, the baby lamb was wrapped up in his arms.

"Good Lad! You will make a great shepherd yet!" Gabriel pointed out the baaing mother, who had finally missed her baby. Looking out at several sheep baaing, Devin didn't know how Gab knew which was its mother, but the boy trusted his word and set the ball of fur down. The happy little lamb ran under his mother and started feeding. "Son, you brought the lost lamb home. Now it's time for you to let me and Ted bring you home." His words were so loving and moving, Devin felt for the first time in his sixteen years, the true meaning of love. As Gabriel stretched out his arms for the lost boy, Devin did not hesitate this time, but welcomed the touch of a passionate father figure. He wanted more of the warm feelings flooding his cold heart.

CHAPTER 35

"Mama, why can't I ask Mary to be my date for the town's fun day?" Teddy sat up in his bed, prayers all said, and looking up serious. "I will be a gentleman, I promise."

"Sweetheart, you are still just a boy and I can't recall ever hearing of a gentle boy." Naomi laughed softly as she, lend down to kiss him. In defiance, Teddy quickly turned his head. "Teddy Jeffery, you are only seven, not seventeen."

"I'm quite grown for my age mother!" he said sharply. "Uncle Jonathan said I was way smarter than those punks living with Ted and Jenny! He said I was ten-times stronger too and that I should remember that if they ever threaten me!"

Jeff walked inside the room and stood by his wife. "Young man, are you sassing your mama? You will not speak to your mama in that manner boy! Do you hear me?"

"Yes papa, I can hear you fine!" Teddy stared back at his father. "I just don't understand what's so bad about my wanting to have fun with my girlfriend, that's all."

"To begin Teddy, Mary is only four-years-old and still very much a child, even if you choose to be a man at seven!" Jeff bent down close to his son. Close enough for Teddy to feel the heat seeping from his breath like the smell of embers burning. "You will apologize to your mother right now, or I will take you outside!"

Teddy pulled the covers up and pulled his stare away and on the loving eyes of his mother. Tears swelled in his young eyes as he reached for Naomi's hand. "Mama, I love you. I'm really sorry I was so ugly to you. Can you forgive me?"

Tears ran down Naomi's face as she took around her oldest boy and felt him kiss her on her lips, like he had done since he was a baby. "Teddy sweet son, I love you more than you could ever imagine and yes, I forgive you."

The hot smell Teddy had smelt earlier had vanished. Had he really smelt the fires of hell from his loving papa, or was his evil grandfather standing there, invisible, watching and waiting for the right moment to collect his bad-tempered grandson. Teddy had felt old enough to take on anyone or anything just a few minutes ago, but now the small boy swallowed nervously, closed his eyes and watched through tiny peeks as his parents walked out quietly, closing the door behind them. He would have preferred their presence all night, but after all his bragging, he wouldn't dare look like a scared child to them. There was only one who could help him, so, he climbed from the bed and returned to his knees and prayed for God to give him strength to fight the evil trying to take his soul and turn him into his once perfectly evil choice, Teddy's own papa.

The day of the Goldsburg Fun Day Picnic came in with perfect weather, mostly sunny with light southern breezes and low eighties. Ted's large family droved down in the two white SUV's and the group of excited children and youth climbed out wearing new short-sets. It was obvious to Jenny and Kathy's great eye for fashion the group was pleased when they got a thumb's up from the entire gang.

"Gee Thanks Jenny and Kathy!" Marble couldn't get over how good she looked in her new yellow short-set. "It's the prettiest thing I've ever owned." She gave a sheepish laugh. "Well, I stole a few really cool duds before, but I've never owned one I could call mine until now."

"I'm happy you like them and you are very welcome." Jenny ran a brush through the twins dangled hair where they had happily looked out the car window on the way down the mountain. "Marble, you look very pretty in them, so, just make sure you act as pretty on the outside." Jenny draped her arm around her best friend. "Looks like we did well with our choices."

"That we did pal." Kathy hit Jenny's upraised palm. "We haven't forgot what it takes to shop for bargains." Miriam walked over between them and touched Jenny's arm.

"Excuse me Jenny, have you seen any sign of Jonathan?" Jenny noticed how radiant the young blonde looked in the yellow top and tan shorts.

"Not yet dear, but Jonathan will be pleased with his beautiful date."

Miriam gave a bashful laugh. "That's very sweet of you Jenny, but I really wasn't fishing for a compliment. Jonathan did say he would wait for me near the parking area." Miriam scanned the crowd until her attention fell on the back of a well-dressed woman wearing a long red sundress, spit up the sides, revealing long shapely legs, well-tanned. Miriam let out a gasp when she turned around. "Jenny, isn't that your Aunt Kris? I know she isn't dressed matronly, but her face could be your twin."

Jenny shaded her eyes with her hand for a better look at the shapely women's back. "She's turned around, so I cannot see her face, but it cannot be my aunt. She has the same height and build as Kris, but I could never see my very proper aunt dress in such a daring outfit. Check out those heels."

"Miriam, Jenny's right. I hardly think her Aunt Kris would dress up so sexy. Much less wear her hair down, hanging straight and over her smooth shoulders." Jenny laughed at Kathy's description and agreed Kristine O'Donnell wouldn't be caught dead dressed like a harlot, her aunt's own words to how she had dressed.

"No way that's my aunt." Jenny laughed out but was cut off when Ted walked up, hearing her and smiled up at the charming lady they were looking at.

"Jenny, I wouldn't laugh in front of Kristine if I were you darling. She has chosen a new life style for herself and I think she's really quite stunning in her red dress even though she apparently ripped it by mistake."

Jenny didn't know whether to laugh at Ted's innocent observation or stare in disbelief at the stylish lady that he just announced was indeed her aunt. She let out her own gasp when the woman turned and started waving at her, calling her name. "Good Lord! It is Aunt Kris!" Some of the gathering crowd separated and Jenny finally saw her grandmother standing near Kris. Jenny watched in silent shock as they walked their way and she hoped she could talk natural when they stepped up. Seeing the two familiar faces coming their way, Mary and Martha ran up to greet them.

"Wow Aunt Kristine, you look young!" Mary smiled shyly as Martha pushed her way in.

"You look great! What happen to you?"

"Girls, maybe Aunt Kris needed a change." Jenny tried to act normal and not stare, but found she couldn't pull her eyes away from the incredible change in her aunt.

Matthew had been helping the youth with the layout of the festivities when he noticed the small group around Jenny and Ted. He moved over beside Kathy for a better look and instantly recognized Bessie O'Donnell but he had no clue who the other lady was that stood next to her.

"Hi Bessie. Didn't Kris come with you to join in the fun?" before the older woman could respond to his question, Matthew moved over to Ted and whispered. "Ted, I know I have seen that face someplace before, but I cannot put my finger on where."

"Kristine" came the deep voice causing everyone to look over and see who had spoken. Jonathan only had eyes for her. "You look radiant this morning." He waved his hand toward the cloud drifting over the sun. "You shine so brightly with beauty that the sun even hides its jealous beams. Perhaps a walk down by the lake."

Jenny instantly looked up at Ted, worry filling her beautiful eyes. He pulled her close and whispered "We'll discuss this later darling. I know what you're thinking and there is some truth in it." In total disbelief, Jenny then heard Kris speaking, same voice, different tone.

"Jonathan, that sounds lovely, thank you. The lake is so enchanting this time of year."

"Jonathan, have you forgotten you have someone waiting for her date with you? I would think your fiancé might enjoy that walk with you if she's to be your future wife." Ted stared into his cold eyes as he pulled Miriam up beside him. Miriam stood proudly, head arched high, and looked Jonathan in the eye.

"It is better I learn what Jonathan is capable of now Ted than to wait until after we're married and I'm fat with his baby! Maybe I said yes to your proposal too quickly, Jonathan Wineworth!"

"Jonathan, I never knew it was Miriam you were engaged to." Kris looked genuinely upset. "And she is having your baby?"

Jonathan was beginning to feel traped so he would choose his words wisely. "Listen to me Miriam." He took both her hands. "I intend to spend my day with you darling. Did I not tell you this on the phone." He touched her lips before she could respond. "I hope these words you speak to me come from a misunderstanding heart. I love you, Miriam, God as my witness."

"Then what did you mean by asking this woman to go for a walk with you? Telling her how beautiful she was!" Miriam still felt insecure where Jonathan stood with her. She had personally witnessed the way he was looking at Kristine O'Donnell.

"Kristine is a beautiful person who has been traped inside an old secure place far too long." His eyes fell warmly on Jenny's aunt.

185

"Such a warm-giving person should never be traped within the walls of loneliness. Kristine needs someone to love her, bring her out of that shell of emptiness and into the world of the living."

"Miriam, Jonathan is right about me. I was traped inside a very old worn-out shell, the hope of finding love long gone from my heart." Kris smiled at her mother, then Ted and Jenny. "Not the love that lives in my heart for all of you, for my Lord. The kind of love every woman seeks, like you Jenny darling. What you have with Ted. Or you Kathy, the love you feel for Matthew. Jonathan saved me. He helped open my eyes to what I was missing and he helped me realize, I am never too old to love and be loved."

"All those things have made you a different person, only in the sense that you have found that to love yourself as God intended will awake whatever dead feelings you had and renew your life. To see you so happy is a joy to each of us, but why agree to a walk by the lake with Jonathan? What is your reason for excepting with such happiness?" Ted knew what her real reason was but he knew Kristine would give him a different reason.

"Ted, just to listened to his continued guidance in how to move forward." Kris looked over at the man who took her virginity after so many years of being pure. The man she had fallen in love with.

"Kristine and I have become very good friends, Miriam. The ideal to help her came when she agreed to help me with a sermon I was working on about age. As a man of God, I want to reach out to those people who are traped in a body too young for the age they are feeling, like this dear Christian woman." Jonathan glanced over at Ted, but found it hard to read his feelings. "Normally, this should remain private between me and my student, but I don't think Kristine would get upset if I explain what we talked about."

"By all means Jonathan." Kris smiled at an uncertain Miriam. "Anything to ease your lovely fiancé's mind. I'd rather her know than to think something immoral is going on between us."

"You are an angel Kristine." Jonathan once again gathered Miriam's hands in his. "Sweetheart, I wish you could have at least trusted me and my loving devotion to you. But, sense you don't, I will tell you enough to satisfy your suspicion. "I wanted to take that walk with Kristine to tell her about a man. About her age, who could make her very happy. I will not share with you the man's name because I feel that should be told only to Kristine."

The Lost Sheep

Miriam turned a bright shade of pink when she gave Jenny's aunt an apologetic look before putting her arms around Jonathan. "Oh, Jonathan, I'm so sorry. I really feel foolish. I promise to never mistrust you again."

Ted walked over between them and pushed Miriam aside, then pulled Jonathan under some trees for privacy. "Jonathan, you are walking a thin line, even though the path you have chosen to take is wide! Miriam is young and believes she's in love so that's why she, trust you. But, I do not trust you or your motives where Miriam or Kristine are concern!" Ted eyes never blinked. "I will be watching you Jonathan, as will your brother, Jeff and if you think you can get past us, the very angels in heaven will come down on you!" Ted's eyes softened as he placed a loving hand on Jonathan's arm. "It's never too late to turn around, Jonathan. Your heart once beat for Jesus. We are here for you and we only want to bring you home."

Jonathan's eyes softened briefly, but Satan had a firm grip on his son. "Save your salvation Ted, for someone who wants it!" Once again, his eyes blazed. "Stay out of my way, Bible thumper! You, my worthless brother and your angel father! You want to battle with me? Bring it on!" Jonathan smiled, revealing sharp teeth. The smell of a burning fire arose from his flesh as he turned and made his way slowly to Miriam.

CHAPTER 36

Ted and Jenny stood back watching as Matthew tried to strike the bell with the weight. Each try brought it closer, so the third and final try, Matthew swung the hammer as hard as he could, expecting a ring, but got nothing. "What? I know I hit it hard enough that time!"

"Alright son, that's your third and final try. Step aside. Better luck next time buddy." The game attendant chomped on his gum and looked over Matthew's head. "Next!"

Ted started to step up when Blaze moved past him, gave him a slight push then reached for the hammer. "Let me show this wimp how to hit the damn bell!"

"Hey you! Wait your turn!" Matthew held tight to the hammer. "Ted was here first moron. You go after him!"

"Let him go ahead first Matthew." Ted took the heavy hammer and handed it to the rude teenager. "Go ahead son, it won't hit the bell, but give it all you got."

Fire moved her attention from her boyfriend to Ted. Never had she seen any man like him before and she really liked what she saw. Fire stepped up next to Ted and yelled out to her friend. "Show him what you got Blaze! Make the young stud sorry for jumping to the wrong judgement about you, lover boy."

While Ted ignored the flirty girl, Jenny watched the outspoken girl staring at her husband, obviously checking him out. "Ted, that young flirty girl must be the one they call Fire." Jenny didn't like the way she kept staring at her Ted so Jenny glanced up to find Ted looking down at her.

"Jenny, I know to stay away from that girl. She's trouble, my love. The Father warned me of her motives and yes, her name is Fire."

Blaze lifted the hammer and brought it down on the lever causing the weight to swore to the top, but it barely missed the bell. Sweating and determined to win, the teenager tried a second time and the exact same thing happened. In anger, Blaze threw down the heavy hammer with a thud and stared at the man in charge.

The Lost Sheep

"Look buster, this damn thing is rigged! I always ring the stupid bell!"

"Ha! Maybe it's you who is stupid fellow and maybe you're not as strong as you claim you are!" Matthew tried to avoid looking over at Ted. "The only thing big about you buddy, is your big mouth!"

"Matthew?" Ted walked over and gave him a warning look. "Let me show this young man the game is not rigged. This is not a real carnival son, this is just a town outing." Ted held out his hand for the hammer. "May I?"

"Suit yourself small fry!" Blaze gave a sarcastic laugh as he handed the hammer to Ted.

Matthew narrowed his eyes at the youth before giving Ted a word of hope. "Give it your best shot Ted."

Ted smiled over at Jenny, ignoring the remarks. "Sweetheart, pick out a prize. I will hit the bell on the first strike."

"Yes, I believe you!" Jenny walked over to check out the available prizes, while keeping one eye on her husband. Ted lifted the hammer with ease and came down gently sending the weight to the top as the bell rang out, loud and clear.

Matthew watched in wonder and yelled out "Shit Ted, you actually hit the ding-a-ling!" Feeling Ted's stare, he grabbed his mouth and gave a sheepish smile down at Kathy. "I'll win you a prize at the duck shoot honey. That, I'm good at."

"You're good at a lot of things sweetheart." Kathy gave him a hug and a thumb's up to the prize Jenny was holding up for her to see. "A glass angel. How appropriate! Good choice friend."

"Congratulations Ted, looks like the better man won." Fire walked up smiling, ignoring the looks from Jenny." Blaze told me about meeting you both on your mountain. I can see why the man upstairs finds you special and permits only you to climb 'His' mountain. It's finally good to meet the Neenam's."

"You and Blaze seem to be on your own in this large crowd." Ted looked around for Jonathan. "I know you arrived with Jonathan and you are his responsibility."

"Ted, Blaze and I are not children. We are capable of looking after ourselves." The young sparsely clothed teen smiled up seductively. "Jonathan wanted some alone time with Miriam and he trust us to be left alone among such friendly town's people." Her heavily made-up eyes stayed on Ted. "I like what this town has to offer Ted and I'm beginning to like it here more and more."

"Jasmine, this town is a short stopping point in your walk of life." Ted's eyes showed love, but not the kind she was hoping for. "Be careful that you choose the right path, my young friends. The wide path may seem glamorous but it pulls you in like a magnet, offering you riches, worldly things, lustful rewards while fooling you into false beliefs." Ted spoke with sincere words, to help guide these, misguided youth. "Dear ones, the path to righteousness is narrow but what it awards you with is more precious than anything this world can offer you, this path leads to one thing, eternal life."

"Well, mister Bible scholar, doesn't the wide path also lead to eternal life?" Blaze had recalled Jonathan preaching on descending into hell to receive your rewards and living among Lucifer and the demons forever.

"My son, you have been misguided about the rewards of hell. It is true you will live forever in hell, but your reward will be through torment and the fires that will consume your soul, can never be extinguished." Ted remained in a loving state as he compared both choices. "Only in heaven will you really be alive, feel young forever, never know pain or grief again, only joy and overflowing love that surrounds you endlessly."

"Ted, how can we find this path you speak of." Fire suddenly froze, at the sight of Jonathan staring at her. Her thoughts raced to say the right words. "Reverend Wineworth, we were just having a discussion on life's paths."

"I gathered as much, young lady." His black eyes froze hers on him. "That is a subject I will take up with you later. As for now, you're both here to have fun, not to bother Ted and his lovely wife."

"They are really no problem Jonathan. Just misguided kids longing for the truth." Ted drew his attention so the girl could break out of Jonathan's trance. "Run along children and have some fun. If you ever wish to know the truth, ask me. I'm not hard to find. You're both welcome on Goldsburg Mountain anytime."

Fire took note at how the handsome young man with the long hair broke her trance with Jonathan and she knew now was the time to break away. Fire grabbed her friend's hand. "We're off then, to ride the roller coaster."

"And Ted, Jonathan is our teacher. If we have any questions about the two paths, we'll ask him. He goes by the same book you do." Blaze held tight to Fire's hand as he looked up at the tall dark man. "I'll keep her straight Jonathan. We know where we want to be."

"Good boy! Now, have fun and be careful Fire, rides can prove dangerous." Jonathan's eyes flashed fire. "Accidents have been known to happen when you're careless." He stared after the couple as they hurried away.

"Jonathan, where did you leave Miriam?" Jenny broke his concentration "I noticed she is not with you."

"Not to worry, fair Jennifer. I left her playing bingo with some of your older youth." Jonathan checked his watch. "She will be playing for some time so I thought I would seek out Kristine and have that talk."

"Talk?" Ted spoke softly as he sent Jonathan a message through spirit thoughts. "No more sex with Kristine or the marriage is over before it gets started."

Jonathan stared at Ted as he returned his thoughts. "Think you're clever reading our act, although the lady enjoyed every lustful moment. She feels alive now because of me. Can't you let her be happy?"

"Happy for having sex under your spell and causing the poor woman to fall in love with a man she will never have." Ted stepped up close to Jonathan unafraid of the tall man standing over him. "Break it off now Jonathan so she will be free to find love on her own."

"Touching that you should care so much." Jonathan spoke out. "Break her heart? I cannot do that." He laughed mockingly. "Find someone for her to love, I can do. Now, if you will excuse me, I have a lady waiting for my help."

As Jenny and Ted made their way to the children's bingo game, she could not resist asking what the silent conversation with Jonathan was about. "Ted darling, what was that all about back there with Jonathan?"

"I'll tell you later sweetheart, but now, it's time for the children to ride the rides before lunch." Ted waved for the smaller children and smiled when they raced toward him, Melaki and John close behind them. "How did the children do at bingo?"

"All the kids won at least one prize." John laughed as he pointed to the childish prizes. "Mary and Martha really racked up, ten games each."

191

"And they played them fairly, if you're wondering. Your sweet girls noticed some of the children not winning and let them pick out a prize for themselves." The young angel beamed with pride. "So, each twin ended up with just one prize like everyone else."

"Look what I picked out dad! It's a robin, like the one that sings outside our window every morning." Martha held up the carved bird for her father to see. "Mary picked out an angel, just like yours, mom."

"Look sis! Here comes Teddy and Jacob!" Mary's eyes lit up with joy. "They look so dreamy."

"And they look so hot in their black shorts and red shirts." Martha breathed out a sigh. "I was beginning to think they weren't coming."

"Jenny, you're right my love. I certainly see my Jenny in our girls." Ted pulled Jenny close to him as she looked up helplessly.

"I agree. They know how to spot a handsome hunk and set their sights on him. But, I was already thirteen before I wanted a boyfriend. Our babies are only four!"

Teddy Jeffery and Jacob spotted the twins at the same time and took off running their way, Jeff and Naomi close behind. Jeff moved up next to Ted, watching their children laughing and talking.

"I'm sorry we're late Ted. I was replacing one of Teddy's pictures at the last minute." Jeff stared over at his oldest. "It looks like Jonathan found my poor art work and took an instant liking to the evil paintings. He carelessly let our son pick out one to put up in his room. Brother Jonathan informed Teddy they were painted by his papa and young Teddy should be honored to have one of his own."

"These are the same paintings you had hanging in your room before you found love?" Ted had seen the evil drawings the night he had gone to the castle for Naomi and bring her home after Jeff had raped her.

"The same! I had them hidden in the attic. I guess those two wild teenagers found them and told Jonathan.

Naomi had been listening and looked up innocently. "Jeff wanted to burn his paintings but I could not bring myself to letting him. I knew they were evil but at the same time, they were a part of Jeff. We just assumed we would tuck them away for safe keeping and never tell our children they existed.

The Lost Sheep

"Excuse me for asking, but you said you were late because you needed to exchange one picture for another." Jenny glanced at her watch and counted the hours they were late. "In less than an hour, the picnic will start. If the children don't ride some rides now, they will have to wait until after we eat."

"Then, let's get these kids on rides, then we can talk." Naomi bent down to her boys. "Jacob, you can ride the carousel with Martha. Teddy, you can ride with Mary. Choose two horses side by side boys and help the girls up. We will be watching so behave."

"Heck mama, what do you think we're going to do? Ride off the carousel and into the sunset like Mary Poppins?" Teddy said so serious, everyone laughed except Mary who was watching the carousel slow down so they could be next.

"Teddy Jeffery, your mama was referring to your wondering hands, always trying to touch me." Mary took everyone by surprise. "It's not happening!" she looked over the wooden horses and started running toward one. "I'm getting the white one wearing a blue saddle!" she reached the hoppy horse and draped her arm on the one beside it. "Hurry Teddy, this black horse is yours!"

Teddy Jeffery laughed and took off toward the black stallion with a red saddle, almost knocking over a chubby boy eating cotton candy. "Watch it tubs! You better look for a fat horse if you're riding this carousel!"

"Teddy Jeffery!" Naomi turned a bright red when she turned to the heavy boy's mother, who was twice as big as her son. "I'm really sorry for my son's behavior. He's seven, what can I say?"

"I'd say a little less cotton candy." Jeff stared at the fudge in her chubby hand and on her lips. "And, a whole lot less fudge, then maybe his butt could sit on a regular hoppy-horse."

"Jeff!" Naomi tried to smile at the angry mother as she watched her grab her son's hand, turn up her nose, then gram the last large piece of fug in her mouth.

"Come on Timmy, let's go get in line for the picnic!"

"Yeh! Maybe we'll be first!" the heavy boy snuck out his tongue at Jeff and Naomi, then threw down his candy cone wraper. "Mama, can we swing by the candy apple stand?" The mother nodded her head, threw down her empty box and charged off.

Jeff's eyebrow went up as he watched them waddle away, then stared down at his wife picking up their garbage and tossing it in a near-by waste can. "I suppose Timmy could always ride the elephants at the zoo."

Naomi heard the gang laughing, so she finally smiled as the merry-go-round played its cheerful song.

After putting the children on the pony's, Jenny persuaded Ted to play the age guess game. "Ted, this is one game I know we will win." Jenny gave him a smile as she handed the attendant a quarter. "Can you guess this fellow's age?"

"Mumm! We do have a two-year window, over or under. Let me see. Young, obvious." The older gentleman removed his hat to scratch his head. "I would say he is eighteen-years-old."

"I knew It! Ted, you haven't aged a day since we met!" Jenny almost appeared upset instead of being happy for winning.

"He's older?" the attendant looked puzzled. "I could ask for an ID. How old are you son?"

"I'm twenty-five, sir." Ted knew Jenny looked younger than her age too, so he pulled her up beside him. "What age would you guess my pretty wife to be?"

"Ted, I really don't want someone guessing my age." Jenny felt embarrassed seeing other people gathering around to watch. "This clever fellow will probably know exactly."

"Mumm! I can easily say this lovely lady is close to your age, young man, somewhere around twenty-four, twenty-five." The man smiled with confidence that he was right this time.

Before Jenny could react, Ted answered. "Jenny, my darling, looks like you haven't aged a day since we met." He took her hands. "You look beautiful Jenny and I love you very much." He smiled at the attendant. "Close enough. It appears we tied this game, Mr. Wilson."

"Mum! You guessed my name!" So, the little lady can pick out two prizes!" the jolly man gave Jenny a wink.

"Then we won?" Jenny reached up and kissed Ted, bringing on loud cheers from the growing crowd. "I'm looking at my prize darling, you."

Mr. Wilson sighed. "You may pool your wins and pick out one of the big prizes. The fluffy bears are a favorite with the girls, young man."

"Then I'll take the white one." Ted pointed to the white fuzzy bear with the twinkling eyes. The attendant shook his head as he wondered how he had missed seeing that one white bear among all the black and brown ones. Collecting the beautiful bear, Ted handed it to his smiling wife, who snuggled it in her arms. "I'll win you another one at the duck shoot, darling."

"Jeff, let the man guess your age sweetheart." Naomi winked at Jenny and Ted, knowing her husband looked every bit as young as Ted.

"Sure, why not." Jeff stared down at the silent man nervously staring up at the man in black. "Do you think you can guess this old man's age, Clarence?"

"Maybe you boys need to have my job, each of you knowing my first and last name." The nervous little man studied Jeff for a moment before speaking. "Old man? No, not old, just a mature deep voice, but definitely young. My guess would be seventeen or eighteen, no more."

"Go ahead and pick out your prize sweet one unless you want this expert to guess your age." Watching Naomi quickly shake her head no, Jeff pulled out his driver's license and showed Clarence Wilson. "I'll be turning twenty-five this October 31, just like my friend did this spring."

After hearing the attendant tell her she could double her prize since her husband knew his name, Naomi happily picked out a baseball and bat for her sons.

Matthew and Kathy walked up laughing, Jonah riding on his father's back, holding a big black bear. "I won it shooting by knocking down all six ducks! The poor little quacks never seen me coming!"

Leah had joined the group just in time to hear Matthew bragging about shooting six ducks so she stomped over and slapped his arm while shouting "MATTHEW, YOU MURDERED SIX INNOCENT LITTLE DUCKS, JUST SO YOU COULD WIN A STUPID TEDDY BEAR?"

"Stupid? Listen big mouth, I'll have you know those dumb ducks did not feel a thing!"

"OF COURSE, THEY DIDN'T, YOU HEARTLESS JERK! YOU BLEW THEM AWAY!" Hands on her hips, Leah was ready to fight.

Ted walked up and grabbed her arm. "Leah, why are you saying such mean things about brother Matthew?"

195

Joan Byrd

Leah squinted her eyes on Matthew as she spoke softer to Ted. "Because he shot those little ducks, that's why."

"Leah, is that all?" Ted and Jeff were aware that Leah thought the plastic ducks were real and wanted to see how long it would take for her to catch on. Leah opened her eyes wide in disbelief at Ted's statement.

"IS THAT ALL? TED, MATTHEW SHOT THEM! INNOCENT LITTLE DUCKS! AREN'T YOU GOING TO DO SOMETHING?"

"Relax Leah, Ted and I are going to do something?" Jeff winked at her bringing on a big smile over at Matthew. "Ted and I are about to shoot their little butts over the rail now, so we can win us a teddy bear."

"WHAT?" Leah stared up helplessly.

"Leah sweetheart, the ducks aren't real, they're only plastic." Ted rubbed her head. "Now, stop worrying and please keep your voice down before they run us out." He took her hand. "You may come and see for yourself if it makes you feel better."

"I believe you Ted." Leah gave him a big hug. "I should have realized you could never shoot an innocent duck. Jeff maybe, Matthew, without a doubt, but never-ever you."

Jenny laughed and gave the red-head a big hug. "Leah darling, why don't you go with Rachael and Rebecca. The three of you can help Esther and Robert get those baskets out of our car for the picnic. We will be right over as soon as the two sharp shooters are done knocking down the plastic ducks."

"That suits me fine Jenny. Even though the little ducks are plastic, I would still feel sorry for them." Leah laughed and ran to catch up with her Christian sisters.

196

CHAPTER 37

Jonathan had found Kristine strolling by the lake and ran up to join her. He looked around to be sure they were alone, then pulled her into his arms. "I cannot get over how lovely you look, my Kristine."

"It's all because of you Jonathan." The once proper Kris O'Donnell felt funny blushing at his flattering comment. "It has been such a long time since my first love's death, I almost forgot how to love a man."

"But, yet you do love a man, darling." Jonathan spoke low and seductive. "Am I right, Kristine?"

"Yes Jonathan, my heart tells me I do." She ran her hand over his handsome face. "I know I shouldn't. but I do love you, Jonathan."

"Dearest Kristine, how easy it would be to fall in love with you, if I were not already engaged." His lips parted over hers, causing her to breathed deeply, feeling passion swell inside her. "Thoughts of you being my lover has cross my mind, but such thoughts are wrong for a man of God." Jonathan pulled her into a tight embrace as he spoke in her ear. "This man I spoke of, how shall I put it, He is fairly handsome, wealthy, and healthy-active, ready to make any lady feel wonderful in every way."

Kris gently pulled away and looked out at the water. "Jonathan, I'm not sure I could just jump from you to someone else." Her heart was breaking. "How could anyone ever replace what I feel for you?"

"Not replace Kristine darling, just fulfil the needs you now have." His hand gently moved down her back. "It won't be any easier on me, my love, letting you go to another man. But Kristine, I care for you too much to watch you become the woman you were before, lonely, living in an empty shell."

"Very well Jonathan, I trust you to introduce me to someone I might care about, if only for a little."

"Kristine, you are a very special person, any man would feel lucky to have you." Jonathan's fingers ran over her breast. "Such lovely breast. Tis a pity I will not taste their sweetness again." He

197

once again kissed her and he could feel her body was desiring him. "Or to feel me hot inside you."

"Jonathan, why do you torment me so, knowing we cannot make love again?" Kris remembered his words before he made love to her the first time, so with a small amount of hope she whispered "Jonathan, darling, as before, you are still not married. Could one more time hurt, to satisfy our need for one another?"

"Dearest love, I would but jump at the chance if it were possible, but I'm afraid Ted has given me no choice." His eyes smiled with mischief into hers. "He forbids me to have anymore sex before I marry Miriam."

"Ted knows about us?" Kristine's eyes grew big. "But, how could he? Surely you didn't tell him, Jonathan?"

"Ted has ways of knowing things Kristine, before or after they happen." Jonathan could see she was feeling nervous over this revelation. "I know it must come as a shock, darling. I don't think he has told your niece about us yet. I suppose he is waiting for the right moment, but it's just a matter of time before she knows too."

Kristine pulled away, suddenly ashamed of her actions. "Jonathan, you are right about us parting and putting an end to this relationship instantly. I often wondered how women got themselves into relationships with married men. I thought them careless and foolish. I've been known to say, they go in with their eyes shut because they get so desperate for a man, not stopping to think about all the people they are hurting. Now, I find out I'm behaving the exact same way!"

"Kristine, you are not like them, darling." Jonathan felt threatened, like his evil scheming was backfiring on him. "You cannot mean what you're saying. Don't you love me? Was that just a foolish remark to hurt me?"

"Jonathan?" Tears filled her eyes as they caressed his. "I do love you. I suppose I always will. For the first time in many years, I felt so complete, so happy. I guess I was hoping you had fallen in love with me too, then would have broke off your engagement to Miriam for me. It was just a beautiful dream. I should have known by your choice being Miriam, a young and exciting woman, Not me, middle-aged and never in the running."

"Kristine? I?" Jonathan suddenly felt strange as he listened to this beautiful woman pour her heart out. Was it genuine pity he was

The Lost Sheep

feeling or was it something deeper.

"If this man you know is a good Christian man, Jonathan, and not married or engaged..." Kris pulled out a tissue to wipe her eyes. "If he respects me and does not expect me to go to bed with him just because I chose to with you, then I will meet him."

"Kristine, perhaps the man I told you about is the wrong one for you." Jonathan suddenly didn't want to see this woman with someone else and he could not understand why he was feeling that way. "Let me look else ware. I need some time Kristine." Jonathan took her hands lovingly and this time Jenny's aunt felt a different kind of love flooding her body as she thought, could he be falling in love with her?

"Whatever you think best Jonathan. It's because I love you, I trust you." She reached up and gave him a gentle kiss. "Now, go find your beautiful young fiancé. I'm sure she must be wondering where you are." Kristine turned and walked away, Jonathan staring after her.

199

CHAPTER 38

"Gab, we have ridden the carousel, swings, and roller coaster, and every time you stayed off and watched us ride." Devin looked up at the angel in wonder. "We watched you wave at us every time we came around."

"Devin's right! You just about scared the shit out of me!" Marble stared at the tall figure, wide eyed. "What 'sha do, fly?"

"Something like that." Gabriel smiled brightly as he rubbed a silent Willy on his head. "Cat got your tongue son?"

"It was like…magic!" Willy, finally spoke. "We crept up on the roller coaster and at the top before flying down, we all waved at you standing on the ground below us. Then, on our second trip up the roller coaster, it just came to a stop, right at the very top, where we heard you laugh directly behind us and start speaking."

"I did! I recalled saying, sweet loving Creator, I can almost touch your stars in heaven from up here! What a view!" Gabriel gave a cheerful joyful laugh. "I had seen other ride this big wheel that rose high in the sky for many years and thought it looked like fun, but since this was the only ride here that climbed to the sky, I decided to give it a try."

"But, why did you make it stop at the top before it suddenly jerked and started down, scaring the daylights out of me? Surely your town has fairs? Why haven't you, ever rode a ride before now?" Marble walked quickly to catch up with his wide steps as Devin punched her arm.

"Marble, will you stop asking so many questions!" Devin could not understand anymore than his two friends but he knew something was different about this man, just like Ted, Jeffery and Jonathan. "We're just in the presence of a very special person who has been gifted with many gifts,"

"Well spoken, my fellow shepherd." Gabriel spotted his son and the rest of their group forming a long line at the food-filled table. "There's our family. Move quickly before the blessing is lifted up."

Spotting Mary standing beside her father and Martha behind them with her mother, Devin smiled to himself, thinking, "For someone just four-years- old, that gal is hot!"

"She looks rather cool to me in those shorts, Devin." Gab had read the youth's thoughts. "That little gal is still just a baby in her grandfather's eye." Devin paused to wonder how he could have read his thoughts and the young teen concluded this man was even more special than he thought.

"For this food Father, we give you thanks! For this drink Father, our thanks we give! For these friends both young and old, guide, protect, wherever they go! Feed our body, feed our soul, with love from thee, to one and all! Amen." Ted squeezed Jenny's hand when he heard her whisper. An instant poem. Smiling, he looked around at his large group.

"Stay together my ones. Get one plate, do not overfill it and move over to where Matthew is waving under the big oak trees. Our long picnic table has been sat up so listen to brother Matthew. He will tell you where to sit, now began."

The well-behaved group moved quickly down each side of the long food table, politely picking out things they liked. Ted had directed Miriam, Jonathan, Rachael and Andrew to go in front of the line to help guide the children, then take them over to relieve Matthew, so he could get in line with Kathy and Jonah.

The large group ate quietly, speaking in soft tones to those sitting beside them. Miriam had noticed how quiet Jonathan had become since he returned from speaking to Kris O'Donnell and decided to wait and ask him when they were alone. Gabriel relived his adventure riding the roller coaster to Ted and Jenny, and they couldn't resist smiling at each other seeing his childlike excitement. Ted had all the children and youth rest under the trees before doing anything else and informed them they had only a couple more hours before they had to load up and drive back up the mountain.

Jenny stretched and smiled over at a yawning Naomi. "I know how you feel Naomi. Days like this can always wear a person out."

"Yes, I suppose you're right." Naomi laughed softly after giving another yawn. "I guess I should be used to it after chasing two active boys around all day."

"And some times those boys can really make thing tiring for their parents, like this morning." Jeff looked over at his oldest son, who lay whispering to Mary.

"Teddy didn't want you to remove your painting, did he?" Ted

201

caught Jeff's attention. "Some times we must go against our wife's wishes, Jeff. Those paintings must be destroyed."

Naomi knew she had never gone against Ted's wishes, but her love for her husband was incredibly strong. "Ted, I just feel they are a part of Jeff, even if it was his past self that painted those horrible paintings. I am aware they show evil and I know they are despicable to look at, but none the less, it was his hand, the hand I love, that painted them."

"Sweet angel, no one doubts how much you love Jeff. I, of all people, can testify to the extent of this great love for him." Ted's eyes held hers lovingly, not with judgement. "These paintings can only bring harm to your family, like this morning, when Teddy Jeffery was angry at you for wanting to remove his painting. His hissing and hate fill words spilled from his young lips as though Satan himself had control of him."

"Ted is right sweet one. Those paintings do harm and they can lead to evil and bad things happening." Jeff gathered her hands in his. When I painted them. I was filled with so much hate, I could have and would have destroyed my own son for speaking out to me like he did. Those pictures tell a story, sweetheart, my life before I found love. Some people have a diary, I never wanted words, I wanted to see my work in front of me. They inspired me to seek out a victim and take their soul so I could paint the horror they had faced." Seeing her tears, Jeff clutched her in his arms. "Naomi, I need to destroy those paintings before the evil returns within them and takes over our son."

"Oh Jeff, what exactly was our son looking at? Was it a painting I had seen hanging in your room?" Naomi had refused to look to see which painting Teddy Jeffery had chosen to hang in front of his bed, then watch him hitting his father as he took it down and grab it away, holding it tight against his small chest.

Jeff noticed Ted's nod to go ahead. He looked down and closed his eyes, never wanting his beautiful wife to ever know about this one painting. Speaking just above a whisper, Jeff spoke. "The painting was of a naked woman, lying stretched out on my bed. Tears were flowing down her beautiful face while I raped her."

Naomi grabbed her mouth, hot tears stung her eyes as she tried to speak "Jeff, not...not"

"Yes, my love, it was you, the only woman I had to rape to have."

CHAPTER 39

"I just cannot believe Jonathan would actually give a seven-year-old boy a painting of his father raping his mother!" Jenny had taken a fresh shower and sat brushing her long chestnut hair. "What sort of man does something like that?"

"The son of Lucifer, Jenny." Ted had removed his clothes and was stretched out on their bed, his eyes shut, tired from the busy day.

"Speaking of Jonathan, what is going on between him and Aunt Kris?" Jenny glanced over at her husband resting, smiled at his handsome body, then climb in next to him. "Please don't tell me he's after her soul?"

"Then I won't tell you." Ted kept his eyes close and Jenny poked him, squinting when he kept them closed.

"Ted? Don't you dare go to sleep!" she waited until he cracked his eyes open and smiled. "What's up with Aunt Kris?"

"Kristine is in love with Jonathan." Ted reached over and pulled his wife in his arms. "Jonathan and your aunt have had sex, in his church bedroom."

"Had sex? In a church…bedroom?" Jenny sit up and hit Ted's arm. "Ted, churches do not have bedrooms, for God's sake!"

"No, not for God's sake, but for Jonathan's sake." Ted spoke sleepily as he kissed Jenny then slid down under the covers. "Now, go to sleep, Jenny."

"How can I sleep?" Jenny pulled at his arm. "How can you sleep?" once again Ted peeked open his tired eyes.

"Jenny, I can sleep because I'm tired. We had a busy day and it's getting late. We'll make love in the morning, darling."

"Oh? Suppose I will be too tired to make love in the morning, Mr. Neenam?" she pouted "Just go ahead and sleep! I will ask Jeff tomorrow."

"Jeff? Jenny, get serious." Ted tried to prop up and opened his weary eyes. "Very well, Jonathan is after Kristine's soul, but we won't let him have it. Besides, Kris has already walked away from him on her own." He yawned. "Your aunt is smart Jenny, just like you. Now, get some sleep. I'll see you when I return from the mountain in the morning."

"Hey husband! What about us making love in the morning?" Jenny looked down hurt.

"You said you would be too tired to make love in the morning, remember?" Ted rolled over and smiled to himself.

Jenny slapped him on the rear and stared down. "Ted Neenam, if you don't make love to me in the morning, I'll..." Ted rolled over and grabbed Jenny, then kissed her passionately.

"Why wait, Jenny! I'm wide awake now!" Hearing her beautiful laugh, Ted climbed over and made love.

Before as the day's events were winding down, Miriam had asked Jonathan if anything happened between him and Kris O'Donnell because of his being distant and distracted during the lunch. His hands collected hers as he tried to explain his emotions.

"Kristine is a beautiful person who has recently found a purpose for living after being traped inside a worn-out body, devoted entirely to her mother. Now, she has fallen in love with me but realizes my devotion to you, Miriam and knows you are the one my heart chose to marry." Jonathan's attention wondered down the path where they had met. "The good Christian woman knows she can never replace you, nor does she want to interfere with our happiness. Kristine is a very mature lady and faces defeat with her head up."

"How terribly sad Jonathan." Miriam clasped her hands together, her heart feeling real pity for Jenny's aunt. "I thought you were going to introduce her to a fine gentleman you knew. Someone more her age. She is a lot older than you are Jonathan."

"Miriam, you will learn when you get older, age is just a number." Jonathan's eyes held a tenderness the young woman had never seen in him. "There are many young men who fall for older women. Ted for instance. I could easily fall in love with someone older than me, even Kristine, if you had not already found that place in my heart."

"Oh Jonathan, I do love you very much." She reached up on her toes and kissed him, only this time, Jonathan did not return it as she would have liked. While Miriam was trying to sort this out in her mind, her thoughts were interrupted by a deeper voice.

"Jonathan, it appears you have not noticed those two wild teenagers you brought did not show up for the family meal." Jeff

The Lost Sheep

stood staring down at his brother. "I see you are preoccupied with your fiancé so I will go hunt them down."

Jonathan jumped to his feet, pulling Miriam up with him. "Never mind brother! Those kids are my responsibility. I'll find the little trouble makers and give them the proper punishment!"

"Nothing too harsh Jonathan!" Jeff's cold stare flashed a warning. "Remember, they're just stupid kids!"

Jonathan glanced down at a concern Miriam and forced a smile. "Don't let Jeffery's over exaggerated words worry you, my future wife. I intend them no harm. I will merely give misguided youth a good talking to and ground them for a week for misconduct." He kissed her hand. "To prove myself right, I am taking you with me. You may be of some help."

Blaze had walked around the outside of the rest rooms, sweating and wondering what had happened to Fire. Surely, she had enough sense not to run away, knowing Jonathan would find her and deal with her badly. Blaze had witness it before. The same man that took him in as a small boy and raised him, showing him so much love, had beat and tortured another girl and left her to die. Blaze never knew if the girl made it or died, he didn't dare go back and go against Jonathan. He had admired him when he was a good man and the sad thing was, he still felt loyalty to him.

As Blaze stared at the girl's bathroom sign, he felt the familiar strong hand on his shoulder. The frighten teen closed his eyes from the pain and spoke up. "Jonathan, I cannot find Fire anywhere."

"When did you last see the girl?" Jonathan had turned him around to face him. "Speak up boy!"

"She needed to use the lady's room sir. Fire has been using the toilet a lot lately, so I didn't think nothing of it." Blaze looked up helplessly. "We had just finished riding the roller coaster for the forth time and noticed it was time to head for the picnic tables." His eyes held sincerity as he said. "We were on our way to join you for the picnic Jonathan, and that's the truth."

"Calm down boy, I'm not mad with you." Jonathan released his tight grip as he turned to Miriam. "Dear, go in the lady's room and see if Fire is still in there. If not, see if there is another way out."

"Shit Jonathan, I never thought of that! Most of these public bathrooms have no windows, or very small high ones!" Blaze felt he had let Jonathan down, But, his worse fears were for the girl he

205

cared about. They waited only briefly before Miriam stepped back out shaking her head.

"She's not in there, sweetheart. I noticed a turned-up trash can had been pushed under an open window. If she's small enough to climb through, my guess would be, that's was how she escaped."

"Damn that bitch!" Jonathan's eyes blazed causing Miriam to step away, never seeing this side of Satan's son come out. "Fire will regret this treason! When I get my hands on her..." his attention fell on Miriam, shaking and wide-eyed. "Forgive me dearest, but these kids can really try my nerves sometimes." Jonathan tried to relax his voice, although he was still seething on the inside. "There are times, this cute little girl can make your heart sing, but other times, you'd like to beat her smart brat ass!"

"We will find her Jonathan. She couldn't have gotten far on foot." Still feeling unsure and nervous from his outburst, Miriam reluctantly took his hand and started back to the group. All she wanted was to get back to safety, to Ted.

Fire climbed out of the old truck and smiled at the nice old gentleman who had given her a ride part way up the mountain road. "This is where I turn around. I'm not good driving up that mountain road. I'm lucky I got this far up. Yep."

"Thank you again Mr. Evans." She glanced up the long road that climbed in front of her. "I appreciate you bringing me this far. I can make it the rest of the way on foot."

"If you sure now, Missy. You are young, so you got that going for you." Barnard smiled, always happy to help young people out. "You be sure to take the road on your right. The Christian home is just a few more miles up."

"Yes, I know." Fire checked her watch. She had two hours before everyone would be coming back. "I've walked this road a hundred times before Mr. Evans. Ted likes us to stay in shape, and walking up this hill is one of the best exercises around."

"You never did say why you left so early missy, all by yourself." He scratched his head. "Peers Ted would want his family to stay safe with him. You could find yourself face to face with a wild animal, if you veer off in the forest. Don't stray to the left, them wolves preying on Black Mountain might mistake you for supper."

"I have no intention of going in the forest Mr. Evans, right or left, just straight up the mountain road. I got permission to leave

206

early sir and Ted knew I was working on a special project and was dying to return home." She checked her watch nervously "I'm all grown up now, Mr. Evans and Ted trust me to keep my word."

"You kids are mighty lucky to have Ted, yes ma'am." Barnard cranked up the old truck and glanced up Black Mountain Road. "I hear there's trouble come back to Black Mountain. I sure do hope it's just a bad rumor. That young fellow Jeffery, just getting himself straightened out and finding that nice girl to marry from Ted's mountain. I thank God for Ted every day and night, sure do, for saving my daughter Holly from that evil castle."

"Whatever happened Mr. Evans, I'm glad Ted saved her, for you, sir and you're right about Jeffery and Naomi, they are a lovely couple." Fire knew time was ticking and she would barely make it up that mountain before anyone saw her. "I hate to rush off Mr. Evans, Ted and that loud bunch of kids will beat me back before I get one note wrote."

"Sure thing, missy. Sorry to have held you up." Mr. Evans waved, turned the truck around and headed back down the mountain to the main road.

Andrew and Thomas had remained on the mountain to watch the sheep, a job that needed doing around the clock. Besides the wolves that roamed the hills, mostly from the neighboring mountain, a mountain lion had been spotted by a neighboring mountain a few miles beyond the Blue Ridge. Ted had given both young men new sling shots and plenty of smooth small river rocks to fight off any danger. Ted had taught each shepherd well how to use the slingshots and had warned them that sometimes you only get one shot, like King David. Make it count.

"It sure is quiet out here this evening, Thomas. I wonder if the family is having a good time?" Andrew and Thomas had volunteered to watch the sheep so everyone could enjoy the fun day. Now, Andrew sat watching the hills in front of them as Thomas carried wood over for the fire later.

"I don't miss going to the fun day picnic. To be honest, I get sick riding most rides." Thomas sat down and pulled out one of the smooth stones and rolled it around in his hand. "Suppose we'll have to use these tonight, Andrew?"

"You never know Thomas. I thought…" Andrew sat up, head perked, ears straining as he listened for the faint sound he had heard in the distance. "Thomas, did you hear something?"

"Nope! Just the usual, baaing sheep." Looking at how tense his partner was, he lifted his head to listen and somewhere in the forest he heard the faint scream. "I heard it. Sounded like some sort of scream." Thomas' eyes grew wide, and showed a little fear. "Could it be that wild cat?"

"It is very possible Thomas, but I swear, I hear two different screams!" Andrew jumped up and grabbed his slingshot and bag of rocks. "Look Thomas, stay here with the sheep, keep watch. If its that mountain lion it could have another animal traped. I'll slip up on him, kill the devil before he spooks the sheep."

"Be careful Andrew, I don't like you going out alone." Thomas rose to his feet, slingshot in hand, ready to defend all the innocent sheep.

"Thomas, we've got our own guardian angel watching out for us. Remember what Ted said: If you feel danger you cannot escape, just whisper his name and he will come."

"Why whisper Andrew? Couldn't we yell it out?" Thomas tried to control his knees from knocking.

Andrew laughed, waved, then call over his shoulder. "I shouldn't be long Thomas. Don't worry, either way, I'll be back, with or without Ted walking beside me."

Fire stood still, frozen in her tracks, too afraid to move, too afraid to breath. Had she escaped the evil hands of Jonathan only to get traped by Satan himself. Would she die before Ted could save her and her tortured soul would burn forever in hell? Fire stared into the angry yellow eyes of her predator, his sharp threating teeth apparent with every devilish scream that it was his intent to attack her and eat her. Fire's heart pounded in fear, knowing it was just a matter of time before the wild cat would pounce on her and no one would hear her final screams out here in the forest. It would surely kill her then drag her body off and no one would ever know she had been eaten by this wild beast.

"Stand perfectly still!" Came the calm voice of a stranger. "No matter what you do, do not stare directly in that cat's eyes. Close your eyes now!" Andrew had found the source of the screams. "Now listen to me miss, that cat will make his move soon. I am ready to shoot him, so keep your eyes closed and pray."

"Pray?" Fire had never prayed before, at least not to God. This person standing close by was from Ted's mountain, so if the cat didn't kill her, she could still be saved from the evil that ran through her veins. "Just shoot! Please!" Fire whispered loudly, causing the big mountain lion to make it move. Andrew quickly released the stone from the sling, striking the big cat directly in its temple. It fell silent at her feet.

Fire opened her eyes and stared down at the large cat lying dead at her feet. Seeing the blood flowing out of its head, she wondered if she had been too scared to hear the gun go off. Taking a deep breath, Fire turned to face her hero.

"Are you alright miss?" Andrew had never seen a girl dressed like this one before. Her short shag hair hang loose around her pretty face and even in the late evening shadows, he could see her black lipstick and fingernails. Andrew noticed the pitchfork tattoo on her upper left arm and the black earring in her nose. "Are you lost, miss? The forest is no place to be wondering around, especially this late in the day."

"No, I'm not exactly lost, if this is Goldsburg Mountain." Her eyes fell on the slingshot in his hand. "Where is your gun? Don't tell me you used that primitive thing in your hand."

"It worked, didn't it?" Andrew could not understand this girl's criticism after he just saved her life. "If you must know miss, Ted does not allow guns at our home. There are too many young children living there."

"I'm sorry, I never meant to sound ungrateful." Fire checked out her rescuer and noticed the tall young man was really quite handsome. "Does my rescuer have a name?"

"Andrew Christian. I'm one of the oldest boys on the mountain." Andrew managed a smile at the unusual girl. "What do people call you?"

"My nickname is Fire. My birth name is Jasmine." Fire moved quickly away from the dead cat and walked over closer to Andrew. "I was actually making my way up your road when I heard a car approaching, so I ran into the woods to hide."

"Who are you running away from, Jasmine?" Andrew preferred her birth name over the evil sounding nick name.

"Can you keep a secret Andrew?" Fire needed time to think before facing Ted so she needed an ally to hide her.

"Jasmine, I'll be honest with you. I will be your friend and help

209

you anyway I can, but I will never keep any secrets from Ted, not ever." Andrew could sense the girl was deathly afraid of something besides the mountain lion. "Let me help you."

"You ask to help me, yet you cannot keep my secret!" Fire studied Andrew and saw only sincerity.

"Jasmine, even if I thought your secret was something I felt I could keep, I still couldn't." the young man knew Ted was capable of reading thoughts and he would know what it was as soon as he saw him.

"Why not, for God's sake? Does Ted demand you tell him everything you know?" Her heart beat with uncertainty. Maybe this Ted was no different from Jonathan. After all, Jeffery was his best friend.

"No miss, Ted does not demand anything of us. He is the absolute best man you have ever met and you will grow to love him instantly." Andrew knew the girl was confused. "The truth is, Ted knows things before they happen. He is capable of reading your thoughts. This loving man has been gifted by God Himself, with powers far greater than Jeff's or Jonathan's. And his love is so overflowing, when he looks at you or gives you a touch, you can feel his warm radiant love penetrate your entire being."

"Feel love instead of lust?" Fire spoke softly, mostly to herself as she continued. "Blackheart can do many of those things you speak of, only his look and touch make you feel seductive."

"Jasmine, you came to see Ted, didn't you?" Andrew took her shaking hand. "God led you to this mountain. You heard Ted speak and you felt his love."

"Andrew?" He saw a different appearance on this strange girl's face. No longer defiant, but one of sadness and loss.

"If I don't get help soon, it will be too late for me." Fresh tears came in her eyes.

"Are you in some sort of danger Jasmine?" Andrew felt her hand tremble "Has someone threatened you?"

"I have been threatened Andrew, but I'm my worse enemy." Now the tears ran down her pretty face. "Blackheart has won my body and soul! I have sex like some sixteen-year-olds have pimples and collect CD's! I've aborted a baby because Blackheart hates children! I lust for his sexual body no matter how bad he hurts me!" Jasmine knew her strong words of admission had shocked this decent young man to silence. "The truth for me is, if I do not turn around right now, Satan will win and I'll burn in hell!" She fell into his arms weeping.

"Jasmine, it's not too late to change. It's never to late to ask for forgiveness." Andrew's strong arms held her protectively. "Ted will help you. He can show you how to save your soul. As long as you are living and breathing, this Blackheart will not have you!"

Jasmine pulled away gently to look into his caring eyes and she knew she could trust Andrew Christian and for the first time in her life, Jasmine felt safe.

CHAPTER 40

Kristine O'Donnell opened the door to welcome Jenny and Ted, who she had called to come by for a favor. Jenny gave her aunt a hug before standing back to admire the changed woman.

Aunt Kris, I just cannot get over how you have changed. I never realized how much we resemble each other. It's amazing."

"It is truly amazing, Jenny. I honestly feel pretty, young and alive for the first time in too many years to count." Kristine gave the loving couple her beautiful smile before approaching Ted. "I am aware you know about me and Jonathan, Ted. I suppose I should feel a shame or at least ridiculous for behaving the way I did, after preaching against women who openly had sex with a man they hardly knew. To be honest, something wonderful was happening inside my warn-out dead body. I learned I could still fall in love and it brought me back to life."

"My dear Kris, I have no intentions of being your judge or condemning your actions." Ted's face held sincerity. "I am certain if Jonathan had been married, you would have refused his advances toward you, no matter how he made you feel."

"Heavens no! I have my limits." She blushed. "I found it hard enough knowing he had a fiancé and even harder when I learned who she was."

"Kris, do you know what sort of man Jonathan Wineworth really is?" Ted knew Jenny's aunt had believed Jonathan when he claimed to be a minister at a reliable Christian church and she did not really know much else about him. Ted knew it would hurt Kristine deeply if he revealed this man's true identity.

Kris motioned to the sofa and took the single chair facing it. "To be honest Ted, I really don't know much about Jonathan. The one thing I do know is no matter what sort of person he is, Jonathan truly saved my life, whether it was intentional or not."

"Kristine, there was a time in Jonathan's life he could have shown true love to a lady." Ted reached over to take her hand, filling her with perfect love and peace. "Jonathan is not the same man that followed his heart into the ministry. The heart that once held love,

212

now holds only hate. The man who once had passion now has lust."

"Can you explain why it doesn't feel like lust when I'm in his arms." Kris closed her eyes and pictured his handsome face looking down at her, making her feel beautiful. "I only saw warmth in his eyes and a gentle passionate man who thought of my needs."

Ted remained calm and patient with the diligent woman. "You only had sex with Jonathan one time, correct? Another encounter with him might not have been so pleasing, Kristine."

"Then I guess I will never know what Jonathan is really like. It's over! Our brief beautiful affair is over." Tears filled her eyes as she got up and walked to the window to peer out. "Jonathan may be as evil as you say, but he respects you enough not to jeopardize his marriage to Miriam. He told me as much when I ask for just one more night with him. It might have been selfish of me. But I was in hopes of him letting Miriam go and loving me instead." The big drops fell off her face. "I know how desperate that sounds, my darlings, but God help me, I just love him so much."

Ted got up and moved to the window to put his arm around her trembling shoulders. "It's far better to let him go now Kristine. Not for Miriam's sake, she got herself involved too deep. God only knows if I will let Jonathan marry her. It is for your own sake, Kristine, to make a clean break from Jonathan. Unless we get the miracle, I'm praying for, Jonathan will remain forever incapable of falling in love."

"That makes my decision to leave Goldsburg an even better ideal." Kris reached for Jenny's hand when she noticed her sad reaction to her announcement. "That's the main reason I called you both over today. It will be hard leaving mother. I've been by her side so long." Now both aunt and niece were crying as Jenny reached for the tissues and past one to her aunt. "Jenny, I took the liberty to write your mother. I thought it best, for mother's sake and yours darling."

"Aunt Kris, mother has been gone for so many years, I'm quite certain she would just as soon forget we ever existed." Jenny felt numb with the sudden revelations. "How on earth did you find her?" Jenny had not seen or heard from her mother since she was twelve-years-old, leaving her with her dear daddy for another man. "Aunt Kris, you were so angry with mama, you didn't ever want me to bring up her name when I visited."

"I was quite angry with my sister-n-law. She did you wrong

213

Joan Byrd

child, running off like that, leaving poor Michael for some man she met while working in the bank. She same as killed my precious brother by breaking his heart." Kris pulled out a small stack of letters from the desk and waved them in the air. "Your mother sent these letter to me and mother in the past three years. I am hoping she is at the same address."

Jenny stared at the pink stationary in her aunt's hand and noticed the name on the return address, O'Donnell. "Aunt Kris, didn't mama ever marry that man she ran away with?"

"Your mother always went by O'Donnell, Jenny." Kristine looked sad. "I believe she regret leaving your father but was too ashamed to come back after making such a rash decision. After finding out Michael had passed away at such an early age, I believe Lisa always blamed herself. I found out years later, all those flowers that secretly appeared on his grave for his birthday, Easter, Thanksgiving, and Christmas, came from Lisa. She still loved him and I could say without a doubt, she always will."

"Daddy was the very best, Aunt Kris, but such a sad man after mama left. I would hear him crying at night and I didn't know how to fix his broken heart." Jenny felt her heart breaking just remembering her sad daddy. "I tried to fill that empty place in his broken heart, but no matter how much he loved me, and that was a lot, he just loved her so much more."

"Jenny, my darling, this is why you never spoke of your parents to me." Ted pulled her up into his arms. "Yes Jenny, your devoted father died a broken man, but he sings with the angels in heaven this very day."

"If I could only see him happy and singing as you describe instead of remembering him trying to make me feel wanted and happy while he suffered the loss of the one he loved so much." Jenny hugged him tightly, taking in his incredible love. "I can almost see him now surrounded by powerful love, thanks to you Ted." She kissed him before turning to her aunt. "Kris, where are you planning to go? We love you and wished you would remain with the family."

"I love all of you as well, Jenny darling and I promise, it won't be forever." Kristine reached over to pat her niece's cheek. "I need to get away from Jonathan and my feelings for him. I need time to think and find myself."

214

The Lost Sheep

"You made the right judgement to leave Goldsburg Kristine. You are not safe here." Ted took hold of her arms. "Kristine, if Jonathan desires you, he will find you and you will give in to him. You are not the only one, Miriam is not the only one, Jonathan Wineworth has many women and young girls under his spell. Leaving will set you free of him, but you must not go alone. I will send another victim of his with you. Until then, you and your mother will come and stay with us on the mountain."

"But Ted..." before Kris could speak, Ted continued.

"You are not safe no matter where you had planned to go? Jonathan can and will track you down, like a wolf. Do you trust me, Kristine?"

"With my life Ted." She smiled. "I will speak to mother immediately about moving to the mountain for a while."

Jeff walked in his brother's room and noticed him sitting quietly staring out the window. "Is there no sign of the girl, brother?" Jeff was aware Fire was safe on Ted's mountain, but kept his thoughts hidden from Jonathan.

"She's someplace close, I can sense her near." He continued to stare ahead as if he was lost in thought. "I have taught her well. Fire has blocked out my power to find her. She will live to regret her behavior."

"That sounds like a threat Jonathan." Jeff remained calm as he stood observing his brother's strange behavior. "Do you intend to torture the misfortunate young lady?"

"Torture the girl?" Jonathan laughed out. "That is your behavior brother, not mind. Fire has earned certain privileges that she worked for. I will simply take them away." He finally turned to look at his brother and Jeff thought he noticed sadness in the usual cold dark eyes. "I'm worried about Kristine. I must call and check on her." Jonathan picked up the phone and dialed her home number.

"It was my understanding Miss O'Donnell moved on." Jeff also knew his brother would have no way of knowing Kristine and her mother had moved in with Ted and Jenny and if he tried to call her, he wouldn't get an answer.

Looking puzzled, Jonathan hung up the receiver. "That's funny, no answer. It's still early in the day. An unusual time for those two women to be gone off somewhere."

"Why is that Jonathan? They could have gone shopping or been invited to a friend's house for breakfast." Jeff parted his lips in a smile. "Do you think Kristine and Bessie are just plain home bodies and outside that, they don't have a life?"

"I suppose you're right." Jonathan tried the number again, letting it ring ten times before hanging up. "I just need to talk to her."

"Is there something more going on with you concerning that woman, Jonathan?" Jeff read real emotion in his brother's eyes. "Are you having real feeling for Kristine? You can be honest with me Jonathan, I have no intention of running to father and telling him."

"Kristine is a special lady and I am very fond of her." Jonathan tried to avoid looking at his brother. "Nothing more."

"Sometimes love sneaks up on you Jonathan when it's the last thing you're looking for, like it did with me, when I came upon Naomi who had mistakenly crossed over into my forest." Jeff laid his hand on his brother's back, and with love in his eyes, spoke to Jonathan. "Jonathan, if it's love you feel for Kristine, don't let father take it away from you. No matter how loyal you are to Lucifer, don't ever count on getting any in return. He will only use you to gain for himself, the only one he really cares about."

"If it were only that easy Jeff. To betray father will destroy me, not that I ever would. He lost faith in you because you turned from him, but I will prove to be the loyal son." Jonathan looked away. "There is nothing more to discuss."

"Then shouldn't you be calling your fiancé instead of Kristine." Jeff knew Jonathan was just using Miriam to win her soul and really cared nothing about her.

"I will go visit my beloved later this afternoon." Jonathan walked passed Jeff to the door. "I'm off for a walk to clear my mind and in return, find out where Fire is hiding."

"Then, good luck finding her. And Jonathan..." Jonathan paused, eyes straight ahead as he mumbled 'what'? "I love you, brother." Closing his eyes to block out the tears he felt coming, Jonathan walked quickly from the castle, Jeff staring after him from the window where he disappeared in the thick woods, Destiny at his heels. "I will get word to Ted. He must move swiftly!"

CHAPTER 41

Ted had left Jenny talking to her aunt and grandmother and they had agreed Kris must get away from Jonathan and Bessie would remain at the white farmhouse with Ted and Jenny as long as things below were unsettled. No one knew for certain if Jenny's mother, would show up in Goldsburg, but if she did, Lisa O'Donnell would have to face everyone on the mountain.

Ted spotted John and Simon, who had taken over for Andrew and Thomas, and had kept the night watch. Both young shepherds saw Ted coming and smiled at one another, knowing their long shift was over. "A job well done, my sons. All looks quiet and peaceful since brother Andrew killed the mountain lion before you took over."

"Very peaceful Ted. Only the usual howls from Black Mountain." John, lend on his staff. "There was a full moon after all."

"We were happy to hear about Andrew killing the big cat, just a quarter of a mile up the path." Simon always had a happy smile on his freckled face. "I really enjoyed watching the sunrise over the mountain tops this morning after the scary events last night."

"I haven't spoke to Andrew about his brave hunt, but he returns to shepherd the sheep soon. I'll catch up." Ted patted their backs. "Meanwhile you boys run along home, wash up and have your breakfast before you get some well needed rest. I'll stay with the sheep."

The two weary shepherds laid down their staffs and headed for the farmhouse as Ted gazed out at the gentle sheep, up and grazing, their young lambs nursing. Feeling a familiar presence behind him, Ted smiled. "Father, it's a beautiful morning up on the mountain and there's nothing more peaceful than sheep grazing on the hillside." Their eyes met in a loving twinkle. "Please, join me."

Gabriel took the tallest staff and sat down next to his son. "So, you wait for Andrew and the lost runaway girl."

"They are just beyond those trees watching us." Ted rubbed the smooth wooden handle.

217

"They took refuged in the barn last night. The girl, Jasmine, is nervous about meeting you again." Gabriel had been watching his son rubbed the wood and followed his lead. "Yes, very smooth wood, the work of a fine carpenter. Your work, Ted?"

"I cannot take the credit for the workmanship we hold, father. Andrew is quite skilled in wood carving, as well as carpentry work." Ted smiled up at Gabriel. "Just like our brother."

"Indeed! Jesus was a very gifted carpenter. Joseph taught him well." Gabriel looked up with reverence "But Jesus was an even better son. He was born a King and He died a Savior."

"And this is what we must share with Jasmine, if she is to be saved." Ted stood up and called out. "Andrew, you and Jasmine may come out now. She has had time to prepare. We must speak to her now."

The young couple walked out from hiding, Jasmine looking from Ted to Gabriel and seeing their strong resemblance. She trembled at the radiant light that ingulfed them as they stood looking down at her. Moving even closer to Andrew, she whispered. "Andrew, they seemed to know I was here and knew we where hiding in the woods watching."

"Just as I told you Jasmine, you cannot hide anything from Ted. You have nothing to be afraid of, he only wants to help you."

She looked up into Andrew's peaceful eyes, still clutching his hand tightly. "You will stay with me, won't you? You won't leave me alone with these angelic men?"

"I'll be right here Jasmine. I'm your friend, remember? I'm not going anywhere, I promise." Andrew took her over to where the two angelic men had sit back down, waiting patiently.

"Ted, you know what Jasmine has done, everything under Jonathan's teaching. She has come so you can help her."

"Yes son, this I know from the moment we spoke at the fun day picnic." Ted stood again and took Jasmine's hand from Andrew. "I will help you child. Gab and I are here to turn your evil into good." Ted looked at Andrew and smiled for his faithfulness. "Andrew, you are a strong and faithful son. Not once did you touch this girl inappropriately, even though you lay next to her all night." Ted touched his hand tenderly. "For this, I am proud."

"Jasmine, you have tempted a great many men, including me and in front of my wife with no thought of her feelings." Jasmine looked down, embarrassed, knowing Ted knew her well.

"I admit I did try to tempt you. I lusted for your body, it's true, just like I did Jonathan's. The only difference was, Jonathan had me many times, even the day he was coming here to ask for Miriam's hand."

"I know child. Jonathan has many women under his spell." Jasmine could see only love flowing from this man in front of her. "You never had a real childhood, Jasmine. Your own father molested you when you turned seven and he continued molesting you until you ran away from home at fifteen."

"I...I always blamed myself, thought it was my fault that he molested me." Tears swelled in her green eyes. "He told me it was his way of loving me, only, it never felt like love."

Gabriel walked over and placed his arm around her trembling shoulders. "I recall your mother was no help to you. She was an alcoholic and abusive in her own way. When your father wasn't raping you, she was beating you, probably because she was jealous your father chose you over her, when he didn't pay for prostitutes."

Jasmine stared at both men, each knowing everything about her past. The tears flooded down her cheeks, mixed with the black eye shadow. "I...I guess you know I've been with so many men, I've loss count. I got pregnant with Jonathan's baby and had it aborted! I pretended I was doing it for him, but the truth was, I didn't want to see the kid abused or raped! It was better off dead than being around Jonathan!" Jasmine broke down and started weeping. "I often wished I would die, but then I learn the truth! I wouldn't die, I would burn for eternity in hell!"

Ted held the sobbing girl in his loving arms and instantly she felt a peace and love unlike anything she had ever known, other than the talk she had with Ted the day before. "Jasmine, it's not too late to live your eternity in heaven. All you must do is believe." Ted knew good had won this young girl's heart.

"Tell me Ted, please, I want to live! I want to love! And, I want to go to heaven!" she looked up with hope on her face.

"Jonathan has told you he has won your body and soul, correct?" Ted waited.

"Yes Ted, I'm afraid I gave them willingly to him." Jasmine suddenly felt a burst of fear. "Is it too late for me?"

"Jonathan is a strong disciple of Satan, even though he has yet

219

to give you to Lucifer as an offering." Ted looked serious. "Should Jonathan get hold on you now, he would do just that, for your punishment in betraying him."

"That is why you must find salvation now, young one, and be sent far away where you will be safe from Jonathan and even Satan." Gabriel joined in, looking around after sensing someone approaching.

"It's Jeff! He brings a warning!" Ted looked down when Jasmine grabbed his arm.

"Jeffery Wineworth is working with you?" Fire looked up, confused over this revelation. "But, he's Jonathan's evil twin brother! I've seen his paintings!"

"Jeff was ten-times more-evil than his brother not so long ago, Jasmine, but love found its way in his black heart and now, Jeff is a child of God's, not Lucifer's." Ted had been watching Jeff move quickly toward him from the dark forest.

"A warning my friend." Jeff glanced down at the girl in trouble. "Jonathan is now in the woods behind me searching for this runaway. He means to do her harm, if he gets control of her!" he turned back to Ted. "My foolish brother has no ideal I am the one who controls the wolves on Black Mountain and even now his not-so-trusted companion is leading him in circles. But this jester has only stalled for more time. Jonathan has plans to visit Miriam this afternoon and not only this girl will be in danger, but also Jenny's aunt. My brother has been searching for her. Jonathan has an uncontrollable desire to see her. He tried phoning her twice and was obviously upset when he did not reach her."

"Thank you for the warning, my brother." Ted reached up to hug him. "Be off with your wife and sons. I will be sending Jasmine and Kristine to a safe place soon."

Jeff turned to the frightened teenager and smiled warmly. "Jasmine, trust Ted. He will save your soul. If he could save me, Ted can save anyone through our Lord Jesus."

Jasmine could see the love on Jeffery Wineworth's face for the first time and her uncertainty melted away. It had to be the same way Blaze felt when he had first met Jonathan before he turned to evil. "My heart burns to know the truth Jeffery! My hope has been built even higher because of your testimony. Thank you!" Feeling free for the first time, Jasmine closed her eyes and gave the tall-dark-handsome man a hug and felt only warm Christian love. When she opened her eyes, Jeff had vanished and Jasmine found herself seated in a grassy spot with Ted and Gabriel.

"Jasmine, Jeff mentioned anyone could be saved through Jesus, our Lord. Have you ever heard anything about Jesus, the Son of God?" Ted, spoke in soft tones.

"I have heard this name mentioned in Jonathan's sermons when we have visitors at Sunday services. He preaches more on the cult and acts of Lucifer with the members." The girl pulled her hands in her lap.

Suddenly ashamed of the black fingernails, she hid them. "I would like to hear more about this Jesus."

"God, the Father and Holy Creator of everything, even the fallen angel Lucifer, you have been worshiping, has one son. His name is Jesus. Jesus and the Father are one with the Holy Spirit, and they have been around since the beginning. They saw their first human creation, Adam, and Eve, fall to temptation, and committed the first sin constructed by Satan. The wages of sin, is death, so no one born of Adam and Eve, were free of sin. Now, God loved his children on earth so much, He knew the only way to save them was to be the perfect sacrifice, the lamb without blemish and carry our sins on the cross. to die, once and for all. So, Jesus, the Son of God, was born of a virgin, grew in wisdom, knowing His purpose for coming to earth and doing His Father's will, teaching and healing along the way to the cross, where He suffered, died and was buried. On the third day, as it began to dawn, Jesus, the Son of God, arose from the grave and forty days later, ascended into heaven, King of Kings and the Savior of the world." Ted reached for her hidden hands and she noticed the polish had vanished.

"Jasmine, Jesus, our Savior died for everyone born on this earth, starting with Adam and Eve. He died for you. All you have to do child, is to believe that Jesus is the Son of God and your Savior. Believe that He died for all your sins and confess those sins to him and ask for His forgiveness, then walk in the Light of the Lord forever and you shall inherit eternal life in heaven with Him."

With great drops of tears, Jasmine knelt down and spoke in broken sobs. "Lord Jesus, you sacrificed so much for all of us! For me! I can never repay you but I can give you my love and follow your light. Please forgive all my many sins Lord Jesus. Wash me whiter than bleach! Take the darkness from me and replace it with your light! I believe, with all my heart, that you are the Son of God, King of Kings and Lord of Lords! Jesus, I know you are truly my Savior and that you died for me! Never before have I felt so at peace from the joy of finally knowing you." Jasmine felt the wind blowing gently around her, whispering 'All is well with your soul, sweet child.', then she felt the love from two hands that lifted her up and she knew she had been saved.

"Now we get Kristine and you out of Goldsburg to safety." Ted hurried past Andrew, Jasmine at his side.

"You don't need to take anything with you. God will provide." Ted had called Kristine to join him and Jasmine. "You will be safe with Rubin and when its safe, he will know to bring you back home."

"Won't they be seen going down the mountain road?" Bessie was nervous for her daughter.

"Rubin won't be taking these ladies by conventional means, Bessie. Where they will be going does not require transportation." Ted didn't have time to explain. "You need to trust me."

"Grams, just tell Kris goodbye." Jenny gave her confused grandmother a hug. "Ted knows what he's doing."

"Yes, you're right, I'm sure." Bessie hugged her daughter tightly. "Just do as Ted says dear and I hope things are better real soon."

"Goodbye mother. I feel good about you living here with Jenny and Ted while I'm away. I suppose I won't be able to write you where we're going." Kristine felt strange leaving without her handbag, but she trusted Ted's judgement.

A tall dark-hair man appeared sporting a smart beard and mustache, and bowed gracefully in front of women. "Ladies, this is Rubin. He will take you someplace Jonathan will never find you and where you will be safe even from Lucifer." Ted smiled at the tall warrior angel dressed in jeans. "Are you ready for your assignment, my brother?"

"Most certainly Ted. These two lovely ladies will be as safe as a babe in our Savior's blessed arms." Rubin's smile was brilliant and friendly, helping both Kristine and Jasmine relax. He held opened his arms. "One on either side, please." After the trusting women followed his instructions, Rubin gathered them securely to his side. "Now, this is very important. Close your eyes and do not open them until I give you the go ahead, understand?"

Both ladies smiled one last time at those watching and shut their eyes tightly. Giving a wink to Ted, Jenny, and Bessie, Rubin disappeared with the two trusting girls, just as Ted heard the approaching car coming up their drive. Jonathan had arrived.

CHAPTER 42

Jonathan barely remembered driving up the mountain road from town. Unable to keep Kristine off his mind, Jonathan had doubled back to the castle to get his car, then drove down to the picture card house in hopes of finding Kristine home. He could not understand the uncertain feelings he was having, but no matter how hard he tried, Jonathan couldn't get the beautiful woman off his mind.

Finding no one at home, after repeated knocking, Jonathan climbed back inside the car and noticed his reflection in the rearview mirror. He wasn't prepared for the sad, rejected person looking back. "Snap out of it Jonathan!" He mumbled to himself. "What is wrong with me?" He closed his eyes, seeing her sad face looking up at him and hearing her words to him.

"Jonathan? I do love you. I suppose I always will." Still, with his dark eyes shut, Jonathan could see her tears flowing down her face. "I felt so complete, so happy with you. I guess I was hoping you had fallen in love with me too, would have broken off your engagement to Miriam for me."

Jonathan shook his head, trying to get Kristine out of his thoughts. "You are just getting soft! Father would not be please with these actions!" Jonathan spoke to himself as he cut on the motor. "I'll go visit that ex-virgin hottie. That should make me feel better." Only he didn't feel better, because all the way up the mountain he kept hearing Kristine's voice.

"If the man you know is a good Christian man, Jonathan, not married and respects me. If this man doesn't expect me to go to bed with him just because I chose to with you, then, I will meet him."

"Maybe Kristine is up on the mountain with Jenny and Ted. He has the gift to block my mind of where she is." He, thought back to the male choice he made for Kristine. "I could never let Bill Baxter anywhere near Kristine. That sex maniac would have stooped to raping her if she refused him!" Jonathan saw the farmhouse come into view.

"Oh Kristine, why didn't I listen to you! Take you into my arms while I could!" Jonathan swallowed, remembering her longing for him to make love to her.

The Lost Sheep

"Jonathan, as before, you are still not married. Could one more time hurt?"

Jonathan couldn't control his tears from falling, as he thought back to his answer. "Why did I tell you about Ted? Why, Kristine? It changed everything!"

"Ted knows about us? But how? Surely you didn't tell him, Jonathan?"

"I could see the change come over you darling Kristine and hear it from your enchanting lips I could never get enough kisses from."

"Jonathan, you're right about us parting and putting an end to this relationship."

"Kristine, my Kristine, what have I done to us?" Jonathan put his head down on the stirring wheel and cried.

Ted had watched Jonathan relive his last moments with Kristine and after seeing the great emotion of sadness and regret, he felt there may be more hope for this man than he thought possible.

"There is nothing impossible for me, my son." The wind blew gently in the loving man's ear. "My son Jonathan has gone astray and has lost his way. Bring back my parable son! Bring him back into the fold that will graze on my right side."

"Lord, it will take time and once again Lucifer will interfere to put up his best defense to keep control of his first born. But, knowing truth and love will prevail, we will defeat our foe and win back as many of the lost sheep that Satan tried to steal from you, Holy One!"

"As always, wise beyond your years." The voice grew softer as the breeze began to blow it upward. "I will be with you Ted, each step of the way."

Ted slowly opened the car door and touched Jonathan's shoulder, causing him to jerk his head up, eyes wet from crying. "Jonathan, I can see into your heart. You are on your way back to us but the journey won't be smooth. But for now, we shall speak no more of this, so welcome to our mountain."

Jonathan wiped his eyes, shook his head and climbed out to stretch. "I'm just tired Ted. Tired of waiting to be married. Tired of the ungrateful teenager who ran off after I saved her from the streets and gave her a home. And I'm tired of friends disappearing when you need them most."

"If your choice is still Miriam, then you must wait. As for

225

Jasmine and Kristine, they have moved on." Ted began walking toward the house as Jonathan reluctantly followed. "Cheer up Jonathan, you still have your brother Jeff and that other kid, Blaze, not to mention your growing congregation of followers."

"Of course, I suppose I'm still doing alright. My committed followers are loyal and never miss a Sunday sermon. We understand each other." Jonathan mumbled when he spotted Miriam walking toward him. He knew her love belonged to him but it was Kristine he could not stop thinking about.

A sky as pure as the air that surrounded the extra tall trees, breathtaking flowers of every color to match the perfect rainbow that danced through the clouds. Great groups of angelic men and women, walking back and forth, happily doing what appeared to be work but from their happy faces and smiles they gave to the new comers, it looked more like entertaining fun.

"Where exactly are we Rubin?" Kris O'Donnell looked around at the beautiful island, laden with fruit trees of a variety of different fruits. Flowers that gave off the most enchanting aromas she had ever smelled, especially one type of flower which grew large and white and a smell remarkable. "I can't ever recall seeing anything this lovely before. The flower lover I am, I can recognize many different kinds, only these are all perfect, not one single dead bloom. And the unusual white flower growing under a canopy of low growing vines, has the most beautiful fragrance I have ever experienced. It smells like"

"Heaven!" Rubin beamed. "You want find the Cornacopia on the earth, except in the Garden of Eden, the only place on earth like heaven. A few gifted people can smell the flower when the veil is opened."

"Rubin, I have heard there a people who can smell heaven around a love one who is about to die." Jasmine looked thoughtful, not sure what he meant, unless she and Kristine were actually in the Garden of Eden. Surely, he couldn't mean heaven. She reached down and picked a beautiful lavender flower and smelled it. "Mumm, this has a great scent. What do you call this flower?"

"That dear girl, is a Florasettia, one of the islands most fragrant blooms. The reason certain people smell the Cornacopia when a loved one is near death, is because the veil of heaven is opening for their souls to be brought up." Rubin took a deep breath and his jeans became a white dazzling robe. Both women stared in disbelief as the angel pointed to another flower. "The green and purple flower growing out of the rocks are called, soulpopulus."

"Rubin, a moment ago you had on jeans! Now you are wearing a very bright robe!" Jasmine nervously dropped the flower in her hand and it took root immediately. "Hey, how did that flower replant itself?"

"Nothing dies here Jasmine! And Kristine, that is why you don't see any dead blooms." Rubin laughed. "You may certainly pick any fruit from any tree and eat it, but when you throw down the seed, it will attach itself back on its tree as a live fruit again. This is a place of eternal life!" Rubin smiled down at both women, staring up in disbelief. "More proof ladies? Kristine, you had on a lovely blue jumpsuit when we arrived and Jasmine, you had on jeans and some kind of funky t-shirt." He chuckled when they looked down and found they too had on white robes.

"But how and when did that happen?" Kristine's eyes were wide with wonder. "Tell me I'm dreaming! Surely, this cannot be real."

"Kristine, if you are dreaming, then explain to me why I am having the exact same dream?" Jasmine stared over at her traveling companion helplessly. "Who exactly did you say you were, Rubin?"

"I didn't say. For if I had you would not have believed me." He snapped his fingers and instantly two angels appeared next to them. "Jasper and Eileen, these are the special guest you were told about. They will be in our care for a while until such time young Ted calls them back for their safe return."

"It must have been the hand of Lucifer if the Creator sent them to find refuge on our island." Jasper looked over at the two tongue-tied women. "Quiet for women. My female ward was always wound up, chatting over any and all sorts of things. The shock of being in a new place can put the spark out of a Fire!" His eyes twinkled at Jasmine.

"Mine wasn't much quieter and used to be worse. The forever know-it all. Nag- nag-nag!" Eileen smiled at Kristine. "Again, our Ted saved her and you can see, she found true love."

"Yes brother, it shows on her face." Rubin reached for Kris's hand. "Unfortunately, dear child, it was not to be easy."

"The three of you have been referring to me and Jasmine." Kris O'Donnell was afraid to hear the answer to her next question, but it had to be asked. "It appears Eileen knows me well and Jasper knows everything about Jasmine." She swallowed. "Are you our guardian angels?"

"Guardian angels? Kristine, these people will think we have gone over the cliff or something believing them to be our guardian angels!" Jasmine knew something was totally different in this place but she wasn't sure she needed to know who or what these beings were.

Pulling Jasmine around to face her, Kris tried to block out the fact that no matter how low she whispered, these beings could hear her. "Jasmine, Rubin took around us as we stood in the farmhouse, he told us to close our eyes and seconds later we were standing in paradise. We had nothing with us and I recall Ted saying the Lord would provide and here we are wearing white robes, just like everyone else here. These three robe beings know everything about us so they have to be angels! I find peace in knowing this, so" Kris face the three waiting. "Are you angels?"

"I am Eileen, your guardian angel Kristine. You were always a hand full but cute as a pattlewag!" seeing her questioning eyes, the angel laughed. "I forgot, there is no pattlewag's on earth. It's a cross between a white rabbit and a blue bird. Sweet and cute, just like my little Krissy was at one and two. I remember the time you almost fell in your neighbors well when you didn't listen to your mother's warning about playing in the Conner's yard."

"Oh Gosh! I forgot about that!" Kristine blushed. "I was six, stubborn as a mule, never listen and always had to do things my way. I remember tripping and falling down inside the dark well, when suddenly I felt strong hands grab me and lifting me up toward the sunlight." She looked up into her angel's beautiful face. "You saved me! I heard you say my name and my fear turned to joy."

"Yes child, the creator wasn't finished with you living. He loves you as he does all his children." She smiled as she hugged Kristine. "I love you too, little Krissy."

"If Eileen is Kristine's guardian, then you must be mine, Jasper." Jasmine felt small and helpless, looking at the one who had watched her doing so many bad things. As tears swelled in her eyes, she choked out her words. "You saw every bad thing I did!"

"Jasmine, I have never judge you child. My place is to show you love." Jasper placed a loving arm around her trembling shoulders. "It broke my heart to watch your own father rape you and your mother mistreat her own child. It came as no surprise that Jonathan won you so easily."

"Jasper, would you have let that mountain lion eat me that evening in the dark woods?" she had to ask after hearing Kristine had been saved from drowning in the deep well.

"No child and I was about to distract the big cat when the young shepherd came up to help you. I noticed his angel kept him calm and helped his aim, just like he did for King David. I helped you a great many times, mostly when you were small or your father would have tried to get you even sooner than he did. Most recently, on the roller coaster, when Jonathan assumed he had jinxed the seat you were riding in, but I held it secure, knowing you had heard Ted and felt the message he could bring you and save your soul from eternal fire."

"I can recall how you stopped my daddy from molesting me when I was only three and four. At three, you sort of tripped him causing him to fall and break his legs when he was coming in my room. At four, before he could touch me, a recruit officer showed up at the front door and ordered him to enlist in the army immediately. I was safe for two more years while he was gone and mama didn't start drinking until she caught him molesting me."

"Three-year-old? Her father tried to rape his own child at three?" Kristine turned white as she turned to the angel that brought them to this peaceful place. "Rubin, just, where are we?"

"This is Angel Island, the homeplace of all God's angels in heaven." Rubin smiled, standing heads above the other two angels. "I am a warrior angel, usually a lot taller but came down a few feet to help you get up here. We are on duty all the time to fight our fallen comrades, Lucifer and those brothers who followed him, from trying to re-enter heaven. We are in constant need to help humans, like yourselves, from entering into Lucifer's web and that includes your Jonathan."

CHAPTER 43

Miriam sat quietly, looking at the man sitting next to her. He had hardly spoken three short sentences since he arrived at the home. She could tell his mind was miles away and Miriam knew in her heart, Jonathan was not thinking about her but another woman he thought more about. As she studied his face, Miriam realized she hardly knew Jonathan and she began to question her feelings for him. Was what she assumed to be love was only lust? Had Jonathan really put her into some kind of a romantic trance, just like Esther described and warned her about. Then her eyes caught movement in the rose garden, just outside the living room window. Miriam's heart fell when she spotted Robert, her Robert, kissing Esther.

"Did I give you up too soon, my darling Robert? For a worthless fling, a love affair that created a baby, of which Jonathan wants no part of." Miriam's thoughts turned back to the man she thought she loved, even wanted to marry. There was no doubt that Jonathan had all the qualifications. He was extremely handsome, like his twin brother Jeff. He was mysterious and very sexy, great at making a woman feel good in bed. Miriam quickly looked around to make sure Ted wasn't around to read her thoughts. Just thinking such thoughts in front of Teddy felt dirty and wrong. Then it hit her that Jonathan had not responded about her negative thoughts concerning him. Was he so completely absorbed in his own thoughts, he had not read a single one of hers? She touched his arm, causing him to jump, then turned to face her.

"Miriam, I'm sorry darling. I don't mean to ignore you, but I've just got so much on my mind."

"Its Kristine, isn't it Jonathan?" Miriam felt she was losing Jonathan and she had already loss Robert. "Please Jonathan, just be honest."

"Miriam, I" Jonathan took her hands. "I think perhaps we jumped too quickly into this marriage thing." If he had expected to see Miriam fall apart, he was wrong, Instead, she seemed relieved at his words. "Of course, I'll help you with the baby. That is my responsibility too."

"Thank you, Jonathan, that is very thoughtful of you but our baby will stay here with me." Miriam could read the relief on his handsome features. "If you would like, you may support him with money, just enough to buy him the things he needs until he reaches eighteen."

"I'll have my lawyer draw up such a fund to help support the baby. I'm sure Ted will feel better now that I am out of your life." His attention fell to the scene in the garden, where Miriam kept looking at Robert with Esther. Jonathan took her hand, and looked down sincerely. "You think you have lost Robert too, don't you, sweet girl. Would you like me to speak to him?"

"No Jonathan, Robert is happy, he loves Esther now." Tears filled her blue eyes. "They're happy and in love. It's my fault I lost him."

"Miriam, I believe Robert went looking for someone to replace you." Jonathan looked down lovingly, no evil shown in his dark eyes. "He's still in love with you, Miriam. You would have been his first choice if I had not interfered."

"I cannot go there Jonathan. No matter how much I love Robert, I cannot destroy their lives because I once again made a mistake."

Miriam noticed Jonathan's attention had went from her to the open doorway, and she could read his expression. Someone had been listening to their conversation. Miriam turned around and stared back at Robert.

"Miriam, I don't know what to say." Robert stood frozen, holding two glasses of lemonade. He had left Esther outside to go after some drinks and thought it would be closer to go out the living room sliding door to the rose garden. Robert had overheard their conversation regarding him and Miriam still loving him. "Miriam, you and Jonathan are going to get married."

"We called it off Robert." Miriam felt flushed and embarrassed. "You cannot expect two people to be happy in a marriage when the bride and groom both are in love with someone else, would you?"

Jonathan turned to Miriam, surprised by her words. Why had she included in her words that he too was in love with someone else? Miriam could read the confusion in Jonathan's eyes regarding her words to Robert, so if he hadn't figured it out, she would help him.

"I can tell you are wondering what I meant by my statement Jonathan." Miriam felt for the first time in her life, she was finally

231

growing up. "The type of man you've become you probably don't even realize you are head-over-heels in love. You thought you had loss the need for love sometime back but a woman can tell Jonathan. You never had those looks for me or got lost in your thoughts over me." Miriam took his hand, as a caring friend this time. "You love Kristine O'Donnell Jonathan and she is deeply in love with you."

"Love?" Jonathan tried to laugh but knew deep inside his heart, he would never get Kristine out of his mind.

"So, you really don't love Jonathan?" Robert could only stare. "But, you said"

"Robert, you know me, how I can jump into something with my eyes shut, never seeing what I am really getting into. I speak out, throw the best part of my life away without thinking it out!" Tears ran down her cheeks. "I am ashamed to admit the truth, but what I felt for Jonathan wasn't love at all, it was sinful lust." She looked around for Jonathan's reaction, but he had simply vanished. "He is finally free of me and this baby, His disappearance only proves he can be dangerous" She turned back to Robert, staring at the spot were the tall dark man stood moments before. "Robert, I've lost you, I know. I will not beg you to come back to me. I can see you love Esther now and I only wish for you to be happy. I just ask you to. Miriam broke down. "Forgive me."

"I need time to think, Miriam." Robert glanced down at the lemonade in his trembling hands. Minutes before he thought he knew what he wanted but now, Robert stood confused, his old feelings for the one standing in front of him crying, asking for forgiveness, but not asking him to break it off with Esther. He could see how much she had grown up, right before his eyes. This time, thinking only about his happiness, not herself, as before. "Esther is waiting," Robert rushed out the door, torn with his feelings for two girls.

CHAPTER 44

School had started and the children had settled into their routine. Mary and Martha had advanced to the first grade, along with Jacob Wineworth. Patches and Blake, being six, were in the first grade with the twins and Jacob. Teddy Jeffery had been bumped up from second grade to third, same grade as Ruth. Leah and Rachael found themselves sitting next to Marble and Willy in the same class.

In the mountains of North Carolina, cold weather had already settled in, the first part of October. Jenny sat in a meeting with a few parents and two other teachers to plan the holiday events of the school year. Mrs. Masters, one of the first-grade teachers, raise her hand when Halloween was brought up first.

"We used to have a Halloween Carnival here every year at Goldsburg School! The event brought together the entire town. Many shop owners got involved by donating items or gift cards to use for prizes for the various booths and games. The older students volunteered to run the stands and the gym was transformed into the spooky ghost ride. All the children loved dressing up in Halloween costumes as well as a good-many-adults. Prizes went to the best costumes, children's and adult's." Mrs. Masters face beamed with memories of the successful event. "Can we reinstate the carnival in this year's calendar? It raises lots of money for the school!"

"Sounds like fun! The children will love it as well as every adult in our town." Jenny remembered the school carnivals growing up and getting to be the fortune teller one year. "My only concern is the event being held at night. Would we have police protection to secure everyone's safety?"

"Oh yes, Jenny, the police department donates their security team to guard both the school and the attending crowd!" the teacher giggled. "They, like everyone else, have a wonderful time, playing the games and munching on the great food! There's even a little Christmas shop for early shoppers! Its like the start of the holiday season!"

The principal stood up smiling. "Alright committee, we will take a vote. All in favor of the Halloween Carnival, raise your hand." Making a quick count for every hand in the room, he stated:

Joan Byrd

"Mrs. Masters, its unanimous! We will put you in charge of the committee and get planning. The 31st of October falls on a Friday this year, making it the perfect night for the carnival! Next holiday, Thanksgiving. Any ideal's?"

"The town has a thanksgiving parade every year and I think the school needs to participate in it this year. The school can enter a float and possibly win the number one prize." Tom Vestal spoke with a nasal tone. "My wife Arlene, is a very talented artist and with the right help working on the costumes, we will get that top prize."

"Mr. Vestal, I like the ideal for having a float in the parade, but what sort of float would represent the entire school?" Once again Jenny voiced her opinion. "We all are aware there are many different classes and we need something that relates to all of the subjects."

"What would you suggest, Mrs. Neenam?" The principal smiled at the pretty English teacher.

"The float would be about learning, of course. I am an English teacher, so I would like to see books on the float. Perhaps big books that come to life. The Math book could be dancing numbers, the History book, famous people in history coming to life, like past presidents, and Literature where characters come to life, such as Romeo and Juliet, and Hansel and Gretel."

"Very good, Jenny!" Mrs. Masters clapped with excitement. "That sounds perfect for the school float!"

"Wonderful! Now Christmas!" The jolly principal's eyes lit up. "The children are the happiest during Christmas. I suggest our annual Christmas pageant! Everyone loves tradition! The big open frame in the middle of out stage, high school students portraying the Nativity scenes while the other students sing the many beautiful carols!"

"Oh yes!" Ruth Masters stood up dramatically to describe it further. "The curtain opens and closes for each frozen scene! The cast get into position for each scene, first, just Mary and Joseph with baby Jesus in the manger, frozen still like a picture while the children sing, O Little Town of Bethlehem, and so on."

Jenny loved the sound of the Christmas Pageant so she joined Ruth Masters. "This is Christmas! I would love to be on this team again, sir."

"Sure thing, Mrs. Neenam." Joseph Reynolds had sit quietly

watching the teachers respond to each event. "I have already volunteered to head the Christmas show this year. This old Christmas pageant is outdated and I was thinking more on the lines of a Christmas spectacular, with dancing and secular holiday music. The stage would be set up with live evergreens and fake snow, Colored lights glowing from every corner and tree."

"If we have your show Mr. Reynolds, most of the children will be left out." Jenny smiled down at the stranger seated with his legs crossed. "We are a small town here and we love tradition, sir. We want every child in this school to have a place in their Christmas program."

"But, my dear Mrs. Neenam, change is good. Its fresh and its what this old school needs to bring in the crowds! Not just a few parents cheering on their untalented children!" Joseph Reynolds tried not to show his anger over this situation.

"For starters Mr. Reynolds, our school auditorium is always packed for the Christmas pageant and we have a hard time getting everyone waiting, seated. Second, I believe we should let the children have a say on which program that want!" Jenny stared at the rude stranger. "I say we let the children vote! Its their program! Not mine and certainly not yours, sir!"

Joseph Reynolds heard the small group agreeing with his competitor, so he forced a smile and stood up beside her. "Very well, we shall put it to a vote, Mrs. Neenam. You write down your little boring Christmas pageant and I will write down a first-rate musical event, then we shall see who wins."

"You're on, Mr. Reynolds!" Jenny stood her ground, but silently said a little prayer. "Dear God, please don't let the kids let me down."

"They vote tomorrow darling." Jenny had poured her heart out to Ted, telling him about the meeting and the rude man. "Excuse my choice of description, but, that jerk showed up from nowhere and wanted to take over!"

"Jenny darling, please calm down before you have a heart attack." He took his upset wife into a warm embrace, relaxing her. "I know how our children will vote dearest, all but two."

"Marble and Willy." Jenny looked down at her hands. "I guess I should have stayed out of it and kept my mouth shut."

"Jenny, you stood up for what you believe and it was the right choice." Ted got a small smile from his beautiful wife, who was glad to know at least Ted was on her side. "I'm very proud of you Jenny."

Mary and Martha had been listening and agreed that their mama was a hero for the kids at school. "Don't worry mom! I think most of the kids will vote our way." Mary bit into her apple, before smiling. "Teddy Jeffery may have to persuade Marble to vote for the pageant instead of the big Christmas show."

Ted sat up to look at his daughter. "Mary, what has Teddy got to do with Marble?"

"Marble has been hitting on Teddy Jeffery ever since she laid eyes on him at school." Martha joined her sister. "She told him he looked just like his handsome uncle, the sexiest man alive."

"How did Teddy respond to that girl?" Jenny was glad to get off the pageant.

"Jeffery told miss flirt that he looked just like his handsome papa and wanted to be just like him when he grew up." Mary giggled, recalling his next response. "Then Jeffery told Marble he already had a girlfriend and when she asked who, he said my name!"

"Then the rude girl just laughed and pulled up her skirt so Teddy could see her pink underwear." Martha made a face. "Teddy Jeffery smiled with pleasure, then turned to Mary and ask her to pull up her skirt for him,"

"Why, that little Wineworth brat!" Jenny's eyes blazed at the very ideal. "Mary Neenam, please tell me you did no such thing!"

"O.K. mom, I did no such thing!" she giggled causing Ted to get up and pick her up off the floor.

"Look, young lady, stop being smart mouth with your mama! If you ever and I mean ever, pick that skirt up again, I will spank your butt, understand?"

"Yes dad, I'm sorry." Mary looked hurt and tried not to look at her mother. "I was afraid I would lose Teddy Jeffery to that fast girl."

"So, you thought you would be just like her to make Teddy happy and he would choose you." Jenny took her small hand. "Sweetheart, Teddy will like you a whole lot better if you just be yourself. He had already told Marble you were his girlfriend."

"Your mama is right, little girl, so listen to her." Ted gave her a kiss before setting her back down. "Now, my beautiful girls, off to bed. You've got to be bright tomorrow when you vote."

The large group of students sat quietly in the auditorium as they listened to Jenny describing the very familiar Christmas program they had every year, then Mr. Reynolds lavishly describing his big holiday show. Jenny sat quietly, listening to all the whispers between the many groups of students and feared the change was tempting, especially to the high school students. She took a breath when the principal stood up to speak.

"Alright students, you have heard Jennifer Neenam and Mr. Reynolds describe two very different Christmas programs for this year. We decided, as the holiday planning committee, to let you vote for the show you think will be best received by our audience. Keep in mind, all the students will be in the traditional Christmas Pageant but the new holiday show has a limit of thirty performers, for dancing and singing songs like Jingle Bells. Each student has been given a card to make it easy for the younger children to vote." He looked out at the excited group. "You may vote for only one. A, the Christmas Pageant and Jennifer Neenam, or B, the Holiday Show, with Joseph Reynolds. Please mark your choice now and place the cards in the big box Mrs. Masters is holding at the back of the auditorium, then return to your classes. We will let you know who the winner is this afternoon."

After the cards had been counted by the math and history teachers, the results were handed to the principal. Without a smile, he picked up the intercom to announce the winner. Mr. Reynolds had watched the principal's dreary expression and gave a proud smirk, assuming he had won. The principal glanced over at the smug face before clearing his voice.

"May I please have everyone's attention. The results are in for our choice of this year's Christmas program." Jenny laid down her pencil and closed her eyes as she listened, fingers crossed.

"The vote wasn't even close." The principal turned to look at Mr. Reynolds, who was smiling broadly back. "It would appear Mr. Reynolds will be happy with the outcome, no matter which way it went."

Joseph gave a chuckle as he stood up to be heard over the mic. "Yes, may the best man, or woman, win!" he sat back down, folded his hands behind his neck, sure of the outcome.

"The vote was 250 to 50!" The principal broke into a toothy

grin. "In favor of the Christmas pageant and Mrs. Neenam!"

Jenny's senior class burst into applause for their teacher and from the open door, she could hear loud clapping and shouts of rejoicing throughout the school. Jenny looked up and gave a blessed thank you before joining in the winning celebration.

Mr. Reynolds grunted and stormed out the door and just down the hall, Mary and Martha jumped up to hug one another. Teddy Jeffery ran down the hall to their room and cracked open the door for Mary's attention. She asked to be excused and walked out into the hallway, whispering.

"Teddy Jeffery, what are you doing out of class? You could get in trouble!"

"I got permission!" he pulled her into his strong arms and hugged her, overcome by the outcome. "We won Mary!"

CHAPTER 45

Jonathan had instructed his congregation to be at church on Sunday, October 26th, for what he called members only Sunday. He had placed a huge sign in the church yard announcing the special service and that visitors were welcome to come the following Sunday. As the members filed in, they whispered among themselves as to what Jonathan was going to do. They could see two new black curtains in the church, one on the side wall and the other curtain at the altar. The group of one hundred grew quiet as they watched Jonathan stepping out from the side, where the wall curtain hung. Instead of wearing his usually white robe, the tall handsome man wore a rich red robe and to all the ladies and young girls, he looked exceptionally sexy and handsome. He remained serious as he spoke in his rich deep voice.

"My people, today is the day you learn what our church is all about. First, let me reveal our new church's name sign. When I have finished speaking this morning, each and everyone of you will realize why I chose to place it inside the building instead of outside." Jonathan opened back the curtain and switched on the sign's letters. KILL DEVIL HILLS CHURCH. The words kill and church were in black lights. Devil Hills, in red lights.

"For those who followed me from our old church, this was the name I gave the church, living in the area of the same name. Now, I make my change. When we have outside guest, it will appear as you see it now." Jonathan's dark eyes stared into every face. "But for you, my people, the name is" He hit a small switch and the only words that remained were DEVIL'S HILL.

There were whispers among the people as Jonathan walked to the front. When he turned around, he noticed Joseph Reynolds trying to slip out the back door.

"Joseph Reynolds, you cannot leave this place. Not until I release you." Jonathan spoke calmly as he watched the man try the doorknob and found it locked tight. "Now, take a seat Mr. Reynolds or would you prefer I single you out?" Joseph Reynolds, now sweating with fear, found his seat next to a nervous Tracy. Jonathan

smiled, revealing his sharp canine teeth. "People! My followers!
"The women could only stare, thinking he removed his covers just
for his enjoyment with them. The men froze at the devilish sight.
"People, you are mine, all mine. Each one of you willingly gave me
your soul and in return, I will give it to the one we follow and
worship."

Everyone listening began to grow more and more nervous, each
knowing they had indeed willingly given this man their very soul.
For the ladies, it was for the lust and pleasures only Jonathan could
perform, for the men, it was lining them up with prostitutes or other
wives in the church for sex.

"Yes, now it all comes back to you. Each of you are filled with
lust. Women of my church, those of you who are married have
committed adultery with other men in our church and all of you with
me, at least once. Some of my favorites, like Tracy Reynolds, even
many more times." Jonathan smiled down at her, watching the
beautiful woman blush, before pulling a tissue from her bag to wipe
her brow. "Then you married men, all of you have committed
adultery with paid prostitutes and other women in this congregation.
Look around men, those prostitutes you enjoy are members of my
church as well.

Jonathan's attention fell to the young girls who were smiling up
at him. "Oh yes, my young sluts, you enjoy sex just as much as the
adults and you young men, when you can't find sex with a broad,
you either turn to another buddy or just jerk yourself off!" Jonathan
smiled back at four women sitting next to their husbands. "Don't
worry ladies. No one here cares that you'd rather get it on with one
another instead of your cheating husbands, who had rather get it on
with kinky prostitutes." Jonathan held up his hands. "My fallen
people, do not worry. Our path is wide and filled with riches, beauty
and sex. Lots and lots of sex! Do not let the Bible thumpers pull you
toward the narrow path! Is there a heaven? Absolutely! A place
where you just walk around being GOOD!" Jonathan laughed. "In
Hell, you can continue enjoying the lust you feel here, only ten-
times-better! You will be welcomed by Lucifer, the beautiful fallen
angel and his followers who fell with him into the deep before the
Creator created the earth. The fallen angels believe in Lucifer's
powers. He is strong and he will give you what you desire. He will
not judge you like the Almighty! The only thing Satan wants is you.

The Lost Sheep

Give yourself to him as you did me. Give Satan your soul and become one of us forever!"

Jonathan motioned for the two young girls to come forward. He stared into their eyes as they removed their clothes and stood before everyone naked. He smiled his approval and willed them next to him, where he reached out and touched their breast, causing them to breath heavy with desire for him. Jonathan turned back to the people watching and noticed the men licking their lips and the women fanning their flushed faces.

"Behind this curtain is the very likeness of Lucifer, the leader and God of our church. I would like to thank Mrs. Tom Vestal, the artist who painted this masterpiece for us for the mere price of getting laid by me and bringing her to satisfaction five times." Jonathan smiled down at the blushing woman. "I must admit, she got a bit more than her painting was worth. She couldn't get enough so I flipped her over and gave her a new thrill up her rear. The seventy-year-old bitch went wild! I stopped short of giving her a rear-end baby!"

As everyone broke into laughter, the poor woman buried her face in her hands as Jonathan told the naked teens to open the altar curtain. 'Ladies and gentlemen, young sluts and wild young fellows, Look upon your master. Lucifer, the prince of darkness!"

There was a gasp throughout the entire group as they noticed the strong resemblance between Jonathan and Satan. The men could feel their hearts pounding, wondering if they were actually in the presence of the devil, himself and the women wondered if they had really been having sex with the devil all this time. Jonathan had read their thoughts and knew this would not sit well with his father so he said.

"No, my people, I am not Lucifer, although the resemblance is great." His smiled brought out his wolf like teeth. "But I can tell you I am more than his disciple. I am the devil's son!" with that, many of the women fainted, two of the heaver men suffered a fatal heart attack because everyone was too shocked to help them. Jonathan's laugh filled the church as he proclaimed. "Two have gone to Satan already and they will miss the big celebration I have planned."

"What sort of celebration, Jonathan?" Tracy stood up on shaky legs wanting to run from this nightmare and never look back.

"Tracy, my beautiful sexy Tracy." Jonathan walked back and

241

took her hand, then led her to the front. "On Halloween night, the school will have a big carnival. The entire town will be there. Lots of virgins from high school." His fingers started undoing her buttons that ran up the blouse she wore. She swallowed but found she couldn't move. "We will find six who are willing to follow us to a special place I have set up. All 98 of you will gather there with me at twelve midnight. There will be a full moon,

Friday, October 31st." Jonathan licked his lips as he removed her skirt and blouse, leaving her trembling in her underwear. "Remove the rest, bitch!" his stare increased as she obeyed his order and stood there completely naked in front of the entire congregation. "Now, unzip my pants, woman!" Tracy gracefully removed his black pants, leaving him in the red robe. Jonathan smiled and pulled her into his strong arms. "People, when we get to the cave, there will be six alters set up for the six virgins. Each one of you worshipers of Satan will have the pleasure of removing your clothes. Then I will choose six lucky men to remove the virgin's clothes and prepare them for Satan's pleasure.

Jonathan unzipped his robe and pulled it over his head. His sexy naked body grew out the hunger from every woman watching. Even the men began to get aroused by watching him pick up Tracy and lay her upon the altar, covered by a black cloth. Jonathan climbed on top of her and in front of a lusting crowd, had sex with the starved woman. Then he took his turn on each teenager as the women filed up for their turn. The men took whoever was available after Jonathan had used them.

Slipping back in his robe, Jonathan looked around and smiled. Finding his members on the floor, in the pews, on the steps and almost every space available, he unlocked the doors and walked out. Mission accomplished!

But maybe he hadn't won them all. Being busy having sex with each woman, Jonathan had failed to see a weeping Tracy Reynolds slip out the side door he came through at the beginning of the service.

CHAPTER 46

"Just what kind of a costume do you call that, young lady?" Jenny watched Mary model her Halloween outfit.

"I'm going as a virgin, pure and innocent." Mary giggled.

"A virgin? Mary Neenam, you are a virgin, pure and innocent!" Jenny looked over at a bewildered Ted. "Just where is she getting all this grown-up knowledge, sweetheart?"

"My guess would be Teddy Jeffery Wineworth." Ted motioned her over. "Mary, why would Teddy tell you to dress as a virgin?"

"Go ahead Mary, tell dad. He probably already knows anyway." Martha made a helpless face at her twin.

"Teddy Jeffery ask me to be his partner and that's what he wants me to be." Mary looked down shyly to avoid her daddy's eyes.

"Why on earth a virgin? Why not a princess, so Teddy can be your prince?" Jenny turned when Martha stepped up, hands on her hips.

"That's what Jacob and I are going as mom. Grandma Hannah is almost finished with my princess gown."

"If you do not tell your mama the real reason Teddy ask you to be a virgin, young lady, I will!" Ted set her down in his lap. "start talking!"

"Teddy Jeffery is going as the Devil and he said he would be winning my soul." Mary looked up innocently. "It's only play-acting dad! Halloween is always filled with goblins and ghost. I know my soul belongs to the heavenly Father and I will never give it away to the mean old devil."

"Mary, this is no play-acting for you or Teddy, not to his grandfather. Teddy could get into big trouble pretending to be that evil angel!" Ted reached over to take his wife's trembling hand. "You must choose something else to go as, sweet girl, with or without Teddy for a partner."

"Alright dad, but you cannot tell Uncle Jeff or Aunt Naomi Teddy Jeffery is going as the devil and he wanted me to be his virgin!" Mary looked genuinely afraid. "Uncle Jeff is very strong dad and he could really hurt Jeffery."

243

"Mary, I am not saying the danger will come from Jeff." Ted lifted his daughter's face up. "His grandfather could get the wrong ideal about Teddy going as him. It might even give that Devil the lead he is after to win the boy over to his side."

"Oh! I never thought of that dad!" Mary sat up, suddenly anxious over the boy she loved. "I can talk to Teddy Jeffery and beg him not to go as the Devil. I'll tell him to choose something better for us to go as."

"That my smart girl!" Ted gave her a fatherly kiss and sat her down. "Now, run along and tell Grandma Hannah there's someone who wants to see her, then run off to bed after you kiss your worried mother goodnight."

"I love you dad!" she reached up and gave Ted a hug before running over to kiss Jenny goodnight.

"Mom, I'll pick something really pretty and if Teddy Jeffery don't like it, he can pick another partner."

"Thank you darling." Jenny gave her a hug, then smiled. "I just don't want anything bad to happen to you Mary."

"It won't!" Mary reached for her twin's hand and headed toward the kitchen. "Let's see if your gown is ready. I hope grandma has time to make me a new costume."

"It will have to be in the morning sis. Someone is waiting to see her now, remember?" Martha glanced at her sister before going in. "I wonder how she knows Gab?"

"Son, why such a big secret?" Hannah followed a smiling Ted to the moonlit rose garden.

"Mother, ever since you came back to help when Jenny and I had to go to the coast, you haven't had the chance to see an old friend that has been here helping me." Ted helped her down on the garden bench. "It has been over twenty-six years since you've seen one another, but I am sure you will remember him." Ted gave her a kiss before standing up.

"Teddy, are you going to leave me out here in the rose garden alone to meet this mysterious friend from my past?" Hannah clutched her son's hand, unsure of this meeting.

Ted gave a soft laugh. "Mother, I promise, he will not harm you. He is one of God's own." He released her hand and walked away smiling.

Hannah sat quietly, looking around at the moonlit garden. Peering upward, she saw the stars shining bright in the crisp cool mountain air. She twirled her fingers nervously as she shifted her feet back and forth. "Now who could be helping Ted that I haven't seen for over twenty-six years?" Then out of the stillness she heard the familiar voice speak her name.

"Hannah." The tall handsome angel stepped out of the shadows and stood right in front of her. Hannah stared in disbelief, unsure if she was really seeing the angel who came to her or was she having a very real dream.

"Gabriel?" Hannah spoke his name softly, afraid she would break the spell or wake up.

"Hannah, you are not dreaming, dear one. I am really here." Gabriel swept his hand toward the garden bench. "May I join you?"

"A…yes, of course. Please, have a seat." Hannah suddenly felt like a school girl seeing an old boyfriend. "Gabriel, it really is you." She glanced down at his clothes and noticed for the first time he wore jeans and a t-shirt." Hannah looked away, trying hard not to laugh.

"Like my clothes, do you?" he returned the laughter and enjoyed her beautiful smile. "Ah! That's the smile I remember. I carry it with me everywhere."

"What a sweet thing to say." Hannah lifted her hand to touch his handsome face, then quickly drew it away, thinking it was wrong to touch him.

"It's alright to touch me if you like, Hannah dear." The bright angel took her hand and placed it on his face. "See, I don't bite."

"Our Teddy looks just like you Gabriel." She closed her eyes blushing as she remembered making love to this handsome angel and thinking it was just a dream. "You gave me a baby boy."

"That I did Hannah, I gave you my boy, our baby Hannah." He reached over and let his fingers run over her lips. "I remember kissing these lips, gazing into your beautiful eyes. "Gabriel pulled her closer. "Hannah, I remember everything about my visit to you."

"I also remember that night Gabriel. I did not want to wake up." Hannah looked down shyly. "I did not want you to leave me."

"It wasn't easy to go. I think about you often, Hannah." His blue eyes held hers steady. "I had never laid with a woman before. I wasn't sure if I would even know what to do. I was used to making announcements, very important announcements as you well know from your biblical reading.

245

"I would never have guessed you had no knowledge of making love. You knew Gabriel, believe me when I say, you did everything right." Hannah suddenly felt embarrassed for speaking so boldly to one of God's angels.

"You have nothing to feel guilty about darling Hannah, it was God, Himself, who sent me to help you conceive our baby" Gabriel looked lovingly into her eyes. "I think the Almighty made me fall in love with you so it would come natural to make love."

"In love, with me?" Hannah knew she had feelings of love for Gabriel as well as the love she had for her beloved Peter.

"Hannah, I know how much you love your husband, Peter. He is a good Christian man and a wonderful earthy father to Ted." Gabriel stood and pulled Hannah up into his arms. "I too am aware of your deep love for me. Our time will come, dearest Hannah. When you and Peter past from this life into life eternal, Peter will become like the angels, no longer married. You may visit with him and other love ones as often as you like, dearest."

"Gabriel, I don't understand what you're trying to tell me." Hannah felt her heart pounding.

"It's quite simple. Your place will be beside me, my love, on Angel Island, out of human reach." His eyes fell on her lips. "There we are free to love Hannah, as angelic husband and wife."

"Gabriel, are you saying, we can make love on this Island, away from the human beings?" Hannah knew heavenly bodies could not be wed in heaven.

"The type of love we will share is different from earthy lovers, but the feelings are unlike anything you have felt before." Gabriel bent over and parted his lips over Hannah's and the depth of passion they felt was like no other. This time Hannah did not have to wake up. She was in the arms of her dream.

CHAPTER 47

"Teddy Jeffery, will you hurry it up!" Naomi called up the stairs to their oldest son. "The Carnival is going to be over before we reach the school if you don't come down!" Naomi looked down, when Jacob pulled at her arm.

"Mama, can you help me with this sword?" He looked up the steps for any sign of his brother. "We'll make it on time mama. It just started and it won't end until ten."

Naomi smiled down at her youngest boy, dressed like a handsome prince. "Well now, aren't you the prince charming. Princess Martha is going to be enchanted by her handsome prince." She took the play sword and stuck it inside the sleeve. From the heavy footsteps, Naomi looked up knowing her husband was coming down the stairs, dressed like a Gipsy. Jeff broke into a big smile when he saw his beautiful Gipsy partner, wearing a long black wig and a very Spanish dress.

"There's my little senorita, looking ready to do the dance of the Gipsy!

"And you, my Gipsy partner, looked as handsome as you are smart!" She started to laugh but stopped short when she saw their son walking down behind his father. "Teddy, just what do you think you're doing, young man!" Naomi all but yelled, causing Jeff to turned around to find their boy, red skin and dressed top to toe like the devil.

"Teddy Jeffery, you cannot wear that devilish outfit out of this house! I forbid it!" cold eyes stared down at the boy's smirking face.

"Mother, father, since this is Halloween, the night of vampires and witches, ghost and goblins, I find going as the most-evil person I know, appropriate." Teddy held up his hand before his parents could speak. "Even though I knew you would be angry with me for my choice of costume, I still chose Satan because I know he is wicked and evil." Teddy's eyes softened. "Mother, I know the difference between good and bad and I am aware that one percent of good can win over one-hundred percent of evil. I want to prove to you both and to my evil grandfather, that I can mock him on

247

Joan Byrd

Halloween night, but like my strong papa, I will NEVER let him have me! I belong to God! Body and soul!"

Tears flooded down Naomi's face, listening to this very grown up speech and she felt her son sounded so much older than his seven years. She looked up at Jeff for answers. He walked over and pulled her into his arms.

"Very well son, you may go as the Devil." Jeff stared down at him with a warning. "Just don't act like him!"

"Mother?" Teddy walked over and took Naomi's hand. "I promise to be good tonight, if you trust me."

"I trust you Teddy. You are a smart young man." She felt she had lost her little boy.

"Mother, you have not lost me. I will always be your boy." The seven-year-old looped his arms around her waist in a hug. "I love you, mama." He turned to Jeff. "Papa, I love you both, very much. I'll make you proud, you'll see."

"Mama, can we go now? Martha will be waiting for me. I cannot keep my princess waiting, can I?" Jacob had kept quiet for as long as he could. Watching the old grandfather clock strike seven-thirty, he began to worry about the time.

"We must not keep Princess Martha waiting." As Naomi checked her make-up in the hall mirror, she glanced at Teddy. "Teddy, what is Mary dressing like? A witch or black cat, maybe?"

"Mary told me she was going as Alice in Wonderland." Teddy made his way to the big front door and opened it. "My date is dressed more to suit being with the Devil."

"Your date?" Naomi followed her son quickly to the black car but Jeff reached him first and stopped him from getting in.

"Just who is..." Jeff's eyebrow flew up, knowing. "Teddy Jeffery, what is the meaning of asking this girl Marble to be your partner tonight?"

"Papa, since Mary didn't want to come as a virgin, I ask Marble." Teddy responded calmly. "I realize Marble is not a virgin, but she is just playing one, especially with me. Mary is still my girl."

"Do you know Marble is older than you and she is one of Ted's troubled teens?" Jeff shook his head with discus. "Son, she cannot be trusted."

"Jeff, what will that girl try to do to our son?" Naomi felt sick over the entire situation. "First, Teddy going as the Devil and now

248

learning his 'date' is trouble.

"For her own sake, that little bitch better not try anything with our boy!" Jeff looked down to find Teddy Jeffery smiling, his sharp white teeth sparkling next to his red skin.

"Look mama, papa, I can handle little miss hot pants. I'm ten times stronger than Marble, even though she just turned thirteen last week."

"Look boy, we will be watching closely, so if either one of you get out of line, I'll be ready to put a stop to it!" Jeff checked his watch and mumbled, "We're late! Everyone in. We're in for a long night!"

Mary watched as Teddy knocked Marbles hand off his rear. The little angelic blonde stomped her foot and narrowed her eyes. "What a flirt! A pushy, trashy, flirt!" Ted reached down for her hand, drawing her attention on him.

"Let's go over to the floating ducks and pick out one. Your mama told me they have some really great prizes to choose from."

"Sure dad, anything to take my mind off Teddy Jeffery and his date." Mary noticed the boy look her way before she turned and walked down the hall. "I think Teddy is just trying to make me jealous, dad. Maybe I should have asked one of the nice boys in my class to be my partner."

"Mary darling, you are too young to be worried about that sort of thing. Most girls your age prefer playing with dolls." Ted stopped at the round baby pool filled with floating ducks. "Alright bright eyes, find the one you like and pick it up." Ted handed the high school boy a quarter as he smiled at his little girl trying to make up her mind.

"Gee dad, they all look alike!" Mary looked down at the ducks as they floated by, then glanced up at the shelf lined with wrapped up prizes of all sizes. Closing her eyes, she reached for the second duck and handed it to Ted. "You look dad. I hope it matches box number 12."

Glancing up to see what made number twelve so special to his little girl, Ted smiled at the sign over the open box, two crosses, one for you and one for a friend. He smiled and turned the duck over as her big eyes stared up hopeful. "Number 12."

Mary jumped up and down laughing as she reached out her hand for her cherished prize. She closed the lid and placed it inside her waist pouch. "Dad, let's go throw some balls at mom!" She laughed happily as they made their way to the clown dunk,

"I did tell Jenny I would enjoy knocking her in the water!" Ted joined his daughter in laughter as he pointed to his wife, dressed like a clown sitting high on a platform over a large tank of water, calling out insults to those throwing and missing the target.

Marble walked along proudly next to Jeffery Wineworth, as other girls walked past them, whispering about the handsome young man with the mysterious black eyes and sharp teeth. She glanced quickly behind them and noticed his parents still trailing them. "Teddy Jeffery, why are your parents following us everywhere we go and never your younger brother Jacob? Why is your father always staring at us?" Marble wanted her date all to herself. "You'd think he didn't trust you with a young woman."

"I'd hardly call you a woman, Marble. The truth is, it's you papa don't trust, Marble." Teddy had been watching Mary, and noticed several boys in the fifth grade were checking her out before she walked away with her daddy. "My papa, same as me, knows you want to get in my pants."

"Why, Teddy Jeffery Wineworth, what a horrible thing to say to a lady!" She puckered up her lips. "Be honest, I think it's you who want to get in my panties. That's why you dared me to pulled up my dress and slow you."

"If I did, I certainly wouldn't be the first, bitch!" the young boy pulled his gums back over his sharp canines, causing the girl to jump back. "And before you ask, yes, my teeth are very real. Just like my papa's and Uncle Jonathan's."

"Mumm, Jonathan is a sexy dream boat and he is a real hot man!" Marble mocked. "That hunk knows how to make it with a lady."

"A lady? You?" Teddy laughed out. "I have been made aware my Uncle Jonathan has sex with a great many sluts and you are no exception."

Marble grew serious and started whining. "Teddy Jeffery, I thought you liked me. If you treat me right, I could show you things that would make you feel real, good."

"Yeh, I know, sex!" Jeffery sneered, "When I decide to make that dive, Mary will be my first choice to do it with."

"What?" Marble burst into laughter. "That little goodie-two-shoes! That Bible thumper's daughter?" her laughter grew louder as she grew spectators. "Mary Christian will remain a virgin until her wedding day! You'll have to wait until you're a boring adult!"

Teddy Jeffery's eyes blazed into her laughing face. He reached out and jerked her around, stopping her laughter instantly. "Don't you dare make fun of Mary, you fallen bitch!" Jeffery practically yelled as Jeff and Naomi looked briefly at each other before Jeff dropped her hand and made a dash for his son.

"Teddy Jeffery, you are coming with me!" The very tall dark man stared down at the nervous teen. "Go find someone your own age girl! Behave yourself before I tell Ted and he sends you back up the mountain!" he gritted his teeth. "If you were under my roof, I'd send you packing!"

Marble could feel her legs shaking just looking up into this angry man's eyes. Frightened ten-times more than she had ever been with Blackheart, the girl turned and ran toward the clown dunk, in hopes that Mr. Neenam would be there.

Naomi had watched in horror as Jeff, in total angry, had dragged her son out of the gym. She had promised Jacob that she would wait for him and Martha to finish riding the haunted house ride. When their car came out, they were holding hands, laughing. Naomi walked over, still worried about what Jeff could be doing to Teddy, but she tried not to show it in front of Jacob and Martha.

"Hey, you two, aren't you suppose to be scared after riding through that scary haunted house? Why are you laughing?"

"It was so funny, Aunt Naomi!" Martha continued to laugh as she climbed out. "This evil ghost was waving a very big knife back and forth, causing the kids around us to scream." She glanced toward her smiling companion. "Then Jacob started staring at the knife until it pulled free from the not so brave ghost's hand and waved back and forth in mid-air."

Jacob bent over laughing. "You should have see it mama! That hideous looking ghost started screaming louder than the kids and ran out the back, waving his hands, shouting, it really is haunted!"

"Jacob Wineworth, did anyone else see you do your magic with that knife?" Naomi hoped the ride was in the dark.

"That's what's so funny mama! Everyone thought it was part of the show, causing them to scream even louder."

"Son, you must never do anything like that again, even if you

251

thought it was just a joke. Do you hear me, Jacob?" Naomi took their hands and started for the exit as Jacob looked behind him at all the games he and Martha were planning to play.

"Mom, why are we leaving? Was what I did that bad?"

"I'm just going to check on your papa and Teddy. He was misbehaving too and your father took him outside. They've been gone longer than I like." Naomi searched the dark courtyard behind the gym but saw no sign of her husband or son.

"Papa won't hurt Teddy Jeffery, will he mama?" the younger boy showed real concern for his brother.

"Jacob, your papa loves Teddy, but sometimes he forgets his own strength. Jeff was very angry with your brother and something doesn't feel right. I need to find Ted." Naomi took the children back inside and headed for the clown dunk.

CHAPTER 48

Jonathan made his way through the crowded school, looking over the young high school girls. They all smiled at the handsome stranger as he walked past them. He spotted Esther, playing a game with Robert and two younger teenage girls. Smiling to himself, Jonathan made his way over to pretend he was observing the game. The four players were so in the game, they never saw the tall mysterious man standing behind them until he spoke.

"Esther, I see you and Robert are still together." She jumped at the sound of Jonathan's deep voice and reached for Robert's hand as she put on a shaky smile.

"Jonathan, what are you doing at our school carnival? I would think you'd prefer a different kind of entertainment on a Friday night." Esther noticed his attention was on Rachael and Elizabeth reaching over to pick up ducks. "Jonathan, Robert and I were about to take these girls over to Ted, just as soon they collect their prizes. He wanted all us to meet him at the clown dunk to throw balls at Jenny." She motioned the two girls over after they received their prizes. "Speaking for the school, we're glad you came and hope you enjoy the food and games."

"It's my pleasure, I assure you Esther." Jonathan, smiled down at the blushing young teenagers. "Run along then, I won't keep you waiting." Overhearing Rachael and Elizabeth whispering about his handsome looks, Jonathan reached down to pat them on their head. "Young ladies, my bet is on you. I hope you knock the pretty clown in and get a handsome reward." Jonathan winked at the blushing girls and walked past them, as they watched him disappear in the large crowd.

"Wow! He does look like Jeff! So good looking!" Rachael sighed.

"Just think, two Jeffery Wineworth's walking around!" Elizabeth stood up on her tip-toes in hopes of one more glimpse of him.

Robert turned them around to face him and Esther. "Young ladies, just forget you ever saw Jonathan Wineworth!" he took their

253

hand and nodded for Esther to follow him. "Now, let's go dunk that beautiful clown!"

"I'd love to go for a ride with you Jonathan." Honey Maxwell pulled her sweater on and buttoned it up, to keep out the night chill. "This old fashion carnival is getting real boring and these high school boys are so childish!" The high school senior could not believe her luck getting ask out by this super handsome man. "The truth is Jonathan, I prefer mature men."

Jonathan smiled as he led her out to his car, past Marshall Fields and Jack Jackson, men from his church, and gave them a wink as he passed them a note, naming two senior girls they knew. "Hey fellows, the games are easy and the prizes are fun to pick. I know there's two just waiting for you." Still smiling as he helped the chatting girl in, Jonathan nodded his head toward the gym at Tammie Franklin and Francine Fraser, the two teenage girls who had helped him with the Satanic service at Devil Hills Church. They waved an acknowledgement. They would go inside, befriend a couple of juniors and walked out with the girls. In such a big crowd, no one would suspect a thing about it.

Ted's voice came soft and calming as he found the missing father and son his angel was so worried about. After Naomi walked up beside him, she did not need to say a single word to him, Ted just knew. Now, Ted had left the young woman he had cared for and watched grow in her faith, waiting in the big room inside the emergency room. "Your wife is worried about you, my friend." Ted bent down at the young boy, noticing his wet eyes and the sling a nurse was laying his arm in, covered with a heavy cast.

"I got a little strong with my son." Jeff looked down and closed his eyes. "I just got so angry."

"It was all my fault, Uncle Ted. I didn't listen to mama and papa after I promised they could trust me." Teddy's young hand patted his father's back. "I got mad too Papa, at Marble, for saying bad things about Mary."

"I knew Marble was too old for you Teddy." Ted glanced down at the broken arm, knowing he could fix it in an instant when the time was right. "Although Marble is only six years older than you, now that she's thirteen, the age difference can make a difference after the life this poor child has gone through."

"Ted, is there any hope for the girl?" Jeff looked up, sadness showing on his face. "The poor girl started out with abusive parents then took up with my evil brother." His strong hand touched Ted's. "If anyone can save her, it will be you."

"Marble is difficult. Her mind is set and she hasn't reacted to anything good yet. Even after having a baby, the troubled girl still throws herself on all the young men she wants." Ted locked eyes with his friend. "Jeff, Jonathan has trained that one well and if she does not come around, things might end bad for her. There is one more test we can give her, but in the end, each one must choose good or evil."

Naomi had not spoken a word to Jeff from the moment she saw Teddy's broken arm. Silently, she tucked her boys in bed and made her way inside her bedroom. Jeff stood by the door, giving his wife the space she needed, then watched her pull out a suitcase. His voice came soft and gentle.

"Naomi, my love, don't leave me." Jeff remained by the door, trying not to rush over by her side for fear it might frighten her. As he watched her, Jeff thought back to leaving the carnival and trying to pick Jacob up to place in the car. He could still hear his son's scream as he ran over to his mother's arms.

"I did something wrong, my darling, I know this." Jeff's usual strong voice came out shaky. "God woman, I saw our son tonight becoming me! My old self! I...I lost it!" Jeff broke down. "God, I love you! I need you Naomi! If you leave and take away my family, I'll...I'll"

"You'll what Jeff? Go back to him? Go back to being evil?" Naomi couldn't control her own anger. "You could have killed Teddy! Jeff, you could have killed your own son!"

"No! There you are wrong!" Jeff's hand nervously gripped the door handle. "I love Teddy! I love Jacob! Don't you know how much I hated myself for punishing him to harshly!"

"It could happen again Jeff and the next time, we might not be as lucky!" Naomi started pulling clothes from her closet. "Ever since Jonathan showed up, you've been changing! You cannot control your temper!"

"Damn it woman! I am the son of Satan! You knew this when you fell in love with me!" Jeff staggered out the door. "Leave me then! Take my heart with you! I have nothing to live for! You go Naomi, I die!" Jeff walked away and the front door slammed. Naomi

255

fell down on their bed and cried.

"Go after him angel." Naomi felt Ted's hand on her shoulder and she fell into his arms. "Jeff needs you. He finds his strength in your love. You need him, you cannot never feel whole without his love. I know you are hurting sweet angel, but Jeff is hurting even more. Your life has known love but his life has been, mostly hate and evil. It was Jeff's love for you that changed all that! Don't undo what you have done by walking out of his life."

"Where is he, Ted? I need to find Jeff and tell him how much I love him!" Naomi stood up nervously.

"In the garden." Ted rubbed her face. "Go tell him, sweet angel and I'll look in on Teddy."

Naomi found her husband seated on their love bench, head in his hands, crying in silent sobs. She walked up and touched his long black hair. "Jeff darling, forgive me. I love you with all my heart!"

With strong arms, Jeff reached up and pulled her down into his lap, parting his lips over hers with relieved passion. "Naomi, my dearest love, I thought I had lost you."

"Never Jeff, my heart beats for you." She held him tight, glad to be back in his arms. "I'm so sorry darling and such a foolish woman. I could never leave you. I would die too without you Jeff. You're my reason for living."

Jeff stood, lifting her into his arms and carried the one he loved up to their room, kissing her all the way. Only until they walked in kissing did she remember leaving Ted in the house. She pulled away as they both stared down at the pulled down bedcovers, candles burning and soft music filling the room. Jeff stared at the romantic scene and assumed his bride had prepared it.

"Sweet one, when did you have time to do all of this?"

"I didn't, but I believe I know who did. Our love-match angel." Naomi closed her eyes and thought. "Thank you, Ted."

Jeff laughed softly, reading Naomi's thoughts. "Yes Ted, looks like you have learned what makes for sweet romance." As he locked the door, to assure privacy from both the boys and the houseguest, Jeff was relieved to know his son was no longer in pain. He was certain when morning came, Teddy Jeffery would awake them over his sudden miracle.

CHAPTER 49

"Here my dear, have a glass of wine." Jonathan kissed the overly heated teenager. "So, this will be your first time getting laid?"

"Jonathan, I'd prefer calling it, making love. It sounds, O so much better!" Honey Maxwell smiled through blurry eyes.

"You can forget calling it that bitch! The one taking your virginity tonight hates the word LOVE!" Jonathan smiled, revealing his sharp teeth.

The scared teenager began backing away as she tried to focus, but the room he had taken her to was spinning around. "I…I thought you and I…Take me…home!"

"Oh, I will slut! Your new home!" Jonathan lifted her and carried her inside a candle lit chamber where many church members already waited, naked. He smiled as he laid her on one of the tables then stripped off her clothes as she lay there too numb to move. "One down! Bring in the other five."

After having drugged the other teenager girls, they were brought in and laid naked on the alter tables. Jonathan pulled a black robe over his naked body before uncovering a deep hole in the ground. Members, drunk on wine, started chanting words taught them by their leader.

"Lucifer, prince of the underworld, prince of darkness, come and except these six virgins as your own. They lie naked and waiting for your hot lust to overtake their untouched bodies."

Jonathan took over the chant. "We are here master! Your followers, ninety-eight-fold, and I, your son, their leader. Come great Lucifer! Most powerful Satan, take your prize this moonlit night. Come! Smell! Touch! Lick! Taste! And enter each naked virgin! Old mighty one, the sluts await! Come master!"

Suddenly, the ground below their feet rumbled as smoke rose from the large hole and before the naked group of Satan worshipers, Lucifer appeared. They trembled as his eyes scanned over them before turning to the six naked virgins. A smile crept slowly over his sharp teeth as a strong demanding voice escaped his mouth.

257

"Jonathan, my loyal son." He flew to the far-left table and crawled up on top the frozen teenager. Satan's long, sharp nail traced her face, drawing blood. "So young! So beautiful!" His hand went between her thighs. "So, mine!" he forced himself inside her and pumped the young girl without mercy.

The followers watched Satan repeat the act with each girl until he had satisfied his lust. Lucifer stood up, his manhood still demanding more as he looked over the nervous members until he made a quick head count. "Jonathan! You fool! All your members are not present! I count only 92 of your LOYAL 98!"

Jonathan looked around the crowded chamber, expecting to have everyone's loyalty. He noticed Joseph Reynolds was standing between two women with large breast, but there was no sign of Tracy. The other missing members were an older couple from Kill Devil Hills, two men who had recently joined the church and one of the prostitutes. Jonathan made a mental note to find each missing member and make them regret their decision not to show. Lucifer smiled at his son after reading his thoughts.

"Yes son, they must suffer for disobeying your command! You must see that each betrayer dies before they can be saved from our grip."

"Could we not just punish them this time, father?" Jonathan wasn't ready to commit murder. The overweight men had died from natural causes and the young girl he had beaten badly, pulled through.

"Do not show your followers weakness son. If you wish to please me, you must prove 'your' own loyalty." Satan could read doubt on this handsome son's face. The Jeffery he had would have killed them that instant, without delay. "You pick two, I will take two, and chose one member to take the last two."

"Father, why dirty my hands when I have loyal followers who would gladly do the job for me. This will prove their loyalty to the both of us." Jonathan needed a way out.

"Very smooth my son. Pass out the deed to an even more fool." He laughed. "Then you will pick twelve of your followers to destroy someone!"

"Twelve?" Jonathan looked over at the six innocent girls his evil father had just ruined. "No father! Surely you cannot mean them!"

"AND WHY NOT! THEY ARE MINE, CORRECT?" Lucifer yelled.

"They are not yet one of us, that's why! If they die now, their

258

soul will belong to your Creator!" Jonathan grew angry at his ungrateful father for degrading him in front of his congregation. "Those virgins did not come of their own free will! They were lured here for your enjoyment, damn it! The perfect tradition, the perfect night, the perfect date! HALLOWEEN! A FULL MOON! FRIDAY THE 31th! Let's not forget your favorite desire, SIX VIRGINS!"

A smile fell on the Devil's face. "They were alluring, young, and sexy!

"When they become one of your followers, and they will after they've been with me a while, then they will be obedient to you and you can lust over them whenever you choose!" Jonathan knew by his father's growing manhood, he had hit the right cord with this lustful, evil, Devil.

"Very well son, just see to the traitors, anyway that suits you, but, it must be done soon!" Satan passed by the nervous members as he walked to the smoking hole. "People, you have chosen to follow me, so from now on your soul is mine!" with that warning, Lucifer disappeared.

After considering who he could trust carrying out his orders to kill, Jonathan had given the two men who never showed up to the ritual to his two young teenage girls who had lured two of the virgins as sacrifices for Satan. He told Joseph Reynolds to take care of the prostitute, knowing it had been a favorite of his, and Jonathan, in return, would take care of Tracy Reynolds. The older couple, he'd give a pass, knowing they only followed him because he reminded them of their dead son.

After learning from her husband Joseph, that Tracy had left a note telling him she was leaving and wanted no part of Jonathan or his evil church. Tracy admitted to her husband that she was disappointed in herself as well as him for falling into Jonathan's trap. She had ended her note with, I will never see you again Joseph unless by some miracle, you change! Then it was a simple, goodbye, Tracy.

Jonathan stared at the note in his hand and he knew Tracy would be seeking to return to the Christian faith again. Perhaps, he thought, she never had left it. Tracy had thought Jonathan's new place was still a Christian church and the only sin she had committed was falling in love with him, making her break one of the ten commandments, Thy, shall not commit adultery. After he revealed what kind of church he was leading and how he treated her, Tracy knew where she really stood with him. He had made a fool out of her in front of everyone and somehow, she had slipped away, undetected by him.

Jonathan found Tracy inside a small Methodist church at the out skirts of town. She was down on her knees at the altar and he knew he was too late, but somewhere deep in his heart, Jonathan was happy for the beautiful woman, yet afraid that his evil father would do what he could not. Jonathan knew his time was limited before Satan found them, but he knew he had to help her escape his father's wrath.

"Trace." Jonathan spoke her name softly causing her to freeze, as she stared up at the cross. "Please, don't be afraid of me, I only want to help you while there's still time."

She turned to face him, tears glistening in her warm eyes. "Help me? How, Jonathan, get me to hell?" Jonathan reached for her hand and she jerked it away. "I loved you Jonathan! I gave my heart to you and was willing to leave my husband to become your wife! You lied to me, like you lied to every woman inside that building you called a church!" Tracy's heart was pounding. "I should hate you for humiliating me in front of my so-call friends, but I don't Jonathan." Tears flooded down her face. "I still love you, after everything you did to me! I will pray for your soul Jonathan, whether you want it or not, that you will turn away from evil and go back to God!"

"Trace, it's too late for me, but I am here to warn you." She noticed how sincere he was and saw real tears fill his black eyes. "Satan wants you to die because you disobeyed me! I want you to live Trace!"

"Then, if I die, I will go to heaven Jonathan. Satan will never have my soul." She cried.

"Please Trace, I do not want you to die! Go to him, go to Ted on Goldsburg Mountain!" Jonathan took her trembling hands but this time Tracy did not feel the passion of lust as before, only love. "He can save you. I will drive you as far as I'm allowed to go but we must leave now! At the moment father is preoccupied but when he's finished, he will be on to us."

Reading the raw emotion on Jonathan's usual calm face, Tracy let Jonathan take her to his car and she felt for the first time he was telling her the truth.

CHAPTER 50

"This is as far as I can go Trace." Jonathan reached for her trembling hand as she stared up the tree line road. "Ted will allow me to go no further. You will be safe as long as you stay on the road going up. One wrong move in the forest could get you lost and you'll end up on Black Mountain."

"Black Mountain? Where your brother Jeffery lives?" Tracy spoke softly. "He and Naomi seem so friendly. I can't imagine either of them being evil."

"I'm afraid I brought the evil back to Black Mountain, Trace." Jonathan's dark eyes were tender, not threatening. "Just do as I say and you will reach a big white farmhouse at the end of this road. When you see Ted, you will understand why I sent you to him. Now go, before Lucifer shows up!"

Tracy opened the door quickly, looking back at the man she loved. "Jonathan, I can see good in you and I know there's still hope for you. Please darling, get out before it really is too late! I will pray for you and for your soul."

"Thank you, Trace. I do not deserve your loyalty." He motioned for her to go. "I wish I could have loved you Trace. You are truly a good and beautiful lady."

Tracy felt the flood of tears falling as she turned and made her way quickly up the mountain road.

Bessie O'Donnell walked in the big family den carrying her radio, a worried expression on her face. "Ted, Jenny, as you both know, I brought my radio up here since you don't have one and there's something on you need to hear. "Ted reached for the cord and hook it up for the frail woman.

"It's about those six missing girls from the school carnival, right?" Ted helped Bessie have a seat beside her granddaughter as the frail woman looked around for a hidden radio or television, then shook her head in confusion as to how he had heard about them up here on the mountain.

"The news is filled with the missing teens. Like you said, they went missing on Halloween night and was last seen leaving the

261

school carnival with some high school seniors, also girls." She glanced up, eyes filled with worry. "Now, it's already Sunday and the girls are still missing! Jenny, I took the liberty to write down their names in case you have the girls in your class." She handed the list to her granddaughter who suddenly looked pale.

"Good Lord! All these girls are in my classes. I'm the only English teacher there so I get all the students throughout the school day."

"They were found this morning." Ted looked serious as he took the list of names, as Bessie stared over at him bewildered.

"Alright Ted, where do you keep your radio? Or is it a television set?"

"Grams, Ted just has a way of knowing things before and even after they happen." Jenny stared up at her husband when he handed the names back. "Ted, please tell us these girls have not been killed!"

"They haven't been killed sweetheart, but they might wish they had been." Ted put his arm around her. "I will just share this much with you. The girls were raped brutally. That's all you and Bessie need to know for now." Ted gave her a kiss, got up and walked over to the front door. "There is someone coming who needs our help so I will meet them on the road. You stay with Bessie until I return."

"As you wish Ted darling." Jenny looped her arms around her grandmother's trembling shoulders.

As Ted made his way down the mountain road, his heart beat heavily for the six young girls. He knew Satan had raped them and the satanic group that was responsible for setting them up, had left them laying on the six alters in the dark chamber. Ted was also aware the innocent teens had been set up for the double murder of two men found killed in the same room. He knew the six girls would require a lot of love and guidance to save them, both mentally and physically. Ted slowed his pace and looked up to the heavens.

"My Father, please show me what I must do to help these tortured souls." Tears filled his blue eyes. "Please, loving Lord, tell me they have not received offspring from Satan's lusting over each child?"

"My son" came the soft voice. "The unfortunate victims of Lucifer have been spared from baring his offspring. Lucifer only desired lust concerning the six young virgins, he had no intention of fathering a child with them."

"That is most reassuring Father, but their pain is great and they cry out from within for help." Ted glanced down the road and saw no sign of the one coming. "Father, this woman who comes to seek my help, yearns for forgiveness for her sins. I know you are aware Jonathan brought her to me to save her from his father, Lucifer, who seeks to kill her."

"There is hope for Jonathan. I think perhaps soon we send for Kristine to return, when the time is right." The wind blew the voice warmly around Ted's face, drying his tears. "Tracy comes my son. If she asked for forgiveness, she shall have it. The six teenage girls must be brought up to the mountain, if there's any hope for them. Arrogant men, claiming to be doctors, might try and stop their parents from seeking your help, but trust that I will intervene for you. Take Matthew and Gabriel, then bring them home."

"Thank you, Holy Father!" Ted caught movement on the road. Tracy Reynolds was walking straight toward him, hope on her face.

Never had Tracy Reynolds saw so much love on anyone's face as she did the handsome robed man standing in front of her. Jonathan had been right. She knew without a doubt, this was Ted.

"Tracy" Ted held out his hand and she laid her trembling hand inside it, and suddenly Tracy felt incredible love, peace, and hope, rolled up in one. His heavenly blue eyes held hers as he spoke. "I know you're hurting, dear one. The heavenly Father knows you're hurting. Jonathan has sent you to the right place. Lucifer cannot harm you here on God's mountain." Ted turned to walk back toward the house, Tracy holding tight to his hand, feeling safe as a child again. As they walked, she pictured Jesus looking just like this good young man. Ted smiled, reading her thoughts. "Tracy, remember what you were taught at Christ Church? No one is good but God."

"Oh!" Tracy realized somehow this incredible young man just read her thoughts. She saw the big white farmhouse come into view and wondered just how many souls lived there. "So, Ted, this is where you live."

"Yes Tracy, and there are many Christian souls living inside this home, including my wife Jenny and our twin girls, Mary and Martha." He smiled when she blushed. "You will find many children and young adults here, not to mention, my mother and father, a great helper name, Melaki and at the moment, Jenny's grandmother."

"Are you sure there will be room for me?" Tracy marveled at the size of this perfect's man's family. "I can find shelter in the barn or a shed if I must."

"God provides Tracy. We will find a room for you." He smiled down, giving her a warm feeling, as he opened the door. "Now to meet some of the family." He led her to the large den where he left his wife waiting. "Jenny, my love, this is Tracy Reynolds. Tracy needs a place to stay and salvation in her heart."

Tracy stared up bewildered by his words as Jenny got up smiling after seeing her confused face. "Welcome Tracy, to our full-loving home. I will take care of getting you settled in and leave putting salvation back in your longing heart, to Ted."

Ted led Tracy out to the rose garden as the sun was slowly setting behind the mountain top. He helped her sit, before taking the chair in front of her. "Jenny has placed you with Miriam. I guess you find those arrangements alright?"

"Miriam and I have a lot in common, it appears. We both fell in love with Jonathan Wineworth." She spoke softly as she watched some small children chasing after lightning bugs. "I guess I can be thankful that I didn't get pregnant like that poor girl, and she was with him for only one time." Tracy looked down at her hands. "I'm ashamed to say I lost count from my long affair with him."

"I can see you still love Jonathan, but, you must put him out of your heart, Tracy. I realize your marriage to Joseph has fallen apart, due to his new lifestyle mainly, but nevertheless, he is still your husband." Ted's eyes showed tenderness. "What do you want Tracy?"

"I want to go to heaven when I die." Tracy felt the tears swelling in her eyes. "I feel so lost, Ted. Tell me the truth, is there any hope left for me?"

"My sister Tracy, your faith was always true before Jonathan came into your life. You recall the words of our Lord, Jesus. Our brother said, I am the way and the truth and the life. No one comes to the Father, except through me." Ted reached out for her hand. "We gain eternal life as soon as we believe in and follow Christ. He knows you still love him, Tracy. He heard you at the foot of the cross, weeping and asking for forgiveness."

"Oh Ted, I believe in Christ, with all my heart." Her tears fell down in droplets. "I've always thought of myself as a faithful

Christian, attending church every Sunday. Then everything came crashing down when Jonathan was sent to pastor our church. I have sinned a great sin and I feel so ashamed! How can God forgive me, Ted?"

"Because he loves you, my sister. Love so strong he died for those sins you committed. Now, He lives for you and you are His. He calls you by name." Ted remained calm and soft spoken. "Before, at the cross, you doubted his hearing you. Ask for forgiveness again Tracy, from your heart. Our God will lovingly forgive you and bring you home to hope, grace, and everlasting peace."

Tracy dropped to her knees, eyes fixed upward to heaven as she called up to her Savior. "My Father in heaven, I have always been your child! Jesus, My, precious Lord and Savior, I know you carried my sins up on that horrible cross for me, so my heart ask, please, forgive me, Lord Jesus, of all my sins and take me home into the fold." Tracy Reynolds felt incredible love fill her as she gazed up into the star-filled sky, seeing the one bright star shine its light down over her. With total forgiveness in her heart, Tracy whelped in Ted's arms, as the light flowed down replacing her sin with hope, grace, and perfect peace.

CHAPTER 51

Things didn't go as well for Joseph Reynolds who had followed Jonathan's orders. He waited nervously outside the church office door until the secretary told him the reverend would see him. He pulled himself together and walked in with confidence.

"Well Joseph, I see you are pleased with your job." Jonathan rolled his eyes up at the sweating man, pretending to act casual. "Calm down man, you pulled it off. The law thinks it was a sex act gone bad. Either self-induced or a paid pervert who left her to die after relieving him or herself."

"We were, you know, doing it, when I casually asked her why she didn't show up for the Halloween ritual." Joseph had a pleasing sick look on his round face. "I told her I had looked for her so we could get it on."

"That's when the little traitor informed you that she did not like taking orders. She was her own boss and there wasn't any money involved in it for her, she could give a monkey's ass to waste her time going to a stupid damn Satan ritual." Jonathan stood up and walked around the desk when Reynold's jaw dropped for knowing everything already. "Yes, I know I'm right Joseph but I still want you to describe what happen, every detail on how you killed the bitch."

"I told her I would pay her an extra thousand dollars if she would let me tie her up so I could pretend I was a prostitute slayer." The sweat began to run down his face and onto his white shirt as he swallowed. "She laughed and said it would be easy money, so after securing the bitch to the bed, I gagged her mouth." He started to get excited as he recalled what happened next. "I took one of her stockings and wrapped it around her throat, scolding her about betraying you. I told her that you were her master and she had made a fool of you in front of Satan, who had quickly read the number and found six members missing. I could read the fear in her eyes as she realized this was not just a kinky game I was playing, but I felt turned on, I grew..."

"Lustful! You could not control your need. There she lay, legs

266

spread and tied to the bedpost. Her body was twisting, unable to help herself while you climbed on top of her and the whole time you were making it, you were choking the life out of her!" Seeing the terrible, horrifying scene unfold in front of him, Jonathan turned to face his desk, feeling sick. At that moment, he wished he had not been able to witness that tortured woman's final breathes before facing his father in death. He could hear Joseph Reynolds' excited voice behind him, heated again just thinking about it.

"I had never gone twice before, so close together, but I got so damned turned on!" He laughed. "The timing was perfect master! I came the moment the bitch took her last breath!"

"So, now the police have your semen, you fool!" Jonathan wanted this conversation to be over. "With luck, they won't trace you Reynolds, if you did not leave your finger prints on everything!"

"I was careful!" Joseph Reynolds suddenly felt the walls closing in. "I wore gloves, telling her I had a bad case of poison oak and I didn't want to give it to her."

"Let's hope no evidence shows up to point the finger at you Reynolds." Jonathan walked over to let him out. "I'm warning you, if you're caught, you had better not mention my name or being associated with me except for the fact that I am your minister!" Jonathan's cold black eyes burned down on the nervous man. "Bad things happen to those who turn against me Reynolds! You'll do well to remember that! Now go, lie low for a while!"

"I've got a job to go to! Clients that need my expert attention!" the nervous man stammered.

"Call in sick Reynolds! It won't be a lie!" Jonathan gave him a push out the door, then slammed it shut, knowing four more of his faithful followers were on their way with news of their great victory.

Jonathan sat thumping his pencil on the desk as he listened to the news bulletin over the radio. The news reporter sounded grim as he began. "They say bad things happen in threes and after this week, I am convinced this is a true statement. On Sunday morning a young girl walked inside her grandfather's barn to gather hen eggs and she might never be the same from her grim discovery. Six unclothed teenage girls were found in a daze. Four had been tied up on what appeared to be a Satanic sacrifice table, while the other dazed teens moved slowly around in circles, where two dead male bodies lay dead. It is still under investigation. Saturday night, an old retired couple from the Outer Banks, booked a flight on a private jet to return to the coast. The plane burst into flames before lifting off the ground, killing the pilot as well as the elderly couple. Also, still under investigation. Now for the third murder. On Sunday night, a prostitute was found strangled to death in her down-town apartment. The police have uncovered a few clues as to who committed this terrible crime. We will give you more details as we receive them. Now, back to our regular program."

Jonathan switched off the radio and dropped his head on the desk, depressed. "How did I get here?" He whispered as he felt a presence in the room with him.

"Having second thoughts son?" Lucifer appeared sitting on his desk. "And you're doing so well. Each one of your appointees carried out your orders beautifully, with the exception of Reynolds who bungled his sloppy job." Satan noticed Jonathan's cold stare. "Not to worry son. If the foolish man is caught, he will find turning coward and squealing on his master will prove fatal. He cannot escape either one of us in a prison cell."

"The plane exploding, that was you who created the fireball and killed Helen and Bill Floyd!" Jonathan already knew the answer.

"Did you doubt that I would carry out my part of our bargain? To disobey us is death! They must not have time for SALVATION!"

"Yes, damn it!" Jonathan stood up in his own defense. "I helped a friend! I did not want to see Tracy die! She never chose to follow you and she never lost her faith in God! Her only quilt was falling in love with me, father! That was her only mistake!"

"But yet, you never loved her!" Satan stood over his son, hate dripping from his mouth. "You betrayed my order to kill those who disobey our command!"

"It was me, she disobeyed, not you father!" Jonathan stood his ground. "Therefore, I can take away or by God, I can let live! I have that power over my followers!"

"Yes, I like this Jonathan! You are standing up to me, unafraid, just like my Jeffery!" Lucifer mused as he noticed his son's tightening jaw. "Jealousy, I see, of your perfect brother, my first choice!" The Devil laughed out. "Get use to this, Jonathan. Jeffery has always been and will remain my number one son! One more six, and he is mine for all eternity!"

"Jeff wants no part of you father! Am I jealous of him, yes!" Jonathan spoke loudly. "Jealous that he has found happiness and love! Peace, hope and salvation!"

"And do you wish to return to that dreary life Jonathan, when you are so close to being my number one son?" Satan rolled his eyes over at him. "I think I have lost Jeffery's devotion forever, but you are so much like him, I am turning my thoughts to you."

"How did you set fire to the plane, father?" Jonathan needed to change the subject on which son would be this evil angel's number one. "Did you do it from a distance or let your victims see your venomous face?"

"Fire is what I do best, boy!" he sneered. "The old couple was seated in the back, happy to have escaped from you. I appeared, to their dismay, in the seat directly in front of them and turned so they could face their worse fear. The poor pilot had no clue the Devil was aboard. But the old goats knew as they sat wide-eyed in terror, too frozen to call out for help as I spoke, preparing them for their final destination to hell! The flames shot from my fingers as it crept up their seat and engulfed them. I can still hear their horrifying screams, such a devilish delight! The flames moved quickly to the fuel tank where it exploded in a glorious ball of fire." Lucifer sneered. "They came with me. Unfortunately, the pilot was carried away by his guardian angel! Pity!"

"You cannot win them all father." Jonathan blocked his thought that he was glad for the unfortunate pilot and somewhat sad for the old couple who joined his teaching because of his resemblance to their dead son.

"The young ones you have trained formed a wonderful plan for getting rid of those two men who failed you. The teen sluts come even now to brag over their deceptive plan." Satan reached out and touched Jonathan's shoulder with a hand that burned with heat. "Son, don't be misguided. I do not dwell in hell as you assume. I, along with my fallen brothers, walk the earth, far and wide, winning many souls every second. The holes from which I appear, never consume me or my followers. It just makes for a grand appearance for those chanting my arrival. Those souls that die damned, are the only ones to descend, never to rise up again! I warn you of this Jonathan so you will always know I am near! Do not cross me again!

269

Those people you claim, already belong to me!"

"You need not worry father. I would not dream of crossing you!" Jonathan remained calm. "The youth are just outside my door father. Will you stay?"

"No son, it won't be necessary. I have already witnessed their beautiful work! Drink up the victory son, its yours, you've earned it." Lucifer smiled, knowing this son better than he thought. "By the way Jonathan, it appears two of your females have gone missing, young fire and Miss Kristine O'Donnell. To prove your loyalty to me, find these two, then sacrifice Fire to me, and seek and destroy Kristine, if you cannot change her and win her soul for us!" Satan turned back, and this time the grin covering his face was pure evil. "Enjoy your victory son, then prove your loyalty Jonathan! Make it count!" with those words, the devil vanished and Jonathan felt like the world as he knew it was about to fall in on him.

"It was beautiful master!" Flame, Jonathan's new name for the teen who had dyed her hair a flaming red, laughed, knowing their job would please their handsome sexy leader. "Jake and Phillip were so trusting, they believed every single word we fed them, right Harlot?"

A name more suited for the teen devil worshiper. "Oh, you should have seen us master!" The teen had no clue Jonathan was already seeing all their evil deeds unfolding in his mind. "Flame and I showed up at their apartment, frightened and in tears!" she laughed. "We ask them to hide us from big-bad-you!"

"Those sweet guys felt so sorry for us. Poor lost girls being misguided then asked to do such horrible acts in front of the entire congregation." Flame threw her arms around Jonathan. "Of course, we both loved the sexual service and were honored you chose us to help you."

"I swear Jonathan, Flame and I could have won the best actress' award for our performance when we confessed the horror of witnessing those poor innocent classmates getting raped by the mean old devil!" Harlot giggled. "Poor stupid Jake looked around the darken street nervously before pulling us inside and locking the door."

"The perfect gentlemen let us take a shower to wash away all the lustful feelings." Flame bent over double laughing. "They, wasn't prepared for our prancing out butt naked in front of the two sex-starved men. They never guessed Ben and Rick were waiting outside to grab them when they were making it hot on us."

"I see while Jake and Phillip had their attention on you, Ben and Rick would slip into the door you managed to unlock and knock the young men unconscious." Jonathan fell into a chair and ran his hand over his fresh headache, knowing the four-young people where doomed. "Then the four of you took them to the old barn where we left the six-unconscious high-school girls on the alters, still shot up with strong drugs."

"Why, yes master, but how?" Ben glanced over at the other three, staring at Jonathan with dropped jaws. "We...a...drug the men after dragging them inside and this is the good part! Back in the apartment, the girls started performing oral sex on their unsuspecting partners to collect their semen in their mouth to spit in a cup for later use."

"It was a well-thought-out plan, master!" Rick winked at the two smiling girls. "After drugging the fellows, we untied two of the girls and placed with the men. We lifted the unconscious men's hands and rubbed them all over the helpless little virgins. We knew Satan had already raped them, so all we needed to do was set up the two traitors and make it look like they did the raping."

Jonathan listened as he watched the raw excitement on each teen's face over their heinous crime. He knew he had won them and owned their soul. At this point, they were hopeless. Jonathan could feel the nausea coming back as he clutched his hand to his mouth. "Go on with this! After you raked the girl's fingernails over their faces and backs, you spotted the pitchforks hanging on the barn wall."

"Yes master, it was perfect! The weapons were in reach!" Rick's eyes grew big as he recalled the blood gushing out from the holes across each man's chest. "Ben and I wore gloves as we grabbed the pitchforks and stabbed the cowards in their chest! They moaned, even in their sleep. The blood poured out and death came quickly."

"We had carried the semen and managed to get it up inside all six girls! Three with Phillip's and the other three with Jake's!" Flame ran her hand over Jonathan's chest. "It was such a turn on, master. We remembered to bring Jake and Phillip's clothes and threw them down near them."

Joan Byrd

"The guys then placed the blood-stained pitchforks in the two untied girl's hands!" Harlot laughed. "We killed just for you master and they will blame the murder on the two rape victims! It was the perfect crime!"

"And then you shameless sinners got so turned on over the bloody crime, you had a round on each other, then and there!" Jonathan shouted at their careless actions. "You committed the perfect crime then you took a stupid chance of getting caught by the farmer or one of the girl's coming to and seeing you!"

"Jonathan, we...knew those girls were completely out of it!" Flame swallowed nervously over their foolish actions. "Aren't you proud of us Jonathan? We are all loyal to you."

"She's right master!" the other three chimed in unison.

"Just go! I'm tired!" Jonathan just wanted to be alone. Things were happening too fast, too many people were getting killed in his name. Then there was his father's statement about proving his loyalty. Would he offer Fire as a sacrifice to this Devil and could he find the strength to kill Kristine just to become his father's favorite son?

"How can I kill Kristine?" Tears ran down his face. "Please woman, stay hidden where you are!" he whispered. "If you come to me...I...I" tears clouded his vision. "I could never kill you Kristine. I could never kill the woman I love."

CHAPTER 52

Naomi looked up at Jeff when he found her crying over the morning newspaper. He took it from her hand, knowing already what was printed. "Sweet one, there is bad news in the paper. Three different tragedies in one short weekend." Jeff pulled her up into his safe arms and held her close. "Evil has returned to Goldsburg in a bad way."

"It's Jonathan, isn't it?" Naomi felt sick recalling the many times she had trusted Jeff's brother to be with her sons.

"I am afraid my brother has started something that even he didn't expect would go this far." Reading his wife's mind over their son's safety with his brother. Jeff took her trembling hands. "Sweet one, Jonathan really cares about Teddy and Jacob, that much I do know."

"But, we both know your father is involved in these horrible acts." Naomi gave him a loving embrace before stepping away to the window to check on the boys playing ball just outside, Destiny and Fang guarding them. "Jeff, as long as Jonathan is around, maybe I should take the boys and go to the farmhouse for a while."

"Look, my love, I sent Jonathan away. He lives in town now." Jeff gathered her hands in his strong ones and gazed down into her warm brown eyes. "You will stay here with me! Send the boys if it pleases you!" His words were final. "I will check on the teenage boy that Jonathan left behind."

"Please do darling. Why do you suppose Jonathan left Blaze here?" Naomi knew she would stay to please the man she loved and was happy he needed her so much. "Maybe Jonathan thinks you and I can give the boy what he really needs, knowing he cannot."

"Sweet one, I can protect him from Satan's hand and you have already showered him with your beautiful Christian love and kindness." Jeff gave her a kiss and walked to the door. "As for saving his soul, I will leave that job to Ted and the Lord! I'm off to share some Wineworth wisdom."

Naomi watched her husband walk away, then turned to looked out at her boys happily pitching the baseball she won. She smiled, then whispered "My darling sons, your papa is about to tell a stubborn teenager how to handle Lucifer. Most fathers tell their kids about sex, girls, or how to drive a car!"

Robert watched Miriam as she made her way through the garden gathering vegetables for the family's supper. Her helpers, Hannah and Tracy, were busy chatting about the Thanksgiving parade, which would be held in three weeks.

"Robert, are you going to stand there staring at others working, or are you going to bring me one of those buckets you're holding?" Esther wiped a fallen leaf from her hair and held out her hand. "I'll go fetch the buckets tomorrow."

He turned to see her smiling and handed her a bucket. "I'm sorry Esther, it's Miriam, she hasn't started showing yet. I just thought"

"She would get fat in a hurry?" Esther laughed softly as she picked grapes. "Robert, Miriam is only in her second month. When that baby starts growing, then she will look like she swallowed a watermelon." Esther laughed at Robert's expression. "Relax Robert, it's not yours."

Robert started picking grapes, his mind wondering. "It could have been my baby." He looked over at his companion. "Esther, it's going to be hard having a kid by yourself."

"She's hardly by herself." Esther couldn't control her laughter. "When Miriam has that little baby, most likely with Hannah's help, there will be enough of us to help baby sit while she dates good Christian men. Find that baby a daddy."

Robert moved to pick where he could sneak a peek at his ex-girlfriend, his mind wondering again. "I would have been that baby's daddy." He turned around quickly when Esther said his name.

"Hey Robert, we could even baby sit Miriam's baby together!" Esther said with excitement. "It could be good training for us, so when we have our baby, right?"

"Esther, a baby is a long way off!" he grunted and returned to the grapes. "Just drop it and start picking before it grows dark!"

At the Wineworth Castle, Blaze put the last paint stroke on his birdhouse. He stood back to admire the first one he had every built, then painted. A bead of sweat danced on his forehead as he looked at the sky-blue clouds gracing the wooden house. "What's wrong with me?" Blaze whispered as he looked at his work of art.

"Jonathan will hate it! He'll say it's too"

"Heavenly?" Came the rich low voice behind him. Blazed whipped around to find Jeffery Wineworth behind him.

"I should have painted a dark, moonlit night with bats flying around, instead of..." he swallowed.

"A beautiful morning sky with blue birds flying across the sunrise." Jeff's eyes were tender. "I really like your birdhouse son. I'd like to buy it for our rose garden."

"It's not for sale sir." Blaze looked down, proud to know this man liked his birdhouse. "It is a gift Mr. Wineworth. I made it for your wife."

"Naomi?" Jeff knew this wasn't a reason to be jealous. His loving wife had touched this boy's heart by her kindness. "She will love it Blaze and cherish it always."

"Thank you, sir." Tears came to the young man's eyes. "She has really been good to me, and Mr. Wineworth, I made something for you too."

"For me?" Jeff looked surprised. "Why would you make something for me? I thought you didn't like me."

"I'm somewhat scared of you sir." Blazed moved his hands nervously in his pockets. "The truth is, I really do like you and admire you."

"That is a revelation, young man." Jeff walked over and sat down. "Son, what are you feeling for my brother, Jonathan?"

"He frightens me sir!" his eyes grew tender. "Although Jonathan scares me beyond words, I still love him, Jeff. Please, help your brother! His heart has grown cold but I know he has a good heart. He is just lost!"

"Son, I think you are right about my brother. Ted also thinks you're right." Jeff stood back up and placed his arm around the young teens trembling shoulders. "Somehow, we will save Jonathan."

Blazed reached inside his pocket and pulled out two matching wooden crosses he had carved out and hung on chains. "These are two twin crosses. One for you Jeff, and one for Jonathan." Blazed hung both crosses around Jeff's neck, then buried his face in his strong chest, weeping. "I love Jonathan! I love you, Jeffery!"

Jeff's blue eyes sparkled with tears. "I love you too, son."

275

"You've come to find salvation Marshall." Ted reached out for the lost teen who carefully placed his hand inside the open palm.

"If there is any hope for me sir, please help me!"

"Jonathan taught you about Jesus when he was a true man of God." Ted remained soft spoken. "Then the man you grew to love, changed and pulled away from the very One he was led to preach about."

"The truth lies within me, Ted. I know Jesus is the Son of God. I know He was sent to save us by dying on the cross." Tears filled the young teen's eyes. "I have done some very bad things to prove myself to Jonathan. I turned my back on God too, and Jesus, my Lord! I had chosen to follow and worship the Devil!" Tears flooded down his face. "How can I possibly be saved now? I feel certain Father and Son have turned their back on me! I cannot blame them if they hated me!"

"Hate you? The Eternal God knows only love, son. This is where you are misguided Marshall. The Holy Trinity, Father, Son, and Holy Spirit, have never stopped loving you. All they want from you is to believe in them again, to love them again, follow their path and ask for forgiveness." Ted walked him a little further up the mountain path. "You are one of their lost sheep Marshall and Jesus, our good shepherd, wants to bring you home."

"Will you pray with me Ted?" He watched the robed man kneel by a rock, lower his head as he folded his hands together in prayer. Marshall fell down next to him and laid his head over on the smooth stone.

"My Father, my Holy Brother, young Marshall comes before you to speak from his heart." Ted laid a hand on the young man's shaking shoulders. "Go ahead son, The Holy Ones can hear you."

"Lord Jesus, I know all you have done for us. Loving God, Father, I know how hard it must have been to send your only Son to die for worthless people like me." Marshall Foster spoke through sobs. "I know I don't deserve to ask, but this good man beside me said you still loved me, after everything I have done! Please, Please, forgive me Lord!"

The wind blew gently around both men, heads still bowed, eyes closed in reverent prayer as a still small voice could be heard clearly. "Your sins are forgiven." There came a peace inside young Marshall he had never felt before. The beautiful voice saying. "My brother,

276

you are loved. Welcome back."

The moving words from the Lord made the teen reached out for Ted and cling to him, as his heart pounded with overwhelming joy. Ted waited for Marshall to calm down before speaking softly.

"Hearing the Holy voices is a wonderful blessing, young Marshall." Ted helped the boy stand as he led him down the path. "You will stay with us on this mountain. Jeff and Naomi feel it will be safer for you here." Ted knew Marshall had grown close to the Wineworth's. "When things have settled down again and the Devil is no longer a threat, you may return to Black Mountain if you like."

"Jeffery had told me that Lucifer was after my soul and would stop at almost nothing to keep it!" Marshall shook, recalling Jeff's warning. "He told me Jonathan had me in his control but pretty soon Satan would snatch me away from him and I would be lost forever."

"And that's why he sent you to me." Ted led Marshall back to the rose garden. Ted noticed the pretty young girl reading a book to Mary and Martha and called her over. "Esther, could I ask a favor?"

She jumped up along with the blonde headed twins. "Hi dad! I'm sure Esther would love to show Marshall around." Martha reached up for Ted to lift her on his shoulders.

"Your daughters Ted?" Marshall smiled at the identical girls. "They are the spitting image of you."

"Marshall, were you afraid when God and Jesus spoke to you?" Mary smiled up at his confused face.

"Where they hiding up there someplace, Ted?" Marshall turned to Esther when she laughed softly.

"The girls were not following you and their dad. They were with me, right here on the bench where I sat reading Alice in Wonderland to them. It takes some getting use to Marshall." Esther winked at Ted. "They're more like their daddy every day."

"Esther, if you could show Marshall around, that would be a big help." Ted lowered Martha to the ground and took both girl's hand. "I will take the girls and go find Jenny. Just explain to Marshall how we do things and show him to his room. He will be rooming with Robert and Andrew."

"I remember you." A flash of memory came back to Esther. You came to be with Jonathan. You and your friend, Jasmine, who went by Fire."

"Yeh, that's me." Suddenly he remembered hearing about a girl named Esther who Jonathan took advantage of. How he had bragged to him about taking one of the virgins from Ted's mountain. "I recall hearing how you came to help when Jonathan broke his leg."

"Well, the broken leg is questionable." Esther shivered remembering the night Jonathan took her virginity. "Did you come here for the same reason as your friend Jasmine?"

"Do you know where she is? She disappeared the afternoon of the fun-day picnic and we have searched everywhere for her." Marshall thought this girl was very sweet and strikingly pretty.

"I know Ted sent Jasmine away, someplace safe so the Devil could not find her." Esther took his hand. "Come along with me. There's a lot to see and in one short hour from now, the supper bell will ring and you will be eating with a very large loving family."

"I hope I'm not taking you away from anything." Marshall liked holding Esther's hand.

"Not at all Marshall. I am doing exactly what I'm suppose to be doing. Ted ask me! We all love adding to our big family." She smiled brightly. "Besides, Robert is busy tending the sheep with John and Thomas."

"Robert? Ted told you I'd be sharing a room with him and Andrew." Marshall was beginning to like Esther and he started wondering why she had mentioned this Robert. "Can you tell me a little something about the two guys I'll be bunking with?"

"Andrew is the one that saved Jasmine on the day she arrived. She cut through the woods not knowing a mountain lion had been prowling around the Blue Ridge, and ran right in to it. Andrew heard her scream and left Thomas guarding the sheep. He killed the big cat with his slingshot."

"Sling shot?" Marshall followed Esther inside the large house. "Why not a gun? It sounds a lot safer."

"Not around a house filled with little children." Stepping inside the huge dinning room, Esther pointed to the extra long table, chairs lining both sides and ends. "Every seat is taken Marshall, yet at six o'clock, there will be an extra chair for you."

"I suppose someone will have to make room for it and squeeze me in. Hope I don't crowd out some of the family." Marshall looked at the perfectly spaced chairs and didn't see how another chair would possibly fit in.

"That someone is Ted and believe it or not, he will not have to lift a finger. If you ask him where it came from, he would say, God provides." Esther giggled. "Now to the living room, den and your bedroom."

"What about Robert? Is he special to you?" Marshall felt he had to know before pursuing her any further."

"Robert is my boyfriend." Esther opened the door to the large spacious den, chairs and sofas throughout the room, a piano in one corner, a small bar with wine glasses along one wall and a massive fireplace dominating one entire end. "We've talked about getting married."

"Then, you haven't set a date yet." Marshall suddenly felt depressed over this perfect girl being spoken for.

"As of late, Robert changes the subject when I bring up marriage." Esther looked down sadly. "I think he may be having second thoughts."

"I'm sure it only seems that way Esther." He took her hand after she had dropped his when she pointed out several interesting things in the house. "A girl as pretty as you would make any man a good wife."

"That's a lovely thing to say Marshall." Esther smiled, keeping her hand in his. "Now to show you your room. I think you will like it here."

He looked deeply into her brown eyes. "I already do."

Everyone took their seat at the large supper table and noticed the extra chair next to Miriam. Ted remained standing as he announced a new family member. "Children, we have a new young man who has come to stay with us for a while. Some of you already know him. He used to go by the name, Blaze." Ted watched Patches and Blake look at each other frightened by the newcomer. "There is nothing to fear small ones. You know how you let Jesus in your hearts?" Patches and Blake nodded their head. "Young Marshall has let Jesus back into his heart. We must show him love." Ted turned to the three other teens he brought to help save. All had come to love Jesus and find salvation, except for Marble, who held on to her unbelief to please Jonathan. "Willy, you and Devin can be real friends with Marshall now. He no longer follows Jonathan, same as you."

"I'll never betray Jonathan!" Marble stared at the empty chair. "Will Blaze screw me like before?" She started to reach for bread

279

when Matthew grabbed her hand. She smiled up seductively into his eyes.

"Young lady, we will not allow such talk in this house!" Ted held her stare until she finally looked down at her plate nervously.

"I'm sorry Ted. I'll behave." She spoke softly as Matthew narrowed his eyes at her skeptical.

Ted looked toward the kitchen and smiled. "Esther, you may bring Marshall in to meet the family."

Esther walked in and took Marshall over behind Robert and Andrew. Her empty chair waited between them. "Marshall, I want you to use my chair today and get to know your room mates." Pointing out each boy, she introduced them.

"It's good to know you Marshall. Welcome friend." Andrew shook his hand and pulled out the chair for him.

"There's always room for one more." Robert smiled and glanced back at his girlfriend. "I see you've met Esther. I was wondering where she was."

"Esther was gracious enough to show me around." Marshall looked down the table and spotted Patches and Blake. "There you two runaways are. I'm glad They found you."

"It's more like they found us, Marshall." Jenny blushed, recalling fining the small children hiding under their bed. "We found them hiding in our motel room."

"Good Lord Jenny!" Kathy blurted out. "How long where they there before you found them?"

"I'll tell you later Kath. It's something I cannot share with the family." Jenny heard Ted laugh softly and glance over at him. "Wouldn't you agree Ted darling?"

"One hundred percent sweetheart. Top secret!" He heard Matthew chuckle softly. "Something funny Matthew?"

"Heck no Ted!" Matthew couldn't wipe the grin off his handsome face. "Too bad we missed that exciting discovery!"

Ted could only shake his head before he bowed it in prayer. "Heavenly Father, we come to you with a grateful heart. Give us the wisdom to help all these children. For what we are about to eat, bless it so as to strengthen our bodies to do your will. Please touch each of our hearts with love to welcome Marshall among us. Help him to feel he is a part of our family. In the Savior's blessed name. Amen."

Marshall had known love with Jonathan, then hate, but never in his sixteen short years on this earth was he prepared for the love radiating from this one man. Tears of joy filled his eyes as he took the passing dishes of food from loving hands. Robert had been observing his emotions and after the last dish was past, he lend over toward him.

"I know what you're feeling Marshall. I too was a lost soul when Ted saved me and took me into his family. No matter what life throws at you, you will never lose the love Ted gives you."

"Thank you, Robert." Marshall looked across the table to see Marble smiling at him. He remembered the things he had done to her and how she enjoyed it. He then noticed that she no longer carried the baby inside her and he wondered if she had it and did she know who the father was after it came out. It could have been one of many men and teens she had sex with.

"The baby is fine Marshall." Ted spoke softly while the family chatted among themselves. "It was a boy. We named him Noah. Jenny and I adopted the precious infant."

Marshall stared over at the man who apparently read his thoughts. "I wonder if Ted knows if I'm the father or not?" could he read this thought as well, he wondered.

"Yes son, I know." Ted smiled warmly. "You can relax, you are not the father, but beware the girl, Marble is not yet saved and she might try to tempt you son."

Marshall looked back at the young girl, barely thirteen and checking out Matthew, a married man. He turned back to Ted, real concern on his young face. Not for him but for this young girl. His thoughts returned to the man he admired with love. "Is there any hope for Marble, Ted? She has been with you a long while and I see no change in her bad behavior."

"There is always hope Marshall, for all God's children." Ted noticed they had gotten Matthew's attention and he was shaking his head at them. "Matthew, is it interesting to listen to a two way conversation when all you can hear is one side?"

"Sure Ted! It's like a game." Matthew looked over at Marshall who was wondering if this Matthew could figure out what he had been thinking.

"No Marshall, Matthew cannot figure them out." Ted laughed. "But my friend does have a bright imagination for coming up with crazy assumptions." Ted casually took a sip of milk as he smiled

281

over at Matthew. "Tell us genus what Marshall has been thinking."

Matthew thought on the first response from Ted. "The first one is easy, because your answer mentioned you and Jenny adopting Noah. So, he was thinking about who took the baby after Marble gave birth."

"The next thought?" Ted tried not to laugh.

"That one is even simple enough for a kinder garden kid! He wanted to know if he was the father of Noah but Ted was giving you a warning you could be the father of her next baby if you fall for her advances." Matthew sit back smiling and jump back up when Marshall joined Ted in laughing.

"What about my last thought Matthew?" Marshall continued to laugh.

"Well, should you get weak and fall into the baby doll's web and find yourself a parent, you know there is still hope for you, being a child of God." Matthew looked sure of his answers, despite their laughter.

"Matthew, my friend, maybe you had better stick to watching sheep." Ted stood up and helped Jenny with her chair as she glanced over helplessly at Kathy.

"Poor Matthew. Everyone with a mind knows what Marshall was thinking."

"Jenny is right, poor darling." Kathy put her arm around Matthew as he frowned up at her. "Go ahead and tell him Jenny." Kathy smiled over at her friend, unsure of the right answer.

"Marshall was asking Ted what could he do if he felt himself growing weak over her advances." Jenny smiled over at her husband. "So, Ted tells him there's always hope for all God's children. Right darling?"

"It's true you have a mind that should know, my love." Ted smiled as he watched Jenny tensing up. "Unfortunately, you are wrong as well."

"So, tell us this instant!" Jenny felt embarrassed with everyone watching her.

"And take away all the fun of the guessing game." Ted chuckled and took her hands, looking deep into her eyes. "Some things are not to be shared at the table darling. I'll tell you later."

"Hey! What about me?" Matthew followed him out of the dinning room. "I'm dying to know here!" He had not noticed Marble

282

walking close behind him until he felt her hand on his arm.

"I know what will make you feel better Matthew." She rubbed up against him causing a reaction to jump away from her. "Kathy is busy cleaning off that big dirty table so we have time for a little roll in the hay. There's privacy in the barn loft. Don't you want someone young, hot, and eager?"

Ted stepped back inside the room and took hold of her arm, then led her to the front door as she looked up dreamily.

"So, the invitation sounded too good to pass up, Teddy boy?"

"Young lady, Matthew is a married man! You will behave under my roof or I'll have to send you away!"

"Good! I hate it here!" Marble shouted. No one wants to have fun! You're just a bunch of sick religious freaks!"

"Look young lady, you do not speak to my husband like that!" Jenny took hold of her shoulders. "What's wrong with you? Don't you want to go to heaven where there's eternal life? Where you can live, be happy and stay cool!"

Matthew laughed, but Ted took him and faced him toward the kitchen. "Matthew, get in that kitchen and help with the dishes!"

"The dishes?" Matthew looked helpless. "Oh, alright! But Jenny was funny describing heaven. Happy and stay cool." He walked past the stubborn girl. "Maybe you had rather be on fire forever and stay hot!"

"Matthew, the dishes!" Ted almost shouted causing the young man to dash through the dinning room door toward the kitchen. Ted pulled the girl away from his wife and stared down at her. "I know Jonathan has a strong hold on you child, but God help me, we will get Satan out of your heart once and for all!" Ted looked warmly at Jenny, who had tears in her eyes. "Jenny sweetheart, it's alright. See that the girls are put to bed and wait up for me. I think it's time to show this young lady what she will gain and what she could lose by the choice she must make this night."

CHAPTER 53

Ted took Marble on the far side of the mountain, where both Mountains joined. On Goldsburg Mountain everything was green and alive. Flowers danced among the rocks and the trees stood tall and green, even through it was fall and the changing colors could be found on the drive up but never here.

Just a few feet away stood the ghostly hills of Black Mountain. If one ventured too close to the black rocks where no flowers grew, nor green grass adorned the ground, they would feel the chill of danger run through their veins. The dark leaf trees, now bare, gave the landscape an eyrie sound that mixed with the howls coming from the dense forest.

Jeff had heard Ted's call and was standing just an arm's length away, hidden in the shadow of the growing moonlight overhead. Gabriel appeared in a glowing white robe while on the other mountain, a black-robed figure appeared, staring coldly at the shaken young girl.

"Marble, here you can witness both worlds to come. Heaven or Hell, good or evil." Ted's presence beside her made her feel safe as he spoke softly and full of love. Then the deep voice came from the tall man, whose face shown in the moon glow.

"Marble, if you choose evil and hell, your eternal home will be even worse than the mountain on which I stand." He called up the figure in black.

"I live in Hell." Came the soft voice inside the hood. "In the deepest chamber I live as you will child, should you choose to follow Jonathan. The Devil, our master, is a liar! You will suffer and be tormented. We have nothing to be happy about and live with the fear of knowing our future will be in a lake of fire! You will wish for death, sweet child, but you are already dead. Is this what you choose?"

"My daughter, fear not!" Gabriel's voice was strong, yet kind. "If you choose to give your heart to Jesus, your home will be in heaven. I know what it's like, dear one for I dwell there, on the left side of the Almighty God, our Father and Creator." The large

284

angel's blue eyes held her in his total love. "The beauty of heaven cannot be described by human words, but young child, there is so much love in heaven you can actually feel it, touch it and taste it. The activities are numerous and happy are the children of God throughout the eternal light. Jesus, our Lord and your Savior, walks among all who dwell there. Just looking into His loving eyes is worth the most in heaven's realm. Yet, there's so much more! Jesus gives the best hugs, he enjoys his walks and talks with each individual and His glorious father, his dad, has so much love for the people, to be in his all-powerful presence is like nothing else you've ever known. He shines with a brightness so powerful, even with the perfect vision of heaven, all you can witness is the shining double of His Son, as The Almighty sits on His throne. Heaven is a place of wonder, where there is no more death, no more sorrow, no more pain or sickness, and no hate, only pure love!"

"Marble, I have brought you here to show you what lies ahead for you." Ted took her hands. "No one knows when God will call you home, but if you choose evil, He will turn you away and Satan will take you with him forever."

"It's your choice Marble." Jeff's stare held her frozen. "Which will it be? Good? Or, will your choice be, evil?"

Tears flooded down her chubby cheeks as she dropped to the knees, shaking all over. "Help me Ted! Please!" she looked up to see him knelling down next to her. Ted could feel the frightened girl shaking as he asked her softly.

"What do you ask of me child? Tell me. I am here to help you."

"I don't want to go to hell! I don't want Satan to have my soul!" she cried. "I don't want to burn forever!"

"Then, you chose where you want to go Marble." Ted waited, knowing she must say the words."

"I want to go to heaven! I want to see Jesus!" Weeping, the young thirteen-year-old girl, laid her head over in Ted's lap. "I want to be good, not evil!"

"God loves you Marble." Ted's loving hands held her tight. "Can you tell the Lord how sorry you are and ask Him to forgive you?"

"I've done so many bad things Jesus!" she wept through her words. "I'm so sorry! Please forgive me Jesus!"

"Jesus has heard your voice. You are forgiven child and your name is now written in the Book of Life, which awaits you in heaven." Ted touched her face and she felt incredible love flow through her. "You may open your eyes and look around Marble. You have nothing to fear."

Marble saw instantly the horrible images on the black mountain had vanished as did the angelic vision from heaven, but in her heart, she knew that she had been saved and was heaven bound.

Jeff looked sadly at the dark robed figure standing in front of him. "Thank you for helping that child. It could not have been an easy decision to come up here knowing the trouble you might find yourself in when they find you missing."

"I would never wish any child of God to be traped in the hell I live in. When you sought me out, I felt a joy I had not felt ever since you were born." A robed hand reached up to touch his face. "I only wished I could have lived long enough to see you change son." Gloria Wineworth pulled back the black hood, revealing her chard sad face. "Now my Jonathan has been lured into the Devil's den. I gain one son to good and lose another to his evil father, Lucifer."

Jeff reached out to caressed her face. "Mother" it felt good calling her this with love instead of hate. "I promise to do all in my power to help save my brother from father's grip."

"Jeffery, my beautiful son, I would to God that I had not thrown myself in that fire." Gloria looked up at the castle where she had lived in fear. "That young girl, Naomi, I tried to make her run from you and it was she who saved you."

"Yes, she did mother." Jeff reached for her hand and was glad to find it had cooled down for her sake. If only for a little while. "My love, Naomi, and Ted, the neighbor I hated for so long."

"You have two sons. My two grandsons, I could have loved and spoiled." Tears came to her parched eyes. "Teddy and Jacob look so much like you Jeffery." She looked down. "I should have loved you more."

"What good would it have done you mother. Before I confessed my love to Naomi, I would not have wanted your love Mother." Jeff wanted to be honest to the woman who gave him birth. "I wished you were still alive, still here on the mountain, to share in my joy."

"It's too late for me son." Gloria looked around at everything she remembered while she lived and recalled it hadn't all been bad. "If you had not helped me here today, I wouldn't be able to feel and breath fresh air once more. For that Son, thank you."

"Mother, I don't know if it is possible, but I will speak to Ted." Jeff pulled her into his strong arms and hugged his mother for the first time. "Ted saw what you did today, to help save Marble from going to hell. God's angel, Gabriel witnessed what you did, knowing the severe punishment you could possible have waiting on your return." Jeff looked hopeful as he held on to her. "Maybe, by some miracle, God will forgive you and bring you up out of the torments of hell into the glory of heaven."

"I can almost believe that Jeffery." Gloria smiled for the first time. "Why, seeing the miracle of you changing and becoming a follower of our Lord Jesus, makes it believable." Gloria stood back, hands laying on her son's shoulders and looking into his blue eyes. "But, my beautiful son, even if it's just our dream and once judged it can never be erased, I will always be grateful that God allowed me to come up to help you and tell you how very much I love you, Jeffery."

"I love you too mother." Tears flowed down Jeff's cheeks as he kissed her, and seeing her face one more time before she descended back down, hopefully before Lucifer found her missing. Jeff could still here hear last words echoing through his head.

"Remember me to Jonathan. Goodbye my son."

As Jeff watched his mother disappear he whispered. "Don't give up hope mother." Finding a nearby rock, Jeff sat down and cried.

CHAPTER 54

"Jenny, wake up my love." Ted lay looking down as her blurry eyes tried to focus in on her naked husband. "You fell asleep."

"Oh sweetheart, I really tried to stay awake."

"You're awake now." He climbed over on her and started making love as she let out a satisfying sigh. "I needed you Jenny, needed this."

"You may need this with me anytime we are alone, you sexy, handsome, husband!" She answered out of breath from their increased movements.

Their eyes met when they both released the incredible passion they had built up, then Ted rolled over after giving her a kiss. He smiled over at his satisfied wife who lay smiling with her eyes shut. "My Jenny, my dearest love."

"You are some sexy husband, Ted darling!" She moved over next to him and rubbed her hand over her growing belly. "If I get much fatter with this baby boy, my sex appeal will fly right out the window."

"Then I'll just have to catch it and place it back in its rightful place." Ted lend over for another kiss. "There's nothing more beautiful and sexy to me than the woman I love carrying my child inside her."

"Ted, if it were any other man but you, I would say they were feeding me a bunch of bull." Jenny laughed at his innocent face. "But, coming from you, my wonderful, adorable, husband, I believe every word you say, so thank you."

"Marshall asked if there was any hope for Marble." Ted smiled when Jenny shot up, confused "Well, you did insist that I tell you what he was thinking when I answered: there's always hope for God's children."

"Now I remember. The thinking, game!" Jenny laid back down, remembering why Ted hadn't come to bed with her. "You left with Marble! That's where you've been all this time, trying to save that little fowl mouth sex maniac."

"We had a way to walk." Ted propped up his pillows and placed his hands behind his head. "I took Marble to the two corners, the only spot where both mountains connect securely. Jeff was there to show her what being evil and following Lucifer would reward her with. Like most Devil worshipers, their leader leads them to believe they will be rewarded with great fortune and for girls, many sexy studs. For men, fortune along with as many virgins as they desire. All lies, like everything that comes from Lucifer's deceitful mouth. Then, I showed her what she would win by following good and the Lord Jesus."

"So, you and Jeff threw out reasons of what her future would be like if she chose either good or bad." Jenny laid her head over on Ted's strong tan shoulder. "I bet Jeff's act made her shake with fear."

"Jeff did not need to act it out darling. Jeff had summons a demon out of hell to help convince Marble not to choose evil." Ted knew he had Jenny's attention when she sat back up and stared over at him.

"A demon actually came up from hell to help Jeff?"

"And Gabriel told the frightened girl what heaven was like and what being in the presence of Jesus felt like."

"I am certain Marble was happy she had a choice between the two." Jenny couldn't get past the demon coming up to help save another from their own fate just because Jeff ask them to.

"The demon was Jeff's mother, Jenny." Ted watched his wife's eyes open in surprise. "He called for her and she came." Ted closed his eyes, both from being weary and feeling the desire of his friend and helpmate wanting something that had never been asked of God. "Jeff wants me to put in a good word to the Father on behalf of his mother."

"You said she helped Marble, by describing what hell was really like." Jenny sat up, thoughtfully considering the possibility of a deceased person doomed for hell to be forgiven and lifted up to the third heaven.

"I can see my Jenny has been reading her Bible, to know that heaven was described by Paul as the third heaven." Ted had read her thoughts. "With God, all things are possible Jenny. When our Lord Jesus was crucified and buried, He descended into hell to collect those waiting to be taken up. The fallen angels, knowing who He was, had no authority over the Son of God, so in fear, they backed away from the Savior."

"Then, you are saying that Jesus, Himself, can get Jeff's mother out of that horrible place?" Jenny yawned and snuggled down beside her husband.

"My love, the Almighty God need not leave his throne in heaven to bring a lost soul up." Ted knew sleep would drift upon them with his last words. "All He has to do is think it, Jenny, and it shall be accomplished." Ted pulled Jenny in close and they fell asleep.

"Mother? You saw our mother?" Jonathan followed Jeff as he made his way to the rose garden to work. "What did she say? Did mother ask about me?"

"Full of questions brother." Jeff got down and started pulling weeds. Glancing up, he noticed tears in Jonathan's eyes. "You really care about mother, don't you?" Jeff remembered how disappointed Gloria had been learning how her once sweet innocent son had turned to evil and Satan. Jonathan easily read his brother's thoughts as he looked down sadly.

"She is disappointed in me. Does mother hate me, Jeff?"

"Does it matter what the dear lady thinks?" Jeff began snipping off the dead buds. "You will find out soon enough if you keep running after father."

"She should not be down there!" Jonathan could not believe his brother could act so cruel and cold toward the woman that gave him life. "She is down there because of you, Jeff! You had driven the poor woman mad! She was so frightened of you and what you would do to her, she chose an instant death!"

"Mother loves me." Jeff looked up seriously. "I was extremely bad to mother and I would have tortured her for getting in my way." He stood up, towering over his twin by a few inches. "I would have sent her to hell, gladly, when I followed father!"

"And do you think I could have tortured that woman and sent her to him?" Jonathan flopped down on the love bench. "God forbid I hurt the woman who loved me and sent me away to save."

"And for what Jonathan? Only to lose you to Satan years later." Jeff stared down at his twin. "No, you could never hurt that woman, but at that time in my life, I could and laugh about it."

"Yet, you tell me she loves you Jeffery!" Jonathan shook his head. "If she can love you after what you did to her, does she love me also?"

"What do you think Jonathan?" Jeff sat down next to his brother.

290

"How could she?" Jonathan almost shouted. "Mother hated you when you were evil and mean, before Naomi! Now, I am the evil brother! Of courses she hates me!"

"No Jonathan, mother loves you, and in her private hell she prays for you, for the little baby she sent away to safety. She prays that you find your way back to God!"

"Jeffery, is there nothing we can do for mother?" Tears filled his black eyes. "You have two sixes so that gives you power to the underworld! Father is not there, he told me. His demons are left in charge, so maybe we could work together to get her out!"

"Jonathan, I want nothing to do with hell. If I start showing my authority down below, Satan will find means to come after me again." Jeff remained calm. "Don't you think I know father roams this earth, gathering lost souls like a farmer gathers crops! I know he will not enter into the hell of fire until our Lord Jesus returns to the earth." Jeff took Jonathan by his trembling shoulders. "Brother, even if we both descended down to retrieved our mother, she could never remain on this earth as before. She is a spirit and this is not for us to do. The only one capable of saving Gloria Wineworth's soul is the Living Lord! Jonathan, if you are father's chosen Anti-Christ, you might reign for several years until Christ returns, then you too will be cast into a burning hell. It's not as glamorous as father paints it!"

"Nevertheless, we are Lucifer's sons Jeffery. I must prove myself worthy of him." Jonathan suddenly felt pulled. By a brother who shared his evil past and found salvation through love, and a strong angelic father, who could make him a king.

"Do what you will then, Jonathan. God has given you a choice to make and you have witness both sides." Jeff had sadness in his eyes as he touched his brother's face. "It will be an incomplete reunion in heaven if you choose evil. Three of our family members will be there. Billy, mother and I will miss you."

Jonathan stared in confusion. "You will help her then? A change of heart, perhaps?"

"No brother, that is up to God in heaven." Jeff hugged Jonathan. "Ted is speaking to Him at this very moment."

"You saw her, my Father, helping that child choose salvation. I really believe Gloria has a faithful heart." Ted had walked to the mountain top as the sun was rising to plead for Jeff's mother, who

Joan Byrd

had been weighing heavily on his mind. "You know this dear lady's heart Father and the love for her sons and You."

"Yes son, I witnessed her deed." Came the still small voice. "You wish for me to judge her again?"

"If it be your will Father." Ted looked up with reverence.

"She tried to help save Naomi, the one you call your angel."

"Jeff mother realizes now that it was Naomi's love that saved her son and that's how you came to save him, Lord." Ted spoke softly.

"Gloria's heart is still filled with love for me son, yes, you are right. She prays for both her sons, even in the lower part of hell." God whispered. "I hear her prayers drifting up, day after day. She is not afraid to show her faith, even now, knowing Lucifer can make things even worse for her."

"Her heart is in the right place, even though her soul is in the wrong place." Ted kneeled down and looked up, love filling his blue eyes. "It is not for me to judge, Holy Father. You and only you, can choose her fate. I merely humbly plea for her soul."

"She cannot come to heaven." Came the bold statement and the loving Lord felt Ted's sadness as he reached down and touched his shoulder. "Be not discourage my son, but be of glad tidings, I mean to help her. Gloria just cannot come up now because she is needed here on earth."

"You will bring her out of hell and to the living again, loving Father!" Ted smiled brightly. "Then, she can have another chance with her sons! They can have another chance with their mother!"

"And we need her mother's touch to help win my son Jonathan back into the fold!" Ted could hear the joy in the Creators voice.

"You spoke of Kristine helping him also Father?" Ted felt like singing.

"Yes, dear son. The love I feel between them is strong!" God's voice rang out. "Kristine's good love can easily win over the evil that has blackened Jonathan's heart."

"Praise be to you, great Jehovah, for your love and goodness flows from heaven and touches our heart with total joy!" Ted sang.

"Go quickly my son and tell your brother, his mother, that was dead, is now alive!" the voice blew softly before it drifted away.

Ted smiled toward heaven before he made his way quickly down the hill where Jenny sat waiting, to inform her they would be paying a visit to Naomi and Jeff with good tidings.

CHAPTER 55

"So, why the hurry darling?" Jenny hadn't seen Ted that excited since he informed her they were having a son. "Couldn't we go back for the car and take the girls with us?"

"There's no time Jenny! I've got joyful news to share with Jeff and Naomi and I cannot wait a moment or it will happen before I reach them!" He pulled her in close and had her to close her eyes. "We're traveling light speed so just relax and keep those eyes closed or you might grow dizzy." Within seconds Jenny and Ted where standing in front of the castle.

"Good Lord Ted, are you telling me that you suddenly know Naomi is having a baby any moment?" Jenny stared up at her husband who laughed out.

"What an imagination! Jenny, that is the funniest thing I have ever heard."

"Well, I'm glad you can laugh!" Jenny frowned up at him. "You just seemed so serious, I only thought"

"Sweetheart, don't try to figure it out." Ted squeezed her hand. "You can never guess, so just wait for the exciting news.

"Thank God we made it without me going into early labor with that lighting speed trick!" She took a deep breath.

"Jenny" Ted gave her a hug. "You won't have that baby until Christmas Eve, two a.m."

"What?" Jenny felt flushed. "Is that your big news?"

"For Jeff and Naomi?" Ted laughed as he gave her a kiss. "Darling, that is our joyful news, theirs is something completely different."

"Then I guess the three of us will soon find out." Jenny waved at Naomi and Jeff when they walked around the yard and saw them.

"Ted, you have news about mother?" Jeff clutched his wife's hand, knowing Jonathan was the only one he had told about bringing up his mother to help him. "You helped save her?"

"Helped save your mother? What is going on?" Naomi looked from Jeff to Ted. "Jenny, do you know what these men are talking about?"

"I haven't the slightest Naomi. I only know that I will be going into labor on Christmas Eve at 2:00 a.m." Jenny smiled up at her husband. "Merry Christmas darling! You are getting a boy for Christmas!"

"Jenny, I know these fellows can drive us nuts by knowing things before we do, but I'm still waiting to find out what you meant by saving Gloria! Your mother is dead Jeff! I saw her burn up, remember that horrible night?"

"I remember that moment well, sweet one. You fainted and I caught you in my arms and carried you up to my room." Jeff put his arm around his wife as she blushed, remembering Jeff raping her and how she enjoyed it. To avoid the sudden interest by Jenny, Naomi turned to Ted. "What is this about saving Jeff's mother, Ted?"

Ted suddenly became still, his blue eyes focused down the garden path. Jeff sensed her arrival too as he turned his head to look in the direction his friend was staring at. Seeing their men's reaction, Jenny and Naomi looked down the empty path and wondered what had drawn their husband's undivided attention. Suddenly, like a vision in a dream, a woman appeared and started slow steps toward them.

Naomi stepped forward, as she watched with strange emotions. Somewhere deep inside, she managed to speak with a shaky voice. "It...it can't be! I saw Gloria fall into those hot flames! I heard her screams of anguish!"

"Is there nothing impossible the Almighty God cannot do, my sweet angel?" Ted spoke calmly. "Yes, Gloria was dead, but through faith and the miracle of prayer, Jehovah has restored her life and has forgiven her completely."

Gloria walked straight up to the angelic man in the white robe and took around him. "You are Ted. It was you who ask the Father in heaven to forgive me and bring my soul up from hell."

"Dear woman, God's mercies are bountiful." Ted's loving embrace sent rays of warm love throughout her body. "It was the Lord who made you alive, because He needed your help down here on earth before you can enter into his Kingdom."

"May He lead me to do His will." Tears of joy flowed down her cheeks as she turned to her son and reached out her hand for his. "Jeffery, do you have room in your home and heart for me, son?"

"Mother, you have already found a place in my heart." Jeff pulled his mother into his strong arms, hugging his flesh and blood mother for the first time. "You must know that you are welcome to live in our home, as it was always yours before." He held his hand out for Naomi. "Of course, my better half has to be alright with her mother-n-law living with us." Jeff gave her a wink, knowing what his loving Naomi would say.

"Mother Wineworth, God has lovingly given you back to us." Naomi hugged her tenderly. "You were always good to me so our home will always be your home. Your grandsons, Teddy Jeffery and Jacob have gained a wonderful caring grandmother."

"Bless you child." Gloria held tight to her beautiful and giving daughter-n-law. "I can see why Jeffery fell in love with you and I remember you expressing your love for him after I tried to warn you about your safety. I also recall laughing at your confession of love, knowing the evil one you claimed to have given your heart to. Forgive me child and I thank God for bringing you into his troubled life." Gloria glanced down, sorrow lacing her face. "If only there was someone to bring the same kind of love to my Jonathan."

"There is someone Gloria and our heavenly Lord intends to use her deep love for Jonathan's salvation." Ted put his arm around Jenny before continuing. "Kristine O'Donnell, Jenny aunt, is very much in love with your son and Jonathan has the same great love for her. He struggles with this love he is feeling and Lucifer has read the deep devotion between them."

"Sweetheart, surely you're not thinking about bringing Aunt Kris back, are you?" Jenny had bad feelings about Satan knowing about her aunt's love for his son Jonathan.

"Jenny, it is not I who brings her back, God will be bringing Kristine back, dearest one." Ted held her eyes, making her calm down. "I promise you, Kristine will never be in real danger. I will be close by her side as will Gabriel and Michael."

"Michael? God's mighty warrior?" Jenny relaxed as she remembered how Michael had saved her from the pack of mad wolves on the scary high mountain connecting the twin mountains. "Then, by all means, Kristine should be brought back to save Jonathan, just like Naomi saved Jeff."

"Not quite the same, Jennifer." Jeff spoke, seriously. "Kristine will be bringing a lost sheep home. A man who had been devoted to

Joan Byrd

God and strayed away to follow our father." Jeff looked down into his wife's brown eyes and pulled her into his arms. "On the other hand, I was completely evil and filled with hate for everyone and every living thing, especially God. I was short of one six in becoming Lucifer's Anti-Christ. I was becoming my father and devoted 100% to him." Jeff's hand touched his wife's face. "Then, Ted's angel, my sweet one and dove, flew into my wretched, miserable life, and with her pure 1% of love, destroyed my 100% of dark evil and I found salvation."

"It was quite a miracle from God." Jenny smiled up at her husband. "I'm sure your Naomi would agree it was the love and guidance of Ted that filled her heart with the love that won your heart. Ted's love certainly changed my life for the better and that too was a miracle."

Ted squeezed her hand lovingly and was about to leave when he stopped suddenly and smiled over at Naomi, then Jeff, who was returning his knowing smile.

"Yes Ted, I've known for several weeks." Jeff looked down lovingly at Naomi.

"Then, congratulations! After two boys, she will look forward to a little girl." Still in the dark, Naomi watched Ted reach over and kiss her. "Maybe your daughter will be a match for our Gabriel."

"For heavens sake fellows!" Jenny could tell Naomi was speechless over this new revelation. "Naomi, I can tell you did not even know you were expecting a baby, did you?"

"Heavens no!" Naomi reached up and slapped Jeff's arm as he and Ted joined in laughter. "Well then, tell me great wizards, will my baby girl look like me or Jeff?"

"Our little daughter will be the perfect copy of her beautiful mother who cannot possibly be mad at us wizards for sharing such wonderful news!" Jeff gave her a wink when he heard his mother laugh softly.

A big smile fell on Naomi's beautiful face as she reached around his waist and gave him a big hug. "We just cannot beat these guys at this game, Jenny."

"At least your daughter will look like you." Jenny smiled at the loving couple. "Mary and Martha look just like their adorable daddy and I'm carrying a little Ted inside me."

Ted smiled as he gave her a loving kiss. "Sweet Jenny, there

296

will be another child and she will be the heavenly image of her beautiful mother."

"Couldn't we just have her now and get it over with? Another set of twins, just not identical this time." Jenny rubbed her big stomach. "I'm big enough to be carrying two!"

"And miss all the fun of making a baby?" Ted knew he had made Jenny speechless, when she took his hand, waved over her head at their laughing friends, and started walking toward Goldsburg Mountain and home.

CHAPTER 56

The day before the Thanksgiving parade came in with a light snow on the mountain. The parents, along with their doctors, had gathered in the large den at the children's home to discuss the six teenage girls found inside the barn the morning after Halloween. The group of eighteen sat watching the young man dressed in a white robe and whispered among one another about his appearance. The highly educated physicians considered their skills in mental breakdowns so great, they should never be questioned, especially by this strange young man with long hair. They had been treating the six girls ever since they were brought to the hospital and up until this moment, there had been no breakthrough. After meeting over the situation, the six-specialist decided the best treatment for the six girls was a lengthy stay at the Mental Hospital. The unhappy parents decided to try the young religious man on the mountain.

The group had chosen Doctor Winfrey to speak for them. Rearing back and crossing his arms in defiance, the sliver-hair man began to speak. "Mr. Neenam, we here are all trained doctors in the field of mental breakdowns and have studied for years on a variety of subjects, such as these six unfortunate teens. After a victim, this young, is raped and dealing with the gruesome murder of their rapers, the case takes on a slow and difficult healing period. We tried to explain this to their parents, but they insisted we give you a try." Winfrey's eyebrow went up in anger. "I don't mind telling you, young man, that never in any of our careers have we been so insulted as to think a person such as you, can make our patients well if we cannot!"

"I'm sorry you feel this way gentlemen." Ted remained calm and untouched by their sarcasm. "You have tried the only way you know how. So plainly, the medical treatments have failed. Now, their healing has been turned over to the power of the Almighty."

The doctor closes to Winfrey laughed out. "Faith healing? I might have guess by your attire. This faith healing medicine is just a myth, if you ask me."

Ted was glad he had sent all the family out of the room,

knowing they would all fly to his defense. Turning his attention away from the snobby doctors, Ted gathered around the sad parents. "Loving parents, do you wish for your daughters to come back to you, whole and without fear, with new hope?"

One sad mother sat up, eyes swollen from nights of weeping over her lost child. "Dear sir, if there is anything you can do to save my little girl, I pray that God in heaven will give you the power to do so."

"Thank you for your faith, dear lady." Ted's warm, loving smile spread over the sad group and brought them a peaceful hope for the first time. "God is please with your belief and devotion to prayer, Gail."

Sitting up, she wondered how he knew her name was Gail, as did the other parents when he assured each on of them by saying their first given name. "I will ask that you all remain here, while I have the guard to take the girls to the chapel." Ted turned to the doctors who had been taking in his promises as they listened and shook their head at one another. "I know what you are thinking gentlemen. That I have gave promises that cannot be kept, correct?" he watched them all drop their eyes. "God has the power to do things man can only dream about. One thing that will work for you my brothers, does not require a school education." Ted walked to the door, then turned to see the parents praying while the doctors just stared at him. "The parents have already found it. It is something you should have been doing anyway. Pray!" he left them staring.

As the six girls were led into the chapel, Ted could tell they moved in a daze and took their seats, never blinking an eye. He knew their minds had been blocked from all the trauma that accrued on Halloween night. The devilish-lustful acts of Lucifer, raping each innocent virgin while they laid drugged. Then finding those two innocent young men slaughtered with a pitchfork and made it appear to have been the girls who did the killing and the young men the rapers. For the average police officer, this was exactly what it appeared to be. The set up was made to look like, the two men drugged the girls, brought them to the old barn, where they had planned everything by the six tables waiting to lay their naked victims on. By the evidence found, each man was supposed to have raped three girls each. The girls, in a state of shock, saw the pitchforks and slayed their rapers.

Joan Byrd

Ted could recall that night through the victims sitting in front of
him and he knew the truth, as it happened to them. He sent the guard
outside, and he smiled, knowing he was not alone in the chapel with
the six teens. Stepping in front of them, Ted began to speak softly.
"God in heaven knows your pain. Jesus, out Lord, hears your inward
thoughts and lets them flow over into me. Children of God, you are
loved beyond anything you have ever known." Ted could see the
girls blinking their eyes as they began to slowly return.

"Little children, you will find peace in your heart, as Jesus, our
Savior, enters in. The Father's loving arms are open wide to give
you complete healing." Ted moved at the far end and started laying
his hand on each girl's head, where they opened their eyes instantly
and focused in on the angelic man with eyes as blue as the sky.
"Before you can find complete peace, young ones, we must put the
past events behind you." Ted felt Gabriel walking beside him and
noticed from the girl's focus, they had saw him appear. "As we
relive that terrible night, we shall learn the truth."

The six teenage girls felt safe inside this holy place with this
incredible young man and the very tall one who could pass as his
father. It was as if two angels were speaking to them and they felt
sure of learning what really happened inside that horrible place.

"You are indeed safe inside the Lord's house, my children."
Gabriel's voice came out soft, yet strong. "I sit at the right hand of
God and He has sent complete healing to your mind and bodies."

Ted reached out and touched each of their hand. "You did not
go to Satan of your own free will, therefor, Lucifer has no power
over you. Your bodies are cleansed from within and made pure
again. The memory about Satan will be erased from your memory
forever."

Each girl felt their first breath of joy flow inside them when
Gabriel smiled, his eyes shone like the stars adorning the night sky.

"The two men in the barn, were victims, same as you. God sees
all! They tried to flee Lucifer and he ordered them killed."

Then, for the first time since the girls had gotten drugged, they
actually looked around at one another, each remembering waking
up in the barn and seeing the two, dead corpse, pitchforks in two of
the girl's hand. "Then...we...we didn't kill those young men?"
came the weak voice of one of the girls who held a pitchfork."

"No child, Satan's worshipers slaughtered those men and set it

300

up to look like you had killed them." Ted could see the color coming back into each girl's face. "One of you saw them, but hid your eyes so they couldn't see you watching.

Again, the girls looked at one another, confused as to which one had actually saw the murder. Ted and Gabriel knew which girl but they also knew she was too afraid to come forward. Ted moved in front of the shy girl and knelt down. "Tammy, young child, you must not be afraid. No one is asking you to be a witness, unless it's your will to do so."

"Those evil beings cannot hurt you again child. Be not afraid! You are safe!" Gabriel touched her arms, and she felt his angelic warmth. "The two dead children of God cannot speak their innocents on this earth and many regard them as evil rapists."

"Please tell me these innocent young men were saved." Tammy closed her eyes, hoping for the right answer.

"You have a good heart child." Ted smiled warmly. "Before the devil worshipers planned their fate that took their life, those two young men had gone to their priest and confessed their sins and ask God to forgive them. They live in heaven this day, praying for the souls that killed them."

Tammy sat straight and lifted her head. "Then I must tell you what I saw! Two young men carried their unconscious victims inside the barn. There were two girls, both high school seniors, who came in behind them carrying two cups with a milky looking liquid inside." Tammy looked down flushed, feeling embarrassed by what happened next.

"We understand your feelings child. Those girls pretended to be your friends to lure you here." Gabriel could see what Tammy was thinking and knew that part would be hard to describe. "Those young men had felt sorry for the girls when they came by their apartment pretending to be frightened and wanting out of the cult. Being hot blooded men, they grew weak when those girls stepped from the shower and strolled out naked, so they ended up having sex." He glanced over at Ted and knew he could see everything unfolding as well. "The girls had planned having oral sex so they could gather the boy's liquid in their mouth, then spit it in a cup, so they could smear it on each of you, thus, setting them up for the rape."

"These poor misled teenagers thought they had got by with the

301

perfect crime." Ted's heart felt bad for the trusting young men who had died. "Then you saw the brutal killing when the laughing teenagers stab those young men in their chest with pitchforks."

"It was horrible! I was lying in the corner peeking, praying they would not see me watching. I felt sick, and kept swallowing it back." Tammy felt relieved to finally get the truth out in the open. "I remember praying, please, don't let me throw up or they will kill me too! Then they yanked off their clothes and had sex right there on the barn floor. I finally felt at ease because they were too much into each other to notice me. After they had finished, they simply put their clothes back on and walked out, discussing where to go get a beer and burger."

"The devil has turned those children cold and uncaring, but they will pay for their crimes. It's over now, child." Ted lifted her up. "I will inform the officer about the set up and murder. I will tell him, under the circumstances, the witness will remain anonymous for her safety."

For the first time since the incident, the six girls felt at peace from within as Ted held up his hands. "Dear ones, you are made whole! You are made well! God's power and love for each one of you has filled you with an everlasting peace."

"Praise be to the Lord God on high!" One girl sang out as she lifted up her hands in praise.

"What a splendid ideal young lady!" Gabriel put his arm around his son. "We shall all sing praises to the Lord as we make our way back to the house!"

"Yes father! It will enlighten the heart of every parent waiting!" Ted smiled brightly as he opened the chapel doors and nodded to the officer who stared in wonder at the six smiling girls who sang at the top of their voices, a song of praise!

Jenny, Kathy, Tracy and Hannah had joined the parents when they heard the joyful voices approaching the house. Moments before, Jenny and Kathy had been having a heated discussion with the doctors, who kept putting Ted down.

"That young man doesn't know what skilled doctors know in curing mental illness! He will simply undo everything we have accomplished so far!"

"I know my husband, Doctor Winfrey and if anyone on this earth can heal those poor girls, it is Ted!" Jenny had defended her angelic husband and now hearing the singing, Jenny smiled over at the confused doctors as she made her way to the front door and opened it. The doctors rushed over to witnessed Gabriel waving his arms as he led the singing group of happy girls. He turned to see Jenny smiling from the front door, then gave her a wink before vanishing, leaving the doctors wiping their eyes. Just as quickly, Ted appeared in front of the girls as they walked passed the dropped jaw doctors and into the den. The stun parents jumped up from the sight of their daughters running toward them laughing and singing. Jenny looked over the speechless doctors and cleared her throat. "Gentlemen, I think you owe my husband an apology."

"Well...I..." Doctor Winfrey stuttered.

"Gentlemen, I do not need any apologies for something God did." Ted pulled Jenny over in his arms. "Are you giving our guest a hard time beautiful?"

"Nothing that we didn't deserve, Mr. Neenam." Winfrey smiled down at Jenny. "You have a woman that takes up for you and rightfully so."

"Well, I may be a little outspoken when defending my perfect husband, but darn it, I love him so much!" Jenny looked up and found Ted smiling. He laughed and pulled her in closer before turning his attention on the six doctors. "As I told you earlier gentlemen, medicine can only go so far. God is, after all, the final healer. Think on these words so your next case may be completed quicker through sincere prayer."

Ted looked over at the happy girls, hugging their relieved parents. The six doctors turned to watch the happy reunion. "Look and see. At first, they were lost! Now, they are found! They were sick! Now, they are made well!"

With Jenny's hand in his, Ted walked over to the happy group and spoke out. "To God be the glory! Great things He hath done!"

CHAPTER 57

The teachers were putting their final touches on the school's parade float. Large books representing various classes lined the long wagon. From Math, History, Science, Music, English and Literature. The float was even better than Jenny had imagined when she drew it out. One teacher from each course would stand in front of the class book and Jenny being teacher for both English and Literature, ask Tracy to stand in front of one of her books.

The children had drawn numbers to win a place on the float and each number had what they would be representing. Three winners had come from the children's home on the mountain, as well as Teddy Jeffery. Teddy drew History and would be George Washington. Leah drew Music and became a big music note. Marble would be a big number eight, to represent Math. Jenny's English senior would be a dictionary and the two students chosen for Literature would be dressed like Romeo and Juliet. Dressed in a white coat holding two smoking vials would be Willy, representing Science.

After everyone was dressed in their costumes, they found their spot on the long float. While most of the family went to the parade, Hannah, Kathy, Miriam, and Esther had remained behind to prepare the big feast for the Thanksgiving meal that would be served exactly at 4:00 p.m."

Ted, along with the children from the home, found a good place to watch the town parade and cheer on the school float when it passed by. Matthew, Robert, and Marshall had joined the group to help with the smaller children. Jeff and Naomi walked up next to Ted and sat down. Jacob looked out with excitement, preparing for his first parade. Jonathan walked up and scooped his nephew in his strong arms, planting a kiss on his cheek.

"How's my little buddy?" Jonathan's smile was genuine when Jacob gave him a big hug. "I hear your big brother is in the parade today."

"Yeh! He is the first president of the United States, Uncle Jonathan!" Jacob kept his arms around his uncle's neck as Marshall looked over to watch their closeness. Jonathan smiled down at the boy he had taken in years before, causing Marshall to turned back toward the street.

Jonathan bent down to his brother, speaking softly. "I see Blaze has found new friends."

"He has lots of new friends, brother. Marshall is doing very well." Jeff looked up, a cold, serious expression on his face. "You best stay away from him Jonathan."

"Jeffery, you may not believe me brother, but I am happy for the boy." Jonathan sat his nephew down. "I guess Teddy Jeffery is happy he won a place in this parade."

"Teddy felt sure he was going to win." Naomi looked down the street to see the first band approaching. "I feel sure he got it by some kind of magic."

"Is that so bad, Naomi? The boy has got the gift, should he not put it to good use?" Jonathan knew the younger Jeffery's powers were growing stronger.

"That kind of magic can get dangerous, Jonathan. I want my sons to grow up as normal boys." Naomi looked up at her brother-n-law, knowing Jeff had not told his brother yet about their mother being alive. "I want both my sons to love and follow the Lord. To be children of the Living God!"

"It does sound safer." Jonathan noticed Marshall observing him so he smiled his way and again the teen turned his head from him. Ted had noticed and reached over to touch the boy's arm.

"Son, we must show love to everyone, even those who are our enemies. You will find that sharing love can help the ones who are lost and hurting the most."

"I understand what you mean Ted. Just like the love you shared to me when I was lost and struggling." Marshall glanced over at the man that had taken him into his heart when he had no one else to turn to. The young man felt bad for his previous actions when he noticed Jonathan's sad face watching him. Without hesitation, Marshall gave his old friend a smile and said a silent I love you, then turned back to see Ted's big smile of approval.

"God is proud of you Marshall." As Jonathan watched the angelic man pat the boy he had raised and loved, he felt tears forming in his black eyes and somewhere near by he could hear a band playing. The parade had begun.

Joan Byrd

Everyone cheered for the bands and floats as they passed by and a group of six distinguish judges watched from a high platform after giving out the ribbons for the best float awards. Ted sat up and pointed at the school float approaching as the children began standing with excitement. He spotted his wife, and gave her a thumbs-up for the best looking original float in the parade. Like a natural, Jenny gave him a beautiful smile and continued waving to all those in attendance. When the float stopped directly in front of the family. Jenny pointed to the front of the float where a big, first-place ribbon blew gracefully in the chilly wind.

The mayor walked up to a microphone on the high platform to announced the three winners. "We hope all of you enjoyed our best Thanksgiving parade ever!" A loud burst of cheers and applause fill the mountain air. "It is my honor to announce this year's winners for the best float, the better float, and the most outstanding first place float. We have all three here in front of you so you may judge for yourselves. Third place and a two-thousand-dollar prize goes to Hinkler's Hardware Store!" Again, clapping for the teenage elves pretending to build toys from items sold at the hardware store. "Second place and runner-up, Jingle All-the-Way Christmas shop with a lovely five-thousand-dollar prize." The owners alone with children and youth, dressed like dolls, toy soldiers, boats and cars brought on a big round of applause. "The first-place float is new to our parade this year and it genuinely represents what it is called, Ringing in the School Year! I am proud to award Goldsburg School the prize of ten-thousand-dollars! Congratulations to the teacher who came up with and designed this highly decorated float." The applause was so loud, Jeff and Jonathan had to muffle their ears with their palms. The mayor made his way down to the three floats handing out the prizes, leaving the school float last.

"Jennifer Neenam, the English-Literature teacher at Goldsburg School, congratulations, for an outstanding job!" Loud applause arose as the parade president, Robert Vestal held up little trophies for each school student riding the float and after hearing Jenny tell them they did a terrific job and how proud she was of them, he called out as he passed out each trophy.

"And so is the parade committee! This trophy says it all, number 1, and you are!" Mr. Vestal motioned for a senior holding a basket of red roses and suddenly felt nervous being observed by a man with long hair, sitting near the curb. "To thank all the teachers for doing such an outstanding job, the committee would like to give each lady a dozen red roses."

Seeing the long-haired man stand and make his way over to Mrs. Neenam and four of the children standing with her, Mr. Vestal stepped back, holding the basket slightly behind him. Jenny noticed his strange behavior and reached for Ted's hand. "Mr. Vestal, this is my husband Ted." Jenny took the roses he had held out. "I don't think you have met."

"Who grew these roses, Mr. Vestal?" Without looking down, Ted patted Leah, Marble, Willy, and Teddy Jeffery as they came over to him, but never stopped staring at the basket of roses.

"I never got his name but he was a very kind man who wanted to help out the parade committee. The thoughtful gentleman had a flower stand on the corner of Main and Chestnut and ask if we would have the need of some roses." The committee chairman swallowed, unsure why this young man's question bothered him so. "I think he just preferred to stay anonymous and didn't want every Tom, Dick, and Harry, to beg him for free flowers."

"Did you not ask him what kind they were or how he came by roses this time of year?" Ted knew there was something strange about some of the roses, he just hadn't figured out what it was. "Did you notice there are two different shades of red, in this dozen?"

"They all look the same to me. Just plain, ordinary red roses." Mr. Vestal gave a nervous laugh. "I guess you don't see many roses on top of that mountain, do you son?"

"Are you kidding me, Mr. Vestal!" Jenny laughed and held the roses up to her nose, making a face. "It's obvious, these roses where grown in a green house. They do not have the sweet aroma that Ted's roses have in our very large rose garden on the mountain. Ted grows the most beautiful roses in the world. The only place prettier is heaven!"

"Heaven? Well, I would not know how any flower looks in that place, but I still say, a rose is a rose is a rose!" He looked away nervously, waving to the History teacher. "I hope you both have a happy turkey day!"

"And a blessed Thanksgiving to you and your family." Ted led the group to the station wagons and began loading up. Tracy Reynolds had been speaking to the Math teacher when she noticed the group getting ready to depart. Excusing herself, she made her way across the street and was stopped when Mr. Vestal stepped out to block her.

"Mrs. Reynolds, before you leave, you must not forget your roses." His cold stare held her and she suddenly recognized the ex-church member from Kill Devil Hills Church. Tracy nervously thanked him, grabbed the roses and pushed past him to catch the waiting family.

CHAPTER 58

"Thank you for inviting me to have Thanksgiving dinner with the family, Naomi." Jonathan stood in the kitchen doorway. "If there's anything I can do to help you, please ask."

"That is very sweet Jonathan, but I think Jeff is waiting to speak to you in the library." Naomi smiled up from mashing potatoes. "Supper shouldn't be much longer. I fixed the turkey this morning, along with two pumpkin pies."

Jonathan smiled and made his way down the long hallway to the big library. Jeff had built a fire in the massive fireplace and was warming his hands when his brother stepped inside. "Come over here Jonathan." Jeff rolled his eyes over on his brother as he moved over and gazed down into the warm blaze. "I just built a fire. This big drafty room can get cold so knock the chill off!"

"I suppose where I'm going, I had better reserve all the chill I can." Jonathan tried to make light over his obvious outcome for following their father but it wasn't something he looked forward too and wondered if any great award was worth everlasting fire.

Reading his thoughts, Jeff looked down at his drooped head. "It doesn't have to be that way brother! And it isn't worth everlasting punishment to reign as some king for a limited time." Jeff placed his hand on Jonathan's shoulder. "Stop following that bastard now and ask God to forgive you."

"Stop now, when I am almost ready to take your place in father's heart?" Jonathan tried to laugh as he sat down, and smiled up at his brother.

"Heart?" Jeff laughed loudly, un-nerving Jonathan. "That devil lost his heart the day he tried to take over God's throne!"

Jonathan looked up, tears on the verge of falling. "Jeffery, It's Thanksgiving. Can we just forget that devil for one day?"

Jeff took a seat next to Jonathan. "Why not forget him every day brother! We have a lot to be thankful for, Jonathan."

"You have a lot to be thankful for Jeffery." Jonathan looked over with a sincere heart. "A loving wife, two great sons, a baby girl on the way, and the big family on your neighboring mountain."

309

"You're right Jonathan, I am a very blessed sinner." Jeff took hold of his brother's shoulders. "I was speaking about you and me brother. The two of us have a lot to be thankful for."

"Yes, finding one another was a blessing and..." Jonathan laughed softly. "finally getting along and perhaps, even starting to like each other."

"Jonathan, I love you." Jeff was sincere, the cold look was gone. "I just don't like how you are living and the choices you have been taking, and for what? A stinking, mean father who will end up destroying you."

Jonathan had tears in his eyes as he confessed "Jeffery, I love you too. It's the boy, Teddy Jeffery."

"What do you mean?" Jeff asked unblinking.

"I fear father wants him Jeff!" Jonathan closed his eyes. "I must stay close to father. Make him choose me." He looked deep into his brother's eyes. "To save Teddy, your son!"

"Jonathan?" Jeff felt tears coming. "It's a loving thing you want to do, but Teddy Jeffery must choose for himself. His mother and I pray he will always choose good over evil."

"I am thankful you let me be a part of your boy's lives, and..." Jonathan smiled warmly. "a part of your life as well"

"Same here, brother, but there is another blessing we both share." Jeff returned his brother's real smile. "This is what I was referring to earlier. There is someone standing behind you who came a long way to be with us, Jonathan."

Jonathan turned around quickly and looked into his mother's eyes for the very first time since he was an infant.

After the big family had ate their Thanksgiving meal, they settled down in the large den for each member to tell what they were most thankful for that year. Noah, being only a baby could only laugh and goo, so the moved to the second youngest, Jonah, Kathy and Matthew's son. When they got to Marble, she stood up from the floor smiling.

"There are two things I'm most thankful for this year. The first is getting saved by God through Ted and the second blessing is, being able to give sweet Noah to the two best parents a baby can have. Thank you, Ted and Jenny."

Everyone cheered and clapped as the loving couple got up to give Marble a loving hug. Each child had something beautiful to be thankful for and Leah was thankful for being able to keep silent on the school float when she had the urge to yell out to waving friends and the family. All the troubled kids and Tracy were thankful for Ted and a loving family who made them feel a part of them. Ted finally stood up and looked out among the smiling faces.

"My first thanks always go to the Almighty God, three in one, then each one of you, my beautiful family." Ted held his open arms out for his girls who dash over to get swept up in a loving embrace, then lowered them by his side to lift baby Noah out of his mother's arms and plant a kiss on his chubby cheek before handing him back. Then, as in slow motion, Ted held his hand out for his wife and lifted her from the sofa. "And my most thankful blessing is the love I share with you, Jenny. Without hesitation, Ted lifted his very pregnant wife up into his arms and gently kissed her as the room rang out with clapping.

Everyone had retired for the night as Tracy sat up in bed watching Miriam brush her hair, stopping occasionally to smell the roses Tracy had set on the dresser. "They don't have much of a smell." Miriam pushed them aside and clicked off the dresser lamp. "I never knew people riding on floats in a parade received flowers for doing something totally fun."

"I agree Miriam. I too thought the man's reaction was strange and at first, I didn't recognize Mr. Vestal, a man who use to attend the same church as I on the coast. I never saw him at any of Jonathan's services here, but yet, he showed up in town this morning and was chairman over the parade committee." Tracy was glad her room mate was enjoying the dozen roses even if she couldn't. "I'm just glad the roses are red instead of black."

"Black?" Miriam laughed as she climbed into the other twin bed. "I've never seen a black rose and it's for certain Ted wouldn't grow any up here. "You might find some growing on Black mountain since Jeff apparently loves black. That's all he ever wears and I bet you could never get him out of them." She giggled. "Except when he's hot and heavy with Naomi." Miriam yawned. "Anyway, black roses sound more like Jeff or Jonathan's taste."

Tracy shivered as her attention locked on the vase of roses, remembering Jeff's warning about receiving a black rose from someone. "It's funny you should mention Jeff. He is the one that told me the meaning of receiving a black rose. It is the symbol of death."

311

Joan Byrd

"That's probably just an old myth Tracy. You are perfectly safe here on the mountain." Miriam switched off the lamp and slipped under the cover. "The big clock just struck ten o'clock and six comes early. Goodnight Tracy and hope for sweet dreams and don't worry about black roses."

"No, I Won't." Tracy noticed Miriam was still awake and not quite sleepy herself, felt the need to ask her new friend. "Miriam, is there anything new about you and Robert?"

"Robert keeps his distance from me and I feel sure he is afraid of the feelings he is having where I'm concern." She yawned. "Poor Esther has been spending a lot of time with Marshall."

"Doesn't Robert get upset with Esther for being around Marshall more than him?" Tracy's vision was growing accustom to the dark room and the moonlight brought out objects in the bedroom.

Miriam closed her heavy eyelids and mumbled. "At first, her actions seemed to upset him. I'll   let you...know if...anything changes." Growing quiet, Tracy knew her room mate had fallen asleep. Glancing over at the red roses in the spotlight of moonlight, Tracy rolled over toward the wall, said a soft prayer and drifted off to sleep.

Tracy awoke quickly and feeling groggy wondered what had awakened her from a peaceful sleep. It was obvious to her it was still nighttime, so she rolled over to check the bedside clock on the nightstand that set between the twin beds. When she noticed it was 12:00, midnight, Tracy shivered and started to pull the cover up when her attention was drawn to the rose vase. Something was different. She sat up for a closer look at what appeared to be one tall rose standing in the middle of the other roses, that had gone limp. Tracy wondered if she might be having a nightmare from all the talk about the back rose. Tracy could tell by Miriam's breathing that she was sound asleep, so she slowly slipped from the covers and into her slippers. After moving slowly through the darkness, Tracy Reynolds stopped and stared wide eyed at her worse fear. A single black rose stood tall as if it was looking into her soul and whispering in a deep voice.

"Beware! You deceived me! Now, you must die!" Tracy Reynolds screamed and fainted to the floor.

Miriam had let Ted and Jenny into the room after they were

312

awakened by her scream. The blonde companion could only stare down at her unconscious roommate. "Tracy was apprehensive about those roses some man she knew from the church she used to attend gave her this morning. She kept talking about a black rose Jeff had warned her about."

"That's it! The roses that man Vestal was handing out to the woman on the school float." Ted walked over and stared down at the vase of red roses. "Whatever Tracy saw here has obviously changed back to all red. These roses have been cursed by someone or something. Most likely Lucifer."

"Oh sweetheart, what about the roses in our room?" Jenny grabbed his arm. "They came from the same strange man."

"Yes, they did Jenny, but these Tracy received are the only ones cursed with evil." Ted picked up the vase. "Evil cannot come to this mountain unless someone in the family invites it in. Not knowing, Tracy excepted the evil rose and brought it into this house." As Ted spoke, the deep love he had inside him ran into every rose until all that was left was eleven red roses, alive and perfect. Jenny and Miriam watched in amazement as the dead roses came back to life and the single rose standing in the middle, vanished.

"Ted, the roses looked dead and now they're more beautiful than before."

"One is missing, Jenny. The black rose has disappeared." Ted knelt down by the unconscious woman and took her hand. "Tracy, open your eyes. You are safe here and no evil can reach you."

Slowly opening her eyes, Tracy saw the loving face of Ted. Turning her face to the dresser, the vase of red roses looked prettier than before and she wondered if she had only imagined smelling their sweet fragrance. "The black rose...is no longer there!" her voice spoke in a whisper, afraid it would reappear. "Did...did you see it?"

"Yes Tracy, I can see it even now." Ted's voice remained calm and gentle. Jenny and Miriam looked over at the perfect vase of sweet smelling flowers and counted eleven roses. Jenny knew if Ted said the black rose was there, he had made it invisible for this woman sake, as well as theirs.

"Alright darling, I believe the black rose is in this room, but the vase has only eleven matching size roses! The tall rose in the center must have been the black rose that's no longer there." Jenny ran her hand over the space where it stood. "See, not here, so where is it lying?"

"You just ran your hand through it Jenny." Ted held out his hand for her to join him when she shivered from the creepy ideal while shaking her hand, hoping any evil would drop off.

"Ted, can you get rid of that creepy invisible rose! The very thought of it being inside this house is weird!" Jenny glanced down at Tracy before making her next statement. "Can you take it out or will it have to be the one that brought it inside the house?"

"Tracy does not have to deal with this evil rose darling." Ted wanted to be sure Tracy was going to be alright before taking the black rose away, so he reassured her. "Tracy, I am going to destroy the rose so there is nothing for you to fear. Satan is playing with your mind, he hates to be defeated. Lucifer thought your soul was his."

"I promise to never except anything from an ex-church goer again Ted." Tracy remembered the look in Mr. Vestal's eyes when he stopped her in town. "Jenny, you must stay clear of Mr. Vestal too. I'm afraid he and my poor Joseph have gone completely mad."

"Vestal will lay low from now on Tracy." Ted turned to his wife and Miriam. "Jenny darling, I want you and Miriam to stay with Tracy. It was a good thing I told everyone else in the family awaken by the scream, to go on back to bed."

Ted reached inside the vase and took out the invisible rose, let it reappear long enough for the three women to see he actually held it, then he willed it back invisible. He walked out the door and disappeared. Standing on the mountain top, all was dark below him, but the light on the mountain surrounded Ted with love. In the bright light of the Father, the demon rose was destroyed, never to return to Goldsburg Mountain again.

Earlier in the evening, Thanksgiving at Wineworth Castle had been a happy occasion. Jeff and Jonathan's mother seemed to make the family complete. Gloria's sons had listened as their mother spoke of happier moments in her childhood, growing up in a big family, five girls, six brothers and great parents. Jeff and Jonathan had promised her they would help her search to find what family she had left and get in touch.

After staying up a little longer than usual, Teddy and Jacob were sent to bed. Teddy looked at the number one trophy in his hand and smiled broadly up at his parents. "I'll place this trophy up on my shelf with all my other trophies." He handed it to his father who placed it high on the top shelf next to his football, baseball, basketball and tennis trophies.

"We are very proud of you Teddy and because you are the first born, you really are our number one son." Naomi gave him a kiss as they all smiled up at the shiny new trophy.

Jeff tucked the covers around him and kissed his forehead. "You and Jacob are very special to your mama and papa. You made a great mini Washington."

Teddy laughed as he hugged each parent. "I love you papa! Mama, you are the prettiest mama in the entire world and I love you too."

"Oh Teddy, my dear sweet boy." Naomi felt tears forming as she touched his face. "I love you very much. Now, say your prayers and go to sleep."

Naomi and Jeff walked out the door and as soon as he shut it, he had her in his arms. "My sweet dove, soon our little Teddy will be too old to tuck in and kiss goodnight."

"Not if I can help it!" Naomi stood on her tiptoes to kiss his handsome lips. True, our sons will grow into men, your size no doubt, but I will still be their mama and you will be their papa." She goosed him when he laughed. "We will tuck them in and kiss our boy's goodnight!"

Jeff laughed out loud as he led her down the hallway to their bedroom. "Even if Teddy and Jacob outgrow being tucked in beautiful, you may remove my clothes, tucked me under our sheets, kiss me with passion for the entire night, forever!"

CHAPTER 59

Teddy Jeffery sat straight up in bed when he heard someone whisper his name and Destiny's growl. Sweat was dripping off his young face and even though he was afraid, the room, itself, seemed to be very hot. Teddy realized the growls were coming from inside his bedroom, which meant someone had to have let the wolf in. He jumped when the door opened slowly, then relaxed when he saw his uncle peeking inside.

"Teddy Jeffery, are you alright son? I was still up researching mother's family's whereabouts, when I heard something in your room." Jonathan felt the wolf sniff his leg and patted it on the head as he walked over to switch on the bedside lamp. He immediately saw the boy was very hot. "My God son, you are sweating! Have you taken a fever?" Jonathan felt his forehead and found it cool to the touch. He closed his eyes and smelled the air, then knew who the unwanted visitor was. What reason could Lucifer have for coming in Teddy's room in the middle of the night? The same night the family gave thanks for God's blessings.

"Uncle Jonathan, you know who was in here with me!" Teddy looked down at his pet who had laid down next to his bed. "Whoever it was, let my wolf in! Mother will not be please!"

"No son, I dare say, she won't, especially for your visitor." Jonathan started looking around the room for any signs he might have left behind. "Your grandfather paid you a visit tonight at midnight. Now, to find out why."

"Lucifer? Was in here with me?" Teddy's eyes grew wide with concern. Suddenly Jonathan knew why the devil had paid the visit to Teddy. His black eyes where frozen on the small shiny trophy. Teddy followed Jonathan's stare and slung his covers back. "My trophy! What did he do to my trophy?"

Jonathan easily reached for the trophy and handed it to his nephew. The letters had been changed to: My Number One Choice, and the once golden trophy was now blood red.

"Son, you must show this to your father first thing in the morning." Jonathan walked over to close the door. Pulling up a chair beside the bed, he sat down. "Get some rest Teddy. I'll not leave your side tonight."

"Jeff, tell me you got rid of that thing!" Naomi had been listening to her husband as he told her of Lucifer's visit and the trophy change. "Just when I am not sure of your brother, he ups and does something loving."

"Yes, my one, Jonathan tries to be evil, to get father's approval. For the life of me, I cannot understand why." Jeff felt the red trophy in his pocket. "I feel sure the love of Kristine can turn him around if the love you gave this evil sinner, turned me around. I was far worse than my brother."

"I, for one, will continue to pray for him." Naomi glanced from the window to see Gloria playing with the boys. "And your dear mother will do wonders for both her sons."

Jeff lifted her up for a kiss. "I'm off to bury this devil made trophy, then I will see what I can make to replace it. Teddy was so proud of his number one trophy."

"You are a good daddy, Jeff Wineworth." Naomi gave him a grateful hug. "I'm going up to scrub down Teddy's room." They went their separate way.

Jeff had dug a deep hole, then with his strong hands, he mashed the trophy in pieces before he buried it.

"You may bury it son, but it does not change the writing on it." Lucifer appeared beside Jeff. "Pity, the boy was so proud of that little trophy."

"I'll make him another one, even better." Jeff stared coldly at his father. "And this one, you cannot touch."

"Using your black magic, my son." Satan mocked. "As before, my very first choice is and always will be you Jeffery."

"Too bad Father, this son is not available!" Jeff started walking toward the garden shed and Lucifer followed behind him. "My son is not available either and with God's help, neither will be my brother, Jonathan."

"You were quick to give me Gregory and little Billy." Satan walked inside the shed laughing.

"The truth is, I regret I sent Gregory and Neil to you now." Jeff casually pulled some wood down. "But Billy never belong to you, you lying bastard!"

"Just seeing if you might know the difference." Lucifer smiled

317

down at the wood. "A trophy made from wood? The boy will detest it!"

"Your opinion means nothing to me!" Jeff slowly drew out the pattern he wanted and selected the right saw, then commenced to making the trophy.

"Your mother has gone missing. The demons have searched for her in every corner of hell. It was told me, you summons her recently, but she returned, only to disappear again." Lucifer reached out and stopped the sawing. "We will find her Jeffery! The dead can only last so long above the ground! When we find her, then she will suffer!"

Jeff pushed Satan's hand away and continued sawing. "No father, you will not touch her! She is safe now and you may never have her again!"

"Then, you did bring her back up! You, foolish man! My powers far outweigh yours! You will only lose her again! You cannot protect her! Her soul is mine!" The devil's eyes blazed. "You cannot save her!"

"No father, I cannot save her nor was it I who brought her up this time!" Jeff remained calm. "You are right to say your powers outweigh mine father, but the Almighty God's power outweighs yours, or have you forgotten? The merciful Lord brought mother out of hell and forgave her soul. Now she lives, to give her sons another chance to show their love for her."

"Damn fire, hell, and brimstone! Why does that Creator keep getting in my way? Once mine, always mine! He has no right to forgive a fallen soul!" he shouted.

"Oh, but He does and He can! Have you forgotten, with God, ALL THINGS ARE POSSIBLE!" Jeff stared, only this time there was love in his eyes. "Good is stronger father. You cannot win. The sad truth is, you lose in the end."

"Words, spoken by that Bible freak on the other mountain!" The devil's eyes remained cold. "You listen to him instead of your own father!"

"Ted does the will of God!" Jeff held up the trophy for his father to see. "See father, even a wooden trophy can hold something powerful." A small wooden cross with the words, NUMBER ONE CHILD OF GOD. "It is something you should have done father. Obey your Creators will."

The devil turned angrily and disappeared.

"Jonathan, my son." Jeff's twin had been sitting quietly behind his office desk, his mind too mixed up to plan the service for Christmas. He knew his father needed no announcement from the church secretary to let him know of his arrival. Lucifer just simply appeared, demanding full attention. "You wish to plan a Christmas service at my church?" he mocked. "I am certain you won't be singing the usual boring carols announcing the Coming Ones Birth!"

"Not hardly father. We have our own hymnal, remember?" Jonathan had mixed emotions about his father's sudden visit. On the last visit, he had asked Jonathan to do the impossible. Sacrifice Fire to him and kill Kristine.

"Yes, our collection of songs suits us better Jonathan." Lucifer looked around the room at the bare walls. "Son, you need to have Mrs. Vestal paint you an office picture of me with the family." Satan turned back and smiled at his son. "Me, along with my two favorite sons, you Jonathan and Jeffery, plus my handsome grandsons, Jeffery and Jacob."

"You want a family portrait?" Jonathan walked over to the biggest wall and pointed at the best spot. "Jeff might not be too please with your ideal father."

"Does your brother visit you here son?" Satan knew Jeff had never set foot inside his brother's church office and smiled to himself when Jonathan looked down. "No, I thought not! It will be our little secret."

"As you like father. I will get Mrs. Vestal right on it." Jonathan had hoped his father wouldn't bring up the subject to destroy the woman he loved.

"Back to the service. I think our Christmas service needs to have a sacrifice on the altar." Lucifer let his fingers run along the desk top. "Young Fire, dressed only in holly. Very festive, is it not?"

"Fits the season father." Jonathan watched his father closely.

"Jonathan, I've been doing a lot of thinking as of late and I am lending more toward you as my number one son." Lucifer rolled his eyes up on his son's face. "If you get me Fire and sacrifice her to me on the altar in front of my followers, I will award you with your first six." Satan walked behind Jonathan and bent down next to his ear. "If you get Kristine on the altar and...TAKE HER LIFE, YOU

SHALL RECEIVE YOUR NEXT TWO SIXES!" he whispered temptingly. "YOU WILL BE MY ANTI-CHRIST!"

Jonathan sat staring into space. Everything he had been working for was coming into plan. His heart was racing, knowing he finally could have what he had yearn for. To be his father's number one son. And now, at what cost?"

"Son, I have left you speechless." Lucifer continued to whisper in his ear. "It is what you want! To be over and above your brother. I should have seen that my eldest son was the best choice all along but I was blinded by Jeffery's abilities."

"Father, you wished me dead after I was born! How can I be sure this is not a trick?" Jonathan felt unsure of his father's honesty, being the creator of lies. Could he trust him turning from the son he adored and choosing him instead?

"Jonathan, I do not give these sixes so easily. They must be earned with complete loyalty to me if you wish to gain my highest reward." Satan patted Jonathan on the back and moved over to the door. "It must be your choice son, your freewill to carry out my orders, then all will be yours."

"I have thought of nothing more than to earn your trust father." Jonathan stood straight, his eyes planted on God's powerful enemy. "I have worked at becoming your chosen one."

"Yet, something stands in the way." Lucifer flipped open the hymnal and left it to be seen later. "You have been wondering how you can earn three sixes when your brother already has two."

"It has accrued to me father." Jonathan had skillfully blocked the real reason from Satan. His feelings for Kristine. "Will Jeffery's two sixes disappear when I receive mine?"

"Jeffery's two sixes will remain, branded on him for life. He earned them and was ready to receive them after proving his devotion to me." Satan's smile was cunning. "You should act soon Jonathan. One never knows when something fatal will happen to so call love ones, then people lose faith and return back, where they belong."

"Are you threating Jeff's family?" Jonathan stared over at his father with anger. "Can you not leave him happy and let me be the chosen son?"

"I am an impatient man Jonathan! I do not like to be kept waiting!" red cold eyes stared back into his son's. "You 'will' prove your worth on Christmas Eve, in this church, on the altar, and in front of your people, my followers!"

"You wish me to find Fire and have her here for your sexual pleasure!" Jonathan smiled, his sharp teeth reflecting the one standing near him. "She will be dressed only in a wreath of holly around her neck."

"Yes, excellent! Good boy!" his hand was on the doorknob. "And?"

"And you will award me with my first six in front of my followers." Jonathan was hoping Kristine would not be brought up again, but the angry look from Lucifer proved he was not satisfied with his answer.

"That, Jonathan, is NOT what I am waiting to hear!" His words were harsh, his tone was dangerous. "Christmas Eve, this church, same altar, you WILL KILL AND RAPE THE DEAD CORPSE OF YOUR LOVER, KRISTINE O'DONNELL! Do this, and you will be my Anti-Christ and have as many virgins that pleases you!"

"I am your loyal servant father." Jonathan closes his eyes. "It shall be as you ask."

"Finally, a son I can be proud of!" Lucifer was on him in a flash, giving him a fatherly hug. "Don't let me down! I won't be made a fool of!" with that, Lucifer was gone.

Jonathan walked back to his desk, his attention falling on the opened hymnal. "Hallelujah, The Anti-Christ Is Born!"

CHAPTER 60

Robert sat quietly shelling the basket of corn placed in front of him, his attention fastened out the big garden shed window as he watched Miriam, Leah, and Marble working in the grape vineyard. She had given him all the space he needed to sort out his feelings. The handsome lad could tell she was far long into her pregnancy and he thought the rosy glow on her beautiful face made her laughter somehow reach out and touch him. Caught up in his thoughts, Robert hadn't heard Esther walk in until she touched his arm, causing him to jump.

"Robert, I never meant to startle you." Esther stood smiling and patted the chair next to him. "May I join you a moment?" she pulled out the chair and sat down before he could respond. "Robert, as of late, your mind has been miles away. We seem to have grown apart." When he started to respond, Esther touched his lips. "I need to say what I came in for. Marshall and I are steadies. In short, we really care about one another." She blushed and looked down to avoid Robert's eyes. "Robert, you are a great friend and fun to hang out with. You always made me laugh and feel special, but I think you are still in love with Miriam and I love Marshall."

"You do?" Robert's eyebrow shot up, a little upset that part of his problem for not going back to Miriam was not wanting to hurt Esther. Finally feeling free, Robert took her hand and smiled. "Esther, I'm truly happy for you and Marshall. I guess the two of us were meant to be just fun-loving friends."

"Robert, you are going to tell Miriam you love her, right?" Esther put her arm around him. "You better grab her while she's fat. When she gets that knockout figure back, some guy will snatch her away."

"Well, that kid does need a father." Robert finally knew what he wanted. "If she will have me, I've gained a family."

"Then go tell her." Esther stood, waved for Marshall, who had been waiting for her signal, then pulled Robert to his feet. "Marshall and I will finish shelling this corn. The chickens aren't picky who prepares their meal." Robert shook hands with Marshall, reached down to kiss Esther's cheek, then made his way to the vineyard.

"That's all for me girls! My buckets are full." Miriam pulled a wet towel from her carrier and wiped off her hands and turned to see Robert picking up her buckets.

"Permit me to carry these, little mother." Robert walked away smiling, Miriam tagging along behind him, recalling watching him moments earlier in the shed with Esther, shelling corn. She had looked away before Marshall walked inside to take Robert's place. Catching up with him, she slowed down.

"Thank you. I am honored to have such a thoughtful gentleman help me carry those heavy buckets." Miriam pushed her hair back in place and glanced at her once perfect nails, then chuckled. "This find job comes with its own reward. Beautiful stained fingers and a few broken fingernails."

"They are still beautiful Miriam, no matter their shape or color. It only proves the lady does her share of work for the family." Robert sat down one bucket just to lift up her hand and kiss, then quickly retrieved the bucket and nodded toward the winery. "My lady, to the winery."

Miriam laughed brightly and for the first time since breaking off her engagement with Jonathan, Miriam felt she and Robert was finding their way back to each other.

"It just seems strange mom, that I get to be Mary, instead of Mary." Martha stood still while her grandmother pinned up her costume. I just don't get it."

"That's because your sister has been ask to sing a solo, Little Mary." Jenny smiled up at Hannah when she laughed softly. "I think it was a sweet ideal to start the Christmas Pageant when Mary was a child."

"And it will be even sweeter when our little Mary sings it for her sister who will be frozen in the frame." Hannah patted Martha's head. "All done pinning. Now to hem it up for our little actress."

"Thanks, grand mom, you are the best!" Martha pulled the blue gown over her blonde locks and tried on the head drape. "I guess there won't be a child Joseph."

"Sweet girl, Joseph would have been a teenager at that time in young Mary's life." Hannah smiled at Martha's twin when she came in and tried to hide her giggles.

"You look funny Martha! I thought you were suppose, to wear

the dress, not put it on your head."

"Mom, tell my sister girls back in the Bible wore head clothes! Their pictures are in my children's Bible." Martha flopped down and frowned over at her sister, still laughing. "Stick to singing, sister mine!"

"Hey, I'm only joking sis." Mary turned when she heard a familiar young male voice call her name. Teddy stood smiling at the kitchen door.

"Hi Teddy Jeffery! I see you brought your things over for grand mom Hannah to sew."

"Yes beautiful, that is correct." Teddy winked at Mary and walked in throwing down the material and pattern. "Mom can cook great but when it comes to sewing difficult costumes, well..." the handsome youth smiled up at Naomi. "She really does try."

"I am horrible at sewing. We bought our Halloween costumes but the school sent home the cloth and pattern, so here we are." Naomi laughed and joined Jenny who was working on the angel wings. "I want my shepherd to look real." She smiled at Jenny. "Who are the angels Jenny, besides Ted, of course?"

"In the church program, both the girls will be angels." Jenny held up her first set of wings, heavy cardboard outlined with gold tinsel and garland. "I'm afraid it's as close as I can get to the real thing."

"Oh mom, its beautiful!" Mary tried on the sparkling wings and danced around the big room. "Too bad they cannot make me fly."

"Gab says we can fly in heaven! I bet he knows what real angel wings look like!" Martha glanced over at Hannah when she laughed softly. "It's trued grand mom. We will be able to float above the ground too in heaven."

"Cool! Why not here though? I bet I could float in the air if I used my magic!" Teddy stood still while Hannah pinned up his costume. "Aunt Jenny, are we having our church service on Christmas Eve down in town this year instead of up here in the chapel?"

"I'm really not sure Teddy." Jenny looked up from her art work. "Ted did tell me this Christmas Eve was special and the gift must be shared with all God's children."

"Gift?" Mary's eyes grew large as did the other children listening. She slowly removed the wings and walked over to her mother. "Mom, what gift?"

"Your daddy said it was a Christmas surprise." Jenny winked at her excited daughter. "I guess I'll be the only one, plus whoever is with me, to miss the happy event."

"Oh? Because our baby brother will be arriving on Christmas Eve!" Martha beamed. "Just think, our little brother will be born on the same birthday as Jesus."

"No Martha darling, Jesus was born on Christmas day." Jenny laughed softly. "Our little fellow only missed it by one day."

"I say baby Gabriel will be born December 25th, same day as Jesus!" Mary walked up next to Martha.

"Sorry to disappoint you darling, but your very clever daddy told me Christmas Eve, at two a.m." Jenny touched her fat stomach. "When you both were born, Ted knew the exact time and date."

"Baby Gabriel told us he would appear on December 25th at two a.m.! On the night of Christmas Eve, you go into labor but the baby doesn't arrive until after midnight, the start of another day!" Mary and Martha said in unison.

"Jenny" Everyone grew quiet when Ted walked in and took a seat next to his upset wife. "Jenny darling, I told you the truth about Christmas Eve. You were to have gone into labor on December 23rd but the baby would not arrive until two a.m., making it Christmas eve. Then the Father realized you would miss the Christmas surprise due to having the baby early that morning." Ted's eyes sparkled with love as he took around his wife. "Our son will be born on Christmas morning at two a.m., same as Jesus our Savior, just as the girls have proclaimed!"

"Then I have been blessed by the Almighty God to receive the Christmas surprise, then have our little baby boy on the same day as our Lord!" Jenny had tears flowing down her beautiful face.

"That's right Jenny. The same day and at the same time." Ted smiled as he watched his words sink in the second time."

"He told you this darling?" Jenny felt stun by this revelation that had finally sunk in. "I will have childbirth with Gabriel at the exact moment Mary delivered Jesus in Bethlehem over two-thousand years ago?"

"Isn't it exciting mom? The Father must have informed our little brother of the change so he could share it with me and Martha!" Mary's hand ran gently over Jenny's stomach.

325

Jenny gave her girls a hug and told them to stack up the wings carefully, then turned Ted's face toward her. "Ted, please explain to me how our daughters heard their brother before he's born. How a little infant could possibly know anything about the time of his birth?"

"Jenny dearest love, our children are not like other children. They have certain gifts, certain powers, that will grow stronger with age. They hear Gabriel through spiritual listening and speaking. He has those same links with both his grandfather and the blessed Lord." Ted placed his arm lovingly around her trembling shoulders. "Our children have a lot of me inside them and you just need to believe what you cannot hear and with faith, you shall."

Jenny finally gave him a smile, knowing how blessed she was to be able to witness the special Christmas gift and humbly share the Bethlehem experience with Mary. "God is so good sweetheart. And I know each child God blesses us with will be just like their angelic daddy. There's one thing for certain, things will never be boring in the Neenam household."

Teddy had been taking in all their words about baby Gabriel and lend up on his elbows. "I can't talk to my baby sister yet. She is way too small." The dark eyed boy got everyone's attention. "I do know what she will look like thought."

"Really?" Naomi felt Jeff's hand caress the back of her neck and turned to smiled up at him. "I guess you know what our daughter will look like too, darling."

"Yes, I can see her plainly." Jeff pulled out a chair next to his wife and whispered in her ear. "Before I tell you, I just want to see if our son really knows or merely pretending." Jeff and Teddy stared briefly at each other before Jeff tapped the table. "We're waiting son."

"Then I shall gladly go first papa! Johanna will have long black hair, her face features will be just like mama, beautiful with full lips. Her eyes will be an unusually striking violet-blue." Teddy raised his head proudly, knowing no one had spoken her name until now, nor had they given such a detail description of this enchanting dark angel. "Of course, Johanna will be like me and Jacob when it comes to our special powers and magic, a birthright given by our amazing papa."

"What about Johanna's teeth, Teddy Jeffery? Will her canines grow long and sharp like you boys and Uncle Jeff?" Mary had been watching the handsome boy closely as he gave his description of the sister yet to be born. "And can you tell me why her eyes are not black?"

"She is a Wineworth lady, Mary." Teddy gave her a big smile, happy she had been listening to him. "Her teeth will be just like papa's, but more girlie."

"Wow! What an imagination!" Kathy had been standing at the door listening to the young boy's description of his sister, yet to be born. "Teddy, you should write fiction when you get older kid."

"Kathy, that was no fiction. My son just described our daughter exactly the way she will look." Jeff pulled Naomi into his arms, knowing her full attention was on Teddy Jeffery. "Sweet one, I knew you had been thinking about names for our baby girl and the name Johanna was your favorite."

Naomi smiled up weakly, then noticed Ted was watching her. He was relaying a message through his thoughts directed to her and she heard him clearly. "All is well, my angel. Just believe what you cannot hear, with faith, you shall."

CHAPTER 61

"Kristine, what we're asking of you could be very frightening." Ted and Gabriel had joined the other angels watching the two sheltered women on Angel Island.

"You are safe up here." Gabriel stood next to his son, gazing seriously down at both women. "But your place at this moment is down on earth within your earthly bodies."

"Kristine, we know your love for Jonathan is strong and pure." Ted took her hands in his. "We also know your love for God and His Son is even greater."

"You are right Ted, and you Gab, for saying my place should still be below with family and friends, although leaving this place won't come easy. The peace, beauty, joy, and love shared among one another is like nowhere else." Kristine spoke softly. "On this peaceful island, there are times I seem to get a glimpsed of Jesus. Yet, I have not been off this Island, but just the thoughts of Him makes me sing praises and I even stay on key here!"

"And well you should Kristine." Gabriel chuckled, knowing how vast heaven was and the fact that all the saints can sing with the voice of an angel. "I'm sure you've noticed Angel Island is as big as the earth and it's only a small part of Heaven."

"Heaven?" Kristine felt Ted's strong arms hold her up when her knees buckled. "Then if you sent me here to stay safe from Jonathan, this thing you are asking me to do must really be a living hell."

"Your faith is strong daughter. Your one percent of love can win over Satan's one-hundred percent of the evil he holds over his son Jonathan. Lucifer has offered Jonathan the one thing he has been working for and in return, Jonathan must follow his father's demands out to the last letter." Gabriel didn't have to look at the young teenage girl to know she was taking in every word he was saying.

"Gabriel, what will Jonathan have to do and..." Kristine swallowed, dreading to hear the answers she must ask. "and what will be his reward?"

"Lucifer gave his son two orders. He is to offer Fire as a sacri-

328

fice to Satan and then he is to kill you on the devil's altar before raping your dead body." Ted held Kristine steady as he continued. "If Jonathan does the will of his father to show his loyalty, and if Lucifer can be trusted by him to keep his word, Jonathan will become"

"My God! The Anti-Christ!" Fire blurted out. "That's what Jonathan has been after! Why didn't I see it?"

"The…the Anti-Christ?" Kristine felt faint. "My Jonathan, the devil's chosen son?"

"Ted, tell me and I will believe it to be true." Kristine had calmed down after her shock. "Does Jonathan love me? And if he does, is it enough to win him back over to God?"

"Yes Kristine, Jonathan has been fighting his feelings." Ted had joined Jenny's aunt on one of the many benches in the sweet-smelling garden. "His heart aches whenever he thinks of hurting you. Jonathan has deep love for his nephews and he would be willing to sacrifice himself to save them from Satan. The love he has for his brother has grown closer and now he has the love of his mother, whom the Almighty rescued from the pits of hell to help save him."

"Before Naomi, Jeff hated everyone. The man had no love in his evil heart." Gabriel spoke softly as he held Jasmine's hand. "Jonathan followed our Lord's teaching until his evil father took over his soul. Kristine, I know love can and will turn this prodigal son back to the Father."

"Then I will go with you. I love Jonathan more than I have loved any man." Kristine smiled through her tears. "I believe with all my heart that Jonathan will come back to love. It already lives in his heart. If it means walking up to that altar to declare my love to him, I will!"

"I go too!" Jasmine stood tall. "I will do whatever it takes to win Jonathan back for Kristine, for Blaze, and mostly, for the loving Savior and Father!"

"You have a good heart Jasmine, but it will be far too dangerous for you child." Gabriel gave her a gentle hug. "You may come back with us but you must stay close to the family on the mountain at all times."

"If my life is in danger, won't Kris's life be in danger too?" Jasmine had grown close to the older woman and couldn't bare for anything to happen to her dear new friend.

"We will be close by at all times to whisk Kristine away if things grow to deadly for her." Ted's eyes held total love, calming the young teen down. "Sweet child, although Jonathan may care for you, his greed to become his father's chosen, interferes with his emotions. To get that first six as promised, I can see Jonathan giving you to his lustful father to prove himself."

"But, if you can whisk Kristine away, why not me?" Jasmine felt in her heart she needed to prove herself. "Hear me out! Even if Jonathan did get me on that altar and the devil came to have his way on me, I've been in pain before sexually. I could help make this work! Lucifer expects to have both, remember? First me, then Kristine. She might not be able to help Jonathan in time if I don't become Satan's sacrifice! The devil will see his son as a failure and destroy him before we can save his soul!"

Gabriel scratched his head, his eyes filled with concern. "Son, as bad as it sounds, young Jasmine has a point. We both know Lucifer. If he does not get his way, he would destroy his son before we even have a chance to save him."

"But, to let Lucifer sexually abuse this one is wrong!" Ted paced the silken floor. "We must speak to the Father. He will know the answer we seek."

"You see Lord, to sacrifice one, we gain one! To do nothing, we lose our lost sheep for good." Ted felt at peace speaking to the good shepherd.

"We must take a page from Salomon's book. We gave him great wisdom because he asked for that instead of great wealth or large armies." Jesus produced a white book from the clouds and the pages fell open. "She must be dressed in Holly, covering her gently around and laid upon an altar where evil cannot be found. And when he comes to take her, before a hand can touch, appears the maiden who loves his son, and whom he loves so much. She tells him how she loves him, and all her heart she'll give, if he can say he loves her, then both of them shall live. The angels come from heaven and send the devil home. The girl upon the altar will know the devil's gone."

"This wisdom speaks for what we must do my Lord." Ted held the words in his head. "We go now, to fight the good fight. My love to you, always first! We leave Angel Island for home."

In a flash, Ted, Gabriel, and Michael with his warriors vanished, holding on to Kristine and Jasmine.

"Jonathan, you look like you've got a lot on your mind." Jeff had offered his brother his old room back and he excepted gratefully and after settling back in, walked out to the garden bench. Jeff laid down his hoe and walked over to where Jonathan sat, head in his hands. "Don't block me out brother, tell me what's bothering you." Jonathan's hand gently touched Jeff's shoulder and the truth came flowing out in his fingers. "Jonathan, you don't need to prove anything to that evil man! Do you really expect father to give you three sixes in one night?"

"I know, how can I believe a word he says." Jonathan finally looked up and Jeff saw he had been crying. "I'm so mixed up Jeff."

"Lucifer can do that to you, when you're already confused as to what you really want." Jeff remained calm. "Jonathan, you are not the right person to be Lucifer's Anti-Christ. You hold love in your heart and this, father cannot tolerate. I'm surprise our old man keeps using you. Don't you know what that devil is capable of brother?"

"He still wants you, right?" Jonathan stood up. "I was never good enough for him! He hated me from the start!" Jeff remained tender toward his brother.

"Jonathan, the fact is, you were too good for him. I mean good, in a loving way. Father hated that part of you and he would stop at nothing to change you to suit himself! Destroy the good inside you and replace it with evil and hate."

"Father expects me to find Fire and Kristine and have them on Christmas Eve!" Jonathan blurted it. "Where the devil are they? No one has seen them anywhere! It's as if they've been whisked from the earth!"

"Do you know what father is capable of Jonathan? Do not avoid this question again!" Jeff raised his voice. "Do you?"

"Yes Jeff! God! I know what could happen to me if I don't have Fire laying on that altar for him with a wreath of holly around her and…" tears ran down his face.

"Kill the woman you love!" Jeff shook him. "Jonathan, is that what you want, damn it! Give an innocent girl to that lustful demon and kill the one person you love most in the world, then rape her after she's dead! What reward is worth that? The hopes of being Lucifer's number one bastard son! Living it up a while as a damn evil king, then burning in an everlasting hell of fire!" Jeff clutched his shoulders. "For God sake Jonathan, wake up!"

"Don't listen to him son." Lucifer appeared, where he had been listening and waiting. "Jeffery is a fool. He does not know what our hell is really like. I am an angel and I have powers in hell as well as on earth. There, you will have a great eternal life son with many fallen women."

"Listen to him Jonathan! He is the prince of lies!" Jeff stood his ground. "Heaven is beautiful and filled with love. Why don't you ask father why he keeps trying to get back into heaven, but is blocked by God's warriors!"

"Do not listen to this fallen son! I hate him! He lies!" The devil's voice rang out. "Prove to me your loyalty Jonathan and without a doubt, you will be my Anti-Christ." Lucifer turned to leave, but stopped, an evil smile on his lips. "But, should you fail me, I have another, perhaps even greater." Lucifer pulled Teddy from behind him. "Such a handsome young man. Soon, he will become a man of his own free will. He has proven to be worthy and with time, grows more to my liking. He is checking out in his grandfather's heart."

"LEAVE! GET AWAY FROM MY SON AND GET OUT!" Jeff shouted as he reached for his son.

"It's up to you Uncle Jonathan." Satan smiled wickedly at him. "See you on Christmas Eve." Then he was gone.

Jonathan looked over at his brother holding tight to his son and he knew what he had to do.

CHAPTER 62

Jonathan had moved back to his town apartment, hoping to draw Lucifer away from Jeff and his family. He stood staring out his bedroom window, looking out into the dark quiet street. It was 2:00a.m., December 22nd and he still had not found a trace of Fire or Kristine. His time was running out and in desperation he called out softly. "Fire, I need you!"

Jasmine sat up in bed, awakened by Jonathan's voice. She glanced over at the clock, 2:00a.m., then looked to see her room companion sound asleep. Perhaps she only thought she heard the deep voice call her. The young girl climbed quietly from the bed, trying not to awake Kristine from her peaceful sleep, and walked to the window to gazed out into the darkness when she heard him again, clearly.

"Fire, I need you! Please Fire, come to me!" Jasmine closed her eyes, remembering nights in her past when she welcomed that call and how she enjoyed being in Jonathan's strong arms and making love to him. This time was different. Jasmine knew her life was in danger and despite how bad Jonathan had treated her at times, most of the time he had been fun and caring. The young girl knew what she had to do. She had to go to Jonathan.

Pulling a slip of paper quietly from the desk drawer, Jasmine wrote a brief note to Kristine and one to Ted. She slipped into her clothes and out the door.

Unbeknown to Jasmine, Ted had also heard Jonathan's call to Fire and he had watched her slip from the quiet farmhouse. He kissed his sleeping wife then vanished.

Jonathan had been pacing the floor, worried about failing his father and knowing it would mean a sure painful death for him. He walked back to the window and touched the window seal with sweaty palms. "Fire, how could you have just vanished? I should be able to sense you." Jonathan froze when he felt a small hand touch his arm.

"I'm here Jonathan. I heard you call." At the sound of her voice, Jonathan turned to see the teenage girl looking up at him with serious eyes. "They had me locked up. I tried to get away before but failed." Jasmine had hoped to convince him she had been held against her will instead of knowing the truth.

"Then, you didn't run away to them?" Jonathan pulled her into his strong arms and hugged her tightly. "I thought I had lost you!"

"Never Jonathan. I am always here for you." Jasmine secretly hoped he didn't want to have sex with her. If she faked a period he would know she was lying.

"How did you manage to get away this time?" Jonathan pulled her over to his bed. She noticed it was still made up and he hadn't slept in it. He read her thoughts and took her hand. "I see you noticed I haven't been to bed and its 2:45 in the morning. I couldn't sleep Fire. Satan is testing me on Christmas Eve and if I fail, I could die."

"Then, this is why you want me?" she watched Jonathan sat down on the bed and patted the place beside him, so she could sit down. "It's time for you to offer me to him, for a sacrifice, right?"

"My clever girl, you always were so perceptive." Jonathan's hand ran over her hair. "Are you willing to help me then?"

"Have I not always been there for you Jonathan?" Jasmine felt his strong hand squeeze hers gently. "Jonathan, I don't want anything to happen to you."

"I could say the same thing for you Fire." Jonathan looked genuinely sad. "If Satan has you then I receive a great reward. My first six."

"You haven't asked about Kristine." Jasmine noticed his expression suddenly changed.

"You know where she is?" he spoke softly, his heart pounding.

"Kristine is where she wants to be Jonathan, safe with Ted and the family on Goldsburg Mountain." Jasmine watched him closely and knew what she had heard was true. "You love Kristine, don't you?"

"Again perceptive, child." Jonathan stood back up and began pacing. "I could send her a note, then she might come."

"Is Kristine part of your bargain with Lucifer, Jonathan?" Jasmine felt more relaxed, knowing Jonathan hadn't called her for sex but his upcoming service."

"Fire, I am torn!" Jonathan flopped back down. "The one thing I've been working for is in reach, only the price is higher than I want to give to receive it!"

"What is it Satan asking you to do to Kristine?" Jasmine already knew the answer but could Jonathan bring himself to tell her.

"Father ask me to kill Kristine, the one I love, on the same altar he will have sex with you on." Jonathan buried his face in his hands. "God! That devil wants me to kill her, then rape her, then I'm guaranteed my big reward!"

"Oh, you bet you will Jonathan!" Jasmine grew angry just thinking about how manipulating and conniving Lucifer could be. "You take the life of the one person who can save you from an eternity of hell!" She jerked Jonathan's hands away from his face and stared him in the eyes. "The thing you ask of me Jonathan, I will do! I have been raped and tortured before! Kristine will never be willing to climb on that devil's altar so you can receive your precious sixes after killing her! Why you would want to become the stupid Anti-Christ is beyond me!"

"Outspoken Fire?" Jonathan spoke softly. "Perhaps I was wrong about you. I think Ted might have reached that heart of yours after all."

"You have a heart too Jonathan. I've seen it." Jasmine grew softer. "Blaze is at peace now, and whether you admit it or not, I believe you are happy for the boy you raised. Do you want to know what I think Jonathan?"

"If I said no, would it stop you Fire?" His eyes grew misty.

"No, not in the least!" she smiled. "I think you have a very good heart Jonathan. You just became lost when Satan wormed his evil way into your heart. But now, love is finding its way back, through Marshall, Jeffery, your brother, your nephews, but mostly through Kristine. Fight back Jonathan! Don't let Satan win! He can never destroy you if you belong to the Lord Jesus!"

"So young and full of wisdom." Jonathan took her hand. "I can see Ted did save you, my precious girl. So why are you here? Why help me by becoming Satan's victim?"

"To help you silly." Jasmine suddenly felt they were not alone, but instead of a dreadful feeling, she had a feeling of peace, and knew Ted must be near by watching.

"I feel him too child." Jonathan looked around. "Did he know you would come to me?"

"Yes, I knew." Ted appeared in the middle of the room. "God's plan has been put into motion Jonathan. It is not for you to know as

335

long as your loyalty lies with your father. The time will come when you must choose Jonathan, evil or good. We love you brother and we will do all in our power to win you back. Our Father loves you Jonathan, more than you could possibly imagine, but that great love has given you free choice. The Almighty's joy would be for you to admit your sin and return home."

"Then, everything is set for Christmas Eve." Jonathan stood up to face Ted. "You know father will be wise to what's happening and have his many warrior demons ready to help fight."

"With or without you Jonathan, in the end, good will win." Ted held out his hand for Jasmine. "She comes with me now. When she returns on Christmas Eve, do not expect her to be alone." With those words, Ted and Jasmine were gone.

"We will have Christmas Eve morning service early in the chapel." Ted held Jenny in his arms as they lay in bed. She was too far long in her pregnancy to have sex with her adorable husband, so they were content to hold one another.

"This other service in town will be dangerous." Jenny knew in her heart Ted would be safe but for the others involved things could get scary.

"Dangerous? For Satan's demons and followers perhaps." Ted kissed her forehead. "You need not worry about Kristine or Jasmine. They will not be in any real danger, although they may feel anxious for a while."

"Will Jeff be there to help you darling? After all, it is his brother you're trying to save from their evil father." Jenny was secretly glad Ted had ordered her to remain at home.

"Jeff will be beside me, as will my father, Gabriel." Ted looked out the window. "It's time for me to climb to the top, dearest Jenny. Our Father will fill me in on what must be done."

"You mustn't keep him waiting." Jenny draped her arms around his neck as his lips parted over hers. "This young man will be coming soon then we can enjoy each other completely again."

"A welcoming New Year's present for us both." Ted slipped out of bed and pulled the robe over his head. "Stay in bed a while longer, Jenny sweetheart. I will be back in time for breakfast with my beautiful wife." With that, he walked quietly out the door.

CHAPTER 63

Christmas Eve came in cold and cloudy, the perfect combination for what lay ahead. Jonathan had set the service for seven p.m. He had the chapel draped in black with rich red curtains pulled in front of the altar and his choice of clothes was black pants covered by a red robe. The followers had been asked to wear black hooded robes and to enter quietly for the serious service planned for him and his father. Black candles lined the walls and front of the church, giving the place a frightening appearance as shadows danced across the pews like ghostly visitors.

Jonathan looked out at the large number of members and was pleased that everyone remaining his loyal followers had come. Fire had showed up as promised, dressed only in holly. Jasmine waited upon the altar shivering from the thought of facing Satan for the first time and she prayed that Jonathan wouldn't give her any drugs for she needed to stay alert.

Jonathan looked down at the pretty young teenager and smiled, his sharp white teeth reflecting in the candlelight. What was going through his mind, she thought. Did Jonathan intend to carry out his father's wishes to gain three sixes and be lost forever? His hand touched her face as he spoke softly.

"Fire, my one bright spot in my dreary world, it's time. Do you wish for me to give you some drugs to block out what will be happening to you?"

"No Jonathan. I must know what is happening to me." Jasmine closed her eyes, thankful for the careful placing of the holy that hid all her private parts. Hannah had done a wonderful job with the long vine of holly Ted had found on the mountain top.

"As you wish. Don't say I didn't warn you." Jonathan touched her leg, recalling the many times they had had sex together. "You will find my hard sex will feel light compared to the creator of lust."

"Let's just get it over with Jonathan. Is he here, your father?" she knew Ted had promised her she would not feel the devil touch her but she couldn't control the anxious shivers. She heard Jonathan take a breath when the gruesome organ music began.

337

"It begins." Staring straight ahead, Jonathan walked out through the red curtains. "Welcome to the feast of Satan. If all goes to plan on this night, December 25th at midnight, Christmas day, the Anti-Christ will be born."

"Praises to Jonathan! Oh, prince of darkness!" The followers chanted "Our master, old chosen one, we follow you!" Jonathan finally felt power. On this night he would become the chosen one of Lucifer and his followers would increase in great numbers until he ruled the world.

"O my father, you who have power over lost souls, come to us!" Jonathan chanted in his rich deep voice. "Come and taste the beautiful maiden, waiting upon your altar O great Lucifer! Come before us with your magnificent presence and take possession of what belongs to you. I, your loyal son, obeys your word!"

Everyone was startled to see smoke rise up beside of Jonathan then Satan appeared dressed in a golden robe, his rich black hair flowing in waves over his shoulders. The women marveled at the handsome resemblance between father and son and there was no distinctive age difference between the men. The male followers admired the strength he bestowed as he placed his hand on his son's shoulder.

"My son, this night has come with three rewards, all for you Jonathan." His cold stare held Jonathan's attention. "if you carry out my two demands you will be granted the prized gift and this December 25th shall be for our people, Anti-Christmas. You will be their king and leader and they will be your Anti-Christians."

"Welcome Anti-Christmas with great tidings! Praise be given to Lucifer, King of the underworld and our master! Praise be given to his royal son, Jonathan, our master forever and soon to be the Anti-Christ, King of the world! Sing alleluia!" The congregation sang out the words written in their hymnal.

Jonathan smiled as he opened the red curtain revealing the beautiful girl draped in holly, laying quietly on the altar draped in pure white. Lucifer walked over and looked down at the death-still young woman, her eyes closed ever since hearing his voice on the other side of the curtain.

"Jonathan, tell me you have not sedated this girl? I insist she be alert for my seduction!"

"At her own request father, Fire was not given any drug. I dare say, she will be the first to feel the full impact of your lustful sex." Jonathan heard the gasp of sympathy for this young teenager from the women watching, knowing they had seen her many times with Jonathan.

"Then tell her to open her eyes and look at me!" Satan ordered.

"The girl is young father and afraid to look upon your incredible powerful image." Jonathan remained calm, feeling his own power building with the thoughts of be Lucifer's number one son at long last. "What makes this one special, she comes of her own freewill."

"Really?" Lucifer drew out the word as his eyes dropped on the naked girl covered with holly, just as he demanded. "My dear girl, I mean you no harm. I will have you and I will enjoy you because I lust for your body. I am a powerful angel Fire, and my power may grow stronger within you, but the pleasure I receive will be rewarding. If you permit yourself young Fire, you too will enjoy me, over and over again." Lucifer reached out his hand to touch her but some force caused him to pause and noticed her eyes were still shut. "Young woman, I order you to open your eyes now!"

Jasmine slowly opened her eyes and looked into the face of evil, but she felt the strength to remain calm. Just as Lucifer was about to reached for the holly, he was interrupted by the back door opening and a female's voice echoing through the vast chamber.

"Jonathan Wineworth, I love you!" Kristine O'Donnell stood alone, the only Christian to be seen among the stunned cold eyes of the cult.

"Kristine!" Jonathan tried to catch his breath as he looked down at the woman he loved. "You...you came."

"How can I refuse the man I love so dearly." Kris kept her eyes on his. "Jonathan, my life, my love, is in your hands."

Satan had been watching the little scene unfold and was taken back. "Well now, son, perhaps I have been wrong about your loyalty." Lucifer stared at the older woman, very attractive but hid her sexual beauty with her high-neck long dress. "I never considered you would ever carry out my second command, yet here she stands, placing her life into your hands. Foolish for her, but rewarding for my first-choice son."

"True father, she has come to me of her own free will." Jonathan held out his hand for Kristine. "So, Kristine, you are telling me I can do whatsoever I choose to do with you? You are mine?"

Joan Byrd

"My love, my heart and body are yours Jonathan." Kris placed her trembling hand in his. "My soul and first love belong to my Lord and Savior, the blessed Holy Spirit and the Father of all creation.

As Jonathan looked down into her eyes, his father laughed out. "Not to worry son, it's not her soul we desire, it's her life! KILL HER! RAPE HER! SHE GOES TO HEAVEN, YOU BECOME MY ANTI-CHRIST!"

"Kristine, you come to me freely. Perhaps its more fitting to take a Christian life in exchange for the chosen one." Jonathan picked her up easily, refusing to look back down into her eyes. "Father, her life and I am the chosen one, your Anti-Christ! Promise me this and it shall be done as you command!"

"Yes, of course my loyal son. Kill her, rape her and you would have proven your devoted loyalty." Satan gave a winning smile when he saw Kristine close her eyes in defeat. Lucifer sneered down. "Woman, you have learned love does you no good when my blood runs through the veins of the man you foolishly chose to love." Satan started to move toward Fire, stopped and smiled to himself. "Girl, remove yourself from my altar and stand next to me!" Jasmine sat up and slowly moved off the high altar before moving next to Lucifer, making sure not to touch him.

"Jonathan, since this is my feast, I have the right to change the service around, do I not?"

"Yes father. What is your will?" Jonathan had blocked out the woman he held in his strong arms by putting himself in a trance.

"We shall reverse the order." Satan's smile was cunning as he brought forth a large sharp knife from inside his robe. "First you kill the slut on my altar by stabbing her in the heart, then side by side, father and his new-born Anti-Christ will rape these two whores. Yours dead, mine alive!" Lucifer smiled lustfully down at Jasmine who was staring at Jonathan. "At least, sexy little Fire will be alive when I start!"

Jasmine did not move a muscle as she spoke directly to Jonathan. "If you try to kill Kristine Jonathan, you will be lost forever!"

Satan laughed sarcastically "If? If?" he stared coldly down at the girl as fire shot from his eyes. "Jonathan will kill her, you bitch!" Then Lucifer turned on Jonathan. "Get on with it boy and stop wasting my time!"

340

Jonathan gripped the sharp knife as he laid Kristine on the altar. She had been watching him and knew he was avoiding looking down at her, so her words came softly, for his ears only. "Jonathan, my love, my heart is sad, it's breaking, knowing I may never see you again. How I had wished that I could feel your arms once more around me, kiss your warm passionate lips and make love to you. I know if you take my life, I will never see you again Jonathan and although they say there are no tears in heaven, my heart will always weep for you, my dearest darling."

Jonathan closed his eyes, his heart was pounding as his mind drifted back to their night of passion. Their last walk together when she had asked for one more night and how he had broken her heart because of an engagement that meant nothing to him. Jonathan had tried in desperation to reach her after breaking it off with Miriam, but she had simply vanished. His hand went up, the knife ready to plunge down when once again he heard his name spoken softly, yet firmly.

"Jonathan, my brother, can you slay the woman you love for this evil man?" Jeff appeared next to his brother. "Search your heart Jonathan, do you think for one second Satan will make you his Anti-Christ?

"Don't listen to him son!" Satan yelled. "Your brother is jealous because he lost the chance to be my chosen one. You will be above him! Rule over him!"

"He lies Jonathan! I know him!" Jeff stood strong and calm. "I am ashamed to admit it, but not too long ago. I worshiped this man! He and I were close, real close! Trust me when I say he would chose my son over you."

"He cannot choose Teddy Jeffery, I won't let him!" Jonathan found it hard to breathed as he felt the knife in his hand.

"Jonathan, it is not up to you to save my son. Teddy must choose for himself." Jeff could tell Lucifer was getting impatient. "If you choose to kill Kristine, you will be lost forever. If you choose to love her then you can help me save Teddy through faith. I need you brother. Teddy and Jacob need their uncle and Naomi needs her brother-n-law. Mother came back because she needs you." Jeff touched Jonathan's shoulder. "Kristine needs you Jonathan. Look into her eyes."

Tears filled Jonathan's eyes as he finally looked down at the woman he had given his heart to. Knowing how close he had come to taking her life, Jonathan dropped the knife on the hard floor and pulled her into his strong arms. "Oh my God, Kristine, please forgive me, my darling, I love you!" She clung to Jonathan as he lifted her off the altar and held her tight, his attention going to his angry father growling.

"I KNEW YOU COULD NEVER BE WORTHY OF MY CHOSEN SON! DID YOU REALLY THINK FOR ONE SECOND I WOULD PLACE ONE PRECIOUS SIX ON YOU!" Lucifer yelled, red with hate, he willed the knife to return to his hand. "You, stupid man, you can never replace my favorite, my JEFFERY! NO ONE CAN, DAMN IT!" his stare went to Jeff. "AND OF THAT JEFFERY, I WILL NEVER GIVE UP! WHATEVER IT TAKES, I WILL MAKE YOU MY NUMBER ONE SON AGAIN!"

"You are wasting your time here father. Just leave if you don't want trouble." Jeff stood firm and stared back at the evil face.

"Do you think I am frightened of you?" he laughed. "Watch your brother die for betraying me!" Lucifer lunged toward Jonathan, knife ready for the kill when Ted stepped out causing Satan to freeze in his spot. "The Bible thumper! In my church!"

"If you mean, I carry my Bible everywhere." Ted smiled. "There is no need for the words live within my head Lucifer. If you mean, I share the word and teach the word to others, then yes, I am a Bible thumper."

"Stand aside, holy freak! My son has disgraced me in front of my followers and you are intruding in my church! Jonathan will die so unless you wish to be apart of my followers and watch, then get out!" Lucifer gripped the knife angrily, ready to finish the service with his sacrifice.

"You mean this congregation seated out here?" Ted moved in front of the silent group, confused at the turn of events. "Lucifer calls you his followers. It is your choice to make. Our loving God has given you the free will to decide just that. But first, you must be warned what will happen is you choose evil over good."

"Friends, I foolishly led you down this path and I was wrong. Please, listen to this holy teacher." Jonathan felt Jeff's hand pull him and Kristine behind him after witnessing some angry faces in the crowd and knowing Lucifer was still ready to pounce on his brother.

"You are a traitor Jonathan!" Joseph Reynolds stood up,

shaking his fist angrily. "I for one stand with our master, Satan!"

"Count me in too!" One of the young teenage girls stood up and looked around at her friends. "Come on guys! These goodie-do-nothings can't buy you happiness! Lucifer can!"

"Yes, my people, they lie by tricking you with beautiful words! False promises!" Satan looked out at the group and many of the women saw him looking like Jonathan and still lusted for his time with them, so they all stood up. "Yes, yes, with me, you can have sex forever! Lust over anyone you wish." The clever devil had read their wicked minds.

"What do you have to offer Bible thumper?" one of the male teens yelled out. "Rainbows and violins?" he laughed.

"The eternal love of Jesus and a heaven overflowing with love." Ted's voice came soft, yet strong.

"I choose eternal love!" one woman near the back stood up crying. "I strayed away from Jesus. Will He take me back?"

"He already has Wanda. Just ask for His forgiveness." Ted's love flowed from his words. "Please everyone, have a seat. If you choose good, remain seated, if your choice is to follow evil, then stand."

Half of the people stood up and stared angrily at the young man in the white robe. Gabriel appeared with Gloria Wineworth by his side. "God wishes to give you people standing one last chance! Listen to what this lady beside me has to say, then your choice will be final."

"Lady?" Lucifer laughed out. "This 'lady' lay lusting for me and the results brought forth two sons, twins! Jonathan, the stupid man you followed and my very favorite son, who used to be as wicked as I, my Jeffery." Satan stared at Gloria, who felt safe beside the big angel. "You wicked woman, if they brought you out of hell to help them, you will suffer all the more when you return, you bitch!"

"Lucifer, quiet!" Gabriel shouted. "You have no control over this saved woman or have you just conveniently forgotten to save face in front of your unfortunate worshipers?"

"Listen you over-rated messenger, once in hell, always in hell!" Satan sneered "No one should be reclaimed once they have been condemned!"

"That is true, most of the time Lucifer, but you have been told

343

that she has been set free from her bondage in hell." Gabriel lifted his eyebrow. "My fallen brother, you ought to know with God, all things are possible!" the bright angel held up his hand to stop the devil from speaking, then turned to the congregation. "People, I urge you to listen to this woman. She is your final hope."

Everyone grew quiet as Gloria stepped forward, the need to know what hell was really like. "Ladies and gentlemen, you are looking at one of God's miracles. I threw myself in fames to escape my son Jeffery's punishment and died a painful death and found my soul in hell for all eternity. The horrors I lived there over seven long years were cut short by a loving, forgiving God. I know I was the first and I dare say the last to be saved once condemned." Tears filled her eyes as she trembled. "Every soul in hell are naked. There are many levels of torture, some so grotesque, I cannot speak of them. Flesh falling off bodies, covered with snakes, rats, or spiders! The pains you suffered with while living continue below. There are lakes of burning fire filled with screaming bobbing bodies, cages set on fire over and over with victims traped inside. Demons in every corner, raping, ripping off legs, arms or dismantling entire bodies, they grow back together only to get torn apart again! Being eaten, grow back, then eaten again!" Gloria felt Gabriel reach to hold her up when her knee buckled. "Because I committed suicide by jumping into fire, my personal torment in hell was a repetition of jumping in a blazing hot fire, feeling my melting flesh over and over! Your body arrives in hell exactly the way it was the day you died but not in heaven." She took a deep breath. "Please dear people, choose wisely. In heaven there is no pain, you are forever young, like the angels. There is great joy and happiness when you united with love ones and there is overpowering love that lights the very heart beat of this place called heaven."

Those who had remained seated, bowed their heads in prayer. Many that had stood up, sat back down, their hearts pounding with fear for almost following Satan to this place of torture. Now, they wondered if they would fall victim to Satan's revenge. Tom Vestal stared at Jonathan, then Ted as fear ingulfed him. He reached over and took his wife's arm.

"Dear, we must not follow Satan and wind up in hell! We must choose good! Sit down beside me and don't looked at that devil."

"Are you mad!" Mrs. Vestal had been promised that her

344

paintings would be valuable and she would become extremely wealthy and well known all over the world. Her greed had eaten into her like a cancer. "Stay seated and become a poor nobody! I will be famous! Lucifer promised me!"

"No Hazel, you must not believe him!" Mr. Vestal tried to pull her down and she jerked her arm away.

"Stay here then Tom! You lose and I win!" Hazel walked over next to a smirking face Joseph Reynolds who took around her and stared down at her low-cut top. "Joseph and I will go down the rich wide path together."

Thomas Vestal closed his eyes after seeing only ten people left standing, including his wife of thirty years.

"Then you ten have made your choice!" Gabriel held up his hands. "Your souls are lost forever! You have chosen freely to follow this devil! Your eternal home will be in hell! As of now, your names have been removed from the book of life!"

"They choose life with me!" Lucifer laughed. "Unfortunate for five of them, they will make their journey sooner than expected. As of now, the police approach to arrest…" Satan smiled, turned and pointed to Joseph Reynolds and the four youth. "you five! For the beautiful bloody murders of three people. My demons will see you to hell."

"But…it can't be true!" Reynolds felt hot and filled with overpowering panic as a sharp pain hit his chest. He screamed out before falling to the floor. "My…heart! Please Lucifer, help me!"

"Help you? You fool, I shall!" Lucifer smiled and held up his hand. "Demons of the underworld, far below the earth, far below this world, arise!" There was a moaning sound from beneath Reynolds as demons rose out of the floor and took hold of the frightened man. Within seconds, Richard Reynolds' soul was sucked down with them and his dead body laid stretched out on the church's red carpet.

"See what will happen to the rest of you, my faithful nine." Satan touched one of the young teenage girls and she smiled up seductively. "Yes, you are a luscious slut. I might pay you a visit in your prison cell." A tall angry looking man appeared next to Lucifer. He wore a black suit with black glasses. Gathering the four young murderers, the stranger walked out the door with them.

"Lucifer, what will happen to those teenagers?" Mrs. Vestal

stared down at Joseph Reynold's cold stiff body as another man in black appeared and carried him away.

"Mr. Death will be their lawyer after the police, who have taken them away decide on a trial date." Lucifer stared coldly at the shaking woman who chose wealth and fame, then at her husband who had buried his face to weep for her. Now, for the rest of you traitors who chose to stay seated! My demon warriors will rise up and destroy the lot of you!" Satan yelled. "Then I will gladly destroy my son Jonathan and his lover!"

"You'll do no such thing Lucifer! You are finished here!" Gabriel spoke firmly. "Leave this place!"

"You, a mere spokesman for his majesty ordering me, Lucifer, a very powerful angel, to leave my own ritual?" Satan laughed loudly and it echoed in the walls. "YOU CANNOT MAKE ME!"

The front door flew open and a very tall warrior angel stepped inside. "I CAN MAKE YOU LEAVE SATAN!" Michael stood ready for battle.

Lucifer slung up his arms and ten warrior demons appeared holding fiery torches and great hot swords. "First, we kill you Michael, once and for all. Then we set fire to all my fallen followers!"

"Lucifer, you cannot kill an angel of God! Do you really think I came to do battle alone?" Michael laughed at the sound of heavy marching feet as ten mighty warrior angels lined up behind their leader after coming through the big double doors. Even then, the ten-foot doors were no match for the great warriors, who had to stoop over to march through, their heads almost touching the high arched ceiling. Those witnessing the heavenly soldiers where amazed at how the floor shook under their feet with their entrance. In each warrior's hand was a large flaming sword, drawn and ready to do battle.

The demon warriors began backing away as they trembled remembering the massive size of their enemy who cast them out of heaven. All ten lowered their weapons and coward behind Lucifer, knowing they had rather feel his wrath than fight these warriors again. In his extreme anger, Satan yelled out.

"I WILL RETURN! WHEN I DO, I WILL GET MY CHOSEN ONE!" Lucifer was gone, along with the last five lost souls.

CHAPTER 64

Matthew pulled one of the SUV's up in front of the small church and took in the size, then whispered to his wife. "I don't get it Kath. How, on God good earth, can the entire town fit inside that tiny-little church?"

"Matthew, you know we cannot question Ted's thinking." Kathy wrapped Jonah scarf around his neck. "Maybe the Christmas gift is fitting the entire population of Goldsburg into one tiny church."

"Why would Ted choose Jonathan's church to have a Christian service?" Blaze could remember the satanic services inside those double doors, the walls with no windows. "Light was forbidden except for the black candles on the wall and at the altar, that was draped in red cloth. I shutter when I recall the large painting of Lucifer, staring out at each person attending."

"I think that had something to do with whatever happened here tonight Marshall." Jenny let Matthew and the young angel help her out of the backseat. "It looks well-lit now."

"Ted did tell us to be here at eight sharp." Hannah held tight to Mary and Martha as they waved happily to Teddy and Jacob who had just arrived with their mama.

"Well, we made it time." Naomi followed everyone eyes and noticed that the chapel seemed to be moving out and up. "Is that building growing or is my eyes playing tricks?"

"I wouldn't believe it if I weren't standing out here watching the whole thing for myself!" Matthew took Jonah from Kathy and pointed to the unusual sight. "Look son, this may never happen again. The building is growing right in front of us!"

"Its that one percent of good Matthew!" Mary said excited. "Evil has departed and the love of God is still inside!"

"Look mama!" Teddy Jeffery grabbed Naomi's hand and pointed to the roof. "The plain roof is shooting higher and higher!" his eyes grew wider. "Look! It's as high as a cathedral!"

"Wow! It didn't have windows before, but now there's giant stain glass windows!" Jacob almost shouted with excitement.

347

Ted stepped out and noticed the entire town where staring up in wonder at the large cathedral. He smiled, knowing his family and friends hadn't noticed the gathering silent crowd behind them. "Welcome my friends, to the first service at Top of the Mountain Methodist Church!" his eyes found Jenny and he smiled brightly. She knew Jonathan had been saved and in return, Jenny blew him a kiss.

"Excuse me Reverend Neenam, but isn't this Kill Devil Hills Methodist?" An elderly lady shivered in the night air.

"The name is Ted, ma'am, and as you can see by the huge new sign reading Top of the Mountain, as of this night, this is a house of God." Everyone clapped, feeling relieved after hearing rumors about a cult group meeting in the building. "Please, come inside out of the cold." Ted stepped back for the people to enter. "There will be room for everyone, I promise."

Eighty-two of the seats had already been filled with old members, including Jasmine, now dressed in a long white Christmas gown. Ted had the ushers to place his and Jeff's family on the front row. The solid blue stain glass windows were aglow with candles surrounded by holly. On one huge wall hung a very large painting of Ted's mountain top. Every eye was glued on the unusual artwork that seemed to have an invisible person still painting it. Mary and Martha smiled at one another, then whispered to their mother who had taken out her glasses for a closer look at the painting.

"Mom, it's an angel painting our mountain!" Mary giggled. "It is wearing a painting smock but doesn't seem to have any brush."

"The angel just points at the colors and they start to paint." Martha sit up laughing softly.

"You can see him?" Jenny whispered as she squinted her eyes, trying to make out the angel without a paintbrush painting.

The twins giggled as Martha lend over toward her mama. "It's a girl, mom." She punched her sister's arm lightly and nodded to Teddy and Jacob who had noticed the talented angel.

"Look girls, there's a rainbow appearing near the top of the mountain and rays from a super bright light has appeared above and between it." Then to Jenny and everyone watching, saw a man appeared in a white robe, his hands stretched up to heaven as though he was praying to the Father of all creation. Jenny smiled as tears ran down her cheeks. "Ted" she whispered and turned to see him looking lovingly into her eyes. The painting was completed.

Ted motioned for the children who would be taking part in the service. The twin girls kissed their beautiful smiling mother and made their way to a side room which held their costumes. Jenny waited for the program to begin and thought back at how well the school pageant went on the last day of school before Christmas break. Martha had made the perfect Mary child with her sister Mary singing like the angel she is. Everyone had left the school feeling the Christmas spirit. The presents had been bought and wrapped. The perfect Christmas tree had been found on the mountain and now sparkled with lights and all the children were excited that Santa would be arriving soon. Jenny knew her gift to Ted would be arriving too on Christmas morning, just a few hours away, but for now, the lights had been dimmed and the Christmas story would once more come to life. What Jenny and the rest of the congregation didn't realize was they had just begun to see the real Christmas magic!

Ted's beautiful voice filled the large cathedral as he sang Silent Night. There was a hush over the large congregation as a marble statue seem to rise behind him, then the spots from unknown lights shown down on the life-size vision. It was a very realistic image of the virgin Mary holding the baby Jesus.

Nothing could control the many tears that flowed from those watching when the children appeared, dressed like angels. They raised their sweet voices as they sang Angels We Have Heard on High. Kathy lend over to her friend and whispered. "Jenny, those wings you made look real from here."

Jenny had also been drawn to the cardboard wings and knew instantly they were not made from cardboard, nor did the shine they created come from garland. Jenny took Kathy's hand and whispered back. "Kathy, look closer. Those wings are not homemade, they are the real thing."

"Jenny, don't be silly, they cannot be..." before Kathy could finish her statement, Mary and Martha's wings lifted them up in the air, flew them over to the statue of Mary and Jesus, then sat them down on either side of the virgin.

At the same moment, Teddy Jeffery and Jacob walked out dressed like shepherds. They stopped in front of a huge drawing of hills, a night sky and sheep grazing on the hillside. The boys began singing in perfect harmony, While Shepherds Watch Their Flock. As they began the second verse, everyone could hear the baa of sheep. With eyes as big as the children watching, the adults could hardly believe their ears and then their eyes when the large drawing seem to come to life. The stars twinkled in the night sky, the sheep were moving around and eating while others had nestled down for the night. The drawing had a campfire which had now come to life and Teddy and Jacob had sat down around it. A very big and bright star filled the sky, prompting the boys and the sheep to gaze up in wonder.

Across the stage, there came another animal sound and before the people's eyes appeared three king-like-figures riding fancy dressed camels. They stopped to gaze at the bright star that led them to Bethlehem as they sang in deep rich voices, We Three Kings.

Gabriel appeared, his great wings spread out in suspended flight as he gave his important message. "Fear not! For behold, I bring you good tidings of great joy! For unto you is born this day in the city of David, a Savior, who is Christ the Lord! And this shall be sign unto you. Ye shall find the babe wrapped in swaddling clothes and lying in a manger!"

Then the light spread over the entire ceiling as a multitude of angels filled the air above the faithful watchers. The angel's voices rang out in a beautiful song of praise. "Glory to God in the highest, and on earth, peace, goodwill to men!" As the angels continued to give praises to God, the entire front of the church lit up causing the people to gasp at the miracle before them. All the stage had come together and just like a nativity scene, the three wise men were bowing on one side, their camels laying behind them, A group of shepherds knelt down next to Teddy and Jacob, who sat close to the manger, their sheep watching in silent wonder, two real angels hovering on either side of the stable, with the twin angels knelling on either side of the manger. In the middle of the stable, Mary sat holding the baby, her voice came sweet and clear as she sang, A Way in a Manger, as Joseph looked down. When she finished singing, Mary looked above her and smiled at the lone angel hovering overhead as he sang to the Holy Child, Sweet Little Jesus Boy.

Jenny knew right away it was Ted and she couldn't stop crying from the very real Christmas story she had witnessed with the entire town. This was the special Christmas gift Ted had spoken about and it was far better than special, it was a miracle.

Everyone had wet eyes when the lights dimed and Ted was once again standing alone at the front of the church. Jenny felt a tug on her sleeves and looks down to find both girls seated on either side of her smiling. Glancing down the pew, she noticed Naomi's sons had joined her, and back in the clothes they had worn to church.

"I said you would receive a special gift on Christmas Eve." Ted spoke with more love than anyone there had ever heard before. "This night, God has put Christmas back into everyone's heart." He lifted up his hands and motioned around the large church. "This little church which once held a lot of hate, has grown from 1% of love and although it will once again become a small church when this special night has passed, it will hold a lot of love. With Reverend Jonathan Wineworth preaching God's holy word from this pulpit, good Christians will come to join and to build the very church we witnessed on this night of Christmas miracles."

Jeff walked out with his brother and Kristine. "My friends, we have been given a special gift this holy night." Jeff's voice was rich and strong. "Perhaps you haven't realized the special blessing we have received. Jesus was born on Christmas day. As devoted Christians, we all know this, but what you might not know is, just after midnight, Christmas Eve became Christmas day. If you had been watching your watches, you would have noticed that was the exact time Mary and Jesus appeared on this stage in front of you!"

"Earlier this night, my dear friends, this sinner was saved." Jonathan held tight to Kristine O'Donnell, whom many in the congregation recognized. "I wept tonight, same a you, watching with child-like faith as the Christmas story came to life for us. The doors of Top of the Mountain are always open. We welcome our fellow Christians as well as sinners looking for hope and salvation. This is a vision of what this church can grow into my friends. Please come and join us to rebuild God's holy house with that 1% of love Ted spoke of." Jonathan's eyes fell down on Kristine. "My future wife and I will be here waiting with the love of Christ."

Kristine O'Donnell wiped her eyes as she found her mother watching from the congregation, doing the exact same thing.

"Now, brothers and sisters, we leave to go to our own homes, to share the love of this Christmas spirit to all we meet. Go in peace

Joan Byrd

and in your prayers this night, pray for the child who will be born to me and my loving Jenny. His path is already laid out for him as he will walk in the steps of his father. To work with a full heart for our God, our Savior, and our Holy Spirit."

Ted, knowing the time was drawing near for Jenny to go into labor, walked over and scooped her up into his arms, walked out the door then disappeared.

CHAPTER 65

Jenny lay comfortably on their bed as she watched her husband pace around the room, stopping occasionally to stare out the bedroom window facing the courtyard. She knew Ted was anxious for his mother's arrival. At the church, his first concern was to get his wife home so she could lie down. Jenny was aware that travel back up the mountain road could be slow due to the fresh fallen snow and she wanted to help get Ted's mind off their late arrival.

"Ted darling, please relax." Jenny gave him a reassuring smile and held out her hand for him. Ted walked over nervously and sat down, taking her hand. "Hannah will get here sweetheart. If not..." she teased "you can deliver your son."

"Me?" Ted turned white at the thought and quickly checked the bedside clock, closed his eyes and spoke softly. "I suppose I could, with God's help."

"I think God is much too busy to deliver our baby sweetheart." Jenny couldn't control her laughter at his expression. "Calm down darling, I'm only joking. God, our loving Father, will never let you down."

Ted tried to smile, but it came out shaky. "So, you really truly believe that, Jenny?"

"After what happened tonight, I would believe anything Ted." Jenny thought back to all the wonders. "That painting an angel was painting without a brush, of you on the mountain top, what happened to it?"

"You actually saw the artist Jenny?" Ted was glad the baby was not the subject at that moment. "Graceland wasn't visible for humans to see."

"Graceland, the painter? No Ted, I couldn't see her. Your daughters informed me about the lady painting the beautiful picture." Suddenly Jenny felt her first pain and sat up, squeezing Ted's hand hard.

"Jenny, are you practicing the hand squeeze darling?" Ted almost whispered, afraid to hear her response, although he already knew it was for real.

353

"No practice Ted! It's the real..." the sharp pains came again, this time causing Jenny to scream out. "God! Oh shit, that hurts!"

"Jenny could you wait a few more minutes longer?" Ted swallowed nervously as he watched Jenny look over at the bedside clock, reading two a.m.

"Wait? Are you kidding me? You announced the time, Mr. Neenam and it has arrived..." another sharp pain hit her and Jenny tried not to yell out when she managed "right on time!"

Ted sat up and took a relieved breath. "They're home! Mother is here!" he jumped up and slung the bedroom door open and looked down to find Mary and Martha smiling up.

"We came to tell you and mom goodnight dad." Mary tried to see past her father.

"Then we heard the big grandfather clock strike two." Martha said excited. "Baby Gabriel is about to pop out!"

Ted looked down at his twins bewildered, then spotted Kristine rushing down the hall. "Kristine, can you take the girls?" he looked down the hall for his mother. "Could you?"

"Happy to assist. Come along with me girls. It's off to bed with you if you expect to get to sleep before jolly old Santa Clause comes down that big chimney." Kristine winked at a worried Ted and smiled over at her niece, who was in serious labor. "Stop fretting Ted, your mother is gathering her prepared delivery cart and is on her way. "I'll be back to help as soon as I get these two into their pajamas and say their prayers."

"Thank you, Kristine, but you may go on to bed and get some sleep after seeing to the girls," Ted watched them disappear down the long hall, then turned, spotting his mother and waved her on.

"Roads are slippery Ted dear." Hannah walked in the bathroom and quickly washed her hands before joining the couple. With expert speed, Hannah had Jenny in delivery position, then turn to see her son swaying, his face a pale white. "Ted, sweetheart, please have a seat and please, do not try to take Jenny's pain this time. Just hold tight to her hand."

Ted felt relieved that his mother was in charge of delivering their baby boy. When Jenny had another contraction, and squeezed his hand tightly, Ted remembered how terrible the labor pain was he had endured so he could know what Jenny was feeling. Then he recalled Jeff following his lead and his reaction over the extreme

354

The Lost Sheep

painful labor contractions. Ted had to cover his mouth to keep from laughing, just remembering the strong touch guy yelling in pain and almost crushing Naomi's hand. They both had failed royally.

Jenny once again felt the pain hit, but this time she knew the baby was coming by the incredible pain that felt as though she was being ripped into.

"Yes, keep pushing sweet daughter! I can see his head!" Jenny took a deep breath and pushed while Hannah gently pulled. "Halfway there, brave girl! He is out!" Hannah breathed relieved as the little baby cried out.

Ted had tears in his eyes as he bent over to kiss his beloved Jenny tenderly, then gazed down at the tiny infant in his mother's arms. The little blonde headed boy looked exactly like him.

Hannah smiled down at her handsome grandson as she finished cleaning him off, then wrapped him in a white soft swaddling cloth before laying him in his mother's arms. Jenny felt speechless as she looked down at their small infant, a little Ted. Her heart was so full of joy she thought she could dance if she wasn't so exhausted.

Ted laid down next to his wife, wrapped one arm around her and gently laid his other hand on his little son. "My love, my Jenny, this is the best Christmas present I have ever received. My son." The baby boy opened his blue eyes and smiled. Ted gently squeezed his wife's shoulder. "Sweet, my love, my Jenny." Ted looked into her tired eyes. "Gabriel just told me it is his first Christmas gift ever and he loves us for giving him life."

Jenny gazed down at the smiling infant then back up into Ted's incredible blue eyes, then gave him her beautiful smile. She knew no matter how far fetched Ted's words were, they were completely true and if there had been an ounce of doubt about hearing their son speak, it was erased when baby Gabriel reached for her hand smiling and said, "ma-ma."

Spring had arrived on top of Goldsburg Mountain when the Neemans received the good news about Jeff and Naomi's baby girl arriving just as Jeff had announced. And true to Teddy Jeffery's description, baby Joanna arrived with long shiny black hair and looked exactly like her angelic mother.

The wedding had been set for Jonathan and Kristine for the third Sunday in April, giving Naomi time to get back in shape. She had teased Jeff, many more nights of having sex every day and night

355

when she was able, might result in another baby. Jeff had informed her that he would make sure she would be the first to know, after him, of course.

The wedding service was going to be at Jonathan's new church, Top of the Mountain Methodist Church. Since the Christmas Eve service, the members had tripled in size and the building committee had started a fund to enlarge the church.

Everyone living in the small town had heard about the wedding being held on Easter Sunday. The non-members, thinking the church would be too small had reluctantly given up on attending after invitations went out for everyone in Goldsburg. Then word spread that the wedding was to be held outside the small chapel to accommodate the large crowd. Relieved, the happy citizens gathered their lawn chairs and headed for the church grounds.

Ted stood once again looking out at the large group of people. Easter services had been held inside the small church building with every pew full as Jonathan led them through a meaningful service. Ted and all the family on top Goldsburg Mountain held their own moving Easter service in the chapel.

"My friends, welcome to the wedding of two very special people who are a part of our lives every day. I hope you came to celebrate this joining of their bodies into one body. We who love them so dearly, join in their happiness." With those words, Jeff and Jonathan walked out to stand next to Ted.

The grounds committee had planted a beautiful garden behind the church and it made the perfect spot for this spring wedding. The people looked on as the music began to play and the bride's mother, Bessie O'Donnell was ushered down to the front row next to Kathy and Matthew, handkerchief in hand for the tears that were sure to fall. Naomi walked down between the chairs wearing a long lilac dress. Her raven black hair was adorned with matching flowers. Jeff's heart skipped a beat when he saw his beautiful wife.

Jenny made her way gracefully, wearing a royal blue gown with matching flowers and ribbons, flowing down the perfect brad handing down her silky back. Ted had watched her with adoring admiration and smiled when their eyes locked.

Jonathan waited nervously for the first glimpse of his bride as Teddy and Jacob strolled down like perfect little gentlemen, each carrying a wedding ring. Then Mary and Martha gave bright beautiful smiles as the danced down throwing out rose petals. When the twins reached the front, the wedding march started and every head turned to see the bride being ushered down to her bridegroom by George Pennington. Jonathan could not remember when he was this happy. His smile was frozen on the woman he had given his heart to, even when she dressed downy and plain.

"Dearly beloved, God in heaven will join together this man and this woman in holy wedlock. They have spoken of their love for one another and have chosen to become one. To live together, to laugh together, to share one another's grief, join hands in the work of the Almighty, and to love one another forever, forsaking all others, till death takes them from this dwelling place into the realms of glory where their love will live on for all eternity. Do you Kristine, take Jonathan to be your husband to brighten his mornings and make warm his nights?"

"I do." Kristine spoke softly and with total love for the man who's eyes she had not left since she stepped from the church's side door.

"Do you Jonathan, take Kristine to be your wife, to start each day in love and end each night fulfilling that love?"

"Oh yes I do!" Jonathan never knew he could feel so totally happy being in love with the right woman.

Ted smiled, feeling their devotion to each other as he continued. "There is no greater love than that of our Father, Savior, and Holy Spirit. We cannot measure the depth of their eternal love for us, but to love that special woman God has chose for your heart to love, goes deeper than man can express. I can see and feel this love you share, Kristine and Jonathan. So, as God's humble servant, I pronounce you are now one."

Ted looked down at the two younger brothers holding the rings and motioned for them to hand the rings to the couple. "As you place the ring that binds you, looked at one another and repeat these words, with this ring we are made one."

Jonathan and Kristine lovingly placed each other's ring on as they repeated the words.

"God has blessed you as one." Ted wrapped a white ribbon around their wrist and said a wedding prayer, then removed it smiling. Jonathan and Kristine Wineworth, may your lips confess in a gentle kiss that you are indeed husband and wife.

357

Jonathan took Kristine's face gently into his strong hands and gave her a tender kiss as the large crowd clapped for the happy couple.

Suddenly the happy wedding party froze at the sight behind those in attendance that only they could see. The excitement showed clearly on the Neenam twins and the Wineworth boys as they watched what appeared invisible to Jenny, Naomi, and George. Other than the children, only Ted, Jeff and Jonathan could see all the angels at work.

To calm the confused crowd down, Ted held up his hands. "My friends, as I told you at the beginning of this beautiful wedding between Jonathan and Kristine, the members of Top of the Mountain have worked nonstop on raising money to add on to this church and make it bigger. Most of you saw the Christmas miracle and how each and everyone of you fit inside what began as a small church and ended as a cathedral." Ted knew the people, no matter how hard they tried, could not turn around to see what was happening behind them.

"You face the garden, where moments before you witness the wedding. Behind you sits Top of the Mountain. I am aware how curious you must be and the need to see what's happening behind you is making some anxious. But total logic will not let you understand what is going on until it is complete." "

"This wonderful thing is nothing to fear, I promise you, it's really right the opposite!" Jonathan watched in wonder at the quick work the angels made with their building skills. "It seems the money we raised has by some divine miracle, been enough to purchase the building materials we needed to build our church!"

"Finding enough skill labor workers to build the cathedral we witnessed on Christmas Eve would cost a lot more money than we have saved." Kristine had worked on a great many finance and · building committee's but she had never witnessed the speed of these invisible workers in front of her. "Friends, it would appear there are many skilled workers building extremely fast and their work is free. A gift from heaven!"

"Like Christmas Eve, you have been blessed with what appears to be an Easter gift to the faithful followers of our Lord." Ted couldn't contain his smile. "The good news, my fellow Christians, is that there will be one remaining gift that will even top off the one we are witnessing." Ted raised his hands again to release the hold on those waiting to see for themselves.

"You may see now what the Lord has rewarded you with because of your strong faith. Turn and behold the hand of God, through His angels who have stopped building in Heaven long enough to give us a helping hand."

Without hesitation, everyone turned to see the wonder for themselves. Sitting directly behind them, towering in the sky, was the majestic cathedral they had witnessed on Christmas Eve. Once again, the small windows became tall arched stain glass windows, but instead of plain blue stain glass, the many windows told the different stages of Jesus' life.

Going inside, they once again saw the life-size statue of Mary and baby Jesus. Behind the walnut carved altar hung a huge picture of Jesus, arms stretched out, to welcome all into His love and care. Ted led Jenny over to the painting the invisible angel had painted of Ted on the mountain top. It now was framed in what appeared to be pure gold, then her attention went to Ted, standing with one hand up, while the other hand clutched the hand of a small boy with hair the color of his father. The small boy wore a white robe like Ted and he also held up his hand to the heavens in prayer.

Tears flowed from Jenny's eyes as Ted wrapped his arm lovingly around her. "You can see Jenny, darling, the angel wasn't quite finished with the painting. With our Gabriel, now, it is complete."

Ted had everyone walk back outside for the last gift. As the group stood waiting, wondering what could beat angels building the cathedral back, Ted drew their attention. "Raise your eyes to the steeple and sing praises of thanks to the Creator of every beautiful gift given.

Through the mist of a sudden white cloud came two nailed stain hands carrying an empty cross. He placed it lovingly on the very top of the cathedral as the Lord proclaimed: "Well done, my good and faithful servants!" The spirit of the Lord and the cloud were instantly gone.

CHAPTER 66

The seven-young people who had come to live and be saved by Ted, stared up in wonder at the cross placed on the steeple by their Savior, Himself. Jasmine felt the small hand of her sister Patches clutch hers tightly and gazed over to the pretty thirteen-year-old blonde who had made several visits to the mountain since Ted took her on the mountain top when she was six. Cindy Russell had stepped up for a better view of the miracle that just happened. Jasmine's heart was bursting with joy and she silently thanked God for saving her little sister and her other lost friends. Everyone stood in silence, too filled with emotion to speak. Then out of the stillness, Jasmine caught Ted focused on her with a bright smile and she knew in her heart what he was asking her to do. She lifted her voice in a song of praise.

"Amazing grace! How sweet the sound that saved a wretch like me" she turned to see Blaze watching and he could read her love for him was like a brother. He smiled as she continued. "I once was lost, but now am found" then Cindy's voice came sweet and clear.

"Was blind, but now I see!"

Jasmine felt the loving hand of Andrew on her shoulder and she knew he loved her in the same way.

Marshall wiped his eyes, filled with incredible love as he sang "Through many dangers, toils, and snares, I have already come: Tis grace hath brought me safe thus far, and grace will lead me home."

Esther had walked up to place her arm around the young man she had fallen in love with. After listening to her friends confessing through song, Marble remembered how Ted had taken her to witness both heaven and hell before choosing which path she wanted to take, she too lifted up her voice. "Twas grace that taught my heart to fear, and grace my fears relieved; How gracious did that grace appear the hour I first believed!"

Tracy Reynolds could not contain her tears no longer as she too lifted her voice. "The Lord has promised good to me, His words my hope secures. He will my shield and portion be, as long as life endures."

The Lost Sheep

George Pennington had been so amazed at the heavenly sight, he hadn't noticed the beautiful woman standing next to him in the crowd until her voice filled the spring air. George looked around her and noticed she too seemed to be alone. His eyes fell to her left hand and didn't see a wedding ring, then noticed her hands trembling. He reached down and took hold of one.

When Tracy looked up and noticed the very distinguish gentleman with the incredible eyes, she felt herself blushing from his smile. Her heart seemed to skip with joy as she wondered, was this the promised good, she had just sung about, the secure hope? Perhaps! Perhaps it was!

Miriam had spoken to Jonathan earlier in the week concerning his son's life and he and Kristine wanted very much to share in the boy's life. Robert had surprised her with an engagement ring and a job offer from George who was planning another Pennington Company in Charlotte, N.C. Miriam hated the thought of leaving her home on the mountain, but Robert and her son was her new life now. Hearing the voice of Ted as he started the large crowd singing, Miriam could not control her tears from falling as she watched the families departing as they joyfully sang, "Blessed Assurance, Jesus Is Mine"

Jonathan warmly hugged Bessie, his wife's emotional mother. "Mrs. O'Donnell, when Kristine and I return from our honeymoon, we would find it an honor if you let us move in with you."

Bessie took both of their hand and gazed lovingly up, tears welling in her eyes. "When we first heard you speak Jonathan, Kris felt sure you were looking at her, but I told her she was being foolish. It came as quite a shock to find out just how much my daughter loved you. What I'm trying to say Jonathan, you are a part of my little girl's life, so that makes you a part of mine, but if you're moving in because you think I'm a lonely old woman, the answer is no. If you're asking because you really want to join me, then I welcome you with open arms."

"Thank you mother and it's not because we believe you need looking after. It is something Jonathan and I have wanted to do." Kristine hugged her mother, relieved to know Jenny and Ted insisted she remain with them until the newlyweds returned from the Outer banks. "You see, I'm not through needing my mother. I never had a child to bring up before and I am sure your expert

361

guidance will be welcomed."

"What a joy it will be to have a little one in the old homeplace again!" Bessie beamed. "Now off, the two of you and enjoy one another. You have waited far too long as it is."

With one last kiss, the happy couple told Jeff's family goodbye, then the Neenams's extended family, as they hurried off for their honeymoon.

Hannah had been helping by putting young Noah and baby Gabriel in their car seats when another SUV rolled up, Gabriel behind the wheel smiling. He climbed his tall body out and handed the keys to Andrew. "Here you go son, a gift from Mr. Pennington to accommodate the ever-growing Christian family."

"That was mighty nice of George, Gab. Things were getting a little crowded in just two cars." Andrew started loading up the three SUV's as Gabriel walked over to his son and took him to one side.

"My present journey is done, my son. I return home to God's side."

"I could not have done it without you father." Ted hugged him tightly, dreading for this moment to come. "I hope the time and distance isn't too long this time. I've grown to enjoy your company sir."

"As I you, son." Gabriel felt sadness for the first time since he was created. Sadness did not exist in heaven. The handsome angel tried to shut out his tears, never knowing until now that he even had any. But, when the mighty angel turned to see Hannah watching him, Gabriel felt the unnatural feeling of wet tears. "Ah, sweet Hannah. Dare I tell her goodbye?"

"Father, I think if you should not, she would feel hurt by your lack of farewell." Ted touched his shoulder, and he felt courage run through his son's fingers. "And you sir would regret it. Love runs deep from what I can sense."

"I fear you are right son." Gabriel watched her lovingly. "Through eternity, Hannah will be by my side, but first, she must live her earthly life for herself and Peter, for her grandchildren, her friends and family." Gabriel turned back to Ted. "And Hannah must live for you and Jenny, Ted."

"Go to her father. It will please her heart, as well as your own." Ted squeezed his father's hand. "She has forgotten something in the garden. Mother will go after it so just follow her."

The Lost Sheep

With that prediction from Ted, Hannah looked around franticly for her missing handbag and grabbed Matthew, telling him she remembered leaving her bag on one of the garden benches, then promised to return as quick as possible. Spotting the familiar bag hanging on the arm of the bench, she hurriedly retrieved it and turned when she recognized a familiar voice behind her.

"My Hannah, sweet love." Gabriel looked down lovingly as he took her hands. "I must return home Hannah. My gracious Creator is calling me back and has given me time to say my final farewells."

"Final?" Hannah felt the tears dancing down her cheeks as she touched his face. "Are you going away forever Gabriel?"

"No Hannah." He pulled her into his strong arms. "Did I not say how much I love you and how you would spend eternity in my arms!"

"Yes, you said those things to me Gabriel, but, you said this was your final farewell!" Hannah started shaking uncontrollable at the thoughts of never seeing the angel she loved while living. "Then, perhaps you mean, I won't see you again on this earth, only..." Hannah reached for her handkerchief to wipe away the tears. "only when I die."

Gabriel took a deep breath and shook his head. "I am doing this poorly, it would appear." He led her to the bench and they sat down. His hand touched her face, her lips. "It appears I don't know the first thing about romance. I'm new at this Hannah. The guardians may know because they can witness everything human, but I only know how to deliver important messages from the Eternal Father."

Hannah relaxed at his innocent expression and finally felt like smiling. "Then I guess you're coming back for a visit to perhaps help our son again. You simply meant farewell until you return, correct?"

"You are exactly right Hannah Neenam!" Gabriel let out a relieved breath. "I will thank the Holy Creator for making women wise." His eyes held hers for what seemed like an eternity until he spoke softly. "Hannah, I love you. I could never stay away from the woman I love for a very long time, even though time does not exist in heaven. But, when the earth's time is ready for me to return, I shall come happily."

"I do wish for peace in this small town and that Satan would turn his thoughts from invading Goldsburg." Hannah closed her eyes, knowing the return of Lucifer would bring her Gabriel back down. "I'll keep busy so I won't miss you so much." Hannah laid her head on his broad shoulder. "Who am I kidding. You will be in my thoughts everyday and yet, I still love my husband Peter with all my heart too."

"Yes Hannah, this I know." Gabriel wrapped his arms around her and held her tight. "Being an angel, I should never be jealous, but the thought of dear Peter, who deserves your devotion as much I, spending a happy life with you while I cannot, makes me feel...I believe the word is, upset."

"Gabriel, I simply love you both." Hannah looked back up at the cross that shone brightly on the top of the steeple. "With Peter, I share a life helping lost children. With you Gabriel, I share a very special son Ted, the joy of my existence." Hannah took his hand. "But Gabriel, with you, I share my greatest love and my heart is forever yours, dearest one. I love you so very much."

With those words, Gabriel smiled broadly, then gave her one last kiss and whispered before ascending into heaven. "Until next we meet, my beautiful Hannah, I love you very much." Gabriel's whole appearance took on a brilliant glow as he looked up smiling. "O, sweet Hannah, I never grow tired of going home. Wait till you see its majesty and glory!" Gabriel was gone.

CHAPTER 67

Ted and Jeff walked side-by-side behind their wife's as they made their way toward the white farmhouse. "Seven years." Ted said softly

"Seven years of peace on the mountains and town below." Jeff, like Ted, watched their woman a few steps ahead glance at each other.

"In seven years the twins will be eleven, Noah seven and a half, and Gabriel will turn seven in on Christmas day. My son would have already been making the trip to the mountain top with me. He'll make his first climb at two-years-old." Ted knew Jenny and Naomi were taking in their conversation because they slowed up their step to be closer and they hadn't said a word to each other.

"You are right, friend, they listen to our words." Jeff glanced over and smiled. "Joanna will turn six, Jacob eleven, and then there's Teddy Jeffery, who will be turning fourteen, prime age for Father." Jeff noticed his wife tense up and glance around at him, while Jenny was shaking her head.

"Can you believe those two looking ahead seven years? I, for one, would like for time to just slow down before I need hair color!"

"Jenny, knowing our men, I think they are saying we will be blessed with almost seven years without my devilish father-n-law trying to take over someone's life at the worry and expense of their loved ones! Naomi knew she needed to teach her eldest that his grandfather was to be avoided.

Jenny shivered at the ideal of evil returning to their town and the fact that her birthdays would be flying around right along with her children's. "I don't even want to count to see how old I will be in seven years."

"Gosh! I will jump to twenty-eight." Naomi gazed down at the baby girl in her arms. "And you, my little angel, will be six!"

"Lord, that will make Ted twenty-nine!" Jenny looked down to see four-month-old Gabriel smiling up at her. "My little smart fellow, I guess you know you will be seven at Christmas, seven-years from now!"

Joan Byrd

"Jenny, sweetheart, you will be thirty-six-years young in seven years." Ted smiled over at Jeff laughing when Jenny stopped and twirled around. "Is there anything troubling you, my darling?"

"Really Ted! Life is already flying far too fast as it is without you and Mr. laughing man pulling us all up seven years!" Jenny marched back and placed Gabriel in Ted's arms. "Here daddy! Why don't you tell your son who he is going to meet and fall in love with so he can make his old gray hair mama a grandmother!"

"Jenny?" Ted held tight to his son with one arm and grabbed his wife. "I love you Jenny Neenam and we will share each other's love and bed until the day we leave this home for our mansion in the eternal heavens, together, forever young, my beautiful wife."

With those loving words, Jenny relaxed, knowing Ted was devoted to her, no matter their age difference. Hearing their twins laughing, she turned to see what was going on.

"Teddy Jeffery, that is the funniest thing I have ever heard!" Mary lightly hit his strong arm. "I agree you're strong, but I do not think you are that strong."

Naomi handed the baby to Jeff, walked over to Teddy and turned him around to face her. "What's this about Teddy? Just what do you plan to do young man?"

"Teddy!" Holding the baby in one arm, Jeff jerked his son off the ground. "Do you actually think you will be stronger than me when you reach fourteen?"

"O, yes sir, much stronger." Teddy Jeffery's stared into his father's eyes. "I have been gifted father. I'm the next in line."

"In line for what Teddy?" Martha looked at him confused. "Head football player? Top wrestler in school?"

"That's baby stuff, Kid!" Teddy smirked. "It's much bigger than school sports, doll!"

"Have I not, forbid you to speak to that evil being, Teddy?" Jeff knew his son had been secretly talking to his father.

"It's Jeffery, father, from now on!" Teddy dark eyes were cold as he bared his canine teeth. "Every year I grow stronger and my gifts more powerful! It is my choice!"

"Teddy." Naomi reached up and touched her son's leg, tears flowing down her beautiful face. "Sweetheart, do you love your Grandfather Lucifer more than you love your mama and papa?" the young boy seemed to snap out of a trance as his mother's words

366

sunk in. He noticed the tears coming from the one he loved so dearly, then looked up to find his papa crying as well. With tears coming to his own eyes, his small hand touched Naomi face tenderly as the other hand touched Jeff's.

"Papa, I love you!" Teddy wrapped his arms around his father's neck, before Jeff lowered him to go to his mother. Teddy grabbed her tightly. "Mama, I'm sorry for making you sad. My words were foolish. I was merely bragging for Mary. I love you mama, you and papa, never Grandfather Lucifer."

"Please darling, the next time your grandfather calls, ignore him and come to me or your papa." Naomi looked up at Ted who had been silently watching and listening. "Son, look up at Ted, then promise me Teddy, you come to us."

"I promise mama." Her eldest son kept looking up at Ted's loving face. "Uncle Ted, would it hurt your feelings if I go by Jeffery instead of Teddy?"

"No son, only let it be for the right reason." Ted gently touched the young boy's arm, sending love through his body. "You just wish to be named after your papa, because you love and admire him."

"And I do Ted, just as I admire you." Teddy stood up to give him a hug. "I suppose you would have named your son Teddy if mama and papa hadn't given me that honor first."

"My son's name would still have been Gabriel, Jeffery." Ted smiled. "Now, all you children go inside and wash your hands. Mother and Kathy has supper almost ready."

"Lucifer has set things in motion, now he leaves for seven years." Jeff stared at his son racing the girls and Jacob to the house. "I must be ready to help my son resist Lucifer's false promises."

"We Jeff, we will help Teddy Jeffery together." Ted patted his tall friend's shoulder. "But for now, we will enjoy peace on the mountain."

Joan Byrd

AUTHOR'S NOTES:

AFTER PEACE LASTED FOR SIX YEARS, ON THE
SEVENTH YEAR, ONCE AGAIN EVIL RETURNS TO
GOLDSBURG MOUNTAIN. A MYSTERIOUS ILLNESS
STRIKES ALL THE CITIZENS OF THE SMALL TOWN,
INCLUDING THOSE LIVING ON THE TWIN MOUNTIANS.
ONLY TED AND JEFF, ALONG WITH THEIR CHILDREN ARE
SAFE FROM THE DEADLY VIRUS. THE ONLY CURE CAN
BE FOUND IN ONE PLACE. THE GARDEN OF EDEN!

FOURTEEN-YEAR-OLD JEFFERY WINEWORTH HAS
GROWN INTO A HANDSOME YOUTH WHO'S APPITITE
FOR SEX HAS INVADED HIS THOUGHTS ALONG WITH
THE STRONG POWERS HE CHARISHES.

BOOK # 4 IN THE GOOD SEED/ THE BAD SEED SERIES
TITLED:
IN SEARCH OF EDEN

Made in the USA
Columbia, SC
07 October 2022